BAD ROMANCE

ALSO BY HEATHER DEMETRIOS

Something Real
I'll Meet You There

Bad Romance

HEATHER DEMETRIOS

SQUARE
FISH

HENRY HOLT AND COMPANY

NEW YORK

SQUARE
FISH

An imprint of Macmillan Publishing Group, LLC
175 Fifth Avenue,
New York, NY 10010
fiercereads.com

Our books may be purchased in bulk for promotional, educational, or business use. Please
contact your local bookseller or the Macmillan Corporate and Premium Sales Department at
(800) 221-7945 ext. 5442 or by e-mail at MacmillanSpecialMarkets@macmillan.com.

Library of Congress Cataloging-in-Publication Data

Names: Demetrios, Heather, author.
Title: Bad romance / Heather Demetrios.
New York : Henry Holt and Company, 2017. |
    Summary: "When Grace and Gavin fall in love, Grace is sure it's too good
    to be true. She has no idea their relationship will become a prison she's
    unable to escape"—Provided by publisher.
Identifiers: LCCN 2016035854 (print) | LCCN 2017010360 (ebook) |
    ISBN 978-1-250-15877-2 (paperback)   ISBN 978-1-62779-773-3 (ebook)
Subjects: | CYAC: Dating (Social customs)—Fiction. | Love—Fiction. |
    Psychological abuse—Fiction. | High schools—Fiction. | Schools—Fiction.
Classification: LCC PZ7.D3923 Bad 2017 (print) | LCC PZ7.D3923 (ebook) |
    DDC [Fic]—dc23
LC record available at https://lccn.loc.gov/2016035854

Originally published in the United States by Henry Holt and Company
First Square Fish edition, 2018
Book designed by Liz Dresner
Square Fish logo designed by Filomena Tuosto

10 9 8 7 6 5 4 3 2 1

LEXILE: HL660L

FOR ZACH: HUSBAND, HAPPY ENDING,
AND MENDER OF BROKEN HEARTS
(TSATMAEO)

I want your ugly
I want your disease
I want your everything
As long as it's free
I want your love

—LADY GAGA

JUNIOR YEAR

ONE

Five hundred twenty-five thousand six hundred minutes.

That's how long it takes me to start falling out of love with you. One year. Our own season of love. You do know which musical I'm referring to, right, Gavin? Because there's no way you can be my boyfriend and not know that of course, *of course*, I would bring *Rent* into this. Five hundred twenty-five thousand six hundred minutes of your lips on mine and whispering in the dark and you picking me up and spinning me around and taking my virginity and fucking with my head and telling me I'm worthless, worthless, worthless.

If I were writing a musical about us, I wouldn't start where we're at right now, at the end. I would want the audience to really get how I was able to fall for you hook, line, and sinker. Girls don't fall in love with manipulative assholes who treat them like shit and make them seriously question their life choices. They fall in love with manipulative assholes (who treat them like shit and make them seriously question their life choices) who they *think* are knights in shining armor. You rode in on your fucking white horse, aka 1969 Mustang, and I was all like, *My hero!* But I am so tired of being a damsel in distress. In my next life, I'm going to be an ass-kicking ninja warrior queen. And I will hunt shits like you *down*. Throw your ass in a dungeon and drop the key in my moat and my lady knights will be all, *Huzzah!* and I will sit on my throne like, *Yes*.

But I can't daydream too much about my next life because I have to deal with you in *this* life. Before I break up with you, I want to reflect. I want to go back through us piece by piece. I want to remember why I was so ooey-gooey crazy in love with you. I want to know why it's taken me this long to figure out that you're poison.

So, I'm gonna *Sound of Music* this shit: *Let's start at the very beginning, a very good place to start . . .*

There I am, downstage right, finishing my breakfast at the dining room table. It's my junior year. Winter. A Tuesday, which is better than Monday but not nearly as good as Wednesday. We aren't together yet, Gav, but, as my lusciously crass best friend Alyssa says, I am *so hard for you*. I've just finished my peanut butter toast and I'm thinking about how yesterday I saw you eating a Reese's Peanut Butter Cup and wanted to lick the chocolate off your lips. Because that would be the most amazing kiss—Gavin Davis tasting like Reese's Peanut Butter Cups. YES. You are my super happy place and I am there, la la la, trying to ignore my stepfather (who shall hereafter be known as The Giant). He's pounding around in the kitchen and muttering under his breath, and I know he wants me to be all, *What's wrong?*, but I'm not going to because he is an absolute fuck nut (that's an Alyssa expression, too—she's very linguistically creative) and nobody should have to deal with absolute fuck nuts without caffeine.

The Giant is displeased.

"Where the hell's my lunch?" he growls, louder now, as he paws through the refrigerator.

Today is the day that will change my life. But I don't know that, of course. I have no idea what's in store for me. What *you*, Gavin, have in store for me. All I know is that The Giant is ruining my Gavin day-dreaming buzz and I really want some of that coffee in the pot, but I'm not allowed because they said so. Everything is *Because we said so.*

The Giant slams his lunch pail on the counter and opens it. It is only then that I remember what I'd forgotten to do last night before I went to bed.

I close my eyes and wish I had a Greek chorus to shake their fists at the sky for me (*Oh, woe! Woe!*) because this slight infraction could result in me losing my whole weekend.

"I'm sorry," I murmur. "I forgot to make it."

My head hangs in shame. I am the picture of Contrite and Subservient Female because this is what The Giant needs to see at all times. But that's on the outside.

On the inside, which The Giant can't get to no matter how hard he tries: *screw you, make your own damn lunch, and while you're at it, clean your own car and do your own laundry, especially your boxers, and can I please stop having to clean your bathroom, because your stray pubic hairs make me nauseous?*

I play this role of the beaten-down, cowed girl because I'm scared. Terrified, really. What little freedom I have is like a delicate piece of blown glass. The slightest push can make it shatter into a thousand million pieces. It wasn't always like this. Before my mom married The Giant, there was laughter in our house, random dance parties, adventures. Not anymore. I live in a kingdom ruled by a tyrant bent on my destruction.

The Giant curses under his breath and I want to be like, *It won't kill you to make your own fucking sandwich.* Seriously. Bread, turkey, mustard, Swiss: *boom*—you have a sandwich. Christ.

I hear a door open down the hall and then Mom is coming in with her own version of Contrite and Subservient Female on her face. My mom thinks invisible dirt is real, that disasters are around every corner.

5

She thinks the Grim Reaper hides in the cracks between tiles, on top of baseboards, in the toilet bowl. She is unwell.

"What's going on?" she asks, looking from me to The Giant. Her lips pull down as she glances at me, like I'm already a disappointment and it's not even eight in the morning.

"Your daughter didn't make my lunch *again* and so I'll have to waste money today on getting lunch out *again*, *that's* what's going on." He looks at me and I can almost hear the thought in his head: *You aren't my child—I wish you would get the hell out of my house forever.*

"You better not be expecting to go to the movies on Friday with Natalie and Alyssa," he adds.

Big surprise. Let me guess: babysitting.

Don't get me wrong: even though Sam is half Giant, I love him to death. It's pretty hard to hate on a three-year-old. It's not his fault The Giant's his dad just as much as it's not my fault my dad is a former/possibly current cokehead who lives in another state and forgets my birthday every year.

Mom shoots me an irritated glare and brushes past me into the kitchen without another word. She pats The Giant on the arm, then pulls down a mug for coffee. It says *#1 Mom* on it, which is ten kinds of ironic. I want mug makers to start keeping it real. Like, why aren't there mugs that say *Once Pretty Okay Mom Who Got Remarried and Stopped Caring About Her Kids?* I mean, that's a lot of words, but if you use twelve-point font, you could totally rock that on a mug.

The Giant doesn't walk past me on his way out the door, he *pushes* past me, shouldering like a linebacker so that I'm forced into the entryway, my spine colliding with a corner of the wall. Pain shoots up my back. He doesn't notice. Or maybe he does. Bastard. As soon as he slams the door behind him, Mom turns on me.

"What have I told you about finishing your chores?" she says. "I'm getting tired of this, Grace. First it's not properly rinsing the dishes, then it's Roy's lunch or Sam's toys." She raises a finger in the threatening way of dictators everywhere: "You better get it together, young lady. You're walking on thin ice."

According to her, I'm always walking on thin ice. It's the topography of my life. Cold, about to break, always uncertain.

She doesn't have to tell me what happens if that ice breaks beneath my feet. My dad promised to help me pay for drama camp this summer at Interlochen, this amazing program in Michigan. I've been saving for it like crazy, working doubles on the weekends at the Honey Pot so that I can help my dad scrape together the hundreds of dollars it costs to be free of suburban hell for a few weeks.

I hang my head even lower this time and become Beaten-Down Daughter. She's the cousin of Contrite and Subservient Female, but more tired. If this were a musical, Beaten-Down Daughter would turn to the audience and sing something like "I Dreamed a Dream" from *Les Mis*. There wouldn't be a dry eye in the house.

"I'm sorry," I say again, my voice soft.

It is an act of will not to let the frustration building inside me slip into my voice, my mouth, my hands. In order to stay Beaten-Down Daughter I keep my eyes on my baby-pink Doc Martens because lowering your eyes broadcasts your worthlessness and makes the other person feel better about themselves and increases the possibility of them being magnanimous. You asked me the story of my boots once and I told you about how I found them in a thrift store on Sunset Boulevard and that I was pretty sure the girl who wore them before me did stuff like write poetry and dance to the Ramones because when I wear them, I totally feel more artistic. *Betty and Beatrice are my shoe soul mates*, I said, and you asked me if I named all my shoes and I said, *No, just these*, and you said, *Rock on*, and then the bell rang and I lived off of that two-second conversation for the rest of the day. So even though my mom's being heinous this morning, my shoes manage to cheer me up a little. I mean, everything is going to be okay as long as there are pink combat boots in the world. Someday I will tell you just that and you will pull me against you and say, *I fucking love you so much,* and I will feel like five million bucks.

"*Sorry.*" Mom snorts. "If I had a nickel for every time you said that . . ." She glances at the clock. "Go or you'll be late."

I grab my bag and a sweater, which is all you really need in Cali winter. I consider slamming the door on my way out, but that won't end well for me, so I quietly shut it and then rush down the walkway before Mom can think of some other reason to be mad at me.

I need to go to my happy place. Now. I can't let this be my day. I have to shake it off, Taylor Swift style.

Roosevelt High is less than a ten-minute walk away, and I spend that time with my earbuds shoved in, listening to the *Rent* soundtrack, probably the best thing to come out of the nineties. It takes me to New York City, to a group of bohemian friends, to my future. Some people run or meditate when they're stressed, but I go to the Village. I picture myself walking along the streets of the city, past overflowing trash bins and scurrying rats and cool boutiques and coffeehouses. People everywhere. I'm surrounded by brick buildings with fire escapes and I jump on the subway and I'm flowing under the city, on my way to the Nederlander Theater, where I'll be directing a play or musical. Maybe even a Broadway revival of *Rent.* By the time I get to school, the music is thrumming through me (*Viva la vie Bohème!*). My mom and The Giant and home splinter and fall away, replaced by my real family, the cast of *Rent*: Mark, Roger, Mimi, Maureen, Angel, Collins, Joanne. I'm okay. For now.

I keep my eye out for you the moment I'm on campus. You'd be hard to miss.

You're like Maureen from *Rent*: *Ever since puberty, everybody stares at me—boys, girls. I can't help it, baby.*

You've got this halo of cool that makes people want to bow at your feet, light a candle. Saint Gavin. You leave stars in your wake. Whenever you walk by, I swear sparks fly off you. The air crackles. Sizzles. You steal all the oxygen so that I'm left gasping for breath, panting. In heat.

I want to steal the leather notebook you carry around all the time. Songs are in there and poetry and maybe sketches. All in your handwriting, which I've never seen but imagine as surprisingly neat. If I could, I'd crawl into your vintage Mustang, your bad-boy car, and curl up in the backseat, waiting for you to maybe ravage me or at least sing me a song. I can't get enough of that sexy, shuffling gait, the way your black hair is perfectly mussed up. The faded Nirvana shirt and the low-slung jeans, the black fedora that I've never seen you without. You have these eyes that are positively arctic, so blue I keep expecting to see waves or maybe glaciers in them. Then there's that impenetrable look, like you have a million secrets locked inside you. I want the key.

I like you best when you're playing guitar, leaning your weight forward, left foot slightly in front of the right, muscled hands strumming magic into the air, intent on the music that bleeds from those long, thin fingers. And your voice: gravel and honey mixed together, a little Jack White, a little Thom Yorke. The songs you write are poetry. You close your eyes and open your mouth and something starts spinning inside me, faster and faster, and I would do anything if you asked me. When you sing, I imagine my lips against yours, your tongue in my mouth, your hands everywhere.

You are the most exotic thing in our crappy excuse for a town. A rock god abandoned by cruel fate to an outpost of suburbia, where it's at least twenty degrees hotter than hell. I like to think that as an LA girl forced to move here I could somehow understand you more than the others. I know what it's like to hear car horns and helicopters and music all hours of the night. I know what it feels like to zip down neon freeways and find street art in the most unlikely places. I know what it's like to feel alive. You want all that, I can tell. You look at everything around us the same way I do: with quiet desperation.

Birch Grove has a newness that only towns in Cali can manage—shopping centers popping up like mushrooms, schools and housing developments where once there'd only been a strawberry patch or cornfield. Even though we have a Target and a Starbucks and all that, it's the kind of place that has an annual rodeo. There is only one vintage store and the mall is the opposite of Disneyland: the Saddest Place on Earth. The worst part is that everything here is the same—the houses, the people, the cars. There's no grit. No wild abandon.

I hate Birch Grove with a passion.

One of the few things I *do* like about it, though, is our school: the drama program, the dance program, my French teacher, who's half Egyptian and smokes long, thin cigarettes behind the gym. And I actually like the school itself, like, the buildings. It has a certain coziness to it, a human scale that makes it feel like a second home. I love how the open-air campus is drenched in sunshine, the huge grassy lawn in its center, the outdoor arena with its covered cement stage that looks like the Hollywood Bowl in miniature. It's an idyllic California school, although sometimes I wish I were at an East Coast boarding school with bricks covered in ivy. If I were, I'd wear a sweater set and have a boyfriend named Henry, who plays lacrosse and whose father is a world-renowned physician. That's a pumpkin spice latte kind of world I'll never be in, though.

When Miss B chose me to be her stage manager and chose you to be her lead for *The Importance of Being Earnest*, I ran home and had a dance party in my room. I wanted to cling to you just like the girls in the play and say, *Earnest, my own!* That's how happy I was to be just a few feet away from you every day after school for six weeks. It was too much, those feet. I wanted them to be inches. Millimeters. You gave me a hug once, laughed at one of my rare attempts at a joke. You accepted pieces of gum I offered you. Smiled at me in the halls. Do you know you are the bestower of the perfect half smile: part smirk, all enigma? Of course you do.

I asked you once why a rock god at night is a drama guy by day and you told me you auditioned for *Singin' in the Rain* (that was way back in my freshman year) on a dare and then you got the lead and your mom made you take the part. And you loved it. I wonder if rock stars are all secretly mama's boys who like to tap-dance.

I love you, Gavin. And maybe it's in the most superficial way, like how I can't stand it when you take off your fedora and run your fingers through your hair. Or how you keep those hands shoved into your front pockets when you're walking to class. I wonder, if you took them out and placed them on my bare skin, would I feel the calluses from all those hours of you alone in your room, playing guitar? Would your fingers be warm or cool? I want to know what it feels like to have your palm against mine, like Romeo and Juliet: *Palm to palm is holy palmers' kiss.*

I still can't believe that when you see me in the halls you say hi. You think it's cool that I want to be a director, so I never had to endure that separation between cast and crew that normally happens. It helped that my best friends were in the show, too. We talk about movies and who my favorite directors are (Julie Taymor and Mike Nichols). We talk about music and who your favorite bands are (Nirvana and Muse). I breathe you in like you're air.

I don't see you on the way to first-period French, which I take because how am I going to speak to my future French lover otherwise (François, Jacques?). Natalie and Alyssa think I'm a weirdo. My best friends are taking Spanish, which, as The Giant says, could be used in the real world (as if France is not part of the real world). I have a bit of trouble concentrating on what Madame Lewis is saying, though, because it's Valentine's Day and even though I dressed up in my *Je t'aime* shirt, pink poodle skirt, and red tights, I have no valentine and am thus depressed as hell.

"*Bonjour*, Grace," Madame says to me. "*Ça va?*"

"What? Oh, um. *Oui, ça va.*"

You should probably know that I've never had a boyfriend on Valentine's Day. Either I break up with them before or get together with them after. And by *them* I mean the one boyfriend I have ever had, which was Matt Sanchez freshman year. It's becoming more of a problem now than it used to be, this not having a boyfriend on V Day. Before high school, it was enough to pig out on heart-shaped stuff with my friends and watch *Shakespeare in Love* for the millionth time, but Natalie is getting over that guy she met at her church camp last summer and anything lovey makes her super depressed so she's abstaining from the holiday this year. Alyssa refuses to participate in my celebrations because she says Valentine's Day is a capitalist ploy invented by soul-killing corporations that prey on women who subscribe to the romantic ideal.

Whatever.

If you were my boyfriend, I bet you'd write me a song or, I don't know, maybe do something homemade. You don't seem like a flowers-and-chocolate kind of guy. You'd make cookies that are burned but I still love, or maybe write a ten-page letter filled with all the reasons you adore me. These are both totally acceptable, by the way.

I'm sort of dying to know what you got Summer. What she got you. You've been together for a year, so I bet it's something special. She's a senior like you, a va-va-voom redhead who somehow makes being in choir sexy. I'd like to believe that if things were different, you might pick me, but all it takes is one look at Summer and I'm quickly disabused of the notion. Mom says I have an interesting face, which is just a nice way of saying I'm not pretty. *Sorry*, she says, *you take after your dad's side of the family.*

The bell rings and I'm off to second period—AP Comp with Mr. Jackson. The halls are packed as students bleed out of their classrooms. I walk on my tiptoes, looking for your fedora even as I tell myself I'm not really stalking you. Usually I'm guaranteed a Gavin sighting on my walk to Comp because you're in the classroom across from mine, but nope, you are nowhere to be found.

I sink into my chair just as the final bell rings, resigned. You are likely with Summer, ditching and in love. I am stuck in English, trying not to think about you ditching and in love.

Mr. Jackson turns off the lights so that we can watch the conclusion of Baz Luhrmann's *Romeo and Juliet*, which we started a couple days ago. It's a pretty badass version, with a young Leonardo DiCaprio who could seriously give you a run for your money in the hotness department. You win, though, hands down.

By the time the credits are rolling, half the class is pretending not to cry as Romeo and Juliet lie dead. It's like, we *knew* it was going to end badly but, even so, it guts us to watch it happen.

TWO

*T*he bell for lunch rings and I make my way toward Drama. I've
got the blues and the only thing that will even slightly cure me
is the next forty minutes. The Roosevelt High drama room is
my personal sanctuary. I love the black velvet curtains, how they
hang there like a promise, and the cumbersome wooden blocks we
use in scenes to act as tables, benches, or chairs. You'd never know
we're in Central California, agriculture Mecca of America: we build
kingdoms here, big-city love affairs, and the ancient houses of gods
and monsters.

This is my favorite part of the day, when I open the heavy metal
door, which is extra tall to allow sets to be brought in, and am immediately submerged in the din of voices, laughter, singing.

We are the music-makers and we are the dreamers of dreams.

We thespian types laugh loudly and often, tumble over one another's
sentences, a dogpile of exuberance. *Look at us*, we're saying to anyone
nearby. *Let me entertain you, let me make you smile.* Our ears are fine-
tuned; we wait for applause.

Every time I walk into this room I know that someday, even if it seems impossibly far away, I'm going to New York City, a small-town girl with stars in her eyes like what'sherface in *Rock of Ages*. I'm not forging a new path in my desire to run away from my home, from a mother who squeezes the life out of me and a stepfather who's always two seconds away from a slap—I'm walking, as fast as I can, down a well-trod path. I'm the girl who's desperate to get out of her small town because if she doesn't she knows she'll die. She knows her soul will start to rot, like fruit gone bad.

One more year, I tell myself. *One more year until graduation*. I can make it that long.

I think.

I step through the door and let out the breath I didn't even know I'd been holding in. The whole gang is here, focused on the current obsession over auditions for the spring musical, *Chicago*. I'll be stage managing, a part I've already been cast in, by choice. According to Miss B, it's a stepping-stone to directing. For the first time in a long while I sort of wish I were auditioning—I don't think I could get away with wearing black fishnets and a leotard as the stage manager. I secretly want you to see me like that. I actually had a moment of doubt and told my mom I was thinking about auditioning.

You can't sing, she said.

My mom went to one of those hard-core Catholic schools. She's big on Being Realistic. She's not trying to be mean; she's trying to help me. It's just that sometimes her words feel like a nun's ruler smacking across my knuckles.

Grace and her pipe dreams, The Giant says whenever I talk about directing plays on Broadway. He's big on Being an Asshole. The Giant has a life motto and this is it: *Money is king*. It's the code he lives by. Obviously we don't see eye-to-eye on the whole starving artist thing.

So instead of being in the cast, I'll help run rehearsals and for performances I'll be in charge, calling the show. *Light cue 47, Go. Sound*

Cue 21, Go. Blackout. I always feel like such a badass, like I'm in Air Traffic Control or something.

Today, I laugh and smile with the others, but I'm not paying attention, not really, because on top of dealing with the fact that there are no boys in love with me (especially you), I'm thinking about how to sneak off to the cafeteria to grab my food without anyone coming along. Sneaking off is hard to do when you're wearing a bright pink skirt with a black poodle on it. See, my friends pay with money, but my currency is the little green tickets the poor kids who need free school lunches get. I'd use my own money for lunch, but I need it for stuff like clothes and books and deodorant because The Giant sure as hell won't buy me any of that. I should have gone to the caf first, but what if you came in to say hi before going off campus and I missed you?

The group's up to its usual antics. Peter does the voices of his favorite video game characters. Kyle stands around looking like a young Bruno Mars, occasionally bursting into song. Our whole group is comprised of juniors, except for three seniors: you (Lead singer of Evergreen! Love of my life!), Ryan (your best friend and bass player for Evergreen), and your girlfriend, Summer (boo, hiss).

Natalie and Alyssa are discussing the pros and cons of leggings worn as pants rather than as a substitute for tights. Normally I get all I-read-*Vogue*-every-month when the subject of fashion comes up, but today I just listen: I'm too whatever I am to join in.

"They make everyone look fat," Lys is saying. She nods to a group of freshmen passing by the drama room. "Case in point."

Nat swats Lys on the arm. "Be nice. That is so not cool."

Lys shrugs. "Neither are leggings."

My two best friends are polar opposites. Nat wears a dress to school almost every day and has perfect makeup and hair with flipped ends, like it's 1950. She wears a tiny cross necklace and this thing called a promise ring, which represents how she's going to wait to have sex until she's married (she says she takes it off when she messes around with her boyfriends, LOL). I can totally imagine her as First Lady someday, with pearls and Jackie O sunglasses. Lys has a wild bob, bleached so that it's almost white, and wears sexy manga clothes like she's Sailor Moon. She's always getting in trouble for violating the dress code—she's got this thing for Catholic schoolgirl plaid skirts. Sometimes she wears tulle, like she's just performed in a psychedelic ballet, all neon and crazy patterns. I guess I'm in the middle because I'm the one who wears vintage thrift stuff, scarves in her hair, and lip gloss that tastes like Dr Pepper.

Peter switches from video game impersonation to strutting across the drama room's makeshift stage, busting out his best vintage Britney Spears moves. He's on this whole Britney kick right now. Last month it was Katy Perry. He's not gay—he's got a hard-on for pop stars that he takes to ridiculous extremes.

"Hit me baby one more time!"

"Not that you were ever remotely cool socially," Lys says, "but you've just taken away any hope of that status changing."

Today she's wearing a black tulle skirt over neon-green tights, crazy platform boots, and a T-shirt with a knife stabbing a heart.

"Hater alert!" Kyle calls. He boos Lys and she rolls her Cleopatra eyes.

I scan the students passing by the door, which is propped open and gives a good view of the quad. I'm hoping to spot a certain black fedora.

"Where's Gavin?" I ask, casual. At least, I hope I sound casual and non-stalkerish.

"Probably humping Summer," Ryan says. He's your best friend so I guess he would know. He takes a bite of one of the soggy burritos they sell on campus, oblivious to the horror on my face.

I get a pins-and-needles feeling in my heart. It's kind of like a heart attack but worse because it's a heart attack for unloved girls. This is a medical fact: when a girl hears another girl is engaging in sexual activities with the boy said girl likes, her heart turns into a pincushion. Pure science.

"Humping? Ewww." Natalie wrinkles her nose. "Summer doesn't *hump.*"

I hope that's true. I hope your worst is the PDA you two engage in all over school: kissing against the lockers, your hands gripping the skin at her waist, fingertips under her shirt. Because that is seriously bad enough. But you just *look* like someone who has sex a lot. I'm not holding out hope that you're saving yourself for me.

"Oh, sorry," Ryan says. "Would you prefer *make love?*"

"Or, *do the nasty?*" Kyle says.

"*Get boned?*" Peter adds.

In an unspoken decision to shun the boys in the group, Alyssa, Natalie, and I close ranks.

"This," Lys says, "is yet another reason I thank God I was born a lesbian."

Lys just came out last year and has yet to find a girlfriend. I wonder if that's why she keeps saying Valentine's Day is a social construct of The Man.

"*Oh, baby, baby, how was I supposed to know . . . ?*" Kyle and Peter start up, serenading us.

"Remind me why we hang out with these fools again?" Natalie asks.

"I don't remember," I say.

Lys pulls out her trig homework. "I have better things to do, anyway." She shoots the boys a glare. "FYI, you look like a bunch of asshats. I hope you weren't intending to lose your virginity anytime soon."

"Oh, *burn,*" Ryan says.

My stomach growls and I start edging toward the cafeteria. "I'll be back in a sec."

I turn and hurry into the thick mess of students outside before anyone can react. Despite wanting to be invisible, a part of me is sad because none of the boys in our group seem to notice my departure. None of the boys notice me, period. This sucks, but I'm a drama girl and I know my casting. I'm not the ingenue, the pretty one, the one who bursts with life. That's Natalie. Summer. Instead, I'm somewhere hovering on the edges: of talent, of popularity, of intelligence. I'm in honors classes, but I have to study twice as hard as everyone else to keep up. The only reason I get to be involved in every show at RHS is because I take the part nobody wants: stage manager, assistant director, Everyone's Bitch. I was the sophomore class secretary last year, but that was just luck: I impersonated a stoner in my speech and it won me the popular vote. I know lots of in-crowders (cheerleaders, jocks), but I'd never be part of their cliques. I barely get the slightest glance from them in the halls between classes. Knowing you, *the* Gavin Davis, is weird luck that proves I'm on Dionysus's good side, long may the god of drama reign.

I have just enough time to scarf down the slice of pizza the government paid for and make it back to the drama room before the bell rings. I walk through the door and stop. Somehow, in just a few minutes, a black cloud swept in to block out our sun.

Summer is there *sans* you, her usually smooth auburn hair a frizzy mess. There are dark circles under her eyes and her face is red and puffy from crying.

A little part of me—an evil part of me—lifts. Did you break up with her?

"What's wrong?" I murmur as I come up.

The group's energy has gone from ten to zero in a matter of minutes. Kyle is bear-hugging Summer. He looks . . . stricken. I've never seen him this serious.

Natalie edges closer to me. "It's Gavin," she whispers. My

stomach turns. I don't like the way she says your name, the horror on her face.

"What about him?"

"He . . ." She shakes her head, big brown eyes filling. "He tried to kill himself."

The words fly through my mind, around and around, a dog chasing its tail. *Kill himself, kill himself.* The bell rings and we all stand there, lost.

It can't be true. People like you don't kill themselves until after they're famous. Then, and only then, are you supposed to overdose on heroin or drive an expensive car too fast on Mulholland or do any number of things that rock gods do.

I will later hear that Summer had broken up with you, that you'd gone to her house and sobbed on her front porch and said you would do it, you'd kill yourself. And she kept that door closed on you anyway. It will take me a long time—over a year—to see that her dumping you was an act of bravery.

You'd left her house, your Mustang roaring down the street. Later that night, your parents found you in the bathtub, fully clothed. The only thing that saved you was that you'd cut the wrong way and fainted before you could finish the job.

I learn all this on the five-minute walk to history, where Natalie, Kyle, Peter, and I discuss you at length. The guys can't believe Summer was stupid enough to break up with you—you walk on water for them, too. They fall to competing over who's most in the know about your and Summer's relationship. This knowledge is suddenly a status symbol—whoever knows the most is your BFF. I secretly think Summer's crazy to give you up, but I keep quiet because I don't know you like the guys do—but I've wanted to and here's my chance.

I pull out a piece of paper, suddenly compelled to write you a letter. I still don't know exactly why I did it. I guess the thought of a world without Gavin Davis was too horrifying.

I know we don't know each other really well . . .
If you ever need someone to talk to . . .
I'm here for you . . .

I don't realize now, but this is the moment. The moment when the rest of my life in high school—the rest of my whole life—will change. The moment when I begin to lose a part of myself I'll have to fight like hell to get back for five hundred twenty-five thousand six hundred minutes.

All because of a love letter in disguise.

When I see Ryan in the hall after class, I give him the letter to pass on. You two are like brothers—I know he'll be seeing you at some point today or tomorrow. By the end of the day, we find out that you have been, for all intents and purposes, committed to a mental hospital. Birch Grove Recovery Center is where you go when you do stuff like try to kill yourself in your bathtub. Normally this isn't the kind of thing that makes a girl swoon, but there's something so dramatic and beautiful about a boy whose heart is breaking and my imagination latches onto that, elaborates on your suffering. You immediately reach mythical status for me, a Byron who's given himself over completely to the ecstasy and agony of love. Van Gogh, cutting off his ear.

Of course I'm worried about you and sad, but there's also this feeling of excitement, which I know is probably wrong, but all the same I can't help feeling it. Suicide is taking matters into your own hands and to me that seems courageous, fierce. You aren't just the rocker/actor everyone loves, the one we all think will for sure make it when he moves to LA. Suddenly, you're Romeo shunned by Rosaline. Or Hamlet, suffering the slings and arrows of destiny: *To be, or not to be, that is the question.*

I'm taken with the morbid romance of it all, that someone in our world of drive-throughs and cow patties and evangelical churches has done the sort of thing we've only seen onstage. Something inside me echoes that refusal to participate in the awfulness of life. I admire the guts it takes to give up. Only tortured artists do that, and being a tortured artist is my most fervent longing.

I know what it feels like, the hopelessness you're wrestling with. I feel it every day at home, when Mom treats me like her personal slave or when The Giant raises his hand just to watch me flinch. When Dad calls, drunk, teetering on the edge of surliness, making promises he'll never keep, telling lies he believes. Sometimes I wish I could sit my life out. Like, *Hey, it's cool but I'm over it. Peace.*

> *I understand . . .*
> *I know right now it seems like . . .*
> *You matter, even if you think you don't . . .*
> *You are the most talented person I've ever . . .*

Later, you'll tell me how you read and reread that letter—the only valentine you received. How my words had been a life raft. How—as impossible as it may seem—you fell in love with me when you were imprisoned in that stark white room at Birch Grove Recovery Center, your wrists wrapped in gauze.

I guess crazy is catching.

THREE

*Y*ou haven't been at school for a week and your absence never seems normal. It's not something I get used to. It's like someone turned down all the colors. Still, the rest of us have to go on with normal life, which for me means after-school shifts at the Honey Pot.

The mall is packed, so we've got a line. Since there're only two of us on this shift and Matt, my coworker/ex-boyfriend is in the back mixing up cookie dough, I stay in front, rushing from the oven to the trays of cookies that are lined up behind the glass case. I use a long spatula to transfer the cookies into the customers' bags, trying to be patient as they pick out the specific ones they want. A dozen for twenty bucks or one seventy-five each. Expensive, but worth every penny. My favorite is the sugar cookie—with or without sprinkles. You haven't had a sugar cookie until you've tasted the buttery, sweet, soft delight that is the Honey Pot's Sugar Daddy. Sometimes, when I'm really daring, I'll put frosting on top.

I get to eat cookies all day and drink unlimited amounts of soda. I scoop up dough and pop it into my mouth when no one's looking. I drop batches of cookies onto sheets of waxed paper using a tiny ice-cream scooper that gives me blisters. There's a glass window in front of the ovens and it's no secret that boys sneak glances at the girls as we bend over to put trays in the oven or take them out. I can't decide if I like this or not.

When the line gets to be too much, I run into the back.

"Sanchez! Help, I'm drowning out there," I say.

Matt looks up from the dough and it takes everything in me not to wipe the flour off his nose. We are so not together anymore and that's a good thing, but sometimes I want to make out with him. Nat says this is totally normal.

He salutes me. "Aye, Cap'n."

Matt and I went out for exactly two months freshman year. We were in the same English class and what started as a daily flirtation became a heady eight weeks of declarations and fights and awkwardness. He loves fantasy football and movies about funny dumbasses. I hate sports and love Shakespeare. It was never meant to be. Still, we stayed friends and I was the one who helped him get the job here at the Pot. Being with him was fun—not an epic love or massive heartbreak. But I'm ready for the real deal. A Serious Relationship. *Love.*

By dinnertime the line dwindles and we get a breather.

"Dude, that was insane," Matt says.

"For real."

The buzzer goes off and he crosses to the oven to retrieve the newest batch of cookies. The air fills with their warm, sweet scent: macadamia nuts and white chocolate. I'm about to go snag one when I see you out of the corner of my eye. You don't see me. You're following your parents into Applebee's, head down. You're wearing a long, thin cardigan, unbuttoned over a Muse concert tee. You're pretty much the only guy other than Kurt Cobain who can rock a cardigan sweater. My eyes follow you. They take in how your dad pats your back, how your mom reaches out and grabs your hand. A lump forms in my throat.

"Grace? *Chica*, hello . . ."

I turn and Matt's holding up a yellow cardboard box.

"That special order—how many macadamia cookies did they want?"

"A half dozen," I say.

My eyes float back to the restaurant, but you're already gone. I text Nat and Lys, tell them I saw you. They both respond with emojis. I can't translate what a confused face, a party hat, and a palm tree mean.

I keep glancing toward the Applebee's entrance throughout my shift, but you never reappear. I'm nervous. What if you think I'm a total freak for giving you that letter? What if you never read it?

I blush, thinking about how I'd said you were the most talented person I'd ever met. How obvious can I be about crushing on you?

"Excuse me," someone snaps in front of the register.

I turn around, ready to be fake nice, but it's just Nat and Lys.

"You bitches! I thought the horrible lady from last week had come back."

Long story short: a customer called me uppity. It was a whole thing.

Lys crosses her arms and leans her chin on the glass counter, her eyes—which have glittery blue and pink eyeshadow—sympathetic. "Sucks being a wage slave."

Though you wouldn't know by looking at her, Lys comes from some serious money. She probably won't have to work a day in her life unless she wants to.

"I like to tell myself it builds character," I say. I point to the cookies with my spatula. "What'll it be, ladies?"

"Chocolate. I'm on my period," Nat says.

Lys scans the trays. "I'll have my usual."

I put brownie chocolate chip cookies in one bag and snickerdoodles in the other.

"If I worked here I'd be such a fatty," Nat says. She's reed thin and has perfect posture after an entire childhood spent in a ballet studio.

"Yeah, my mom told me she saw some cottage cheese—aka

cellulite—on my legs the other day," I say, "so I'm taking a break from the deliciousness."

Lys stares at me. "Your mom actually *said* that?"

Nat rolls her eyes. "Are you surprised? That's textbook Jean."

Matt comes through the swinging door wearing basketball shorts and a tee. He gives us a little wave.

"*Adios, chicas,*" he says. "I'm out."

"Does that ever get weird working with him?" Lys asks after Matt heads toward the parking lot.

I shake my head. "Everything's cool between us."

Nat glances over her shoulder, toward Applebee's. "So I'm just gonna say it. Suicide attempt aside, Gavin Davis is back on the market."

Lys grins at me. "So when are you gonna tap that?"

Nat gasps and I laugh. "Nice, Lys. Keepin' it classy."

"Dude. You've been in love with him for, like, three *years*," she says. "Now is your chance."

Nat raises her hand. "Can I say something?" We nod. "As the most responsible of the three of us, I would say go for it, but be careful."

"Why are you the most responsible?" Lys asks.

Nat eyes Lys's ensemble, which includes rainbow tights, platform sneakers, and a pink bow in her hair.

"Fine, you can be the most responsible," Lys says.

I break off a piece of a freshly baked peanut butter cookie. "What do you mean *be careful*?"

"He'll be on the rebound," Nat says. "And he might be a little . . ." She makes the sign for crazy, twirling her index finger next to her temple.

Lys nods. "True. The dude did try to kill himself."

"Guys, I appreciate your faith in me, but there is no way Gavin would ever look at me that way, so I don't really need this advice."

Nat's eyes flash. "You just think that because of the kind of crap your mom says."

I fold my arms. "Like what?"

She ticks off on her hand: "According to her, you have cottage cheese legs, you're not photogenic, you can't sing—"

"Okay, okay. I get it." My eyes flick toward Applebee's. *Maybe you and your parents went out the other door.* "But this is *Gavin Davis* we're talking about. He's going to have a Grammy before any of us finish college. Also, if you compare Summer and me—"

Lys holds up her hand. "Please allow me to give the lesbian perspective. Summer is nice and cool and all of that, but she's really not as hot as you think. I, for one, have never fantasized about her while masturbating."

"OH MY GOD," Nat says, her eyes wide with shock. Two spots of pink deepen on her cheeks.

Lys raises her eyebrows. "Aren't you people not allowed to take the Lord's name in vain?"

Nat gives Lys a dainty punch in the arm and Lys gets into a karate stance and starts quoting *Princess Bride.* "*Hello. My name is Inigo Montoya. You killed my father. Prepare to die.*"

Just then a woman comes up and I try to keep it together while I box up her dozen cookies but I keep snort-laughing. She frowns at the three of us as though we're all hoodlums, her eyebrows going way high as she takes in Lys's ensemble. It's crazy that a socialist lesbian and an evangelical Christian are besties, but that's just how the three of us roll. We became friends our freshman year, when we were put together for a musical-theatre assignment in drama class. We decided to sing the fabulously naughty "Two Ladies" from *Cabaret* (Lys played the emcee), and we bonded over our love for Alan Cumming. I feel like our friendship is like those outfits you see in *Vogue* where nothing matches but it looks totally awesome. We're plaid and polka dots and stripes.

As soon as my customer's gone, I glance at Nat and Lys.

"I wrote him a letter," I say as I start bagging cookies to sell as day-olds tomorrow. The mall closes in fifteen minutes.

"Gavin?" Nat asks.

I nod. "And I . . . I mean, he probably didn't read it. Or, if he did, he'll think I'm, like, the lamest person ever." My breath tightens just thinking about it. "I'm sort of mortified. I don't know what got into me."

Nat's phone buzzes and she glances at it. "Well, you're going to find out tomorrow. Kyle says Gav's coming back."

"Tomorrow?" I say.

"Yep."

"Oh god," I moan. "Why did I write that stupid letter?"

"Because you're fucking cool and fucking hot and he probably fucking knows it and just needs an excuse to fucking make out with you," Lys says.

Nat nods. "I agree with everything she says minus the F-bombs."

Lys places a hand over mine. "You've been crazy about him forever. Now it's up to the universe."

"Or God," Nat says.

"Or Buddha or Muhammed or, like, the Dalai Lama, whatever," Lys says. "Ten bucks says Gavin falls for you before he graduates."

"Ten bucks says he doesn't," I say, holding out my hand.

Nat balls up her bag and throws it in the trash. "May the best woman win."

YOU ARE BACK at school today.

I see you in the halls, joking around with the other drama guys, with your band. You're like a pack of gangly puppies; none of you ever sit still. Somehow you're able to live in both those worlds: the cool-guy band and the nerdy drama dudes.

It's been nine days since The Day happened and from where I'm standing, Gav, it looks like you're back to normal. You're wearing your Nirvana shirt and your fedora is tilted at a particularly jaunty angle. The hat throws me off. I'd expected—what? A black turtleneck and beret in place of your usual outfit? A Greek chorus following you to class? You're wearing the cardigan sweater again and I wonder if it's to hide your wrists. I know I'm not the only one who wonders if there's a bandage, a scar on each one.

My heart speeds up and I suddenly feel foolish. What possessed me to write that letter? What if you think I've overstepped my bounds, that I'm weird? What if—

You turn around.

There are dozens of students between us, everyone rushing because the bell's about to ring. You're holding both straps of your backpack and you stop the minute you see me. Freeze. Your eyes widen (blue, blue like a tropical sea) and then the corner of your mouth turns up, just the slightest bit.

How do boys do that? How do they make your whole body combust just by looking at you?

I hug my books to my chest, Sandy in *Grease* asking Danny Zuko with her eyes, *What now?*

I don't know this yet, but these moments between us are choreography for the movie of your life. This thing you're doing—the look, the stop, the awed stare—you stole it right out of the BBC production of *Pride and Prejudice*. You're ripping off Colin Firth like nobody's business and I don't even realize it. You're two steps away from rising out of a lake wearing a drenched white shirt. It's only later that I'll see you're feeding me rehearsed lines and perfectly timed smiles and gasps and tears that come at precisely the right moment. A year from now I'll be screaming *Fuck you, FUCK YOU* into a pillow because I won't have the guts to say the words to your face.

But right now, a boy is staring at me from the end of the hall and even though he doesn't say a word, he's claimed me.

I'm new territory and you've planted your flag.

FOUR

I walk through the drama room door just as the bell rings. It feels like there's one inside me, too, clanging away. I keep replaying that look on your face when you saw me. The smile. *Ring! Ring! Ring!*

Peter is working on his English accent for the scene he's doing this week from Pinter—I forget which play. Alyssa is helping Karen with the first sixteen counts of the dance they're in for the concert this spring. Kyle's singing "Lily's Eyes" from *Secret Garden*, totally lost in a world of his own, and I listen to him for a moment, utterly enchanted. He has the kind of voice that makes everything inside you sit up straight. If God could carry a tune, I bet he'd sound like Kyle.

I cross the room and plop down next to Natalie, who's sitting on the carpeted floor, cross-legged and deep in conversation with Ryan. From the concerned looks on their faces, I suspect they're talking about you, analyzing your first day back. I want to tell her how you stared at me. I want to use words to trace that half smile.

"How is he?" I ask instead.

She shakes her head. "I can't tell. Summer said his parents are freaking out. They didn't want him to come back yet."

"Well, duh," I say. "He tried to . . . you know."

"Yeah," she says, soft.

It's strange to think that your life is going to go back to normal, that you'll have math homework and run laps at P.E. You're so beyond that now.

Miss B comes out of her office, which is located just off the drama room. We don't have chairs or desks here, just lots of space to play. We turn our bodies toward her. She helped us all through what happened to you—there were whole class periods that turned into counseling sessions.

"Who's auditioning for *Chicago* today—can I get a show of hands?"

I look around—nearly everyone has raised a hand.

"Excellent," she says, smile wide. "Be sure to bring your music to the choir room and comfortable clothes for the dancing portion."

Natalie grips my hand. She has no reason to be nervous—she's a total triple threat. Plus, she's pretty, but she doesn't know it, which is the best kind of pretty.

Miss B passes out new scenes for all of us and I'm paired up with Nat and Lys, as usual. We're playing cheerleaders in a scene from the play *Vanities*. I'm secretly excited about this scene because I've always wanted to be a cheerleader. It doesn't matter that as a smart, arty girl I'm supposed to hate them. Being a cheerleader has always seemed like a way to change your fate, to become something bright and shiny that no one can look away from. Nat and I went to the meeting at the beginning of this year, just to see what the tryout required. As it turned out, we were both too broke to be cheerleaders. You have to buy a specific color lipstick, special shoes, the uniform, bows, warm-up outfits . . . I guess there's a reason why all the rich girls are in cheer.

But none of this—cheerleaders, popularity, becoming a sparkle kind of girl—matters in light of you being back, you being broken.

"Do you think Gavin's going to audition?" I ask Natalie.

She shakes her head. "I have no idea."

How must you feel, knowing that as you smile and sing and dance, everyone will be thinking about what you did, their idea of you reorienting itself around this terrible thing?

"Let's read through it, yeah?" I say, holding up my script.

We jump into make believe like it's a pool on a sweltering day. Here, we wear other people's skins and it helps us forget our own, lets us pretend, for a little while, that we're okay.

THE CHOIR ROOM is packed with actors. I sit a little ways from Miss B, keeping track of everyone. There's only one name I haven't checked off the list yet.

"Hey."

Someone plops down next to me. I turn. It suddenly becomes a little bit harder to breathe. I can cross that last name off the list.

"Gavin. Hey." Everything in me lights up like Christmas.

We've never been alone before, never had a real conversation that didn't include other people. When we were in rehearsals for *Earnest*, you'd mostly talk to the guys. Except for our one or two conversations about music and directing, we've mostly had brief exchanges about stupid, inconsequential stuff. The last thing we talked about was garden gnomes. But now I can feel that letter, hovering in the air between us.

> *I understand . . .*
> *I know right now it seems like . . .*
> *You matter, even if you think you don't . . .*
> *I'm here for you . . .*

"You ready to get up there, show Miss B what you got?" I ask.

You lean in, conspiratorial, forehead nearly touching mine. You wink and it's the goddamn sexiest thing I've ever seen.

"It's in the bag," you say.

Your voice has its usual carefree tone, but amazing actor that you are, you can't hide the tension underneath. I follow your lead, though—if you want to pretend everything's fine, then I will, too.

"Pretty confident, are we?" I ask.

You laugh and I notice that when you do, you look down at your lap and shake your head a little. Soon, this gesture will become familiar to me. Dear.

"Put in a good word for me?" you say.

"I'll think about it." Now it's my turn to wink.

"This is pretty fabulous." You reach out and gently tug on my sweater. It's covered in sequins, one of those cheap five-dollar things from H&M.

"You're the only straight guy I know who can say *fabulous* and get away with it," I say.

You grin. "That's because I'm fabulous."

The first round of singers go up, most of them variations on awful. You actually cringe once and slide lower into your chair, like the sound is physically painful to you. I like that you try to keep this on the DL—you're not a jerk, just a connoisseur.

You turn to me, eyes snagging on mine. "Thank you," you say, your voice soft. "Your letter, it kinda . . . saved me."

I blush, pleasure blooming in my chest. I don't know it now, but there will be a garden inside me soon. And it'll grow thorns.

"Oh," I say. Why can I suddenly only think of expressions from French class? *Je suis un ananas.* I am a pineapple? "I mean, cool. I hope it helped. Um."

I bite my lip, look down at the audition slips I'm clutching in my hands. Nothing ever comes out right. I wish Tony Kushner or some other beautiful playwright could live inside my throat and just say the right thing for me at the right time.

"It did," you say. "Help, I mean."

Something in my bones tells me this moment is important.

Miss B calls your name before we can say anything else and you pass me your audition slip (your handwriting *is* surprisingly neat) and lope to the front of the room. You hand your music to the pianist, then look at us with what my grandpa would call a shit-eating grin.

You're suddenly Billy Flynn, perfect casting for the conniving lawyer. Anyone who wants that part probably gave up the moment they heard you were still auditioning. Like so much, it's yours for the taking.

This is Drama King Gavin: life of the party, the guy who takes nothing and no one seriously. Especially himself. Band Gavin is more like the real Gavin I'll be getting to know: broody, moods shifting like tectonic plates. Vulnerable.

Despite the smile on your face and the magnetism that crackles around you whenever you're onstage, I can feel the apprehension in the room. Everyone leans forward in their seats. I can almost see the neon sign blinking above your head: SUICIDE SUICIDE SUICIDE.

You sing "One Song Glory" from *Rent* and I wonder if this is the song you'd originally planned to sing, or your way of telling us, *I'm okay now*. It's definitely not the kind of jazzy song everyone else is doing and not your band's brand of angst rock. It's . . . beautiful. Delicate and raw, laced with gritty elegance. I want to make out with you so bad right now.

> *One song, he had the world at his feet,*
> *Glory, in the eyes of a young girl, a young girl . . .*

I'm that young girl.

I just don't know it yet.

FIVE

All my guy friends at school are horny. Their favorite thing to do is figure out what each of us girls' porn names would be. I guess a lot of people in porn use their middle name as their first name and the street they live on as their last name. This would make me Marie Laye.

Unfortunate (or perfect), I know.

You, Kyle, Peter, and Ryan think it's the most hilarious thing in the world that I live on Laye Avenue. It's a pretty perfect name for a porn star. It cracks you up and seeing you laugh makes me happy, so I don't care that the four of you are plotting my side career in adult films. I guess if directing doesn't work out, I'll have something to fall back on.

Gavin Davis.

I can't get you out of my head. The air around you is changed, weighted somehow, by what happened. You look older, like you've really been through something. You don't even try to hide your scars. You almost wear them like a badge of honor. Battle scars. I like that. You seem wise somehow. Like you found the answer to a question you've been asking for a long time. I want to know the answer.

The words I wrote you two weeks ago make my fingers burn. I hold them to my lips now and suddenly think, *I wonder what it would be like to kiss him.* Summer has moved from fear and sadness to seriously pissed off at you—she doesn't hang around with us anymore. Lys, who plans to be a psychologist someday like her parents, says that Summer is moving through the stages of grief.

Summer says you're controlling, that you didn't like her having guy friends. I mean, I guess that's not cool but she *is* pretty flirty with other guys. Even I've noticed that. *He wanted to be with me all the time*, she says. *He wanted to be the most important thing.* Sorry, but I don't see what's so bad about that. I mean, if you were my boyfriend, I can't imagine not wanting to hang out with you every second of every day. If that's crazy, sign me up. Attach me to your hip.

The bell at the end of my last class rings, jolting me out of my thoughts, bringing me back to Now, which is not a happy place. I'd like to pass Go and collect my two hundred dollars, but college feels like a long way off. So the bell rings and my heart sinks. I hate this part of the day, when I know I have to go home.

There's a collective happy sigh as Mr. Denson says, "Do your homework or you'll end up homeless. Say it with me: Trigonometry is good."

We all groan out, "Trigonometry is good."

I realize I haven't heard a thing Mr. Denson has been saying for the past hour. This happens to me all the time. I get lost in my thoughts, daydream whole classes away.

Get your head out of the clouds, Mom says.

My house is only a few blocks from campus, so I'm home pretty quick. Pro: I don't have a long-ass walk. Con: I get home before I want to, which is never. You know that bummed-out feeling you get on Sundays—the Sunday blues? That's how coming home is. That's how I feel every second I'm in my family's house.

36

I'm not really sure why my mom had me. By that I mean that I wasn't a mistake baby, like an oh-shit-I-got-knocked-up baby. My mom wanted me. Which is why it's so weird that she doesn't seem to want me *now*. I feel like I've somehow intruded on her, like she and The Giant have a big No Trespassing sign and an electric fence around them and Sam. I am constantly bumping into the goddamn fence.

They don't want me here. In some of our worse arguments, when I threaten to go live with my drug addict of a dad, my mom says, *Fine, see how you like it there*. And I don't know what she means by that. Like, *Fine, I don't care?* Or does she mean the life she gives me is so much better? And if she does mean that, isn't it, like, not really impressive that she's giving me a better life than a drug addict? The bar is set pretty low, is what I'm saying.

To my mom and The Giant, I'm a nuisance first, a servant second, and a person a distant third. My life at home is an endless list of chores. To name a few: scrubbing between the tiles in the shower, organizing the recycling (crushing every individual can first), watering the lawn, dusting, vacuuming, folding laundry, prepping dinner, washing the windows (God forbid I leave a streak), making beds that aren't mine, doing dishes, and babysitting. My mother, she can't stand dirt. Everything has to be spotless, in its right place, and it is my job to do that regardless of my pile of homework or the friends who want to see a movie, hang out. The Giant gets in on this action, too. For example, it's my job to wash his car every week and I'm often stuck doing his laundry.

My friends and I secretly dubbed him The Giant because he has a very *fee fi fo fum* personality. He drinks vodka tonics and has a voice that throws goose bumps over your arms. His word is law. Our house is full of yelling and tears, walls that hide the truth from our neighbors. The Giant can be very charming, you see. When he's outside our house, he's an ogre in disguise, morphing into Friendly Neighbor or

Dedicated Parent. He's an accountant with a business that costs more than it makes, but his true calling, I think, is acting: he's so very talented at pretending to be a good person.

We live in a one-story with three bedrooms. I used to share my room with my older sister, Beth, which is why I have a bunk bed. I claimed the bottom one because it feels like a cocoon, like I can hide there when things get too hard.

I've stuck up pictures of my friends on the wall beside the bed, a mixture of show photos and random candid shots. There's one of you sitting on the edge of the stage, fixing me with a lazy grin. I have pictures of my idols: Julie Taymor (only the best director *ever*), Walt Whitman. There's also my favorite quote, which my freshman-year English teacher had on a poster above the whiteboard: *Medicine, law, business, engineering are necessary to sustain life. But poetry, beauty, romance, and love—these are what we live for.* It's basically my mission statement.

The quote's from *Dead Poets Society*, one of the parts where Robin Williams is in the classroom, teaching his students about Shakespeare. No one had to get me to like Shakespeare. I've memorized nearly all of *Romeo and Juliet*. I understand how trapped they feel, how desperate they are to get out. In eighth grade, I carried it everywhere, reading and rereading it in all my spare moments. My copy is pretty beat-up, but it would probably be the first thing I saved in a fire. The pages are brittle and yellowing already, stained with the hope that bled through my fingers, a new girl in a new town looking for something epic in her life.

I remember the day we moved here from LA. My mom and The Giant had just gotten married, and Beth and I stayed up late in the dark, crying. It was too quiet—we missed the sound of the freeway, the helicopters. It smelled weird, like dung and dirt and broken dreams. We made a list of all our favorite things about LA and then posted it on our bedroom wall. It's still up there: Venice Beach, the Fifties Cafe, Pickwick Ice Rink, standing in line at Pink's, Mexican food.

I dump my backpack on the floor in the entryway of our house just as Sam skips in. Even though I love him, Sam, through no fault of his own, is kind of the bane of my existence. My mom has already told me that my (unpaid, unappreciated) job this summer will be to babysit him every day, all day, whenever I'm not at the Honey Pot. Beth and I used to share the burden, but now it's all on me—babysitting, chores, punching bag. Mom takes advantage of the free labor so that she can spend time on Mineral Magic, this makeup company she does parties for, selling the makeup to her friends and their friends and their friends.

"Gace!" Sam yells.

He has trouble pronouncing his r's. Sam reaches his arms up, smiling, and I hug him to me, pick him up and spin him around. I like the way he throws his head back and how the laughter starts somewhere deep in his belly. Right now, he's not the bane of my existence: he is adorable and sweet and really the only good thing about this house.

"Grace!"

My mom, already calling, impatient, irritated. It's chore time, I just know it. I swing Sam around so I'm carrying him piggyback style and head for the kitchen. Mom's doing her drink ritual: glass, ice, water, lemon wedge, one packet of Equal. Place in glass in that order, stir three times clockwise, three times counterclockwise. She has me make it for her all the time. *Grace, I need a water.* She'll do that, just call me out of my room while I'm doing homework, like I'm some on-call bartender. One time she caught me stirring it four times—I was daydreaming about you and lost track. She screamed at me for wasting the lemon, the Equal, the water during a drought as she poured the contents out, rinsed the glass, then set it on the counter. *Do it again.*

"I need you to weed the backyard," she says. "Take Sam with you and keep an eye on him."

No *Hey, how was your day?* No *Do you have a lot of homework? Did any more of your friends try to commit suicide?*

Ever since last week I kept wanting to talk to her about you because sometimes adults know stuff, but she's always busy with some new project and now I feel like, what's the point? I hate the yo-yo that is our relationship. Sometimes I feel so close to my mom, like we're two soldiers in a trench, clutching our guns to our chest, ready to charge when the enemy comes. Other times, she *is* the enemy.

This is my attempt to not have the worst afternoon ever: "I have to do a ton of trig before work—"

She raises her hand. "You should have thought about that before you decided not to weed last weekend."

The anger in me simmers just under the surface of my skin. It's there, right when I want it. Waiting. I only have an hour to do homework before I have to work the closing shift at the Honey Pot. Now I don't even have that.

"Mom, that's not fair. I had work and then that big project for English to finish, remember?"

"I don't want to hear it."

She's yelling now. It doesn't take much to get her there. Sam digs his forehead into my back like he's trying to hide. My mom is angry all the time. When she talks to me, she clenches her teeth, growling. I'm too old for an actual spanking, but my face, my arms, the back of my head—all that's up for grabs. I'd like to avoid getting slapped around today. I'd like to not hate her.

"Okay," I say, my voice suddenly quiet. Beaten-Down Daughter. I curl my toes. Stare at my Doc Martens. Except I don't do a good enough job of hiding my frustration this time.

"I'm *this close* to keeping you home."

"I'm sorry," I say, contrite, like she's Jesus and I'm asking for forgiveness.

If I skip work today, I could lose my job. I just want it to stop. This constant confrontation—it's exhausting. Mom has three major states: Angry, Depressed, Unhinged. By *unhinged* I mean she'll decide to reorganize the Christmas decorations in July—at three in the morning.

I'm so tired.

When I try to explain how awful it feels here to my friends, when I try to explain the fear I constantly live with that the bit of freedom I have is going to get taken from me—it just comes out sounding petty. Poor me. And their sympathy isn't what I want, anyway. I need righteous anger. I need someone pounding on the front door, ready to tell my mom and The Giant just how lucky they are. I get straight A's. I'm a virgin. The only alcohol I've ever had is a thimble of Communion wine when my Grams takes Beth and me to church. I've never smoked pot or a cigarette or even been in a room where those things are present. I don't jaywalk, I don't ditch classes, I never lie to my mom. In short, I am a really good fucking kid. But they don't see that. They see someone trespassing on a life that would, it seems to me, be much better without me in it.

Please don't ground me. Those are the words that go round and round in my head right now. I was grounded for half of last month because I hadn't cleaned the master bathroom that my mom and Roy share before I went to Nat's house. I was running late and wiped it down quickly, hoping she wouldn't notice. But she did, of course she did. There was a hair on the base of the toilet (*You call this CLEAN?*) and a speck of mold between two tiles (*And THIS. I'm not blind, Grace.*). My punishment: two weeks of imprisonment, which just happened to coincide with a home improvement project that The Giant was undertaking.

Mom's voice turns indifferent—my apology does nothing. "When you're done you can go."

"Are you still okay to drive me?"

The mall is a half-hour walk away and my mom refuses to let me get my license because she says it's an adult responsibility and I'm not mature enough to handle it (except: Straight A's! Virgin! Sober!).

"Let's see how you do on the lawn."

This is how I pick up the pieces of my afternoon, how I hold on to the hope of making it to work on time and thus not losing my job: I nod, wrapping my meekness around me like a cloak.

I change out of my vintage mod dress and into old jeans and a T-shirt, then head out the sliding glass door that leads to the back, picking Sam up on my way. I squeeze him too tight and he cries out and I snap at him, the anger pouring out of me, hot and quick. The guilt is instantaneous. I'm not any better than my mom.

"I'm sorry, buddy," I whisper to Sam as we get outside.

I help him over to his swing set, then pull on gardening gloves and get to work on the weeds.

Being seventeen with fascist parents sucks. You get to feeling like nothing is yours except the thoughts in your head and these tiny private moments.

Don't be a martyr, Mom would say.

Look, I'm not this upset because I have to do one stupid chore or babysit my brother for a few hours after school. It's that things have gotten to the point where everything is bad all the time, so one little thing pushes me right over. Sometimes I wish I had split lips or bruises to show the school counselor—it's hard to explain the torture of living in this house, the way the constant nagging and housework and yelling grinds you down. Before, when there were welts on my skin from The Giant, I was too young to know what to do about them. Now I'd love to present them to a school counselor and say, *See? I can't live like this anymore.* I'm trapped, suffocating. Living in this house is like the time I was in my cousin's pool and a big raft everyone was playing on covered me. I was stuck underwater with it just over my head and for a few seconds I was certain I was going to drown.

It's not bad one hundred percent of the time, but if anything good happens, there are always strings attached. I've learned to barter. Time with my friends, clothes, movie tickets, a night out—these all cost something. Is having fun Friday night worth a weekend's worth of chores or babysitting? I remember once how Lys tried to explain that this wasn't normal, that parents would do nice things for their kids because they wanted to, because they loved them. There was no *you owe me*, no *what's in it for me?* It sounded too good to be true.

I pull weeds, the sun hot on my back. It's unseasonably warm, even though we're used to crazy heat in this part of California—ninety degrees even though it's March. Money's tight, though, so being inside isn't much better. On days like this, Mom only puts the air-conditioning on at night. It's too expensive to keep it on all day. I take a break and look at the sky—the same sky as the one over Paris. I pretend for a minute that I'm there, walking along the Seine. I'm wearing a chic skirt and blouse, and . . . carrying a picnic basket with a baguette, cheese, and wine inside. And of course I'm holding hands with my boyfriend (Jacques? Pierre?). Or maybe I'm in New York City walking along Fifth Avenue, my hand in yours . . .

Mom opens the door and shouts at me to pay attention—Sam is climbing too high on his jungle gym. Every few minutes I have to get Sam away from one thing or another: the hose, the garden tools, the grill. I am never going to finish. I check my phone: 4:15. My shift starts at five. I speed-dial Beth and my perpetually busy sister actually picks up on the first ring.

"Hey, little sis," she says, and I burst into tears.

"Ah," she says softly. "What'd they do this time?"

I tell her about being on thin ice, how I'm scared Mom and The Giant aren't going to let me go to Interlochen. I tell her about you and about weeding the backyard and about being exhausted.

"Why does she have to make everything harder?" I say.

"Because . . . it's hard for her, too. With Roy. You know?" Beth says. "I don't even think Mom realizes she's like this."

Beth has sort of become the voice of reason since going away to college. It's like the distance is letting her see what's happening at home more clearly. I don't know how I feel about that. I don't think it's okay to let Mom off the hook. I liked when we were in the thick of things together, war buddies.

"Are you having the time of your life?" I ask her.

Even though she's just in LA, it feels like she's a million miles away. I want gossiping in the middle of the hottest nights, when we can't sleep because the only air we have is the hot, manure-scented breeze trickling through the open window. I want washing dishes side by side. I want how we'd go from tears to laughing so hard our stomachs hurt.

"I am," she says. "And you will, too. One more year. Chin up, okay?"

"Okay."

When I'm done, I run to the kitchen and make the salad and set the table. I glance at the clock on the stove: 4:40. I really hope Mom doesn't make me walk. It's a couple miles—I'd never make it in time.

I hurry to my room and throw on the white shirt and black skirt all of us Honey Pot girls wear, then grab my khaki apron and purse. 4:45.

Mom comes in from her room and surveys what I've done in the kitchen as she talks on the phone to a friend.

She laughs. "Oh, it's no problem, really. Grace can watch Sam and I'll come over and help you plan the party. Saturday night at six? Perfect."

I hate when she does this, just puts a big X over my weekend. Maybe I had plans for Saturday night at six. But the conversation with her friend seems to be winding down and my heart lifts. She'll hang up, I'll be on time—no. Now she's crossing into the living room, straightening things that are already straight, seeing wrinkles that aren't there.

It wouldn't be the first time that I was late for work (or anything else) for that reason. I'm dying inside (*I have to go, I have to go!*). Why does she always do this? She knows I start at five. She knows you can't be late for your job. I can't say anything, even though it's so hard not to. It's pointless. She'll just wave me away like I'm an annoying fly: *buzz buzz buzz*. It's hard to kill a fly, but it can be done, if you swat at it enough.

I rush to my room and scream into my pillow, just to let some of this out. When I get back to the kitchen, she's off the phone and scrubbing the cutting board.

"Mom?" I glance at the clock. 4:55. I should have just walked. "Can we—"

"I'm not leaving the house like a pigsty," she says. "What have I told you about cleaning up after yourself?"

It's a cutting board, that's all that's out of place. A cutting board I'd already rinsed off after chopping onions and making a salad for a meal I'm not even going to be eating because there's no time to eat and I'd rather go hungry or eat my left arm, if it means I can get the hell out of here. I'm going to be late because of a cutting board? How do you explain that to your boss? *I'm sorry, but there was this dreadful cutting board situation, you know how it is.*

Other than the cutting board, the house is perfectly clean. I mean, you could literally eat off the floor. Put on white gloves and run your finger along the bookcase—your glove will come away white as snow.

There are medical words for the problems my mom has, but my only words for it right now are *batshit crazy*.

These are the worst moments, knowing I can't say a word while something important to me hangs in the balance. How many times have I been late or missed entire events because of a dirty dish or my mom's sudden need to dust or organize a cupboard, water the grass. I've learned my lesson the hard way: pester her, even just once, and *that's it, you're not going*.

4:58—if we leave right now, I'll only be five or ten minutes late. That's respectable. You can blame traffic or a watch that's set too slow.

4:59. My mom hands me the keys. "Go get your brother in the car seat."

I grab Sam and run.

SIX

I see you every day after school for four hours. For most of it, I sit hunched over my copy of the script, writing down the blocking and anything else Miss B needs the cast and crew to remember once we get onto an actual stage. Being a stage manager is serious business. I could screw up the entire show, so unlike you and the rest of the cast, I don't have much time for socializing.

You're Billy Flynn, of course. No surprise there. The first time I ever saw you perform was when you played Don Lockwood in *Singin' in the Rain*. I was a lowly freshman, utterly besotted from my seat in the audience. When you're onstage, nobody can look away. You just have it. You know, *It*. Star quality, that *je ne sais quoi*.

Something's happening now with you and me, but I'm not sure what it is. I catch you looking at me, furtive glances that you hold long enough for me to see. You want me to catch you looking. There are soft smiles that make me blush. And suddenly there are hugs. When you see me, when we part ways. Hugs that last longer than they should, your heat seeping into me. More and more often now you'll come and sit by me and do homework if you're not in whatever scene is onstage.

Or you pretend to do homework—mostly you write funny little notes to me.

When I walk into a room the magnets inside us make it almost impossible to stay more than a few feet apart. But we don't talk about it. Any of it. There are no phone calls, no dates, nothing. Just these magnets.

I worry that it's all in my head. Wishful thinking. I mean, come on. We're talking about Gavin Davis here. I'm not the type of girl that gets a boy like you. And yet.

Nat makes a beeline for me, pulls me to an empty corner.

"I heard something," she says.

I raise my eyebrows. "Don't tell me God spoke to you again."

Every now and then Nat will say that God laid something on her heart, which in Christian speak means God communicated directly with her. It's usually something that she needs to do or fix. Lys thinks that's creeptastic, but I don't know. It's kind of nice, I think.

"No," she says. Then she gets a wicked look in her eye. "Maybe I shouldn't tell you."

"I'll give you my firstborn child if you tell me your secret," I say, contrite.

She laughs. "Fine. Gavin told Peter and Kyle that you're hot."

I pretend to be offended, but inside? DYING. "Is that so hard to believe?"

"Oh, shut up. Of course it's not hard to believe." Her big brown eyes dance. "I think he's crushing on you."

"Don't get my hopes up," I say. But they're already up. This is going to crash and burn so hard.

"Fabulous thespians!" calls Miss B. For some reason, she's decided to have an English accent today. "Gather round while I tell you the schedule." She says it the British way: shed-jewel. I love Miss B. She exudes theatricality. The whole world is her stage. She's got a

48

thousand-watt smile, a chic bob, and when she talks, she uses her hands as much as I do. Her hair's black, with one white streak in the front. In short, she's super awesome.

You catch my eye and I can't look away and we smile goofy smiles.

Nat takes my arm and whispers in my ear, "I think he's imagining having sex with you *right now*."

My face turns bright red and I hit her arm as she guides us to the opposite side of the room from where you, Kyle, and Peter lie on your backs side by side, elbows propping you up, the Kings of Roosevelt High Drama. Your head turns, ever so slightly, following me. Cue soft smile. Cue my blush.

"Uh-huh. Just as I suspected," Nat says under her breath.

"Nothing's going on," I say, adamant. So why are things bursting inside me, stars being born where there'd been only darkness before?

Miss B runs down the shed-jewel: five more weeks of rehearsal after school, then we move into the big, fancy theater we get to use downtown. I could pee my pants I'm so excited. Once we start night rehearsals and performances, I won't have to go home until ten every night. It's the only freedom I'll have until the next play, which is *next October*. (Best not to think about that.) Then Mrs. Menendez comes up, our dance P.E. teacher who choreographs all the shows.

When she gives the rundown on all the things the dancers will need to buy, I thank my lucky stars I'm not in the cast. It gets old being broke. My family's biggest splurge is getting the two-for-one cheeseburgers at McDonald's on Sundays. On my last birthday, I had to use the money my grandparents sent me to take my family to the movies, otherwise we would have had to just stay home and do nothing. I know people are starving in Africa and it's wrong of me to complain, but it's hard, seeing how most of my friends don't get it. I'm so used to *Money doesn't grow on trees, Grace.* I honestly don't remember the last thing my mom or The Giant bought me. Oh wait—The Giant lent me the money to get a soda at Costco last week. Yes, he *lent* me the ninety-nine cents—I shit you not.

After rehearsal, I head toward my house, walking as slowly as I can. A slow walk takes between eight and ten minutes, as opposed to normal walking, which takes only five. I always dread that moment when I walk through the door. I never know what's waiting for me. Maybe I'm already in trouble and I don't even know it. I shove my earbuds in and turn up *Rent.* I'm in NYC, eating lunch with my bohemian friends at the Life Café . . .

There's a honk and I turn around. Your Mustang pulls up, a shimmery dark blue classic, the engine purring. "Hey, girlie," you say, sunglasses slipping down your nose, your voice purposefully creepy. "Want to take a ride with me?"

I lean in the window and grin. "My mommy told me not to talk to strangers." I hold up my hand when you open your mouth. "Don't you dare make a *your mom* joke, Gavin Davis."

You laugh. "Fine. I'll resist the temptation—just this once." You turn down the radio—indie rock of some kind, mellow and deep.

"So . . . ," you say.

"So . . . ," I say.

Smile. Blush. Repeat.

"You want a ride home?" you ask.

My stomach goes all kinds of wonky.

"Oh, I literally live across the street." I point toward Laye Ave. "On the cul-de-sac."

Yes! I want to say. *Let me get in your surrey with a fringe on top, your rowboat in the depths of the Paris opera house.* (Pssst: ten points to you, Gav, if you can guess which shows I'm talking about.) But I can't get in that car. And I really don't want to explain why. *See, my mom has this rule . . .* I'm so tired of having to narrate the crazy that is my home life.

You raise one eyebrow. I didn't know that real people knew how to do that. "Good to know," you say. "Where you live, I mean."

Butterflies! In my stomach!

"Don't use that knowledge for nefarious purposes," I say.

"I make no promises." You grin. "You know, I could really go for a Pepsi Freeze right now." You point to me and then to the passenger seat.

Me. Freaking. Too. Are you asking me out? What is happening?

I take a breath and give you the rundown, which is: "So, I don't know if, like, Kyle or Nat or anyone has told you about my weirdo family. One of my mom's million rules is that I'm not allowed to drive with people she doesn't know."

"Even to the gas station up the street?" you ask.

"Even there."

"Sucks. And you don't have a license?" you ask.

"No," I say. "Parentals don't want to pay for insurance, blah blah blah."

"Lame."

"Pretty much, yeah. But it's . . . you know, whatever, it's cool."

"Don't go anywhere," you say. "Promise?"

"Um. Okay?"

You turn back into the school parking lot, park, then walk over to me. I like watching you do this, the way your shirt rides up a little so I can see the skin at your waist. The cool you exude with your Ray-Ban Wayfarers and skinny jeans.

"Gavin, you really don't need to walk me home," I say when you get to me.

"I'm not." You grab my trig book out of my hand. Why, hello, Gilbert Blythe. "How long do you think it will take us to walk to the Pepsi Freezes?"

"Gavin . . ." I shake my head. "Seriously—"

"Half an hour there, half an hour back?"

51

Twenty-six minutes, not like I know or anything. I nod.

"But I can't just—I need permission? And my mom, she's . . . Maybe I shouldn't."

"I'm super good with parents." You grab my hand and pull me toward my house. So. Freaking. Smooth.

You're holding my hand, you are HOLDING MY HAND.

There isn't much time to talk on the way, but you don't let go of my hand and I'm worried mine is sweaty but I try not to think about it because that will make it more sweaty and then if you realize it's sweaty—hell. I am in hell. But, like, with a view of heaven.

I'm not religious but I literally pray to whatever is out there that my mom isn't screaming at Sam or fighting with The Giant when we get to the house—how mortifying would that be?

When we walk up to my front porch, though, it's unexpectedly quiet. Our house is *never* quiet. I unlock the door and you hover in the hallway, so close I can feel the heat of you. I can't enjoy being this close, though—I'm about to break out in hives because if I have a friend—especially a friend of the male species—inside the house without anyone else being home, I will be dead. Like, *so dead*. My mom can't handle people being inside unless it's just been cleaned.

"Any embarrassing baby pictures for me to look at?" you ask. Wow, do I love that gravelly drawl of yours.

"Sorry," I say, grabbing my trig book out of your hands. "We have a no-baby-pictures policy here."

"Somehow I think you're lying."

I roll my eyes, open my bedroom door, and throw my backpack and book inside.

"Your house smells like lemons."

"Pine Sol Lemon Fresh, to be exact," I say. Other people's houses smell like life: food and maybe candles and dog.

"No pets?" you ask.

I laugh. "My mom would probably have an aneurysm if there was an animal in the house." I seriously can't imagine what she'd do if there was dog hair in here. "I guess we can go."

This is an adventure I might pay for later, but it'll be worth it. On our way out, I see a note on the dining room table for me in my mom's looping handwriting.

> *Went to Costco. The laundry needs to be folded and the front and back porch swept. Also, you forgot to clean the baseboards in the dining room last Friday, so that needs to be done before we get home. Put the roast in the oven and make a salad.*

The effing baseboards. Mom's invisible dirt and microscope eyes. There's no reasoning with her, either. You just scrub until she can't see it anymore.

"Is this for real?" you ask, reading over my shoulder. You're so close I can smell your cologne, a woodsy, spicy smell.

"Yeah." I hate it when people find out about my family for the first time.

I do some time math in my head. No Costco trip is shorter than an hour and the long list of chores suggests Mom's planning on being gone awhile, maybe running other errands, too. That should buy me at least another twenty minutes, maybe more. I can always say rehearsal went long if she and The Giant get back home before I do. Which isn't technically lying because rehearsal went five minutes longer than it was supposed to.

Good enough.

I push you out the door. "We have to power walk."

"I was in the *Guinness Book of World Records* for power walking," you say.

In my fifty-seven minutes with you that evening, I learn three things:

1. You're the only other person I know who looks up at the sky and imagines you're somewhere else.
2. We both cried at the end of *Hamilton*.
3. You've always wanted to get to know me but were too intimidated.

"Intimidated?" I say. "By what—my efficient stage management skills?"

You shrug. "You've just got this thing. . . ." You start in with some Billy Joel: *"She's got a way about her, I don't know what it is, but I know that I can't live without her . . ."*

I love being around a boy who sings all the time. And sings old-school songs only our mothers know.

It's a perfect first date, even though I know it's not actually a date. I walk around the house in a daze and when I get an apple to snack on, I catch myself twisting its stem, playing that game from when I was a little girl. You twist the stem around and each rotation is a letter of the alphabet. The letter corresponds to a boy. A-Andrew, B-Brian, etc.

The stem breaks off at G.

SEVEN

I stumble out of the bathroom and crawl into my bed, weak. I think I'm finally done throwing up. I'm at the dry-heaving stage, which is pretty much as low as you can go.

It started in the middle of the night, a nausea so strong I had vertigo. It was noon before I was able to text the girls—I didn't want Miss B to think I was ditching the show. When I'm not throwing up or curled into a ball of pain, I try to imagine what's going on at rehearsal. I can picture you lounging offstage, trading jokes with the guys, or maybe in a hallway by yourself, going over your lines. I see Nat and Lys practicing a tap routine. Miss B looking slightly frazzled.

I drift in and out of sleep. When I look out the window I notice the sky is getting darker—rehearsal will be over soon. I'm pissed that I missed a whole day of seeing you. You sent me a selfie at lunch—in it, you made yourself look totally depressed. You texted, *This place sucks without you.* A few hours later, during one of my many trips to the bathroom, you left a voice mail singing a naughty sea shanty. I listen to it for the fifth time, propped up on two pillows. This is evidence of how close we've gotten over the past few weeks. It wasn't that long ago that we didn't even have each other's phone numbers. Now I have hundreds of texts from you. I set down my phone and slide back under my thick duvet, fluffing the pillows until I get comfortable.

The doorbell rings and I hear my mom pad down the hallway. She's paranoid about getting sick—she can't handle the germs, so I've pretty much been a prisoner in my room. She's been talking to me through the door all day, leaving the occasional tray outside of it with crackers or a glass of water or a bottle of Pepto-Bismol, which makes me nauseous just looking at it. I'm not allowed to open the door until she's out of range. I think she's about two seconds away from calling the Centers for Disease Control.

I'm just falling back asleep when there's a knock on my door.

"Grace?" Mom says. "Are you decent?"

"What? Yeah." I'm wearing a pair of baggy pajama shorts and a tank top that my grandma bought me when she went to Wisconsin that says Somebody in Racine Loves Me. Because I'm sexy like that. It occurs to me that I desperately need a shower.

I hear some mumbling outside the door and then it opens. I sit up on my elbows, my hair a rat's nest, my eyes bleary.

It's you.

"Now, I'm only shutting the door because I don't want Sam coming in here and getting sick," my mom says.

I stare at her. I don't know how you sweet-talked your way into this house, let alone my room.

"Hey, beautiful," you murmur after the door shuts behind you.

The surprise of seeing you in my bedroom almost trumps the fact that I look like death. Wait, did you just call me *beautiful*? I search blindly for a rubber band. I realize I'm not wearing a bra. I pray I don't smell like I've been vomiting for the past fifteen hours.

"Gavin, what are you—"

56

"Doing here? Like I wasn't going to make sure you're okay. What do you take me for?"

You set your backpack, a grocery bag, and your guitar down before kicking off your shoes and crawling onto the bed. You sit cross-legged in front of me, your hands resting lightly on my knees.

"Um, I might be contagious—"

You shrug. "Misery loves company."

A sharp pain shoots through my stomach and I lean back onto the pillows. "It kind of hurts to sit up," I say.

You lie down next to me, your head propped up on your elbow. I lie in the fetal position and we stare at each other for a moment. You're not wearing your fedora and your hair falls into your eyes. I want to brush it back, but I don't.

"Everyone missed you," you say.

"How was rehearsal?"

"Madness. Utter chaos. This production can't survive without you."

"I'm glad I'm indispensable." I smile. "How did you convince my mom to let you in here?"

"I told her I needed her help in making a grand romantic gesture," you say. For me. A grand romantic gesture *for me*.

"I also threatened to start serenading her."

I laugh. "I can't believe you charmed my mother. That's seriously hard to do."

You know women, Gavin. I'll give you that. You know just what we need to hear, don't you?

"She seemed nice, but . . ." You frown, searching for the right words. "Formidable."

I snort. "Then you caught her on a good day."

I've told you a little about my family situation, but not all the gory details. I've been trying to figure out how to introduce you to my mom without making a thing about it. I'm sort of glad it happened this way.

"I like your hair," you tease, fingering my tangled locks.

"Not all of us can wake up in the morning looking like James Dean," I say.

You laugh quietly. "Do you still feel like shit?"

"I think I'm in the post-feeling-like-shit stage, but before the feeling-better stage."

"I can help with that."

You sit up and rummage through the grocery sack. You hold up a bottle of ginger ale and a plastic container with what looks like soup inside.

"Chicken soup?"

"I asked my mom to make it for you," you say. "It's a total miracle cure."

My eyes widen. "You had your mom make chicken soup for me?"

You set the container on my desk. "Yep. She had today off work. I swear you'll feel better after eating it."

"Wow. That's . . . you're amazing."

"Why, thank you." Your lip turns up. "I may have promised to bring you to dinner when you're not contagious."

My stomach flips. Holy fucking shit, you want me to meet your *parents*.

"I promise they don't bite." You hold up a spoon. "You hungry?"

"I better wait," I say. "Unless you enjoy being vomited on."

The corner of your mouth turns up. "I draw the line at being vomited on." You look around. "So this is your room."

I try to see it through your eyes. A poster with a shot of New York City from above, a *Rent* poster I got on eBay, a map of Paris. A bookshelf stuffed with Nancy Drew mysteries and old copies of *Vogue*. Knickknacks line the windowsill—seashells from Malibu, Happy Meal toys that Sam gifts me with.

"I like it," you say. Your eyes land on the collage of pictures next to my bed. You move closer. After a minute, you see the one of you and my face goes pink.

"That was a good day," you say.

We had finished tech rehearsals for *The Importance of Being Earnest* and we all ordered pizza and ate it in the quad before playing flag football—without a football or any flags.

You point to a picture of Beth and me jumping from a high dive together. "Who's that?"

"My sister—Beth. She's two years older than me. She's at UCLA now."

"My dream school," you say.

"Yeah?"

"I auditioned for them in the fall. Should be finding out sometime soon."

I need this reminder. Whatever's going on between us now, it can't last. You'll be moving to LA when I'm starting my senior year. But I don't want to think about that.

"You'll get in."

You shrug. "Maybe." You reach for the ginger ale. "Think you can keep this down?"

I nod and take it, grateful. "All my mom gave me was water."

"What's the deal with her? I felt like I needed a hazmat suit to get in here."

I sigh. "That's just . . . Mom. She's got a thing about germs." I reach out a hand and squeeze your arm. "Thanks for taking care of me."

You smile. "Best part of my day."

I bite my lip, casting about for something to look at, anything but your eyes.

"What's in that bag?" I say, pointing to the tote.

"Ah, yes."

You grab it, then crawl back onto the bed, settling in next to me.

You pull a stack of picture books out of the bag. "When I was a kid and got really sick, my mom would hang out in my room and read books to me. They were a good distraction."

As opposed to my mom, who, since I can remember, always stays a good ten feet away from me when I'm sick.

"Are you going to read me stories?" Because oh my god that is the cutest—

You nod. "Which one do you want first?"

My eyes catch on yours and you smile. Then you reach out and slide the back of your fingers across my cheek. For a second I can't breathe.

You hold up *Goodnight, Moon*. "This one was my favorite."

"Then I want that one," I say.

You rest your back against my pillows, then reach out so that I'm lying in the crook of your arm, my hand against your chest.

"Comfy?" you ask.

I nod. "Perfect."

I can feel your heart beating under my hand. You cough slightly, then begin, your breath gently stirring my hair.

"In the great green room there was a telephone . . ."

I lose count of how many stories you read me. You do all the voices. If there's a song you sing it. You hold me close to you so that, by the end, my head is against your chest. The smell of you is crack to me— that spicy cologne and whatever else makes you *you*. If I hadn't been throwing up my guts all day, I might have had the courage to kiss you. But probably not.

"Feeling any better?" you murmur after you close *The Very Hungry Caterpillar.*

I nod and look up at you. "I hope I don't get you sick."

You smile, running your hand through my hair. "It'd be worth it."

I want to stay in this moment, suspended forever. I don't know yet that this tenderness between us will be impossible by the end. I have no idea how much you will hurt me.

You stay for another hour, playing your guitar as I eat. Your mom's chicken soup is delicious.

At nine my mom knocks on the door.

"Grace? You need to rest now if you're going to get to school tomorrow morning."

"Okay," I call.

You stand up. "That's my cue."

You insist on getting me comfortably settled, then squeeze my hand.

"How are you sick and pretty at the same time?" you say.

"Flattery will get you everywhere."

You shake your head. "Good night, Miss Carter."

"Good night, Mr. Davis."

You shut the door behind you and I lie on my side, turning off the lamp. My pillow smells like you and it's still warm from where you'd been leaning against it. I hug it to me.

I'm asleep in seconds.

EIGHT

After that night, I allow myself to think that you might actually be falling for me.

I can't believe it, but I really think you are. There are the looks, those searing glances that own me. The hugs you don't give anyone else. The way you've started appearing at my locker between classes. The texts that say things like *Thanks for getting me through the day* and, as a joke when you were walking behind me, *Nice ass, Miss Carter*. Little gifts: Pepsi Freezes during rehearsal, a light for my clipboard so I can see backstage, bags of food when I have my long shifts at the Pot.

And a song.

You grab my hand and pull me into an empty classroom before rehearsal. You're carrying your acoustic in the other hand.

"I wrote you a song," you say, without preamble.

I stare at you. Did I just hear Gavin Davis tell me he wrote a song for me?

"It's rough," you say. "I couldn't sleep last night and I . . ." You rub the back of your neck, your cheeks going the softest shade of pink.

"Are you *blushing*?" I say, half laughing, half turning into a pile of mush.

"Shut up." You grin and play the first chords, a midtempo sound that reminds me a little of Ed Sheeran.

"I never thought I—" You stop. Clear your throat. "God, you're making me nervous."

I smile and slide behind you, so close I could kiss your neck if I wanted to, which I do—want to, that is.

"Is this better?" I murmur, my lips close to your ear. Who is this secret vixen living inside me and where has she been all this time?

You reach one hand back and I take it, let you pull me around so I'm facing you again.

"I want to see your face," you say with that perfect half smile. "That's the best part."

You let go of my hand, look down, take a breath. Then:

> *I never thought I'd find a girl like you*
> *Someone who makes me feel so damn brand-new*
> *She never turns her nose up at me*
> *She never tries to fucking change me*
> *She never leaves without saying good-bye*

You shrug as your fingers leave the strings. "That's just the first verse. It still needs a lot of work."

I stare at you and something like panic flits across your face.

"I said too much," you mumble. "You hate it? I know that second line is shit."

I shake my head, find my voice. "I . . . I love it. It's . . . Gav, I—"

A goofy grin spreads across your face.

"What?" I say.

"I love when you call me Gav."

I hadn't even realized I'd done it.

This is us now. For the past few weeks we've been skating around whatever *this* is, running headlong into a heart-shaped mystery. People are starting to notice. There are lots of raised eyebrows, especially from Nat and Lys.

"So. You and Gavin—spill," Nat says as she slides into a perfect split.

We're working on a new combo for dance P.E. and I keep screwing it up because I can't help replaying the last hug you gave me. It was so long that I'm pretty sure it qualifies as holding.

"I have no idea what's going on," I answer, honest. "I think he likes me, but—"

"You *think*? That boy is head over heels for you, anyone can see that," she says.

"Yeah?" I ask, grinning.

"Um. *Yeah*." She shakes her head. "Who would have thought—you and Gavin Davis."

It's like winning the boy lottery.

I smile. "Who would have thought."

You say I'm the only person who understands you. The only person who doesn't judge you. We can talk to each other about anything. And yet we're not together. We haven't kissed except for on the cheek or the few gallant times you've kissed my hand. It's almost like we know that if we *kiss* kiss, that will be it. We won't be able to fool our parents, our friends, *ourselves* any longer. Right now, we can say we're taking it slow, that of course we're considering how maybe it isn't good for you to be in a relationship right now. You *did* promise your parents you wouldn't date anyone until after you graduate. Which, by the way, will happen in a few months—and that brings us to the other reason we shouldn't be *we*: Guys in college don't usually have girlfriends in high school.

But then this happens:

"I want to kiss you so bad," you say. You're leaning against the lockers, holding my books while I work on the combination. I go still. "But we shouldn't. I mean, we're like . . . a frouple."

I've lost track of the numbers and have to start over.

"A frouple?"

Thirty-nine, ten, twenty-two . . .

"Yeah. You know. Friends that are almost a couple. A frouple. And froples don't kiss because then they'd be . . . couples."

"You're so weird."

"You're so perfect."

So each week we get closer to . . . something. I can feel it, like a tide dragging me out to sea.

On opening night, I pull you into a dark corner backstage. It's the middle of April and rainy, the thunder outside loud and insistent. My Gram always says that's God bowling. Everyone's worried people won't come because of the weather and I've spent half the afternoon reassuring nervous actors. But now *I* need some reassurance.

"What's the real reason?" I say, apropos of nothing.

You furrow your brow. "The real reason?"

"That we aren't together."

You smooth your Billy Flynn tie and look behind you, toward the stage. No one's around. You set your palms against the wall behind me, boxing me in. Classic sexy move.

"Grace, believe me when I say that there is nothing I want more than you."

We're so close your lips are almost touching mine.

"So *why?*"

"I'm trying to save you from me."

"What's that supposed to mean?"

You look away. "If you saw . . . if you saw the real me, you might not want—"

I rest my fingers against your lips. "Shut up," I whisper.

There's a small cough behind us, but instead of jumping away from me, you press your lips against my fingers before turning around.

"What's up, Nat?" you say.

She looks past you, toward me, apologetic.

"Sorry to . . . uh . . . interrupt. Miss B is looking for you—they can't find Roxie's last costume."

I nod and move away from you. "Okay."

It's too dark for her to see my blush, to see the pride in my eyes. *Believe me when I say that there is nothing I want more than you.*

She and Lys ambush me after the show, yanking me into the prop room. We're surrounded by shelves of theater junk—revolvers, candlesticks, knives, a rubber chicken. Like we're about to start an epic game of Clue. I open my mouth, but Nat puts a hand up like, *Stop right there.*

"Okay, were you guys, like, *making out* back there?" Nat asks.

"No! We haven't kissed, I swear. I would tell you guys."

"What the hell is he waiting for?" Lys asks. She sets down her massive purse and pulls a feather boa out of it, throwing it dramatically around her neck.

"It's complicated," I say. "Because of . . . you know. His parents want him to stay single until after graduation."

Nat frowns. "Is he still . . . suicidal?"

"God, no. He's doing great," I say. At least, I hope so. You say being with me is like taking a happy pill.

Nat and Lys exchange a look.

"What?" I say.

66

"You know we are very pro you-and-Gavin, but we've been talking and we thought you should maybe think about how, like . . . he's, like, really . . . intense," Nat says. "Are you sure you're up for that?"

"We don't want to see you get hurt," Lys adds. "Summer's still fucked-up about it all."

"I *live* for intense," I say. "I want someone who will write me songs and who's arty—like *bohemian*—and who gets me, you know? Someone in our world."

Lys chews on her lip. "What if he does it to you, too?"

"Tries to kill himself?" I ask, my stomach turning.

She nods.

"He won't," I say.

We tell each other so much, but you still haven't gotten into that day. I'm afraid to ask. I don't know if it's Pandora's Box—maybe we should just leave well enough alone. You're okay now. You've moved on, gotten over . . . whatever made you do that. Right?

Nat looks like she's going to say more but then Kyle throws open the door wearing a Jason mask he found in one of the dressing rooms and we all screech.

He pulls it off, grinning. "Evening, ladies."

"You bastard," I hear you say somewhere outside the prop room, but you're laughing along with the guys.

Miss B herds us all into the parking lot and I jump into Nat's car since you're riding with Peter and Kyle. I give you a wave, but you're looking down at your phone and don't see. A second later my phone pings.

The real reason is that I don't deserve you.

My heart does that zapped thing it does whenever you say or do something so perfectly perfect. I respond right away.

> *That's a stupid reason and you know it.*

I'm going to college next year.

> *Okay, but that's six months away.*

My parents won't let me be in a relationship.

> *So lie to them. It seems to work for all the other lovers in the world.*

Romeo and Juliet—not so much.

> *They're a cautionary tale. I promise I won't drink poison if you're banished to Mantua.*

I promise I won't be dumb enough to believe you would drink real poison.

> *So, we're good. Next reason?*

"Are you sexting him?" Lys asks.

I blush. "No. I don't *sext*."

"Yet," Lys says.

"I think a boy is coming between us," Nat says. "Chicks before . . . well, you know."

I roll my eyes. "It's not either/or. I love you guys, you know that."

"Imma bring this waaaaay back," Lys says before she starts in on the Spice Girls. *"If you wanna be my lover, you gotta get with my friends . . . Make it last forever, friendship never ends."* Nat joins her, dancing in her seat as she drives.

> *They're singing the Spice Girls in here.*

Damn. That's rough.

When Lys is done she takes her bows in the backseat, then leans forward and plants a wet kiss on my cheek. I'm pretty sure her sparkle lipstick is all over me.

"We just don't want Gavin to steal you from us," she says.

"And we don't want you to be someone's rebound," Nat adds. She and Lys exchange a look and I realize this is something else they've *discussed*.

"Dude, what is up with you guys talking about all this shit behind my back?"

That word—*rebound*. I hate it. Every time it sneaks into my mind, I push it away, but here it is, right back where it wants to be, front and center.

"We're not talking shit," Lys says. "We just, you know, we love you. Some guys are grenades, you know?"

"He's not a grenade," I snap.

"But he is maybe possibly kind of on the rebound," Nat says, her warm brown eyes settling on me as we wait at a stoplight. There's no judgment there, nothing but love. My best friends are just trying to have my back—something you will one day hate them for.

"Maybe," I say. "I mean, maybe that's how this started or whatever. But now . . . You guys, this is . . . special. Like, so totally the real thing."

"Just keep in mind that the dude has some unresolved issues," Lys says. "And it's not your job to fix them."

I turn around. "You're starting to sound too much like a professional psychologist."

She beams. "Thank you."

I'm a rebound. Is that it?

You take too long to answer and something inside me starts to crack. But then:

> Sorry, Kyle was trying to steal my phone. You are
> NOT a rebound. Trust me.

But maybe Nat and Lys are right. Maybe we should be slowing down.

What's the real reason?

I'm running out of answers.

So . . .

So.

I lean back and sigh. "Boys are weird."

"Now that," Nat says as she turns onto my street, "is something we can agree on."

"Also, you owe me ten bucks," Lys says.

I turn around. "For what?"

"I seem to recall you and I making a bet. I said Gav would fall for you. . . ."

I grin. "That is one bet I'm happy to lose."

I call my sister as soon as I'm home.

"My sistah! What's up?" she says, not drunk but on her way. I can hear voices and music in the background—dorm life, my dream.

"Tell me the truth," I say, "am I a rebound?"

"With Gavin?"

"Who else?"

"The truth? Yeah, probably," she says. "Look, I don't know Gavin personally, but he seems like a tragic teen if ever there was one."

"What's a tragic teen?"

"Like, *tragic*, you know. Emo shit."

I roll my eyes. "First of all, Gav hates emo—"

"What I'm saying is that the dude is *Shakespearean*. And don't get excited, because I don't mean that in a good way," she says. "People who try to commit suicide have issues. Is he on meds?"

I shrug. "I don't know. I mean, that's super personal. I can't just ask him."

"Um. Yeah, you can. If this guy wants to be with you, you need some guarantees that he's not gonna get all Byron on your ass."

I decide this isn't a good time to tell her that I sort of love Byron.

"I want to be with him," I say.

"Well, duh," she says. "He's a super-hot rocker guy. Maybe you should talk to Summer—find out what happened with them. Wait. Hold on." She pulls the phone away from her and I hear muffled conversation, then, "Dude, I gotta go. Just . . . follow your heart but keep your eyes open. 'Kay?"

"Okay. Love you, Bets."

"Love you, Gracie."

Before I go to bed, I get one more text from you:

It's 11:11, make a wish.

I wish for you.

NINE

I am in love with your parents.

I'm practically shaking with nerves when I walk up to your front door, worried they'll think my pink Doc Martens and Princess Leia buns are weird, but it's too late to go home and change into a normal girl. I'm wearing a lacy babydoll dress I know you like and my jean jacket and black tights with tiny pink hearts that I got on sale at Target. I can hear piano music and the clanging of pots and pans and as soon as I knock, your dog, Frances, starts barking. I wonder if she can smell the fear on me.

You open the door, your hair still wet from your shower. You look me up and down and then shake your head.

"How am I supposed to not jump you during dinner?" you murmur and I laugh. I've never been jumped before. I now have a new life goal.

"I have a feeling your parents wouldn't approve of that."

You usher me inside and I instantly feel at home. Your house is like those children's books where the animals live in trees or underground or whatever and everything is cozy and safe. There are overstuffed chairs and pretty paintings on the walls and thick woven rugs on the hardwood floors. It smells like lasagna and I love how there's a sweater lying over the back of one chair and a half-finished game of chess on the living room table. Your backpack is leaning against the couch and there's a stack of magazines on an end table. It's delightfully messy. Frances bounds toward me, very keen to be paid attention to, so I get on my knees and scratch her Labrador ears and let her lick me.

"Ah, here she is," your dad says as he stops playing the upright piano in the living room. He stands—he's very tall, your dad, but you look just like him—and, instead of holding a hand out to me, he pulls me into a bear hug.

"It's nice to meet you, Mr. Davis," I say, flushing.

"You too, sweetheart." He glances at you. "I don't know what you see in this hooligan."

I laugh. "Oh, he's not so bad, once you get to know him."

You beam. "I told you she was perfect," you say, and now I'm speechless.

Your mom bustles out of the kitchen wearing a *Kiss the cook!* apron.

"Grace! I hope Frances didn't slobber all over you."

"Just the right amount," I say.

She also gives me a hug. "Aren't you adorable? Dinner's almost ready. I'll let Gavin give you the tour."

Your house is my dream of what a house could be like. On one wall is one of those sepia-tinted photographs of you all dressed in Western gear, the kind you can get at Disneyland. You guys have a whole book-shelf filled with board games. There's dust—oh, heavenly dust!—and ratty old toys of Frances's lying around. Another shelf filled with books—mystery and sci-fi and fantasy. Outside is a pool and I love that there are weeds and that your patio furniture has seen better days. It's clear your mom doesn't make you spend hours scrubbing and weeding and sweeping.

"And here," you say, pushing open the door to your bedroom, "is where all the magic happens."

You have four guitars—one acoustic and three electric. A poster of Jimi Hendrix and, of course, Nirvana. A kittens calendar that the guys bought you as a joke gift last Christmas. It's still on January even though it's April. You don't have a lot of books on your bookshelf, but you do have *The Alchemist*. I pick it up. There's a folded piece of notebook paper inside.

"Favorite book?"

You blush a little. "My parents gave it to me when I was . . . after . . . you know."

"Oh." Fuck. Now what do I say?

You cross to me and take the book out of my hands and flip to a dog-eared page, then hand me the book.

"I thought of you when I read this," you say, pointing to an underlined passage.

You will never be able to escape from your heart. So it's better to listen to what it has to say.

"That's beautiful." I want to know so badly what your heart told you. I want to know why these words made you think of me.

You nod and hold up the piece of paper.

"Not as beautiful as this."

"What is it?"

You smile, soft, and hand me the paper. I open it up. And see my own writing.

> *I understand . . .*
> *I know right now it seems like . . .*
> *You matter, even if you think you don't . . .*
> *You are the most talented person I've ever . . .*

My letter. The paper soft and wrinkled, like it's been read hundreds of times.

I swallow. "I was so afraid you'd think I was a total freak for writing this."

"Not even close. You know, my parents wanted me to stay out of school an extra week, but I couldn't. I had to see you."

I look at you and my heart is like a diver, waiting to jump. "Really?"

You lean your forehead against mine. "Really."

"Gavin! Grace! Dinner!" your mom calls.

You take my hand and lead me to the dining room, which is more like a breakfast nook off the kitchen. A huge tray of lasagna sits in the center of the table, with a salad and bread.

"I hope you're hungry, Grace, because I made enough to feed ten of you," your mom says.

"This looks delicious—thank you so much."

You squeeze my hand and then we sit down. Dinner with your family is how I've always imagined a family dinner could be. Instead of The Giant criticizing my mom's cooking or interrupting me every time I try to speak, there's laughter and good conversation, where the adults actually listen to what you have to say. Your dad calls your mom a kitchen goddess and you heartily agree. She keeps doing TV mom stuff like trying to put more food on your plate and running her hands through your hair.

"How much time do you two have before you have to get to the theater?" your mom asks.

It's hard to believe we only have two more performances of the show. Time flies, I guess.

You glance at the cuckoo clock on the wall (your family has a *cuckoo clock*—how cute is that?).

"A couple hours," you say. "Ish. Grace has to get there earlier than

75

me. I just have to look pretty and remember a few things—she's doing all the real work." You wink at me and I hope your parents can't tell what a turn-on that is for me.

"So, Grace, Gavin tells us you're pretty much running the show these days," your dad says.

"Yeah. It's kind of amazing. But the cast makes it easy—they're all super great."

"You excited about this cast party tomorrow night?" your mom asks. "Kyle's mom told me she's going all out."

And just like that, the warm fuzzy feeling I've been nursing is gone.

"I'm actually . . . grounded." I can feel how red my face is getting and this is so freaking awkward. "So I'm just, you know, going home after the show."

"Oh, that's too bad," your mom says.

"It's okay," I lie.

"Ask her what she did," you say, and you don't even bother to hide the anger in your voice.

"Gav . . . ," I say, soft. "It's fine."

"It's *not* fine." You set down your fork, shaking your head, and I love you for how pissed off you are on my behalf. "She's grounded because she forgot to turn on the dishwasher. The *dishwasher*."

Your dad cocks his head to the side, as though he's trying to figure out a difficult trig problem.

"Er . . . what?" he says.

"My thoughts exactly," you say. "She's been working her ass off on this play and—"

"Gav. It's not a big deal," I say. I turn to your parents, hoping they don't decide to keep you away from me because of my crazy family. "My mom needed some of the dishes to make something for this event she was doing for her makeup company. So, you know . . . she was almost late because she had to hand-wash the . . . anyway, it's fine."

76

When I told you at lunch, you didn't buy my it's-no-big-deal rap then, either. God, you already know me so well. *You don't have to pretend with me*, you said. *This fucking sucks and your mom is being a psycho, end of story.* I am so afraid that my family is going to scare you off.

"Well." Your mom stands up. "It's obvious that the only thing we can do now is eat sundaes."

You turn to me and smile. "This is how my family deals with a crisis."

We eat sundaes piled high with whipped cream and fudge and cherries. Your mom tells me a little bit about how it was for her growing up. Her parents were strict, too.

"Aaron got me through it, though," she says, putting her head on your dad's shoulder.

"Wait, you guys were high school sweethearts?" I say.

"Disgusting, isn't it?" your dad says with a wink.

We hang out with your parents for another hour and it's not lame or boring at all. They're funny and kind and when it's time for me to go, your mom wraps her arms around me and I realize I can't remember the last time my mom hugged me. Tears prick my eyes and I blink them away quick before anyone can see.

"It'll be okay, Grace," your mom whispers. "If you ever need to talk, you know where to find me."

I feel safe here. There is so much love in this house. No one here cries themselves to sleep at night or wonders what would happen if they stuffed a backpack full of clothes, walked out the door, and never looked back.

"Do you think your parents would consider adopting me?" I joke as we drive to the theater.

"Yes, but I can't allow it—we would be incestuous, it'd be a whole thing," you say.

I laugh. "Yeah, I guess that would be pretty gross."

"You totally rocked it with them, by the way. I bet I'll get home and it'll be all *Grace this* and *Grace that*."

"Do you guys ever fight or do you get in trouble or anything like that?"

You shake your head. "Not really. My parents are pretty chill and they respect me. I respect them. It's all good."

"I seriously can't even imagine that."

You're quiet for a minute. "I wish I could protect you from them," you say softly.

I rest my hand over yours. "You do." I smile. "Whenever we're together, you help me forget about them. You're . . . my happy place."

Your lip turns up. "That sounds dirty."

I hit your arm. "You know what I mean."

You stop at a red light, then pick up my hand and kiss my palm. I hold my breath. Your lips are warm against my skin and goose bumps fly up my arms.

"You're my happy place, too."

I lean my head on your shoulder like your mom did with your dad and I wonder if that will ever be us, sitting at our dining room table with our teenage kid and the girl who's in love with him.

Now I look at that girl who adores you, who thinks she's safe with you, and I want to scream at her to jump out of that car and run like hell. Because you won't be her happy place for long.

TEN

When I was a kid, my mom would call us the Three Amigos: me, her, and my sister. Every weekend we'd get up on Saturday morning and do something unexpected—we called it our Adventure Day. A bike ride along the beach. A drive through Topanga Canyon, plastic water bottles filled with soda. Walking around the mall. Even though we didn't have money to buy anything, we got a snack and window-shopped and that was kind of enough.

There was this one nasty-looking purple house in our neighborhood in LA and every time we drove past it we'd all cry, "Eww, the purple house!" I loved that. We always said the words slowly, with relish. *Eww . . . the . . . purple . . . house.* We singsonged our delighted disgust in unison. I don't remember anything about the house except that it was purple—a garish shade, bright, like Halloween decorations in March. It was our thing, part of what made us the Three Amigos. When The Giant came into our lives, he took the purple house away. And Saturday adventures. And smiles. We learned to live without these things. Eyes down, lips shut tight, hands clasped in our laps. We became a flinch, waiting for hands to slap skin, words to cut through bone.

Beth and I asked WHY WHY WHY and all Mom would say was *I love him.*

And I thought: *but what about* Eww the purple house?

The Giant's the one who made us move here, forcing us to leave our family and LA, where there were wonders around every corner. He made us come to the armpit of California, a suburban Our Town between San Francisco and LA. Beth and I got used to waiting on him hand and foot. He said we had to earn our keep.

In return, he made my sister and me beg. For money, for free time, for a ride to work. He told us we were lucky, we had it easy. "Easy" was him pushing Beth into an eating disorder after she quit playing volleyball. Her body had quickly gone from tomboy to girlish curves and The Giant wasn't okay with that. She is gorgeous, with long, thick hair and wide hazel eyes. And she has the most beautiful singing voice. And when she laughs, she laughs with her whole body, leaning forward and holding her stomach while she shakes her head. But The Giant only saw a fat girl.

This was a typical dinner:

My sister reaches for the butter.

"You sure you need more of that?" The Giant says with a mocking tone. He gives a pointed look to her stomach.

Beth's face turns red. My mom laughs uncomfortably and swats at him—it seems playful until I see the desperate sadness in her eyes.

But she doesn't say a word.

My sister's hand moves away from the butter and she looks down at her plate. Her long dark hair slips forward, hiding her eyes.

Shame. It works every time.

"Dude, he's a dick," I tell Beth after each of these dinners.

"Fuck him," she says.

"That's Mom's job," I say.

We laugh mean-girl laughs. It's Us against Them.

But it didn't matter how much I told Beth to ignore The Giant, how much I made her laugh—his words found a home somewhere deep inside her. First there were the baggy clothes she wore to hide her figure, then there were the skinny limbs, jeans falling off her waist.

Home became a place that wasn't safe and it's been like that ever since.

It's late on a Monday night when the house phone rings. The Giant yells from the living room for me to get it, even though I'm in my bedroom down the hall and he's a few feet away from the phone. I throw down my AP History book with a huff and head out to where the phone is attached to the dining room wall.

The Giant turns from where he's watching golf on the couch. He's maybe the most unattractive man in the world. No, that's not true. I guess he's okay-looking, but he's ugly to me. Thin blond hair, a matching goatee. Give him horns and a pitchfork and he'd be a dead ringer for the devil.

We don't say a word to each other, just exchange one wary glance before I pass the living room.

I grab the phone and as soon as I say hello, there's a gravelly, "Hi, honey."

"Dad." I can hear the uncertainty in my voice, almost a question. *Dad? Is this really you? How many lies are you going to tell me this time?*

I wonder what I will tell you about my dad, if you ever ask. The important things first: he joined the Marines after 9/11 and they sent him to Iraq three times and Afghanistan once. By the time he came back from his second tour, he wasn't my dad anymore. Someone had taken his happy-go-lucky personality and replaced it with a very angry, very sad man. He and Mom got divorced not long after that, when I was about six.

I don't know what went down during the war, but whatever it was turned my dad into an addict. Whiskey. Cocaine. Heroin. After my dad checked into rehab the first time, I heard the term PTSD: post-traumatic stress disorder. *The war fucked me up good*, he said once, when I was eight or nine.

We don't see him much.

"How's it going, hon?"

"Fine."

I don't have lots to say to someone who is little more than a shadow on the periphery of my life. Someone who breaks promises as often as he makes them. He lives in another state, just a voice on the phone: nice enough guy one moment, anxious, furious man-child the next. I wish I didn't love him, but I do. It's hard to write off your own flesh and blood, even when they take a jackhammer to your heart.

"Well, good, good," he says. "Got a new job. Construction. Pays shit, but it's under the table, so that's cool."

"Nice."

But my heart sinks. His words run together, like he has to get them out fast or they'll scamper away. I can't tell if he's drunk or high this time. I think I know why he's calling.

"Don't know about *nice*. I've . . . got some problems," he says, "but it'll be okay." He pauses. "I don't have the money right now. For that thing. The drama thing. I'm sorry, sweetheart."

The tears come hot and fast, but I hold them in. I knew the summer theatre camp at Interlochen was a total pie-in-the-sky dream but my dad, when he heard about it, insisted he could make it come true. I should have known better than to trust him. To trust that he'd be able to stand on his own two feet for longer than a few weeks at a time—long enough to get me to camp.

"What problems?" I ask, already weary. *Here we go*, I think.

"Well, you know, my doc at the VA gave me these fuckin' meds. Fuckin' doc doesn't know what the fuck he's doing."

This is normal. He gets angry, fast. A switch flips and then you've got a *US Fuckin' Marine, motherfucker* on your hands. All I can do is listen until I can pass the phone to my mom so they can argue about child support and then he'll go off on her until she's screaming back and one of them hangs up the phone.

Twenty minutes into my dad's rant about the VA, I start daydreaming. I'm in New York, walking through Washington Square Park. I'm a student at NYU and I'm on my way to acting class. . . . You're there, holding my hand. You lean down and kiss me, soft, like—

"Making me fall asleep," Dad's saying.

Did you mean it when you said you didn't love Summer anymore, that you aren't even sure if it was *ever* real, true love? Because—

"Hel*lo*!" Dad yells.

"Sorry," I say. "What?"

"I said the fuckin' medicine is making me fall asleep on the fuckin' job and I—"

"Dad," I say, serious. "You have to stop taking that medicine. Or at least take it at night, so you can sleep."

"Yeah, yeah. Maybe. Hey, your mother keeps nagging me for child support." Dad does this—he's all over the place when we talk. "Think you can get her off my back?"

I've gotten so used to this. One parent says this, one says that. I have to give my mom credit, though: she doesn't badmouth him or try to put me in the middle. That's classy. And probably takes a crapload of restraint. I wonder if it's because a little, very hidden part of her still loves him. Or maybe she just feels bad for him. They got married so young and it's like she's the only one of them who ever learned to be an adult.

"We're kinda broke, Dad. I mean, that's why she's asking for it," I say.

Never mind that a father is supposed to provide for his kids. That ship sailed, like, a million years ago.

"You got a boyfriend?" he asks, out of the blue.

You take my hand and turn it over. Kiss the palm.

"Nope. No boyfriend."

And I don't. Have one, that is. Unfortunately.

"Well, let me tell you something, honey. All a boy wants is for you to give him a blowjob. Better than sex."

My stomach turns. Why does he tell me this stuff? This is sick.

"Dad . . ."

He laughs. "I'm serious!"

What the hell is he *on*?

"Dad! Eww, stop."

"You need to know about these things. All boys care about are tits and fucking."

"No, actually, they don't. Not all of them."

I think about you sitting backstage with your black notebook, writing songs, your lips moving slightly. Or how you'll give me one of your earbuds so that we can listen to a song together. The way you exaggerate choreography to make everyone laugh, your perfectionism when it comes to music.

"Yeah, they do, honey. You ask 'em. Tits and fucking, all day, every day."

"Dad. Seriously, I don't want to talk about this. It's, like, totally inappropriate?"

He just laughs.

I have four vivid memories of my dad and here they are:

When I was a little girl, maybe seven years old, he had me for the weekend. He lived in San Diego at the time, near the Marine Corps base. We went to the beach and we were there all day because the beach is my dad's version of heaven. I had a blast. But then we got home and I realized I hurt so bad all over. My pale skin had turned a fiery red everywhere. Some blisters had developed over the burns. I cried all night. Dad had forgotten the sunscreen, but not the cooler full of beer.

When I was in sixth grade, my dad went to Afghanistan again. Before he left, I got to see him walking into a roomful of Marines and all of them stood and saluted him. Pride filled my chest. We got ice cream after—mint chocolate chip.

I remember how later that day, my mom dragged me onto the tarmac where rows of men stood. Where is the money? *she yelled.* You don't just get to go and leave these girls stranded. *This was in the desert—29 Palms. It gets cold there at night and you can see thousands of stars in the sky. There are snakes that hide under the sand. If you aren't careful, their fangs will latch onto your skin, fast as lightning.*

My most recent memory of my dad was when I went to visit him over the summer when I was in junior high— seventh grade, going into eighth. He'd had a lot to drink and we were sitting in the living room of his bachelor pad. He sat in a beach chair because that was all he could afford.
I killed people—bad guys. They were planting bombs next to the road, killing our guys left and right, fucking us up, *he said, his eyes glassy, his whole face zeroed in on people and places that I couldn't see.* I saw a lot of my friends die. They're just . . . gone.

Mom walks into the kitchen and I put my hand over the phone. "It's Dad," I say, my eyes begging her to let me off the hook. She sighs and holds out her hand for the phone and I pass him to her mid-rant (now he's onto politics) and then I run to the backyard and find a hidden corner to cry in.

Tradition.

I want to call you so bad, tell you about Interlochen and my dad. I want to hear your voice telling me it's going to be okay. But would my family situation make you less into me? Would it make you run in the other direction? I know my family isn't normal. We're fucked up. I'm sure there are lots of non-fucked-up girls who could make you happy.

I sit on a patch of grass and pull up the blades as I think. My mind plays hopscotch, jumping from you to Dad and back again. Instead of the trip I was supposed to take, I think about how you come up behind me in the hallways at school and wrap your arms around me. I think about how you hold my hand backstage, secretly so no one can see. You belong to a different world from the one at home. A place where I'm seen, where there's gentleness. Hearts that beat in time.

I take a risk and call you. You answer on the first ring.

"How's my favorite girl in the world?" you ask.

"Whoa," I say. "My status has been seriously elevated since last we talked."

"Since last we talked? Nuh-uh. You've been my favorite girl for a while now."

"Is that so?" I say.

"It is so."

I break down crying. I can't keep the sobs in. You ask me what's wrong and when I tell you everything—about my dad and Interlochen and how fucked-up everything is—all you want to do is come over. But you can't.

"It's a school night," I say. "My mom has this rule—"

"What is up with these *rules*?" you growl.

Since you can't come over, you do the next best thing. You grab your guitar and sing me "Somewhere Over the Rainbow," putting your own Kurt Cobain angst twist on it. I can't get over the fact that Gavin Davis is serenading me over the phone. That you're upset because you can't see me. That I'm your favorite girl in the world.

"Feeling any better?" you ask after you finish the song.

"I'm perfect. Great. You're amazing."

You laugh softly. "You bring it out in me. You bring all the best things out of me." You pause. "I want us to be together, you know that, right?"

There are fireworks inside me. I press my phone closer to my ear, as if that could somehow make you less far away.

"Do you?" I breathe.

"Yes, hell yes," you say. "I just don't want to go too fast and fuck it up, you know?"

"Yeah," I say softly, "I know."

We talk for another hour while I stay in the backyard, huddled on Sam's jungle gym. You tell me corny jokes and secrets and all the unhappiness in me seems to get whisked away, as though the sound of your voice has the power to banish badness.

We hang up when my mom calls me inside, but just before I'm about to go to bed, you call me back.

"I know you," you say. "You're going to lie in bed and think about Interlochen all night. Am I right?"

I grudgingly admit that you are.

"Not on my watch," you say. I hear you strum your guitar.

My life has become a fairy tale. Evil stepfather, prince in disguise.

I keep my phone against my ear and let you play me song after song until finally I fall asleep to the sound of your voice, to words that say everything you can't yet say to me.

ELEVEN

*T*wo weeks later:

There's a tap at my bedroom window and I wake up, scared. But it's you. You point in the direction of the sliding glass door. It's three in the morning. All I'm wearing is a tiny pair of shorts and a cotton tank top. No bra. I should get decent, but I don't.

I listen for my mom. For The Giant. But they're sound asleep. The door slides silently open and your eyes travel from my feet to my knees, to my thighs, to the way my nipples press against the thin cotton tank. You lean against the doorway.

"You're torturing me. On purpose."

I smile. Bite my lip. Lean closer. (Who IS this girl?) "Is it working?" I murmur.

"Yes," you breathe. Your lips are close, but you don't lean in. We haven't kissed, not yet.

"Want an adventure?" you ask, eyes sparkling.

I nod. Because I'm pretty sure it'll involve kissing, it has to.

But it will also involve lying and sneaking. I still remember the first time I lied when I was a little girl—the shame and fear over one measly cookie. Worrying about getting caught—and then getting caught—was so not worth that Oreo. I logically concluded that it wasn't in my best interest to lie.

The one time The Giant caught me in a lie—I said there was a meeting after school for drama, but I was really getting Pepsi Freezes with the girls—I was grounded for a solid month. So I just . . . didn't lie. Pretty much ever. And then you came along. Lately, I catch myself lying all the time, little fibs that buy me extra minutes with you. Instead of feeling bad about it, I feel liberated. Being a good kid hasn't been working out for me. So I let the bad girl in. Each lie is something that's mine, that my mom and The Giant can't take away from me. Each lie reminds me I'm an actual person with rights and desires and the ability to make choices on her own. Each lie is power—control over my life.

So I sneak out, chasing that power, chasing *you*, wearing next to nothing. You grab my hand and we sprint down the street, to where you parked your car well away from my house.

"Don't distract me while I'm driving, you minx."

I hold up my hand. "Scout's honor."

The streets are empty. The night is ours. You turn into one of the new housing developments and stop in front of the skeleton of a half-finished house. You grab a blanket and pull me inside. You lay the blanket in a dark corner, where the moonlight can't touch. Above us, the sky. Just rafters where the roof of this house will one day be. You pull me down onto the blanket and there is no space between us, not even a centimeter. You want me, I can feel it. You're hard and you press against me and I bite my lip and you groan.

"You better lie next to me," you say.

I love that I'm torturing you.

"And why is that?" I press closer and you close your eyes for a second.

"Because I'm about two seconds away from ravishing you," you say.

I actually have no problem with this, but I laugh and slide off you. We lie on our backs, staring at the constellations. And then—a shooting star. We gasp at the same time and you reach out and grip my hand.

"I've never seen one before," I say.

You smile. "It's a sign."

"Of what?"

"That we're meant to be together."

You bring my knuckles to your lips and your mouth moves across my skin. You keep your eyes on me as you kiss each finger. You drop my hand, your mouth moving closer to mine. I can't breathe. You put your fingers on my lips and lean over me, studying them.

"You better fucking kiss me, Gavin Davis."

The corner of your mouth turns up. "Oh, yeah?"

"Yeah."

You laugh softly and rest your weight on your elbows, eyes roving over my face. I am dying. I want to scream. You smile.

"This is the best part," you whisper, nuzzling me.

"What?" I say.

"The before."

You bring your lips to my ear. "Are you sure you want this?"

"Yes." There isn't the slightest hesitation in my voice.

Your lips brush my earlobe, snake across my jaw, and when they finally fall onto my own we are hungry and want more, more, more. You crush your lips against mine and I open my mouth to let you in. You taste so good, like cinnamon. We roll around and now I'm on top of you, kissing you like it's the only chance I'll ever have to feel your lips against mine. Your hands slide up my thighs, under my shirt.

"Tell me when to stop," you whisper as you pull the tank top over my head, then pull off your own shirt.

I don't want to stop, not ever.

I forget about parents and rules and all our empty promises to each other to take it slow and I can't think, I'm dizzy. Your hands are everywhere and I'm a door that's thrown wide open and I let you in. We kiss and we kiss and we kiss.

"Fuck," you whisper, "I left the condoms in the car."

I shiver, hold you closer. "We shouldn't, anyway. Until . . . until we figure out what we are."

I'm not losing my virginity to a guy who isn't my boyfriend. I don't care how much I like you. Also, WHY AREN'T YOU MY BOYFRIEND?

"Voice of Reason," you murmur, your lips finding mine again.

All that want of the past few weeks washes over us, drenching. This is something else I will learn while I am with you—not now, but later: there are so many ways to drown.

IT'S LUNCH AND we're in the drama room. You're about to go off-campus—only the seniors get to do that—and Lys has caught you kissing my cheek, whispering sweet nothings in my ear.

"Oh, hell no," Nat says from where she lies sprawled on the floor, using her backpack as a pillow.

You look back at her, frowning at the scowl on her face. "Um . . . ?"

"You just cursed," I say to Nat, smirking. She calls cursing the "height of uncouthness"—the fact that she uses words like *uncouth* is part of why she's my best friend.

"This calls for it," Nat says, sitting up. She smooths her hair and turns to Lys. "It might be time to do that thing we've been talking about."

Lys nods, serious. "Yep. The time has definitely come."

They get up and cross the room.

"You," Nat says, grabbing you by the arm, "are coming with us."

"I am?" you say.

"Yep." Lys crosses her arms. She manages to look intimidating despite the Alice in Wonderland–style dress she's wearing, complete with white tights and her signature platform sneakers. "We want to know what your intentions are toward our best friend."

I roll my eyes. "Oh my god, you guys."

Okay, but seriously, what *are* your intentions? Because this sneaking-around thing is getting old. But I'm too afraid to say that. I don't want to scare you away.

"I assure you they're honorable," you say.

"Uh-huh," Nat says. She starts pulling you out of the room.

"You guys!" I say. "Stop being dumbasses."

"You'll thank us later," Lys calls over her shoulder.

You look back at me. "If you don't see me by the end of lunch, call the police."

You flash me that half smile (so sexy) and then you're out of the room.

The bell rings half an hour later and you still aren't back. A tiny knot of worry twists inside my chest—I hope my friends aren't screwing this up for me. Whatever *this* is. I start heading toward English when someone grabs my hand—you—without breaking your stride.

"You survived?" I say.

You're holding my hand in public. This is a good thing. They must not have freaked you out too badly.

"I did," you say. "Though they threatened to cut off my balls if I break your heart."

"That sounds like them."

You laugh. "Those girls do *not* fuck around."

"I don't know if I even *want* to know what you guys talked about."

"Let's just say that they were satisfied with my answers."

You pull me out of the stream of students, to the deserted area around the science building. No one is around. Your lips are on mine in seconds. You gently push me up against the wall and slide your tongue in my mouth while your hands slip under the hem of my shirt. I press against you and you moan, the sound vibrating in my mouth as you deepen the kiss. The bell rings but I don't care. I'm not even afraid of getting caught.

"God, I want you," you murmur as your lips move to my neck. I shiver. I think I want you just as much. More. I've never wanted someone like this. I feel a little crazy—I have to force myself not to slide my hand down your pants. I can feel you smile against my skin and then you pull away and give me a sneaky look.

"What?" I say, breathless.

You take both my hands and squeeze them. "I have a surprise for you. Tonight."

I bite my lip, uncertain. "I don't know, Gav. I can't keep sneaking out. If my parents catch me, I'm dead. They're not like your parents. My life will seriously be in jeopardy."

You and your parents are a perfect unit of three. They adore you, give you lots of freedom. The last time I was at your house, your dad sat down at the piano and started playing Lady Gaga tunes and then your mom insisted we have a dance party. These aren't the kind of people who ground their kid for the rest of his life. You don't have invisible dust and a giant. You can't even comprehend what that's like.

"Please," you say, begging in that sexy way of yours, chin down, eyes intense, mouth set in the tiniest pout.

"You're taking advantage of me," I tease. "You know I'm a sucker for The Look."

"Is that a yes?" you ask, eyes lighting up.

"It's not a no." I sigh. "This surprise can't happen during business hours?"

You shake your head. "Hell no. My surprises happen only during rock-star hours. We open at midnight sharp."

It doesn't occur to me to be annoyed that you don't seem to care what the consequences of your surprises are or that you don't hear my distress. This is you, building your castles in the sky, whisking me away from The Giant, from my mom. After years of being trapped inside my house, I'm finally being rescued. In fairy tales, the princess doesn't tell her knight in shining armor that he came at a bad time.

I don't see how good you are at manipulating me with your pretty looks and your teasing and your slight but insistent pushing. It will take me months not to fall for that shit. Every. Single. Time. Right now, I just see *you*.

And I can't stop looking.

"Aren't you sort of regretting falling for someone with an eleven o'clock curfew? And psychotic parents?"

"Nah. Gives me more to write about," you say.

"I don't get it," I whisper.

"Get what?"

"You could have any girl in this school—some of the guys, too. Why me?"

You tilt your head, studying my face.

"You get me," you say. "Nobody gets me like you do." You lean your forehead against mine. "It doesn't hurt that you're the sexiest girl in school."

I snort. "I was with you up until *sexiest*."

"Wait." You pull away. "Do you seriously not see what I do?"

A blush creeps up my neck, reaching for my cheeks, red ivy that spreads the longer you stare at me.

"Gavin. That's . . ." I throw up my hands. "Just patently untrue."

"You think this because of your fucked-up parents. They don't appreciate you. They don't *see* you."

I look away, considering. I remember how last year's Christmas card picture didn't have me in it. Mom said she couldn't find a good one of all of us, so it was one of just her, The Giant, and Sam.

"I don't know," I say softly.

"I do. You're fucking perfect." You put your finger under my chin and turn me so that we're face-to-face again. "I mean it."

I spend the rest of sixth period with my mouth on yours and we don't stop kissing until the bell rings.

"I'll see you tonight," you murmur.

I smile, drunk on you. "This better be good."

You grin. "Oh, it is."

TWELVE

*T*here's a soft knock on my window.

I've been waiting for it. I slip out of bed, fully clothed in my skimpiest sundress, now that it's May and the nights are warmer. I wave and you smile, tipping your hat like a proper gentleman.

I hesitate at the door, listening hard. Silence. I look at the window, almost ready to call it off, but you're already gone, waiting by the sliding glass door for me, no doubt. We've done this almost every night since you kissed me, so we have a system in place.

Is he worth it? Beth asked on the phone when I told her about all the sneaking out.

Are you worth getting in trouble for? Are you worth maybe being grounded for the rest of my life?

Yeah, I said. *I think he is.*

Nobody could possibly understand how you and I feel about each other, how deep this goes. It didn't take long for you to become the most important person in my life. The most important *thing*. I don't tell anyone this, especially not you, but I'm pretty sure you're my soul mate. I like to imagine us old together, our hands gnarled and veined and spotty and still clutching at each other. I like to think that you won't be able to stop looking at me, even when you're wearing bifocals and have cataracts.

I slip out of the room and tiptoe down the carpeted hallway, careful to step over the places that squeak.

"Where are we going this time?" I whisper once you and I are clear of the house.

Your eyes slide to mine as your lips turn up. "You'll see."

We zigzag down the street, jumping from shadow to shadow. It becomes a game—who can jump the farthest? Five minutes later, we're in front of the school. You pull me toward the thick, dark shadows clustered near the library just before a cop car goes by. In our empty suburb, it's not unusual for cops to stop pretty much any young-looking person after ten p.m. That's when a notice goes up on the news: *It's ten p.m. Do you know where your children are?*

I almost sob with fear—I don't even want to begin contemplating the punishment I'd have if I were caught. I'm pushing my luck, I know it.

"Gav, maybe we shouldn't . . ."

"Almost there," you whisper, squeezing my hand.

I pull back, shake my head. "Seriously, you have no idea how bad it could be for me."

"What are you afraid of?" you ask, running a finger along my jaw.

"Everything." Being with you is like being in free fall, with no place to land in sight.

"Which is exactly why we need to do this," you say as you plant a kiss on my forehead. "You won't regret it."

I wish I could be brave like you. I wish I had an adventurer's heart. I stand still for a few breaths, thinking. *Is he worth it?*

"Okay," I whisper.

"That's my girl."

My girl.

I shiver, grinning as you lead me to the outdoor amphitheater.

There's a nearly full moon tonight and it bathes the campus in silvery light. Without all the students and general chaos, the school becomes mysterious, magical even. I feel like I could be directing a scene from *Midsummer Night's Dream*. I'd put you in the amphitheater downstage right, where the moonlight's the brightest. You tug me toward it.

"Okay, stay right there," you say, letting go of me.

You walk deeper into the amphitheater and pull your guitar from a dark corner—the acoustic you named Rosa.

If I were directing us, I'd have me scoot farther downstage so that my back isn't facing the audience. Cue soft lighting—cream and blue on you and me with the rest of the stage staying dark. This is so good it should be on Broadway.

> Gavin and Grace stare at each other across the stage. She
> crosses her arms, hugs herself, suddenly shy. He smiles
> as he moves closer.

> ### GAVIN
> (strums guitar, singing, a wailing acoustic vocalization similar to Jack White):

> White walls
> Black heart
> My mind breaking
> itself apart

> Crumpled paper
> Dark blue ink

Words from her heart
That bring me from the brink

The edge of sanity
The losing season
Gotta love you, honey
Don't need no reason

Soft kisses
Warm hands
She's putting me
Back together again

Her words are glue
She gets me through
Her eyes inspire
Reignite my fire

Soft kisses
Warm hands
She's putting me
Back together again

So tell me, baby
Tell me true
Do I make you feel
Brand-new too?

Take my hand
Let's do this now

Be together
I don't care how

The edge of sanity
The losing season
Gotta love you, honey
Don't need no reason

The edge of sanity
The losing season
Gotta love you, honey
Don't need no reason

Don't need no reason

                    GAVIN
(Stops playing. He takes the last few steps across the
stage, sets his guitar on the ground, then falls to his
knees):
        Grace. Be my girlfriend.

Grace starts crying and Gavin stands, picking her up. He
spins and she leans her head back, laughing.

                    GAVIN
(whispers against her lips):
        Tell me this was worth the risk of getting
        caught.

She tilts back his fedora and presses her lips against
his.

                    100

GRACE:

It was worth the risk.

UNIDENTIFIED VOICE:

Hey!

GAVIN:

Fuck.

He sets Grace down and they run hand in hand off the stage
as a security guard shines his flashlight on them. They race
through campus, past the library and the cafeteria. When
they reach Gavin's car, Grace lies on the hood, laughing.

SO WE ARE officially together.

I'm not over the moon, I'm *on* the moon. It's surreal, this happiness. I'm scared the universe will notice and take you away from me. Because it isn't fair, how good I feel.

I have no idea the sacrifices that are ahead of me. I'm so clueless, Gavin. So fucking clueless.

"Hey," you murmur, "I gotta ask you something."

We're sitting in your car—it's only been a couple hours since you sang your song to me, but the sky is already getting light. I'll need to go soon.

I kiss your nose. "Okay."

"Now that we're together, I think we should share, like, what we've done with other people."

It takes me a minute to figure out what you're saying.

"You mean . . . physical stuff?"

You nod. "We should just get it out of the way, you know?"

We're each in our own seats, lying on our sides, hands intertwined across the parking brake.

"I don't know, Gav. . . ."

Your grip tightens. "I mean, it's not like you've done that much . . . right?"

I can hear the slight tinge of panic in your voice. I shake my head.

"No, not really."

"Okay, then, so . . ." When I don't say anything, you sit up a little. "I want us to be able to tell each other everything. You know?"

I think about my mom and The Giant, about all the secrets they have; all of The Giant's don't-tell-your-mom's and Mom's what-Roy-doesn't-know-won't-hurt-him's. I don't want to be like them. Ever.

"It's no big deal," you say. You hold up my hand and kiss it. "I'll go first."

You tell me about Summer. How you did everything but have sex. I'm shocked that you're a virgin. I never would have guessed.

"Why didn't you?" I ask. "Have sex, I mean?"

You play with your keys, eyes on them.

"She's religious. And . . . it just never felt right." Your eyes slide to mine. "So . . ."

I take a breath and tell you about the three boys I've kissed. About the older boy whose hands I let under my shirt, down my pants, way back in eighth grade.

You go pale. "Did you . . . do anything to him?"

This beautiful, perfect night is suddenly ruined. I can see the war inside you. It plays across your eyes. You're wondering if you actually want to be with me. Maybe you'll dump me before first period. That's only four hours from now.

"Yes," I whisper.

I tell you how I'd never seen a penis before, how I'd held it in my hand. *Look what you do to me*, the older boy had said.

"I'll fucking kill him," you mutter.

"Gav. He's, like, far away."

"How do you know?" you ask. "Do you guys keep in touch?"

"No. God, no. It was a summer fling. Camp." I reach out and squeeze your hand. "It was a long time ago. Forever ago."

I suddenly feel guilty, like I cheated on you. You won't look at me and you feel miles away, like what I'd done with those guys has put up a wall between us. I feel dirty, ruined. I wonder if you think I'm a slut. Without warning, I burst into tears.

You glance at me, stricken. "Grace! Oh my god, I'm sorry. *Shhhh.*" You pull me over to you so that I'm sitting in your lap. "Don't cry, baby," you whisper. "All this shit's over now. It's just me and you. That's all that matters."

"But I can tell how grossed out you are by me," I sob.

"Grossed out?"

"Because, like, I've done stuff with other guys."

You smooth back my hair. "I'm not grossed out. I'm angry. And not at you. I just hate the thought of anyone but me touching you like that."

I look up and you gently kiss me, soft and sweet. When you pull away, you lean your forehead against mine and you say the words that seal my fate for the next year:

"God, I love you."

My mouth opens and a soft gasp escapes my lips. "Don't say it if you don't . . . I mean, you don't have to make me feel better."

"Grace. I. Love. You. Got it?"

Your ice-blue eyes are dark with feeling, tears brimming. In this light, you're all charcoal lines and velvet shadows. Something inside me breaks open and the words fall out.

"I love you, too." I smile. "I mean, duh."

That's how the worst year of my life starts—in a Mustang with steamed-up windows, with a beautiful boy who cries.

THIRTEEN

I used to dream that I'd been switched at birth. For years I had a fantasy that I was the daughter of a Greek shipping magnate or the princess of a small but wealthy country. Maybe a young heiress—a Vanderbilt or Rockefeller—had me as a teen and I'd been left in the hospital and the woman I call my mother and the man I call my father didn't realize I wasn't theirs or maybe or maybe or maybe . . .

My grandfather was a jock. My mother was a jock. My sister was a jock. Football, tennis, volleyball. Long, lean muscles, eyes on the scoreboard, that's them. Me? Soft and bendy, dreamy, eyes on the stars, head in the clouds.

I am the one who doesn't fit.

There are no intellectuals in my family. No crazy aunts who live in Europe and paint. No father who once dabbled in jazz. Here, where I live, there are no ivory towers. Nobody using words like *serendipity* or *existentialism*. Nobody wears flowy scarves or reads Brecht or has a ring they bought in Barcelona. Nobody's been in a band, in a play, in a *pas de deux*.

I ache—I mean literally *ache*—for the streets of New York City,

Paris at night, Moscow in winter, like Lara and Dr. Zhivago. I long for cobblestones, mist curling around gaslit streetlamps, kissing in the rain. These are things I can't find in Birch Grove and so I magic them into being, gathering everything that is Other around me, like a hen with her chicks. I listen to Mendelssohn's Venetian gondola song in the dark, the only light a few candles. It makes me cry, this song. It makes me yearn for a time and place I know nothing about. I close my eyes and I am there. I read poetry, my eyes hungrily scanning the lines, heart beating in iambic pentameter: *Now is the winter of our discontent.*

When I feel trapped, afraid, lonely, I only have to look up at the sky and think: this is what people in Morocco look at when they see the sky. And India, Thailand, South Africa. Korea and Chile and Italy. The world, I remind myself, is mine, if only I have the courage to grasp it when the opportunity is given to me. *I know there is that within me, I know not what it is, but that it is in me.* Walt Whitman said that way back when because he's the man and a prophet and he gets what it feels like to be me so hard.

This is my secret self. The part of me I hold as delicately as a violet plucked from a meadow. It is the me who lies awake in bed late at night and imagines what Verona is like, what it would be like to say, *Be but sworn my love and I will no longer be a Capulet.* It is the me who takes French, dreaming of trips to Paris: *Je m'appelle Grace. J'ai dix-sept ans. Je veux le monde.*

The first time you hurt me was when you took this secret self and squashed it between your thumb and index finger like a bug. You didn't mean to, but that was how it felt.

We are sitting beside your pool, legs dangling in the water. It's the middle of May: spring. New beginnings. The sun is setting, the warmth of the day an exhale. You are the sun to me, shining so bright I can only look at you sideways. I allow myself to think that maybe I am your moon—luminescent, enigmatic—until:

"You're not very deep." You say these cutting words thoughtfully, to yourself, almost as though you're surprised. They hit me somewhere below my ribs.

Inside: I'm Broken Girl Blown to Smithereens: explosions, not the good kind—a blitz, unexpected, flattening anything in me that had dared to stand up around you. Just as I'd suspected, I'm not artistic enough to be on Gavin Davis's arm.

Outside: I'm Dull-Witted Girlfriend, a shrug of a girl; heat screams up my cheeks and I look away, toward the shallow end of the pool. *Shallow.*

I think of the dictionary app on my phone that I have to use all the time when I'm reading stuff like *The Master and Margarita* or *The Awakening*. Or that one time when I missed *sophomoric* on a vocab quiz. And how I totally don't get why girls love Jane Austen. You're right: I'm not deep.

"Yeah," I say. "I know."

The words hurt, but The Giant has been telling me the same thing for years, except he uses synonyms: *thick, dumbass, use your fucking head, Grace.*

And Mom: *Ivy League? Honey, be realistic.*

I didn't know how to pronounce *respite*. I read it in a book, I can't remember which one, and I confess I thought it was res-PITE, not RES-pit. I knew it generally meant "a break from something that isn't all that great and that you'd like to get away from in some way," as in *I'd like a respite from my entire fucking life*, but I'd never heard the word out loud. My family doesn't generally use SAT-level vocabulary, except when my mom tells me that the things I do are *asinine* or that I'm being *obtuse*. I didn't know the difference between an epiphany and an epitome, not for a long time. I learn words when I read and so I do this nearly every day, pronouncing things wrong. When someone points it out, it makes me feel stupid. Like I'm wearing a dunce cap while everyone else is wearing fedoras and berets. Can you believe they used to make kids wear those? Hey, Stupid. Put this shit on your head while we laugh at how dumb you are.

That's what's happening right now. I feel naked. It was no trouble for you to blast through the armor I wear with everyone else, the shield I spent years building out of my hurt and confusion. You have the power to hurt me so bad, Gavin. Like in *Spring Awakening: O, I'm gonna be wounded . . . O, you're gonna be my bruise.* Maybe the only way you really know you love someone is if they can break you with a single sentence.

You look down at the songs you've written in your ever-present black leather journal, the ones I didn't understand when you read them to me a minute ago. This disappointed you—here you are, trying to share your heart, the essence of you, and your girlfriend—the one person who should understand—doesn't. I don't measure up. This disappoints me, too. I thought I'd be able to get the words that you'd dragged up from your soul. But I don't know what they mean.

You sigh and try again:

Me, alone
You, twisting around bloody
roses
Eugenics
Euphoria
Eucharist

What's *eugenics*? And a bloody rose—does that mean I'm, like, attacking you with thorns? What did I do wrong? Or is this about Summer?

This is me, then: not the brightest bulb. Not the sharpest knife.

You take my hands and look into my eyes. I'm trying really hard not to cry because I know guys hate it when girls cry, but the tears spill over.

"Fuck," you say. "Baby, I'm sorry—I didn't mean . . . like, you took it the wrong—"

You wrap your arms around me and pull me closer. "I just meant we're different and that I *like* that," you whisper. "I can't tell you how good you are to me, *for* me."

"How can I be good for you if I don't understand your songs?" I mumble. I'm crying into the ROCKSTAR shirt I bought you and it smells faintly of baby powder. I close my eyes.

"What I need is someone who is there for me no matter what," you say. "I need someone *dependable*."

This doesn't make me feel better. It's like saying I'm a Volvo or something. I don't want to be dependable. I want to be a Ferrari—sleek and fast and sexy as hell. You lean back and run your hands through my hair, gentle. I wanted to get it cut like Lys's, but you told me no, you love it this way. I should have cut it, Gav. I should have done whatever the fuck I wanted to. But I didn't, did I?

"We fit. Like . . . a puzzle. You know?" you say.

I thought I was the one that didn't fit anywhere, but maybe with you that can change. Maybe.

"But . . ." I look at you, helpless. "The opposite of deep is *shallow*. Do you think I'm some ditzy, pea-brained—"

"I didn't mean *deep* as in . . . like that. I meant . . ." You frown and look away for a moment. Take off your fedora and run your hand through your hair. "You're perfect, Grace. That's what my dumb ass was trying to say. I meant that you're not, like, a tortured person. You're good and sweet and that fucked-up shit doesn't make sense to you because it's fucked up." Your eyes mist over. "*I'm* fucked up."

"Gavin—"

"No, I am. I mean, what kind of guy tells the girl he's in love with something like that? I don't deserve you."

You deserve someone better. That's the problem. I can't imagine ever earning my place by your side.

You stand up and reach out your hand.

I take it, wordless, and follow you to a corner of the backyard your parents can't see from the sliding glass door. You sit down in the grass and pull me on top of you, my legs on either side of your hips. By the time you're done with me, I don't know which way is up, only that I want more, more, more. I forget that you don't think I'm deep and I forget the hurt inside me. You kiss it all away.

FOURTEEN

I can't stop thinking about what you said. For a week it bothers me, needling under my skin. *You're not very deep.* You ask me what's wrong and I say, *Nothing, I'm fine.* Smile, smile. And I am. Except when I'm not.

I find myself watching every word I say to you, wondering what they say about me. I look for disappointment in your eyes, get nervous whenever you play me a new song. I've been walking on eggshells for a week. You're up north this weekend visiting your grandparents, so I spend Saturday with the girls, secretly relieved to have a little break from you. A break from the me I am with you.

"It's time for some broke girls' food," Nat says as she pulls into the Wendy's drive-through. She glances at me. "Dollar menu?"

"Is there any other kind? Fries and chili for me," I say. "And a Frosty."

"Lys?" she asks.

"Same."

She makes the order and we pool our money together, then head toward Lys's house, which is in a fancy development a few miles outside of town.

"Are you still a virgin?" Lys suddenly asks, leaning forward. "Inquisitive minds want to know."

"Oh my god, where did that come from?" I say.

"Come on, like we weren't gonna ask," Nat says.

"Yes. Still a virgin."

"I thought he would have deflowered you by now," Lys says. "I mean, when he and Summer were together, it was obvious he was hot for her, but with you he's like . . . *obsessed*."

I smile. "Good."

Last night you insisted that we fall asleep together, so we set up our phones on FaceTime. I was the first to fall asleep. When I woke up in the morning, you were curled on your side, your hair falling over your eyes. Shirtless. You're pretty adorable when you're sleeping.

I glance at Nat. "Speaking of obsessed boys . . . what's up with you and Kyle?"

"Yeah, dude. He's gotten super touchy-feely with you lately," Lys says.

Nat can't keep the smile off her face. "We . . . may have made out last night."

Cue screaming. "WHAT? Details *now*," I say.

"Okay, when I say *made out* I don't mean like the way you probably make out with Gavin. We kissed. For a while. That's it," Nat says.

"Tongue?" Lys asks, clinical.

Nat goes beet red. "Yes. A *little*."

"What does Jesus have to say about this?" I tease.

Nat sticks her tongue out at me. "I didn't consult him."

"I want someone to make out with!" Lys falls back against her seat dramatically.

I reach back and squeeze her hand. "She's out there somewhere."

"Yeah. Like Antarctica," Lys mutters.

When we get to Lys's we change into our swimsuits and go sit in her Jacuzzi.

"You okay?" Nat asks.

I was zoning out, going back through the conversation I'd had with you on the phone this morning, wondering if I'd said something stupid.

"What? Yeah, I'm fine," I say, sinking farther into the water.

"No you're not," Lys says. She cocks her head to the side, studying me. "What's up?"

I don't want to be disloyal to you, but I have to get this off my chest.

"Gav . . . he said something last week that . . . I mean, it's nothing, but—do you guys think I'm deep?"

"Deep?" Nat says.

"Like, can I be philosophical or, I don't know, *deep*. You know?"

Nat narrows her eyes. "What exactly did Gavin say to you?"

"Nothing."

Lys points at me. "Liar."

I slip farther into the Jacuzzi, the water bubbling all around me.

"He . . . said I wasn't deep."

"What. The. Fuck?" Lys says. "Are you serious?"

"He didn't mean it in, like, a bad way."

Nat shakes her head. "There's no good way to mean it. How could he say that to you?"

I shouldn't have said anything. "Guys, don't make a big deal out of this. Seriously, he just . . . misspoke."

"Don't make excuses for him," Lys says. "That was a dick thing to say."

I know they're right. But there's nothing I can do. It's not like we can change the past. And I know you'd take back the words if you could.

Nat reaches underwater for my hand. "You're one of the deepest people I know. He's an idiot. A *hot* idiot, but still an idiot. I mean, you freaking read *War and Peace* for fun and, like, listen to NPR podcasts.

Yesterday you said you wanted to direct a Brecht play and then explained *The Communist Manifesto* to me."

"And you can quote *Leaves of Grass* and tell classical composers apart," Lys said. "Remember when we were in Macy's and you were all, I love Vivaldi!"

I smile a little. "I remember because you gave me shit for it."

"Girl, that's because you're a bougie motherfucker and I love you."

Nat's phone buzzes and she dries her hand on a towel before reaching for it.

"Peter's parents are gone for the weekend and he's having people over tonight. Are we going?" she says.

"Who's gonna be there?" I ask.

She shrugs. "I'm guessing the whole drama crew."

Lys nods. "Let's do it." She glances at me. "This one needs to let loose."

"I'm fine," I say. My phone buzzes and I glance at it, then smile.

"What?" Nat says.

I hold up my phone so they can see. It's a picture of your grandparents and underneath you've typed, *This will be us in eighty years.*

Lys pretends to vomit. "What did I say?" she says. "He is totally obsessed with you."

"I still can't get over the fact that I got Gavin Davis. How the hell did that happen?"

Nat frowns. "The real question is, how was he so lucky to get *you*?"

PETER'S HOUSE IS in the country, about fifteen minutes outside of town, a sprawling ranch-style home on a couple of acres of land. When we get there all the lights are on in the house and the music is just short of blaring.

"If my parents find out I'm here, they'll kill me," I say.

"What they don't know won't hurt them," Lys says, adjusting the pink wig she's wearing. "How do I look?"

"Fabulous," I say. "Me?"

I'm wearing 1950s capri pants, ballet flats, and a 1940s blouse.

"Very Audrey Hepburn," Nat says.

Lys leans forward. "I'd just like to point out that Nat's wearing her sexiest dress."

It's still conservative—J. Crew, neat and tidy—but it hugs her Cuban hips and booty.

"That has Kyle written all over it," I say.

Nat turns pink. "It's not too short?"

I pat her on the arm. "It's just short enough."

There are maybe fifty people here and I know most of them—fellow drama geeks, choir kids, and random friends from school. For just a minute I stand in the doorway, basking in the glow of being a normal teenager. For once I'm not spending Saturday night babysitting Sam or doing chores.

"Hey, you guys made it!" Kyle says when he catches sight of us. He's wearing a top hat and his bow tie, signature Kyle party wear. "Drinks are in the kitchen." He turns to Nat. "Can we . . ."

"You two go make out. We'll see you later." Lys grabs my hand and pulls me away, both of us giggling at the shocked look on Nat's face.

The kitchen counter is covered with bottles of liquor and a nearby cooler is filled with beer. I grab a Coke while Lys mixes herself what looks like a particularly stiff drink involving tequila and Sprite.

We head into the living room, where an impromptu dance-off has started, drama geeks against choir nerds.

Peter catches sight of us and waves us over. "These little choir fuckers are kicking our asses. I hope you guys have some moves up your sleeves."

Lys hands me her cup as Beyoncé's "Single Ladies" starts playing. "I'm on it."

I squeeze onto the couch, half sitting on Peter's lap as Lys struts onto the floor and proceeds to kill it. I had no idea she had the whole dance memorized. I'm laughing so hard I'm crying. She steps back to let the choir girl who's challenging her go for it, but Peter just shakes his head.

"No contest," he shouts. "This one's ours." Peter holds up his phone. "Selfie time!" He and I press our cheeks together and smile. "Posting this shit right now. Caption? *Hot Motherfuckers*."

I laugh. "Nice."

Lys comes over to us, doing the running man. "Don't hate me cuz I'm awesome," she says, sweat dripping down the sides of her face.

I laugh, handing back her drink. "That was hella hot."

She grabs it and takes a big swig. "Your turn."

I set down my drink and pretend to do some serious stretching. "Baby Got Back" comes on and I throw myself onto the dance floor. Peter comes with me and we bust out our best moves—something between disco and hip-hop. We look like total idiots, shaking our asses, trying to go as low as we can to the floor without falling over. Peter pretends to spank me and I look scandalized. Just as we go to sit back down, I see you. You're standing in the ring of people that had been watching the dance-off, staring at me.

"Gavin!"

I run to you but when I throw my arms around you, you don't hug me back. I don't notice, not right away, because I'm still buzzing from dancing and a night away from The Giant.

"I had no idea you were back in town!" I murmur against your cheek. "Why didn't you call me?"

I pull back, grabbing hold of one of your hands. Did I ever tell you how much I used to love your hands? Strong, thin guitar-playing fingers that fold over mine, that twirl locks of my hair, that caress me in all kinds of goose-bump-inducing ways. I didn't know then that those hands would hurt me. I was so used to you touching me like I was made of glass—so careful, so gentle.

"I thought you were spending the night at Lys's," you say. Now I can hear the accusation in your voice, but I still don't know why you're so upset.

"I was. But then Kyle told Nat that Peter was having a party. What's wrong?"

"What's *wrong*?" you growl.

I've never seen you pissed off before. It throws me, this other Gavin, his mouth an angry slash, eyes cold. This Gavin who looks at me, furious.

"Gav, I—"

You grab my hand and pull me away, upstairs. You, Kyle, and Peter practically live at one another's houses—you're as comfortable here as if it were your own. You go into what must be Peter's parents' room and shut the door. A small bedside lamp is on beside a king bed. The room is decorated with country kitsch—wooden hearts and little plaques with Bible verses on them. A stenciled quote covers the wall above the bed—I wish I'd paid more attention to it:

> *Love is patient, love is kind. It does not envy, it does not boast, it is not proud. It does not dishonor others, it is not self-seeking, it is not easily angered, it keeps no record of wrongs. Love does not delight in evil but rejoices with the truth. It always protects, always trusts, always hopes, always perseveres. Love never fails.*

"What the fuck, Grace?" you say.

I am so confused.

"What? Why are you so pissed off?"

"I saw you—sitting on his lap, fucking dancing with him like you're about to have sex."

116

"Wait, this is about *Peter*?"

If you weren't so upset it'd be funny. Peter, who's basically been like a brother to me ever since I met him. Peter, whose wardrobe consists of free promotional T-shirts. Peter, who has serious acne problems and talks with his mouth full. And you, Gavin Davis, are jealous of him?

"*Yes*," you explode. "It's about Peter. About the fact that my fucking girlfriend is going behind my back—"

"Whoa, Gav." I take a step closer to you, put my hands on your shoulders. "Peter is just a friend. And I wasn't going behind your back. I had no idea you were in town. Plus, I didn't know about this party until, like, a few hours ago."

You shrug me off, then cross to the other side of the room, hands on your hips, eyes on the floor.

"I don't know if I can do this, Grace."

The words cut deep. You have no way of knowing this, but that's exactly what my father said to my mom before he walked out the door for good.

It always protects, always trusts, always hopes, always perseveres. Love never fails.

"Gavin." My voice breaks. In just a few weeks, you've become my center. The thought of having to face The Giant and my mom without you there to sing me to sleep at night or kiss the tears away threatens to gut me. "I'm . . . I'm so crazy in love with you. This . . . it's nothing. Nothing."

Your eyes go to mine then, softening a little. "It didn't look like it downstairs."

I hesitate, then cross the room and take one of your hands. You don't pull away.

"I'm sorry. I wasn't thinking," I say. You're right to be upset. If I'd seen you dancing like that with another girl I would have lost my shit. God, I am so bad at being a girlfriend. "Honestly, it really was nothing."

You sigh, your eyes on our hands. "Summer would do stuff just to torture me," you say. "I have no idea why. It was all this . . . power shit with her. Like, she'd flirt with guys right in front of me. And she'd lie to me about where she was going. One time I caught her at the mall, hanging out with this guy from her math class. She said they were just friends, but . . ." You shake your head. "That's not what it looked like."

I have to ask the question that nobody seems to be able to answer.

"Is that why you guys broke up?"

Your hand tightens around mine. "I found out she'd been having these, like, nightly calls with him—the guy from the mall. When I confronted her about it, she just . . . went crazy. Said all this shit to me and I just couldn't take it. By the time I got home I felt . . . worthless. Hopeless. And I—"

Your voice is shaking and you look away, clear your throat. This is the closest we've ever gotten to talking about that night.

"I'm such a fucking pussy," you mutter.

"Hey," I whisper. I gently place my hand on your cheek and turn your face back toward mine. "I will never hurt you like that."

You don't say anything and I wrap my arms around you and you are paper thin, so fragile. I realize that there will be days when I'll have to be strong enough for both of us. You hug me back, tight.

"I will never hurt you like that," I repeat.

"Okay," you say softly.

You let go and sit on the bed, then draw me onto your lap.

"It drives me crazy when I see other guys touching you," you say.

I love how possessive you are. You want me all to yourself. At home, I think they'd get down on their knees and praise Jesus if I disappeared.

"When do other guys touch me?" You give me a look. "Okay, I mean, other than with Peter tonight."

"They hug you, like, all the time."

"As friends!"

"I just . . . Can we have a rule? Like, no touching someone of the opposite sex?"

"You don't trust me," I say, my voice flat.

"I do. It's them I don't trust, okay? I know they think you're hot. You have no idea what a turn-on you are."

I blush. "Gav . . ."

"I'm serious." You tuck my hair behind my ear. "Just promise me. No touching."

I can't think when we're this close. When you smell so good and look at me with those bedroom eyes.

"I mean, if it's that important to you . . ."

"It is."

You reach into your pocket and hand me something wrapped in tissue paper.

"I got you something at this store near my grandma's house," you say.

I smile. "You didn't have to get me anything."

You brush your nose against mine. "I love getting you things."

I unwrap the tissue paper and inside is a silver bracelet fashioned into an infinity sign.

"Because," you say, tracing the bracelet, "that's how long I want to be with you."

I slip it on, then pull you to me. I tell you how much I love it—love *you*—with my lips and hands, with the fast beating of my heart, with everything in me.

"I'm ready," you murmur against my collarbone. "Whenever you are."

I pull away for a second, my eyes on yours. "Is it okay if I'm not ready yet?"

"Of course." You smile. "I don't think you'll be able to resist me for long."

I laugh. "Probably not."

We go back downstairs and you grab a beer. In a matter of minutes, someone is putting a guitar in your hands. I curl up on the couch next to you as you play whatever people request. A few weeks ago, I would have been just another admirer at the party, standing in the semicircle around you. I love how, every now and then, you lean over and kiss me, not caring that we're in front of everyone.

I don't know it now, but this will be one of my happiest memories of us. It's before the screaming and crying, before the guilt trips and the uncomfortable silences. Before I stopped wanting to be the girl you kissed.

FIFTEEN

"*D*oritos are essential to life," you say.

We're at the grocery store, picking up snacks for a movie night at your house. Your mom and my mom have both accepted that we're together even though your parents really didn't want you dating again so soon after your last breakup. It sucks, though, because my mom's imposed all these rules about how often we can see each other and your mom watches us like a hawk. She likes me and everything but will not, under any circumstances, allow another girl to break your heart. *It scares me*, your mom said to me once, when you were in the bathroom, *how much you two already love each other.*

Mom thinks the whole high school/college thing will only end in tears. She doesn't like that I want to spend so much time with you.

You're in high school, she says. *You shouldn't be this focused on one boy.* But I think about how happy your parents are. They met in high school. Besides, it's not like I'm going to take love advice from my mom. She married my dad and The Giant. Enough said.

My mom says we're only allowed to see each other three times a week and, even if you come over for five minutes to bring me a Pepsi Freeze, that counts as one of the times. My mom's a fascist dictator, but you and I are strategic. We're so good that the military should hire us. I invite you over for dinner each week and you make Mom laugh, love on Sam (you call him Little Dude, which makes him ecstatic), help with the dishes. You're cordial with The Giant, but mostly try not to get on his bad side (which is hella easy to do, as you well know). Mom's gonna cave and let me see more of you. I know she is.

Later, I will realize that she should have stuck to her guns—it would have saved me a hell of a lot of heartbreak. I will come to realize my mom and I are both suckers, perpetually won over by male charm and our own loneliness. She and I, we dig our own graves. Then we lie down in them, cross our arms, and wait for boys to pour dirt over us.

"I hate Doritos," I say as you throw the worst flavor—spicy nacho—into the shopping cart.

You stare at me, aghast. "Tell me you're joking."

"I'm not. Sorry."

You shake your head, aggrieved. "Wow. I can't believe you didn't tell me this before. I don't know if you and I are gonna work out. . . ."

I laugh and you toss a second bag into the cart, daring me to protest, then grab my hand as Ed Sheeran's "Thinking Out Loud" comes on over the store speakers.

"And, darling, I will be loving you 'til we're seventy . . ."

"What are you doing?" I squeal as we proceed to tango up and down the aisle.

"Dancing. Duh."

You twirl me and I laugh, but I also can't help but notice that everyone in the chips aisle is looking at us. Not bad looks, but still looking. My face heats up and I keep my head down. This is exactly why you're an actor and I'm not—I can't stand people looking at me.

When the song stops, you plant a kiss on my cheek. "You're totally mortified right now, aren't you?"

I nod and you turn to our fellow customers. "Thank you!" you say, with a sweeping bow. "We'll be here all night."

"Oh my gosh." I drag you out of the aisle.

"Come on," you say, laughing, "was that so bad?"

I take stock. Was it? You're the most uninhibited person I know. Other people might think I am, too, because I'm a theatre nerd, but they'd be dead wrong. I worry suddenly that I might be a disappointment to you. Summer doesn't care what anyone thinks of her, but me—I care. I care a lot.

"Yeah, it was bad," I admit. "I think. Yes. I don't like people watching me."

"I'm going to keep that in mind." You don't say that like, *Okay, I won't push you.* You say it like we're about to embark on a grand experiment. An adventure of epic proportions.

A few days later, it begins.

Prom is a few weeks away and everyone's talking about it. I'm not certain you'll ask me because you told me you might not go at all. The prom is for seniors only and nearly all of your closest friends are juniors like me.

But then I get the first clue on Friday morning, handed to me by Kyle on a small square of notebook paper. I know it's from you because your handwriting has already become very familiar to me. You like passing me little notes throughout the day—I have a cigar box full of them at home.

On one side of the paper Kyle hands me is the word *WILL*. On the other side, a directive:

> *Walk like a penguin to the library. Someone will give you the next clue upon your arrival.*

"Is he serious?" I ask Kyle.

He grins. "I don't know what it says, I just know Gavin's watching you."

I look around, but there's no sign of you. How often does this happen, me looking around, wondering if you're watching? In less than a year, I won't be looking around with hope. I'll be scared. Paranoid. I'll see conspiracies in kisses, ulterior motives in hugs.

"I can't believe he's making me do this," I mutter under my breath.

I know you're asking me to prom. I mean, come on, the first clue is WILL. And instead of flowers or maybe a song—hey, you're a rock star, why not a song?—I get walking like a goddamn penguin.

The school is crawling with students. The library is on the other side of campus. Knowing you're watching makes me feel even *more* self-conscious. I'm going to look like an idiot in front of the one person I'm desperate to impress.

I take out my ponytail and try to hide my face with my hair. I stare at the ground and begin to walk like a penguin, waddling from side to side like Charlie Chaplin.

Penguins aren't very fast. By the time I get to the library I'm sweating and my face is ten shades of red.

Peter is standing beside the glass double doors and he starts guffawing—a real stage laugh—when he sees me making my way painfully toward him. Of all people, you chose the prick of our group to witness my penguinness.

"Oh my god, this is priceless!" he yells, following me with his phone. Great, now he'll post a video of my humiliation for all the world to see.

I just shake my head and pray no one got a good look at my face.

Peter hands me the next piece of paper, but only after I beg in a

Mr. Penguin voice, which he informs me is very high and snooty sounding. From the next clue, I can tell you're going to make me work for it. *YOU.*

> *Crawl on all fours and bark like a dog in the drama room*
> *during lunch. Someone will give you the next clue.*

By the time I make it to the drama room, my stomach is a knot of nerves. I'm not sure if I should be angry at you or not. You know how introverted I am. But you're always telling me I need to learn how to live on the wild side. I wish I could be more like you: stick my head out a car window with the wind rushing over my face, yell Shakespearean monologues on the football field during P.E.

But that's just not me. Am I not good enough as I am?

I throw my backpack down and get on all fours. *There's always,* I think, *room for improvement.*

"What the hell are you doing?" Lys asks.

"You don't even want to know," I say.

I crawl. I bark.

I want to cry.

Nat looks murderous. "This is so stupid," she says to no one in particular.

Ryan rushes to me. Leans down. He grins, but there's something in his eyes—a flicker of sympathy he can't quite tamp down.

"Clue number three," your bassist says softly.

Is there pity in his eyes? I can't even tell at this point. I've only been looking into *your* eyes for so long now, learning their language. I don't realize that I've begun seeing myself this way—through your eyes. Only through your eyes.

I open the paper: *GO.*

Sing the national anthem outside your sixth-period class-
room. Someone will give you the next clue.

I do it. I do all the things and by the end of the day, I want to
change my name and move to Guatemala—get as far away from here
as I can. *It's worth it*, I tell myself, when you walk up to my last class with
the final word in your hand. You whip out your guitar and suddenly
all the guys are with you—the band, whoever's around—and you're
singing a punk version of "My Girl."

When you're done and half the school is applauding the impromptu
concert, you wrap your arms around me, tight.

"I'm so proud of you for doing all that crazy shit. You must really
love me. I was afraid you'd give up."

I hide my face in your neck, still mortified. "Were you, like, *test-*
ing me?"

"I wouldn't say *testing. . . ."* You grin. "But you passed."

"Gavin!"

"Don't be mad, I love you! We're going to prom!" You kiss me
before I can say anything else.

With your lips on mine, your song still in my ears, I forget that I
never said yes, that all of it—the dance, us—was a foregone conclusion.
You told me to be your girlfriend. You didn't wait for me to answer
about prom. I gave you my heart on a silver fucking platter and you ate
it, piece by bloody piece.

YOU HAND THE policeman your ID. Again.

We're not even to the dance yet.

"You were swerving a bit there, son. Have you been drinking?"

My face goes beet red and I sink into my prom dress, which you
insisted on picking out. ("I know what looks best on you. Besides," you
added with a devilish smile, "I need to make sure it's easy to take off.")

You wouldn't let me buy it, either. I guess you'd overheard me telling the girls I'd have to work extra shifts at the Pot to cover prom. It's a gown that goes all the way to my feet—you said the super-tight and short ones were for skanks who wanted to make their boyfriends jealous. Depending on the light, it shimmers pink, tangerine, gold. I want to hide underneath it, turn it into a fort. My hand strays to the necklace you gave me: intertwining ribbons threaded with beads that match my dress.

"No, I haven't been drinking, sir. I swear on my mom's life," you say. "My girlfriend was . . . um . . ."

I lean toward the window and give the officer the most charming smile I have in my arsenal.

"I was kissing him," I say. "On the cheek only, but it totally distracted him. I'm *so sorry*. I promise it won't happen again."

The officer frowns as he takes in your tux and my fancy updo.

"Prom night?" he asks.

You nod. "I'm a senior. At RHS. And . . . a totally responsible virgin."

The officer laughs. "All right," he says. He hands you back your license. "You two be safe now." He fixes us both with a stare. "And stay virgins."

"This is the kind of story we'll tell our grandkids someday," you say as you pull back onto the road.

I raise my eyebrows. *"Our?"*

The corner of your lip turns up. "I'm thinking we'll have ten."

I go all warm and gooey inside. You want to be with me forever, don't you?

THE DANCE IS magic. You are a perfect gentleman. In every photo I look happier than I've ever been—I'm always mid-laugh or grinning or kissing your cheek. During slow songs you sing softly in my ear; during fast dances you pull me close.

"How did you do it?" you ask.

"Do what?"

"Be the most beautiful girl here."

Something about you in a tux makes me want to do a striptease for you right there on the dance floor. I love how you lose the bow tie almost immediately, how the top two buttons are undone. And your sleeves, rolled up to the elbow so I can see the muscles in your forearms from all that guitar practice. Oh, and the way you carry your coat slung over your shoulder, one finger holding it up like an eighties movie star. Perfection.

Girls stare at me with jealousy. I know they're wondering how I snagged you. I'm the luckiest girl in the world.

After the dance, you get me into the backseat of your Mustang and we kiss so much my lips get swollen. Someone raps on the window, shines a big flashlight at us.

"Kids," the security guard says, "clear out."

I look out the window as you scramble into the driver's seat. We're the only car left. When we got here, the parking lot was full.

For the next hour we drive to some of our favorite make-out places: the Mormon church parking lot (a favorite among local teens—who knew?) and that fancy neighborhood across town that doesn't have that many streetlights. Except someone in one of the houses calls on us.

The cops come by *again*. After they let us off the hook, we both burst out laughing.

"I have some pretty salacious stuff to write in my diary tonight," I tease.

"You have a diary?"

I nod. "Ever since I was in kindergarten."

"Damn. Do you write about me?"

"Of course I write about you. But don't worry—it's well hidden."

We end up at a dark patch of street in your neighborhood, in the backseat once more. It's surprisingly comfortable. You bunch my dress up around my hips and I run my hands through your hair. Your lips, your tongue, your fingers—they're all over me. I should be embarrassed by what you can see and taste, the moans coming out of my mouth, but I'm not. I close my eyes and a shudder of pure bliss rolls through me and I get it, I know what that is. And I love you so fucking much.

My eyes snap open and you wipe your mouth on my knee, smiling against my skin.

"God, I love doing that to you."

"Really?" I whisper.

"Are you kidding? *Yes.*"

Natalie would say *sick*. Mom would . . . god, I don't even know what she'd do.

I know it's not true, but I can't help feeling that no one in the history of ever has felt this way about each other. How can anyone have wanted another person this much? Or felt like they were a part of them?

I sit up and reach for your belt. "Come here," I whisper.

I remember one time a cheerleader in my geometry class was talking about Justin Timberlake and said something like *I want to have his babies* and I thought that was so weird.

But I have that thought, out of nowhere. I want to have your babies. I want you inside me. I want to melt into your skin so that I'm with you all the time.

"I love you," I whisper against your lips.

Your mouth turns up in a love-drunk half smile. "I love you more."

I'm obsessed with you. When you said that to me, I felt proud. *I can't stop thinking about you. Sometimes I can't sleep until I write a song about your lips, the sound of your voice, the way your middle finger curves slightly to the left.*

We stop before we go so far we can't turn back and when I catch my breath, I feel relieved. I don't want anything to ruin tonight. As much as I want you, I don't want to lose my virginity on prom night. I don't want the first time I have sex to be a cliché.

We get back into the front seat and head toward my place, the college indie station playing quietly. It's nearly curfew—Mom is letting me stay out until midnight. This is a good thing, her rule. It keeps us from going to the housing development that's still being built, the one where we first kissed. You know I don't want to have sex yet, but we talk about it all the time. You're not pushing me. I want you just as much as you want me. I don't know how much longer I can hold out. I'm just scared. Sex seems like a huge step, one I can't ever go back from. I don't want to be one of the girls in my high school who have sex. It would just feel . . . wrong. Like suddenly belonging to an alien race. All of my friends are virgins. I don't want to be the first to lose it. And I don't want anything between us to change. I'm scared what will happen if we do it.

I want to be your first, you said the other day. Then you changed your mind: *I want to be your only.*

I still can't believe you've never had sex. *I am so going to deflower you*, I'd said. You laughed your head off, told me no one makes you laugh like I can.

We're almost home when I feel the atmosphere shift from blissful giddiness to something . . . bad. I have no idea where it's coming from. Your hands tighten on the wheel. Without realizing it, everything in me tenses up. The happy evaporates. This is how I'm supposed to feel at home, not with you. Never with you.

"I'd really like to read it," you say quietly. "Your diary." You turn to me. "Can I?"

"What?" I shake my head. "Wouldn't that be weird?"

You shrug. "I mean, if you're not hiding anything, what does it matter?"

I sit there, quiet. Thinking. I don't know why, but it just doesn't feel right.

You rest a hand on my knee. "I just want to be as close to you as possible."

Some of the fear inside me melts away. You love me. You want to know me inside out, just like I want to know *you* inside out. But still. I can't shake the wrongness of the question—that you even asked it.

"I know," I say. "But . . . it's my *diary*."

You frown. "I read you my poems, my songs. That's like my diary."

That's true. Except you get to choose which ones you read to me. My diary—I don't leave anything out. The whole mess of me is in there. Matt's in there. You already hate him, hate that I'm working with my ex and that he gets to see me more than you.

"I trust you—why don't you trust me?" you say.

"I do."

"I just . . . can't be with anyone that isn't up-front with me. Summer . . . she had a lot of secrets."

Summer is the magic word. I think you know this. I don't ever want you to think I'm like the girl who pushed you toward suicide. I see it that way now—as though you slitting your wrists were somehow her fault. I'm not like her. I'll keep you safe. You'll keep me safe.

So I cave.

I read you parts of my diary the next day. You're sitting on the hood of your car and I stand in front of you, your arms around my waist. After several entries, your hands drop away. You're angry—why? I left out the Matt parts, like when I kinda wanted to kiss him when he had flour on his nose that one time. So what is there to be mad about?

"I know you're skipping parts," you say. You reach for the diary. "Come on, let me read it."

You're right—I have stuff I'm hiding. Entries where I wonder if you're really the one. Entries that list your faults. Like, I think it's really dumb you're super into He-Man. You have the figurines from the eighties and you and the guys are always all *I have the power!* But maybe that bugs me because you once said I'm not as hot as He-Man's sister, She-Ra. I'm sure you were joking, but still. Stupid little nitpicky things like that.

If I don't give you this diary, you'll know I'm hiding something. And you'll force it out of me. You asked me a few weeks ago if I'd ever masturbated and I lied, but you could see the lie all over my face. You pushed me to tell you how I do it, what I think about.

You better only think of me, you said. You weren't teasing—sometimes I think you'd set up security cameras in my mind if you could.

I hand you the diary. But I'm strategic. I flip to a page where it says how much I love you, how maybe we might get married someday. This is the truth and I want you to know it.

After you're done reading the entry, you pull me closer. You're beaming.

"See," you whisper, your lips brushing my hair, my neck. "That wasn't so bad."

"No," I say, relieved. "It wasn't."

I never write in my diary again.

SIXTEEN

I like that you tell me your secrets. Sometimes you get so sad you can't stand it. And you don't know why you feel this way and you're terrified your parents will find out. *They watch me all the time*, you say. *Every word, everything I do—it's like they're analyzing it. They think I'll . . . that I'll try to hurt myself again.*

You confess that the sadness is eating you alive. That the only thing that's saving you is music . . . and me. *Me.*

"Do you ever feel so trapped you can hardly breathe?" I ask you one afternoon. We're at your house, pretending to do homework but really just kissing every moment your mom isn't in the room.

"All the time," you say. "I mean, I love my parents, but this town, this life—it's their version of heaven. I just totally don't get that."

"I know—Nat and Lys are the same way," I say. "Sometimes I feel like I'm the only person in this entire school who actually has a dream. Like, a big dream."

Nat and Lys have dreams, sure. But they're human-sized. Nat wants to be a nurse, Lys wants to be a psychologist.

"Which is . . ."

"Bohemian starving artist," I say immediately.

"Ha! You would say that."

I swat at your arm. "What's that supposed to mean?"

"Hmmm . . . let me think," you say, rubbing your chin. "Remind me—how many times have you seen *Moulin Rouge*?"

"Well, okay. But even you have to admit that would be a cool life."

"Grace, are you telling me your life goal is to be a whore dying of consumption?"

I will not be swayed.

"If that's the only way I can live in *Belle Epoque* Paris, then yes, yes I do want to be a whore dying of consumption."

"You're crazy."

"Come join me," I say. "You can die of syphilis—it'll be so much fun!"

You laugh, shaking your head. Your fedora topples to the ground and you pick it up as you turn to an imaginary audience and gesture to me.

"Ladies and gentlemen, I rest my case." You reach up and brush your finger against my cheek, smiling that soft smile that's just for me. "I need you. You're the only good part of my day, you know that?"

I bat your hand away, blushing. "I'm sure that's an exaggeration."

You take my hands and lean closer. "You're so good at this."

"At what?"

"Dealing with me."

"Gav, I don't *deal* with you. You're . . ." I bite my lip.

"God, I love when you do that," you say.

"Do what?"

You shake your head. "I'm not telling you—you'll get self-conscious and you won't do it anymore and then what am I supposed to day-dream about in class?"

Lines, these fucking lines of yours—why can't I see that they're all

134

too perfect? How would things have turned out differently if I hadn't fallen for every single one of them?

"So. I have some news," you say. "I've actually had it for a while, like over a month, but I've had to do a lot of thinking, so . . . yeah."

My stomach tightens. "College news?"

You nod. I try to smile. I knew this was coming. We both did.

"Okay," I say, quiet.

"Don't be sad."

"I'm not."

You gently push me. "Liar."

"Okay. I'm a little sad. Maybe a lot sad. Just tell me and get it over with."

"I'm not going to UCLA."

I stare at you. "What? How could they have not chosen you?"

You shrug. "Their loss."

I feel so guilty for being happy.

"So what are you going to do?"

"Well, I thought you might like to know that I'm staying here. Going to State."

I blink. "But you're supposed to move to LA and be a rock star and forget all about me."

You lean your forehead against mine. "First, I could never forget about you."

"Once you have groupies you could."

You laugh and brush my lips. "You're the only groupie I need."

"I'm trying really hard not to be happy about this," I say.

"Why? Were you planning on breaking up with me in September?" you tease.

"*No.* But you hate it here. You're going to be miserable."

"Can't be miserable when you're around. It's just one more year,

135

Grace. When you graduate . . . we can go wherever we want." You grin. "The world is our fucking oyster."

LAST NIGHT MY mom grounded me from eating eggs for a month because I forgot to wash the pan I'd cooked them in. A few days before that, she threatened to pull me out of the school dance concert if I left the laundry in the dryer again. The ridiculousness of all this has quickly slid to the number one spot in Reasons My Mother Is Crazy.

Now, it's almost eight in the morning and my SAT test is at eight-thirty. The test center is twenty minutes away and I'll need a few minutes once I get there to prep. Mom is taking me because I don't want to make you wake up on a Saturday at an hour you consider to be, and I quote, the ass-crack of dawn. But Mom said we couldn't leave until I'd folded the laundry (The Giant's tightie-whities and undershirts) and now I'm about to start crying and am so stressed because *I need to go take my fucking SATs, you bitch, I hate you.*

"Mom, the laundry is done, can we go?"

She looks over the pile of clothing, refolds the top items, then nods.

I run outside and jump into the van and just after Mom turns the key in the ignition, *this* begins:

"I don't think I locked the front door," Mom says. "Go check it."

"I saw you lock—"

"Grace. Go check the door."

I fucking saw her lock it because I knew this would happen, I knew it. I make a big show of trying to open the very locked door. I get back in and Mom ignores me as she pulls out. Talk radio is on way too loud and my head is spinning and I am totally going to fail this test. Next week is the last week of school. I don't want to have this hanging over my head all summer.

We're halfway down the street when Mom stops the car.

"Crap," she says. "The back gate. I doubt Roy locked it when he took the trash cans out."

Mom starts to do a three-point turn. The clock on the dash says 8:05. I point to it.

"Mom, please. I'm gonna be late."

"The Hendersons had their yard broken into last week," she says.

"They have a totally jumpable gate!" I say. "And it's eight in the morning, Mom. I'm sure all the thieves are sleeping. . . ."

She ignores me. We're back in the driveway. I jump out before she tells me to, run, and—sure enough—the gate's locked. I sprint back to the car.

"Okay, okay, we're good. Let's go," I snap.

"Do *not* take that tone with me, young lady. I'll just sit here and wait until you can be respectful," she says.

Tears well up in my eyes and I bite my lip. If I start crying I'll get a headache; I'll say something I'll regret.

"I'm sorry," I mumble.

"What was that?"

"I'm sorry." My words this time are louder, the defiance stuffed way down deep where she can't see it. I am Totally Remorseful Daughter.

Suddenly she pushes open her door, pulls the keys out of the ignition.

"Mom! I said I'm sorry!"

"My curling iron," she calls over her shoulder, hurrying to the door. "I left it on, I'm sure I did."

No you didn't!!!!!!!!!

8:10

8:15

I'm crying now, tears blurring my index cards, each one neatly printed with an obscure piece of vocabulary, but the only words running through my mind are:

Obsessive

Compulsive

Disorder

I am tired of invisible dust.

Doors that unlock themselves.

Creases in smooth sheets.

Cold irons burning.

Since I'm grounded from my cell (long story involving a forgotten broom on the front porch), I compose an imaginary text to Natalie:

Can't make it. Good luck. I fucking hate my life.

I hear the door slam and now the dance really begins. Mom locks the door, goes down the porch steps, turns, checks it. Still locked. She walks down the path, pauses. Starts to turn. Her eyes meet mine. I am silent. Tears running down my face. I can see the battle she fights inside herself—*check it again*, her little demons tell her, *one more time*. My eyes beg her to get in the car. Her eyes beg me to understand. But I can't. I won't.

She holds up a finger. *One more time. Better safe than sorry.*

8:45

We arrive at the testing center. They tell me I'm late. They tell me I can't take it. I turn to my mom.

"I hate you," I say, quiet.

She knows I mean it.

"I'm sorry to hear that," she says. Her voice is a shrug, but I can see the misery in her eyes. She won't admit it's her fault, though. She won't admit she needs help.

We don't talk the whole way home.

SEVENTEEN

*T*he entire sloping lawn in front of the school's outdoor auditorium is packed. Hot sunlight burns down, turning anyone with pale skin pink. I sit squished between Natalie and Alyssa, waiting for the end-of-the-year talent show to start. Waiting for you to knock everyone's socks off.

It's the last day of school and finals are over. It wouldn't be Roosevelt High without this annual tradition. Even though it's just a school event, there's a carnival feel to it all: summer is here and you can feel the rapture of the school year coming to an end. We're animals in a cage who are so so close to being free. At least, that's what we tell ourselves. *Freedom is an illusion*, Lys says. *The Man invented summer vacation to make us forget that he's keeping us down the rest of the year.*

"It's so stupid they still call it Air Guitar," she says, taking a bite from the In-N-Out burger she's gotten at one of the food trucks parked around campus for today. "Like, *hello*? Everyone is actually playing guitar."

You and I have had this conversation before, about how the yearly talent show has gone from lip-synching to the real deal ever since your freshman year, when you and your band decided to turn the mics on and plug the amps in.

"I would just like to point out that my boyfriend has revolutionized the entire RHS talent show system," I say. "Can you imagine how much this would have sucked if it was all lip-synching?"

Nat rolls her eyes. "Well, it should be pretty fun watching Peter, Kyle, and Ryan try to be One Direction."

"Gav tried to talk them out of it—it's on them," I say.

Poor Ryan, getting roped into their scheme. Now, instead of just being the cool bass player of Evergreen, he'll be remembered as boy band wannabe number three.

You laughed your ass off when they told you they would be lip-synching and doing a choreographed dance to "What Makes You Beautiful." The only person willing to be their fourth boy band member was a freshman.

"I can't wait," I say. "Mostly because I'm going to take a million pictures and use them as blackmail for the rest of their lives."

Nat laughs. "I told Kyle he's lucky I'm not dumping him."

She and Kyle have pretty much been together since Peter's party.

Lys nods. "For real."

My phone buzzes and I check my text—it's from you.

Peek-a-boo

Where are you?

In a super secret rock star location. I'd tell you, but then I'd have to kill you.

Can you see me?

Oh, yeah. Your boobs look good in that shirt, btw.

Do you ever think about anything else?

Sorry, I didn't catch that. I was busy imagining my girlfriend with her clothes off.

"Is he nervous?" Lys asks.

I laugh. "No, I don't think so."

You never seem to get nervous. You take all the attention in stride, like it's your due. I think you've probably always been this way. Taking things as your due, I mean.

The first act comes on, a group of three girls singing an old Destiny's Child song. I'm annoyed by their general lack of clothing. Wonder if any of them flirted with you backstage. Wonder if you flirted back.

"Skanks," Lys mutters under her breath.

I wish I could say I didn't laugh, but I did. Nat hits her, though.

"You're the worst feminist ever," she hisses. "Didn't you read *The Vagina Monologues*?"

Lys flashes an evil grin. "Let the record show that Nat just said *vagina*—in *public*."

When you and the rest of Evergreen go onstage, the entire school's energy spikes.

That's my boyfriend, I think, proud, as guys whistle and girls scream. I'm not jealous of the girls this time—you're mine.

You're always hot, but with your electric guitar in your hand and your hair in your face as you strut across the stage, you are gorgeous. You really do look like a rock star.

When you get to the center mic, you pull the guitar strap over your shoulder and when you do, your Ramones shirt cinches up a little and for a second I see a swath of skin. Skin that I've touched, kissed, licked. Those narrow hip bones, unexpectedly delicate.

You pull your mic closer, then look out over the audience. And I know you're looking for me. I wave and your face breaks out into a grin and you wave back. It's like having a neon sign over my head that says GIRLFRIEND. I love it. You're wearing the necklace I made you—a guitar pick strung on a braided leather choker—and your fingers touch it once, for luck maybe. For me.

You guys launch right into a cover of my favorite song, "California Dreamin'." You didn't tell the guys why you chose it, but I know why and it's the sweetest, most romantic thing anyone has done for me. It's a great cover—true to the song, but its own thing entirely. You guys went for a real California vibe—Sublime mixed with the Chili Peppers, with a reggae riff here, punked-out Green Day bass there. It's all my favorite things mixed into one. Every now and then you look out and sing to me, your mouth close to the mic.

I hold my breath the entire time and I know I'm not the only one. I watch your hands on the strings, the way the muscles and tendons strain against the skin. The way you seem possessed by the music, how it takes you and you let it. You launch into a guitar solo filled with longing, desire, a raw need I see in your eyes every time we shed our clothes like second skins.

The way you growl the part *Well, I got down on my knees and I pretend to pray* is so sexy I can't stand it. The audience erupts and you smile a little, the same smile you get after we've messed around. Satisfied. A knot of longing builds in my belly and I imagine running backstage, grabbing you, and taking you into the nearest empty classroom.

When the song finishes you get a standing ovation—the only one of the afternoon. I scream and wave my hands as the band shuffles offstage, suddenly awkward boys again—the potion of the music has worn off. You're different, though. You just walk off, like the whole thing doesn't matter anymore now that the music's stopped. You don't even look at the audience again, even though you're the real deal—no potion necessary.

I feel the lack of you deep in my chest, just like I always do when a door shuts behind you, when I hear the dial tone in my ear.

Later, we go swimming at your house. Everyone's there, including your mom, whose job, it seems, is to keep the pizza coming. We go to your room after everyone leaves. Your parents tell us to leave the door open and we do, but it doesn't matter because they're in the living room watching a movie and the last time you went by there to grab us some drinks from the fridge, they were asleep.

"You were amazing today," I say against your lips.

I'm sitting on your lap, straddling you, and your hands are busy untying my bikini top. You don't say anything—compliments make you bashful—but you sing "California Dreamin' " softly as your lips travel down my neck toward my chest. My arms are wrapped around you, my hands in your hair, and I slowly sit up on my knees so that your hand can slip more easily into my bikini bottom.

"I bought some condoms," you whisper in my ear. "Just in case . . ."

"We . . . can't . . . Your parents . . ."

I gasp and you laugh softly as you lay me on the bed and unbuckle your pants. We lie against each other, naked. You press closer to me.

"Are you sure?" you whisper.

I want to lose my virginity to you. I just don't know when the right time will be. I think I'll just *know*. I'll feel it in my bones.

"Not when your parents are home," I whisper.

I find the Grace inside me who's got her head on straight. But she looks nothing like she used to. I roll you so you're on your back and then I slowly make my way down your torso, past that patch of skin I coveted when you were onstage. Lower and lower.

Your hands snake through my hair and I smile against your skin, feeling powerful, feeling like I'm the only thing that matters to you right now. I'm finally the most important thing in the world to someone.

When it's over, I wipe my mouth and look down at you. I wish I could paint. No, I wish I could sculpt. I want to turn you into clay, run my hands along every part of you. I want you under my fingernails and stuck on my skin. I want to know exactly what you're made of, what's inside.

I look at you and look at you and look at you.

WHEN I SEE you in your cap and gown, I cry.

I'm sandwiched between Nat and Lys and they both, as if by silent agreement, wrap an arm around me. This makes me cry harder.

You give me a tiny wave from where the seniors are lining up behind the bleachers.

Lys tries to redirect my attention. "How are things with your parents?"

"They're still pissed as hell at me," I say, wiping my eyes.

Which is why I'm grounded from seeing you all summer, your last summer before college.

> You tap my window and I'm at my bedroom door seconds later. Underneath my skirt I'm wearing the lacy underwear you bought me.
>
> I'm sliding back the glass door when it happens:
> "What the hell are you doing?"
> The Giant. Oh god, to be caught by HIM of all people.
> My hand falls from the door handle. Your face is nearly as white as the stage makeup for mimes.
> I turn and say the first lie I can think of.
> "I couldn't sleep, so I called Gavin. We were just gonna hang out on the porch and talk until I got sleepy."
> "You better get home right now, Gavin," The Giant says.
> He turns to me. "Congratulations. You just lost your summer."

"At least they didn't ground me from you guys," I say.

That was on the table for a while.

144

The girls tighten their hold around me, a cocoon of best-friend love. I have my new version of the Three Amigos. No *Ewww, the purple house*, but this will do.

The ceremony goes by faster than I thought it would—months of dread for one and a half hours of good-bye.

"I'll see you in a few minutes," I say to Nat and Lys as I hurry down the bleachers.

I get to see you before you go off to a party with the senior class. We've agreed to meet on the baseball field before you find your parents.

"Hey," you say, wiping away my tears. I hate that I'm all splotchy. "I love you. Nothing's going to change that."

I nod, miserable. "I just love you so much and what if—"

You press your lips against mine, soft and sweet. I hold on to you, greedy. I don't care who sees us.

"I have to go," you say, pulling away. "There's no way I'm not seeing you all summer—we'll figure it out. Promise."

I sleep over at Nat's and she, Lys, and I spend the night eating popcorn and chocolate. If it weren't for them, I would have been inconsolable tonight. We talk about you going to college and how, even though it's local, it's an entirely different world. No—an entirely different planet.

"He's going to be this hot rocker guy and all these college girls are going to throw themselves at him," I say miserably.

Lys nods. "Yeah. Sorry, but . . . yeah." Nat hits her and she says, "What? It's true."

Nat puts an arm around me. "He's obviously in love with you. I think you guys will make it next semester . . . if you want to."

"Of course I want to," I say. I can't really picture any scenario in which we're not together. "Okay, no more boy talk, it's too depressing."

"Agreed," Nat says. "Can you believe we're officially seniors now?"

Lys reaches for the bag of kettle corn. "I know, right? Time to blow this Popsicle stand."

The future is creeping up on me. The possibilities, I realize, are endless. I'd forgotten that over these months with you. My already tiny world had shrunk to the circumference of your arms.

"Am I losing myself?" I ask suddenly. "Have I become *that* girl?"

"That girl" is the one who ditches her friends for a boy, a girl whose whole life revolves around him.

Nat hesitates. Takes a long sip of her Pepsi Freeze.

"Well," she says, weighing each word in that thoughtful way of hers. "Maybe a little."

I reach for her hand, then Lys's, and squeeze them. "That's lame. I'm sorry."

Nat shakes her head. "You're happy, right?"

"With Gavin? Yeah," I say. "It's my parents who are making everything with him so complicated."

"Then that's all that matters."

Happy. This time next year, Gavin, I won't be happy. I won't be desperate to see you. By this time next year, I'll be ready to say good-bye.

EIGHTEEN

*Y*ou have the perfect family.

I like to just sit back and watch you together—your mom, teasing you, kissing your cheek to reassure you when you take her ribbing seriously. I love how when she kisses you, she makes a smacking sound. *Mwah!* That means she really loves you, in case you didn't know. Your dad: absentminded and sweet, always walking into whatever room we're in, looking for his glasses (or maybe checking up on us, I don't know). You're an only child and it's obvious: you are their entire world. They worship you just like everyone else does—your first acolytes.

"Grace, I wish we could just put you in one of our suitcases," your mom says. "You're such a tiny thing, I bet we could manage it."

"A carry-on bag would be better," you say. "Then she wouldn't have to stay in the bottom of the plane with all the other luggage."

Your dad chuckles. He thinks you're the cleverest boy in the world. I do, too.

You come closer and kiss my head, expression serious. "I can't believe your mom said no. I thought for sure—" You break off, sighing.

"I know." I look away when my throat starts to close up. I've been crying so much lately.

I am so in love with you, Gavin Davis. I love how messy your hair is and how you wear the same three outfits all the time. I love how I can hear you playing guitar when I walk up to your house. I love that you're the only person who knows that I'm unbelievably ticklish on the inside of my elbow.

"It's criminal," your dad agrees.

Your parents are taking you to Hawaii for ten days and they offered to pay my way as a graduation present to you and my mom said no. *Hawaii.* A tropical beach and hardly any clothes and you you you.

It *is* criminal. I hate my mom. I know that's a horrible thing to say, but it's true. I think she's jealous of me, that I have a guy that doesn't walk all over me, that I'm young and thin and happy. That I have lots and lots of orgasms. Sometimes I'll catch her looking at me with real dislike. And she's become more critical of me lately. I have fat rolls in my stomach when I hunch forward, I don't have nice enough knees for short dresses and skirts, my favorite color (red) makes me look pasty. She even got pissed when I weighed myself and realized I'd lost a couple pounds. *Just wait until your metabolism slows down,* she said. *You take after your dad and look at the women in* his *family.*

"Absence makes the heart grow fonder," I say. I'm practicing having a stiff upper lip. *Chin up,* as Beth would say.

"That's the spirit," your mom says as she places a Coke in front of me—she knows how soda deprived I am at home, how it's considered a luxury on my family's grocery list.

"Thanks, Anna," I say. I like that she refuses to let me call her Mrs. Davis. *You're one of the family now,* she says. *He loves you,* she says, *so we love you. It's that simple.*

And it really is. Your parents have become parents to me, too. They give me advice, they worry about me, they feed me. Your mom even insists she and I have girl time together. Manicures or lunch. It's all the things I hear about other moms doing, but didn't know they actually *did*. When you told them what happened the morning I missed my SATs, your mom actually started crying. You made me promise that from now on, you're my ride for anything important.

She squeezes my hand. "When you two get married, we won't have to deal with this crazy anymore."

By now I'm used to your family's openness, but I had no idea your parents approved of me that much.

You smile at the surprise on my face. "Yeah, we talk about you behind your back" is all you say.

I blush. You will always be able to make me blush, no matter what. You plop down next to me and bury your face in my shoulder. It's been days since we've made out, since we've gotten to touch each other. *One more chance*, Mom said, after the night The Giant took my summer away. *Next time, you're breaking up with him.*

I think I might die if I had to break up with you. The thought of another girl in your arms, lying beneath you—it kills me.

"Anna, Grace's parents aren't crazy." Your dad looks from your miserable face to mine. "Okay, maybe a little."

"This sucks," you grumble.

My mom's attempt at a peace offering is letting me be here to say good-bye. Then it's back to being grounded from you all summer. You have these amazing parents who've embraced me, made me part of your family, and I have a mom who locks me up and throws away the key. It's like I'm Rapunzel without the romantic tower and gorgeous hair.

"If I were a better parent," your mom says to you, "you'd be grounded, too, after what you pulled, going to her house in the middle of the night."

"You can't ground me," you say. "I'm eighteen."

I feel like I will *never* be eighteen.

"I'll ground you until you're forty if I feel like it," she says, trying to hide her smile.

You turn to me. "Don't your mom and The Giant—"

Your dad swats you on the arm with his newspaper. "Don't call him that." But I can see the little glimmer in your dad's eye.

"Don't your mom and *(cough)* The Giant *(cough) Roy*"—you grin at your dad and he just shakes his head, his lips twitching—"realize that when they ground you, they ground me, too?"

"Yeah, I don't think they care about that," I say.

There's a honk outside—your shuttle to the airport has arrived. The sound is like a punch to the gut.

You grab my hand and pull me toward your room. "We'll be right back," you call to your parents as they start bringing stuff outside.

"Don't make me a grandmother!" your mom calls.

"Har-har," you say.

She's joking, but it's her way of reminding us of boundaries and responsibility and all that. She doesn't sweep sex under the rug. Your parents talk to us about it and they know we're both virgins. Your mom even took me to Planned Parenthood because she knows my mom would never in a million years do that. It seems like those would be horribly awkward conversations, but they aren't. Your parents are . . . cool.

When we're alone in your room, you press me up against a wall and kiss me, hard. You taste like coffee and sugar and I grip your hair in my fists and rub against you.

"I wish I could slip inside your skin," you murmur against my lips. "Be as close to you as I can."

How often does that happen, where words you say to me become a song? You'll play this one for me when you get home:

I wish I could slip inside your skin
Be as close to you as I can
Live inside your heart
Own it like a home.

We kiss a bit more and then you pull away, your hand lingering just under my shirt, gripping the spaces between my ribs. I love that your room is already familiar to me: the guitars on their stands, the amps, the little aquarium with two goldfish in it.

"You're going to fall in love with an Australian girl in a string bikini," I say. "I just know it."

No girl can resist the power of the black fedora or that voice of yours. You're bringing your acoustic. She'll hear you playing and it will be like in those stories with fairies, where they lure humans in with their otherworldly music. Oh my god, you'll write songs about her but later tell me they were about me.

"Why Australian?" you say, trying not to smile. "P.S. You're being very silly right now, you know that?"

I shrug. "That's just what my intuition tells me—Australian. String bikini. *Yellow* string bikini."

"Come here."

You wrap your arms around me and I sink into you. You rock me back and forth, call me *sweetheart, my love.* I like how you get old-fashioned when you're most affectionate. There's another honk outside—that's your cue to go. I pull away and your shirt is off in an instant.

"Sleep in this every night," you say, handing it to me. "Promise me."

"Gav, I can't take your Nirvana shirt."

You smile. "It'll be safe with you."

You reach for a small box that has been hiding behind one of your amps and hand it to me as you grab another shirt at random from the pile of clothes on the floor.

"And wear this every day," you say, nodding at the box in my hand.

"Gav—"

Another honk.

"Hurry." Your eyes sparkle in that way they do when you know something I don't. "I want to see it on you before I go."

Inside the box is a small silver star dangling from a chain.

"It reminded me of our shooting star," you say.

"It's beautiful." I reach my arms around you and hug you tight. You put it on me and we head toward the front door, hand in hand.

Just before you get to the airport shuttle you turn and grab my chin—not hard, but the way you do with a child when you want them to focus on you. It feels strange, being touched this way by you. Parental.

A siren goes off in the back of my mind, but I ignore it. (Oh god, Gavin, why did I ignore it? Why couldn't I see through you?)

"I trust you, Grace. Even though I'll be an ocean away and every guy in town is going to be buying cookies from you at the Honey Pot, I know you'd never screw around on me."

I suddenly feel nervous, even though I have no reason to be.

I nod. "Promise you won't make out with Yellow String Bikini Girl."

You laugh softly. "I promise." You lean in for a kiss, wait for me to meet you in the middle. "Call me every night," you say.

"I will."

And then you're gone.

I watch the van turn the corner, then start walking home. I'm not crying anymore. I'm not even sad. Just confused.

Why does it feel like a weight has suddenly lifted?

NINETEEN

*T*here's this rule in the theatre that if you show a gun in the first act, it has to go off by the second or third, the idea being that there's no way the audience will see that gun and forget about it. Something has to happen with it. After a whole summer of being grounded from you, I start to realize that *you* are that gun, that you're going to go off and I'm not sure which one of us will be left standing in the end. Maybe a part of me has always been waiting for the other shoe to drop. You're too good; *this* is all too good. It's not my narrative—I was never supposed to be the girl who got the guy everyone wants. So I wait for you to end it, to come to your senses. In the meantime, I try to be there for you.

You're sad. You say it's like a black wave that drowns you and the only time you rise to the surface is when we're together. I am your oxygen, your breath of fresh air.

But I'm not enough.

You're angry. At yourself, at the emotions that spin inside you. They won't leave you alone until you write a song and when you sing it to me I feel every inch of your pain. Sometimes you punch walls, doors, anything to break the skin that's holding in the demons.

"I need to see you, Grace. This is insane!"

We're on the phone when normal teens would be on a date, at the newest action movie, making out in a car. We're only halfway through this miserable summer—there are thirty more days until I'm officially allowed to see you again.

"I know," I whisper. "I'm sorry they're so crazy."

There's a long pause and then you say it: "This isn't working."

First: shock. A punch to the chest. We're so close already. To untangle me from you would be like tearing out pieces of my flesh. I'd bleed everywhere. Mom would be furious. It'd be such a mess.

But in my gut: relief. I can stop feeling so bad about how strict my parents are. I can stop feeling like I'm holding you back. This whole summer I've been waiting for you to break up with me. Seen it coming. Every time we've talked, you've been upset by the end of our conversation. I'm already starting to see how different our worlds are. My life is all rules and your life is none. I live my life in black and white. You live yours in color. You stay out however late you want, come and go as you please. There are literally no rules in your life except maybe don't kill people or steal. I can't go to any of the shows you play, any of the parties you're invited to. I can't swim in your pool or watch movies on your couch or sit next to you in a restaurant.

"If . . . if you want to break up I . . . um . . . I understand," I whisper.

It was too much to expect, that someone would love me like this for very long.

I'm dead weight.

The future lies out before me, lonely and bleak. No more dancing in grocery aisles. No more being serenaded. No more surprises around every corner. No more being saved from The Giant. We've been loving at warp speed, not caring about anything or anyone else. We've made each other everything. Our own little universe.

It isn't enough. Not for you.

"Why did I have to fall in love with you?" This is a growl. It comes from somewhere deep inside you, as if you've been asking yourself this question for a very long time.

"I'm sorry," I say, quiet.

What am I sorry for, exactly? Existing? I don't know. But these are the words that always jump out of my mouth whenever you're upset, because I assume it's my fault. I'm not fully aware yet that there doesn't have to be a reason for you to be unhappy. The sad swims through your veins, dives right into the middle of your chest with no help at all from me.

"I'm a legal adult," you say. "I mean, what am I supposed to tell people at school? *Oh, sorry, you can't meet my girlfriend because her curfew is before the party even starts. Oh, my girlfriend can't come to my shows because she's a minor.* I mean, Jesus Christ. What are we doing?"

"I'm holding you back," I say.

You're quiet. Which means you agree. A Muse album playing in the background abruptly turns off, like someone ripped Matt Bellamy's voice away from him.

I take a breath. "I'm sorry—"

"Stop fucking saying that!"

I'm sorry.

I cower. If I had a tail, it would be between my legs.

There's a bang and then you curse under your breath. You've hit something and now the bruise on your knuckles will be my fault. You'll think about me every time you see it.

"Don't hurt yourself," I whisper. "I love you."

Nothing.

"Gav . . ." My voice shatters and I bite my tongue, hard, to keep from crying, but a sob slips out.

Your voice immediately goes soft. You can't stand it when I cry. You say it breaks your heart.

"Baby, don't cry. I'm sorry. I just . . . fuck. I'm really sorry. I feel like I'm losing it. God, I'm such a dick."

Now the tears fall fast and hard. You tell me you love me, that you're taking out your anger at my mom and The Giant on me.

"I don't deserve you," you say.

"No, *I* don't deserve *you*." It's true. You're too good for me. It was an accident, me getting you for these past five months.

"Baby, no. Listen." You sigh. "God, I just . . . I want to be with you. You're crying and I can't even come over and give you a hug and it's *killing me*."

"I thought you wanted to break up," I say.

I have no idea what's happening right now.

"It would end me, not being with you."

And I melt. There I go, all over the kitchen floor.

In the silence that follows I can feel us get closer, as though all the bits of you you've given to me and all the bits of me I've given to you are tightening their grip. But then:

"I'm thinking about it again," you say, soft.

"What are you—"

And then I understand. *It*. Suicide.

"I'm coming over," I say.

"You're grounded!"

"I don't care. I'm coming over."

I throw on exercise clothes, then lie to my mom, tell her I'm going on a run to burn off some calories from all the cookies I've been eating from the Honey Pot. My mom's always dieting, so she doesn't think twice about it.

156

I get to your house in record time—five minutes.

When you open the door, I throw my arms around you.

"I love you," I say, over and over.

"I'm fucked up. I'm sorry," you say.

"No, no, you're perfect."

Your parents aren't home. We don't know when they're coming back. We don't care. You pull me inside, kiss me until I'm dizzy, then practically drag me to your room.

"Baby, maybe we should talk about this," I say. "This is really ser—"

"I need you," you say. "I need to be as close to you as possible. You're the only thing that makes me feel real."

You slide your hands underneath my shirt. "As close as possible," you repeat.

"I don't know if I'm ready," I whisper, suddenly scared.

"I need you, Grace," you repeat. You bring your lips to my ear. "Please."

You've had to put up with so much shit from my family. I owe you this. And I want to give myself to you, I do. I'm not sure what's holding me back. I look into your eyes, fall into those blue pools and get lost in them.

"Okay," I whisper.

This isn't happening in slow motion, like a movie where the girl and the boy decide that tonight's the night and he's filled his room with candles and tries to clumsily set the mood. No. This is rash and now now now. In seconds there are no layers between us. Dusk settles over our skin and I shiver because you are beautiful and you are mine, one of those forlorn boys with pouting lips in an oil painting. An angel wrapped in colorful swaths of fabric, a young prince lounging in his palace.

I press my lips to the scars on your wrists and you inhale sharply.

"I love you," I say again, like the words are medicine, like they'll keep you here on Earth for the next hundred years.

You lay me down on the bed and climb on top of me.

You pull a condom out of the box next to the bed.

I close my eyes, take a deep breath.

"Are you okay?" you whisper, just before.

I run the tips of my fingers over your face; they shake a little because I'm thrilled and scared and full of a want that is threatening to crush me.

"I'm okay."

You push into me and it hurts. I bite my lip to keep from crying out and you bring your forehead down, rest it against mine.

"God, I love when you do that," you whisper, kissing my lips.

You are gentle, checking in with me every few seconds, whispering poetry in my ear. Your fingers move across me like I'm the strings of your guitar, the music, the everything. When it starts to feel good I wrap my arms and legs around you, tight, and we are a ship at sea, alone and surrounded by nothing but moonlight.

After, we lie side by side, staring at each other.

"Forever," you whisper as you take my hand and kiss my palm.

"Forever," I agree.

THE GIANT IS being nice to me, which I swear is a sign of the apocalypse. Up next is, like, a plague of locusts. He caught me crying while I was sweeping the back porch and now we're sitting out on the patio and he's giving me one of his Klondike bars, which is The Giant's equivalent of signing the Treaty of Versailles.

"So what's up?" he says. "Boy trouble?"

Boy trouble? Since when does he care? He doesn't say this in a mean way, but I'm not seriously going to discuss our relationship with him . . . am I?

I swallow. "Sort of."

I glance at The Giant as he takes the wrapper off his ice-cream sandwich. He's wearing his usual polo shirt and khakis, his eyes squinting at the sun. I know I can't trust him. But at the same time, I do need to talk to someone. There aren't a lot of opportunities for heart-to-hearts around here.

"Lay it on me, kid," he says.

I get the echo of a warm fuzzy feeling and suddenly I just feel unbearably sad because is this what it's like to have a dad?

"Gavin and I got in a stupid fight about a totally hypothetical situation and now he's saying he doesn't believe that I really love him. . . . It's so dumb."

"What was the fight about?"

It's been weeks since anyone in our house has really talked to me beyond the usual orders and yelling and threatening. It's nice. It's really, really fucking nice, and so I decide to pretend that The Giant actually cares, that he's suddenly seen the light and realized he's been a shit excuse for a dad. Look how I beg for scraps, Gavin. Look how goddamned grateful I am.

"He was talking about how someday, like when the band blows up and they're on tour, we're going to have so much fun on the road and I was like, well, that would be cool but I'll probably be in rehearsals for something—I mean, this is the hypothetical future, so I'm assuming I'm directing and everything—and then he's all *Wait, you wouldn't come on tour with me?* And I was like, *Well, of course I'd go if I wasn't doing a show but, like, Taylor Swift was on tour for seven months this year and, like, I need to do my art, you know?* and then he was upset and said I wasn't being supportive and like how could I be cool with him being surrounded by groupies and then I was like, *That's pretty egotistical* and then, and *then* he said he has groupies *now* and like I guess there are all these girls who have been coming to the shows Evergreen plays and it's just like, what am I supposed to say about *that*?"

It's ironic, talking to The Giant about this stuff because part of the problem is that he won't let me go to any of your shows. All I can think about are these fucking bitches in short skirts trying to fuck my boyfriend and I am going insane. And you're punishing me because after you say the groupie thing I look on Evergreen's concert blog and it's all these pictures of you and hot girls. I mean that's not *all* the pictures, but there are a lot like that, them screaming in the audience and posing for pictures with you. And they're all posting stuff online when they're at the show and saying all this shit about how they want you and all I can do is sit at home and do NOTHING. You're pissed because I won't sneak out of the house anymore and you say you're the only one making sacrifices in our relationship and so your new strategy is to let me know just what I'm missing.

"Sounds to me like he's trying to make you jealous," The Giant says.

Thank you, Captain Obvious.

"Yeah, well, it's working."

The Giant lifts his legs and rests his feet on the patio chair across from him.

"Gavin's a nice kid," he says, "but I'll tell you something: a guy like him—the kind who wants you to follow him around like a puppy dog—they're the ones you have to watch out for."

"Why?"

He frowns as he takes another bite of ice cream. "My sister and I used to be really close," he says. I know he has a sister, but we've never met her. "Then she married a controlling sonofabitch. Jeff. At first it was small stuff, like what Gavin's doing with you. He wanted to be with her all the time, expected her to drop everything for him. He hated if she went out with her friends, stuff like that. Then he wanted her to quit her job—stay at home, even though they didn't have kids. She loved her job, but she said she wanted to make him happy. He beat her up one night and I kicked his ass for it. She wouldn't leave him, though, and he wouldn't let her talk to me after that. It's been five years since I've heard from her. My aunt says they've got a couple kids now."

"Jesus," I say. How can his sister not see how bad this dude is for her?

He nods. "Do what you want, Grace, but I'm telling you—guys like Gavin, they're real snakes in the grass."

He stands as he finishes his ice-cream sandwich and crumples the wrapper. Mom opens the sliding glass door and pokes her head out. She frowns when she sees me.

"There you are," she says, annoyed. "I need you to watch your brother. I have to run to the store."

"I'll come with you," The Giant says. "I need to pick up more propane for the grill."

Bonding time is over and Sam runs out and wraps his arms around my legs. I suddenly feel guilty for selling you out to The Giant. This is the guy who has kept us apart all summer and I just let him in, all for the price of an unexpected Klondike bar.

"Thanks," I say to The Giant as he turns to follow my mom inside. "But Gavin—he really is a good guy. I don't think he means anything by . . . I mean, he loves me."

I feel the need to defend you. You're not a snake in the grass and, as much as I appreciate The Giant trying to help, I can't really take relationship advice from a guy who regularly calls his wife a bitch and controls every cent she has. I mean, the way he described this Jeff guy, he might as well have been describing himself. The Giant has zero self-awareness. Why the hell should I listen to his take on you?

He shakes his head. "It's your funeral."

I stare after him as he goes inside. Just when I thought he might be the tiniest bit okay . . .

You're lucky I didn't have a dad with a shotgun, the kind who'd say he'd blow you to pieces if you broke my heart. You're lucky it was The Giant warning me off you and not someone I respected, trusted. And you're lucky you called me before anything The Giant said had time to sink in.

My phone buzzes and I slip it out of my pocket and it's you. It's been sixteen hours since our fight.

I hold the phone up to my ear. "Hey."

"I'm a fucking asshole and you're the best thing that's ever happened to me and I'm so sorry," you say.

I'm quiet. I can't get those pictures from the band's blog out of my head.

"Grace?" There's fear in your voice. You think I might actually have the courage to break up with you. Don't worry, Gavin. I won't grow a pair for ten more months.

"Did you cheat on me?" I whisper.

"Oh my god, Grace. No. Fuck no. I love you. I would *never* cheat on you."

Sam's in the swing now and he shrieks for me to push him harder. He pumps his little legs and laughs at the sky. I wonder if I've ever been that carefree.

"Those pictures . . ."

You sigh. "I was trying to make you jealous. Nothing else was working."

"What the hell, Gav?"

"I know. It's stupid. I just . . . I need you there, Grace. I can't play right without you. That's why I freaked out about the whole tour thing. You're my muse. You have no idea what having you there means to me. What it does for me. And I realize I've never made that clear. You're so fucking essential to me, it's not even funny."

Fuck you for saying the perfect thing, Gavin.

"I still can't come to your shows," I say. "My mom said if I sneak out again, she'll make me break up with you."

"We'll be careful," you say. "Please, baby. I need you. I'm not trying to push you, I swear. And if you say no I'll shut up about it. I promise."

I sigh. "When's your next show?"

SENIOR YEAR

TWENTY

The long summer is finally over and we go back to being allowed to see each other three times a week. You cheat and visit me at work, but that's definitely not quality time. You got a job at Guitar Center, which means that there are times when I'm free, but you're not. It's Saturday and we're getting ready to go out when I get a surprise call from my sister.

"Turn around, little sis."

Beth is standing across the street, leaning against her car. Cue lots of screaming. She looks different—older. But she still smells like oranges.

"Guess who you get to meet?" I say to her.

"Is he tall, dark, and handsome?" she asks.

"Yes. And he's mine—keep your paws off."

She laughs and I hook my arm through hers and bring her to where Sam has roped you into drawing on the front porch with sidewalk chalk. You're so good with him.

"Nice, Little Dude," you say, grinning at his mess of squiggles.

"Ta-da!" he says, adding another flourish.

You crack up. "Gimme five." You reach up your hand and he smacks it.

"I love you, Gab," he says, putting his chubby arms around your neck.

"I love you, too, buddy." You squeeze him until he squeals.

I don't know what it is, but seeing you being so sweet with him makes me want to jump your bones.

"So," I say, gesturing to you like you're a prize on a game show, "this is Gavin."

You turn and it takes you a second, but then you recognize her from the pictures in my house.

"Is this *the* Beth Carter?" you ask, standing up.

"The one and only," she says.

"Beff!" Sam shouts. He vaults off the porch and into her arms.

You grin your lazy grin and shake my sister's hand. She takes in your skinny jeans and faded concert tee. The fedora. The bad-boy car.

"You look like trouble," she says in such a way that I can't quite tell if she's joking or not.

"It's my middle name."

Bowling isn't really your thing, but it makes my sister gloriously happy, so I insist we go. Beth's up for the weekend, a quick visit while her apartment's being fumigated. You're upset because you had plans for a romantic date, but I haven't seen my sister in almost six months, so no matter how much you beg, I'm not ditching her.

"I think I'm open to friendship with termites," I tell her later as we check out the assortment of bowling balls up for grabs. "I mean, if that's what it takes to get you to come visit . . ."

She laughs. "Dude, you know why I don't visit."

Just one more thing to blame The Giant for. I remind myself that he shared a Klondike bar with me. Maybe there's hope for him after all.

The bowling alley is old—it doesn't seem like a thing has changed since the seventies. There's wood paneling with cutouts of bowling balls and pins. The air smells like stale nachos and grease. Across from the main counter is a small arcade with PacMan and some kind of army shooting game. There's one of those claw games, too, where you try to get a stuffed animal or other prize with the claw. Oldies music plays on the loudspeaker and the sound of bowling balls hitting the shining wooden lanes echoes off the walls.

"Okay," you say, coming up to us with your bowling shoes in one hand and a ball in the other. "We're lane seven. I insisted on a lucky number."

I grin. "You think we're gonna need it?"

"If your bowling is anything like your singing . . . *yes*," you say with a laugh. You let me put on the *Rent* soundtrack in the car on the way over and I sang along to every song, doing all the parts.

I hit you on the arm and generally try to pretend that didn't hurt my feelings. Beth shoots us a concerned look that you miss. I just roll my eyes. She looks like she's about to say something but I'm saved by Nat and Lys, who squeal when they see her.

Bear hugs all around. We head over to lane seven and you tug my hand to keep us back a bit.

"What's up?" I say.

"I think I'm gonna head out."

"What? But Beth's here. She wanted to see you. See us, like, together. You know?"

"Have your girls' night. I'm gonna hang out with the guys." You squeeze my hand. "I'll see you tomorrow."

"You're upset about the date."

You nod. "But I understand."

"They're gonna think we got in a fight or something."

You shrug. "I don't care what they think."

"I do," I say. "I care what Beth thinks. She's my big sister. Come on, Gav . . . please."

You sigh. "All right. But you owe me."

I kiss you on the cheek. "I love you."

"Yeah, yeah."

It's the most awkward night ever. You and Beth seem to have gotten off on the wrong foot. You bicker with each other about the scores, music, movies. It pisses me off that neither of you is trying to get along, at least for my sake. I think about your parents and how nice I am to them. I'm exhausted, trying to referee between you two and annoyed because I keep getting gutter balls.

"Hey, I think I know what your problem is," says one of the guys who works at the bowling alley as I'm making my way back from the snack bar. I'm guessing he's my age, but he could be in college like you.

I put my hands together like I'm praying. "Help me, please!"

He laughs as he leads me to a rack and hands me a six-pound ball.

"This happens to be my favorite ball in the alley," he says. It's sparkly and pink.

I raise my eyebrows. "Oh, really?"

He nods. "The glitter gives it extra speed." I laugh and he smiles. "With the eight you're using, you don't get the lift and—"

"Hey, what's up," you say, coming up behind me.

"Tim here is giving me some pointers," I say. I realize after saying his name that it's a mistake—it makes it look like we've gotten to know each other when, in fact, I was just reading his name tag.

"Well, Tim, I'd appreciate it if you got the hell away from my girlfriend," you say in a calm, measured voice.

Tim frowns. "Dude, I'm just doing my job."

I hug the six-pound ball to my chest. "Gav, he was only—"

You point to the counter where a line is forming while the other guy on staff runs around getting shoes.

"*That's* your job." You give him a little wave. "Bye."

Tim glances at me once more, then shakes his head and makes his way over to the counter. I hear him mutter *dick*, but I don't think you catch it, which is good because you've got this testosterone-pumped look on your face and it's about to get all Sharks and Jets up in here.

"What the hell, Gavin?" I say, whirling on you.

I can see Beth, Nat, and Lys out of the corner of my eye, all of them unapologetically eavesdropping.

"Grace. Don't play innocent. You were flirting with him right the fuck in front of me."

Beth's on you in a second. "Hey. Do *not* talk to my sister like that. What the hell is your problem?"

You narrow your eyes at her. "What the hell is *your* problem?"

I step between you two. "Okay, you guys, seriously, it's not a big—"

"Yes it is a big deal," Beth says. "Look, I've stayed out of your relationship—"

You: "Good, because it's none of your goddamn business—"

"Even though, *frankly*, I never thought it was a good idea. But this shit that just went down," Beth says, ignoring you, "is the kind of stuff The Giant pulls with Mom."

Beth knows how to hit me where it hurts. I stare at her. I never in a million years would compare myself to my mom when it comes to matters of the heart. Is she serious?

You turn to me. "Your sister is comparing me to Satan incarnate and you're okay with this?"

My eyes fill with tears and I turn and run off to the bathroom like the coward I am. Nat and Lys come inside seconds later. I'm at the sink, furiously wiping my eyes with scratchy paper towels. I'm a mess—my makeup is everywhere.

They don't say anything, just hug me. I feel like my whole world has turned upside down. A few minutes ago you were my wonderful boyfriend and now . . . I don't even know *who* you are. Just yesterday we played an epic game of *I love you more, No I love YOU more* and no one loved each other more in the world than us in that moment, I'm sure of it. I think we called it a draw after an hour, by which time we were both naked on your bedroom floor.

"I love you more," you whisper as you unbutton my shirt.

"No, I love YOU more," I say as I unbuckle your belt.

You grin and bring your lips to the side of my neck. My breath catches and my head tilts back.

"Nope," you murmur against my skin. "I definitely love YOU more."

Your palms slide up my back and you unhook my bra, throw it to the side.

I reach for your zipper. "Nuh-uh. I love YOU So. Much. More."

The door opens and Beth comes in.

"Hey, little sis."

"Am I really acting like Mom?"

Something like pity crosses her face. "A little bit, yeah. Does he talk to you like that all the time?"

"This was the first time," I say, dazed. Did what just happened out there really happen? "I mean, we've been kind of fighting because we never get to see each other—Mom and The Giant are ridiculous, you know how they are."

She nods, sympathetic, then turns to Nat. "Can you give us a ride home? Gavin already left."

"Wait," I say, heart pushing against my chest, "he *left*?"

I brush past her and run out to the parking lot. You're just pulling out of your parking spot and I sprint to you.

"Gavin!"

Your window is up and your music is blaring. I have to jump in front of you to get your attention and you hit the brakes.

"Jesus, Grace!" you say when I come around to the driver's side.

"I'm sorry," I say. "About all of it. I don't know what got into Beth—"

You leave the car running but get out and lean against it.

"Yeah, your sister's kind of a bitch."

"Whoa. Gav. You don't even know her."

You snort. "Well, I don't want to now."

"This is so stupid," I say. "Can't you see that? That Tim guy, he was just being nice."

"No, he was trying to get down your pants."

I start crying again, frustration trumping calm, and you pull me against you.

"I'm sorry I talked to you that way," you say. "That anger wasn't directed at you, it was at him."

"Well, it's over now. Can we just . . . get on with the night?"

You shake your head. "I don't think so, Grace. But go and have fun with your sister. I'll see you . . . whenever your parents let me see you again."

There's nothing to do but kiss you good-bye and go find the girls.

Later, back at the house, Beth climbs up to her old bed, the top bunk, and dangles her legs over the side.

"So that was awesome," she says drily. Her long dark hair is up in a messy bun and her eyes stay on my face, watching me.

I collapse onto my bed and groan.

"He's usually not like that, I swear. It's just been hard lately. With school and stuff."

We've been fighting a lot since college started. You're realizing just how lame dating a girl in high school is.

171

"I didn't know it'd be such a big deal," you say. "But, man, I tell people my girlfriend's in high school and I get these looks like, 'What the fuck?' Like I'm a fucking pedophile or something."

"I'm sorry."

Why am I apologizing? It's not like I can control being seventeen any more than you can control being eighteen. But I feel like I have to. Like, by being who I am, I've done something wrong.

You sigh and rest a hand on my thigh. "Well, at least I'm getting laid now."

I shoot you a look and you laugh.

"Don't look at me like that, you know what I mean," you say.

Do I? Because I'm not so sure. What am I to you now? An embarrassment? A piece of ass? Because that's how I feel. But I don't say anything, just crawl into your lap and pretend things are okay. Because if things aren't okay with us, then nothing's okay.

"He giving you a hard time about being in high school?" she asks. My sister has always been kind of a mind reader.

I sigh. "Gav says people react like assholes when they find out."

Beth nods. "That makes sense. I mean, going to college, you really leave everything else behind. High school seems so *young*, even if it wasn't that long ago."

"Do you think he's gonna break up with me?" I ask.

She shrugs. "I don't know. That's up to you guys." She hesitates, then slips down the ladder and sits beside me on my bed.

"Are *you* happy being with him? Because you seem stressed."

"I—"

I'm about to say, *Of course I'm happy, everything's great*, but then I realize . . . I don't know if that's true.

"I guess I just feel kind of confused," I finally say. "Between stuff here at home and Gavin being in college, everything feels like a mess."

"You want my advice?" she asks.

"Yeah. Always."

"I think he's hot and I know him being a cool rocker guy adds to his appeal. But . . . he's not very *nice*. Do you know what I mean?"

"No, I don't," I say, my voice hard.

"Come on. The comment about your singing?"

My face reddens. "He was just kidding."

"What about him freaking out on that guy?"

"Gav is . . . overprotective."

You've started making more and more comments about guys lately and I can't tell if it's me or them you don't trust.

Beth snorts. "That's one word for it." She slings an arm around my shoulders. "I'm getting a bad vibe, little sis. And you know my vibes are always right."

Unfortunately they are.

"I love him," I say.

"I know. That's the problem."

My phone buzzes—it's you.

"I'll be back in a few minutes," I say.

"Don't be gone too long—I want quality sister time. There's Ben and Jerry's!"

I promise to hurry. I answer the phone on my way to the backyard.

"Hey," I say as I settle into one of the patio chairs.

"Hey."

Neither of us says anything for a minute.

"Was that our first fight?" you say.

"Well, we've been kinda fighting a lot lately. I'd say that was our first *big* fight."

"I think I know how to avoid this kind of stuff," you say.

"Okay . . ."

"We should make a rule—about being with the opposite sex. Like, I'm not allowed to be alone with any other girls and you're not allowed to be alone with any guys. Then we can avoid shit like this."

I've already been following your no touching rule. I haven't hugged any of my guy friends for months. It was harder than I thought, which made me realize maybe you were right to make that rule all along. I was definitely too touchy-feely. But I'm not sure I'm up for another rule.

"That's kind of impossible if a conversation in public counts as 'alone,'" I say.

"Well, tonight you could have just said thanks and *I have a boy-friend* and left it at that," you say. "Like, don't keep talking to him."

I'm quiet for a while. If I tell you I don't like the rule, you'll think I want to hit on a bunch of guys all the time. But if I agree to the rule, then I get peace of mind knowing you're not having study dates with hot college girls.

"Okay," I say, "let's try it and see."

You're building a wall around us, keeping out everyone I know and love. Soon, that wall will be too hard to climb back over.

TWENTY-ONE

I'm sitting in the theater, orchestra third row, watching Peter screw up again. Miss B is sick so I'm running rehearsals today.

"Line!" he calls, shading his eyes against the stage lights as he looks for me out in the house.

"Peter, we open *next week*," I say. "What are you going to do when there's an actual audience out here?"

He's the lead in *The Crucible*. It's not my favorite play, but Miss B had to choose it because it goes with the English curriculum.

"Just give me the line, Grace," he says.

I sigh and look down at my script. *"Can you speak one minute without we land in Hell again? I am sick of Hell!"*

He repeats the line and I make a note that he's got to deliver it with more passion. He killed it at the audition, but his Proctor is pretty rough around the edges.

A few minutes later, he's calling for his line again. I imagine I'm Miss B as I stand and move toward the stage.

"I'm not giving you your line this time," I say.

"What the fuck?" he says.

"Don't talk to me like that," I say, channeling Beth. Firm, calm, in control. *I am a badass director*, I chant to myself. "You need to figure out how to move through the scene if you go up on a line."

"Dammmmnn," Lys says, nodding approvingly. Every time I look at her, I have to try not to laugh: Lys in a Puritan bonnet is priceless.

Peter throws a murderous glare my way, then continues with the scene, ad-libbing or getting prompts from the other actors as needed. I think about the personal statement I have to write for my NYU application, which is due in a few weeks. Maybe I should talk about how overcoming adversity in my personal life is helping me to be a better director. Life with my mom and The Giant has allowed me to hone my conflict management skills and prepare for catastrophe. I already know I'm going to have to be backstage feeding this fool his lines.

I give notes at the end of rehearsal, my notebook paper filled with suggestions for improvement. Everyone takes me seriously—even Peter, jackass that he is—and it's probably one of the proudest moments of my life.

You pick me up after and I'm walking on cloud nine. Things have been a little weird between us since my sister's visit, but we're generally working through it all. It's October, and we're getting more used to you being in college.

". . . And then Lys was all *dammmmmnn* and basically I'm a badass," I say.

You laugh. "Of course you are—I already knew that."

We stop at Denny's for some food before you take me home.

"I wonder if they have a class in college about having to deal with actors like Peter," I say, sliding into a booth. "Dealing With Divas 101."

"If they do, you'll ace it."

The waitress comes to take our order and pour our coffee. I add cream and three packets of sugar to mine, but you drink yours black.

I lean forward. "So. When were you going to tell me that you emailed my sister?"

You take a sip of coffee. "I figured you'd find out eventually."

I rest a hand on your arm. "Well, you scored some major boyfriend points. Thank you."

"I was a dick to her. And since she's probably going to be a family member someday, I figured it'd be good if she didn't hate me." I blush and you grin. "Don't look so surprised. There's no way we're not spending the rest of our lives together."

"Stop being perfect," I say and then I take a big swig of coffee to burn away the lump in my throat.

I could have ended up like my mom, with someone like my dad or The Giant, but the universe gave me you.

"How'd you even get her email address?" I ask, going back to the topic of you being a top-notch brother-in-law.

"Your phone."

"That's pretty sneaky."

You smile. "It is. Did it work?"

"Yeah, I think so. She's willing to give you another chance, anyway."

"That's all I was hoping for."

Our food comes and I pour copious amounts of syrup over my pancakes. You grab a bite and I bat your hand away.

"So . . . who's Dan?" you say.

"Hmm?"

"Dan. I saw a couple emails from him in your inbox."

"You read my emails?"

"Not on purpose. It was just, you know, *there*. When I was looking for Beth's address."

I frown. "He's a guy in my Brit Lit class. We're partners for an assignment."

"Okay." You take a bite of your burger and I grab one of your fries, chewing thoughtfully.

"Have you read my emails before?" I ask.

I try to keep my voice casual but I can hear the anxiety in it. The *What the fuck* in it. You have the security code for my phone, just like I have yours. It never occurred to me to go snooping through your emails or texts.

I try to tell myself it's fine, we have no secrets. But it's no use—this feels wrong. Really wrong. See, Gav, I should have listened to my intuition right here. I should have remembered that the women in my family know stuff before it happens, like how my great-gram would know who was calling her before the phone even rang. I should have known that you doing this means you're a snake in the grass.

"No." You hold up your hands when I glare at you. "I swear! My curiosity just got the better of me."

"Because you don't trust me."

"I do." I shake my head and angrily stab at my pancakes. "Grace, I swear I do. I just . . . couldn't resist. I was only in there to look for Beth's address. Promise." You raise your eyebrows. "It's not like you have anything to hide, right?"

"What the hell, Gav?"

"I'm kidding!"

"I don't believe you."

You lean forward and kiss the tip of my nose. "I love you to the moon and back. Okay? Now eat your pancakes."

I love you to the moon and back—you read that in one of the picture books you brought to my house when I was sick. It's become this thing with us. I melt. And you knew I would. You've got all these aces up your sleeve—a real card sharp.

"You owe me a song," I say, pointing my fork at you. "Something romantic about how much you trust me."

You grin. "I'll start working on it tonight."

When you're a stupid girl in love, it's almost impossible to see the red flags. It's so easy to pretend they're not there, to pretend that everything is perfect.

Beautiful rock gods who can kiss you until you're dizzy always get away with murder.

IT'S CLOSING NIGHT of *The Crucible* and we get a standing ovation. The cast makes Miss B and me come onstage and they present both of us with huge bouquets of roses. We take a little bow and I catch your eye in the front row. You yell the loudest and raise your hands over your head when you clap.

Tomorrow I'll be back to help strike the set and get everything out of the theater the school is renting, but tonight my mom is letting me stay out until midnight because we have our cast party. I'm wearing a cute little black dress from the sixties with red tights and my Doc Martens. Since it's Halloween, I've added cat ears and used thick black eyeliner to give myself cat eyes. I've been too busy to think of a costume, and, besides, you think dressing up is dumb. It's been getting pretty chilly at night, so I go backstage and throw on a leather jacket I found at Goodwill for five bucks, then grab my purse to meet you out front.

"We're gonna head over to Peter's place now—you want to drive with us?" Nat asks.

She and Lys are both in the cast. Nat's dressed as Audrey Hepburn in *Breakfast at Tiffany's*, and she sticks the long cigarette holder Audrey rocked between her teeth. Lys is dressed as an existential dilemma, wearing a black unitard with questions like *Is there a God?* and *What's the point of life?* stuck all over her. Of course, she's also wearing knee-high sequined boots and a blond wig because she's Lys.

I shake my head. "I'll see you there. Gav's here, so he'll take me."

Nat frowns and I roll my eyes. "I told you guys, he feels really bad about what happened with Beth."

It's been over a month since that night we all went bowling, but Nat and Lys still haven't gotten over it.

Lys mimes locking her lips and throwing away the key. I stick out my tongue and they both blow me a kiss, then head out with the rest of the cast.

I meet you in the lobby and when you see me you grab me in a bear hug and spin me around.

"I missed you so much," you say, keeping an arm around my shoulders as we head out to the parking lot.

"I missed you, too."

We haven't seen each other in over a week. My senior year and your freshman year are kicking our asses. It seems like every time I'm free, you're not. And when you're free it's past my curfew.

Your eyes travel upward as you take in my outfit. "Do you always dress like this when I'm not around?"

"What do you mean?"

You run your hand down the length of the dress. "This is pretty . . . short."

I raise my eyebrows. "Yeah . . ."

You pull me closer. "Only wear this for me, okay? I don't want the guys at your school getting any ideas."

"What? Baby. Are you serious?" When you don't say anything I just laugh because you're being silly, but you frown. "*Anyway.* What did you think of the show?"

"It was cool," you say.

I deflate a little.

"Just *cool*? I was hoping for something more along the lines of *brilliant, life-changing, phenomenal . . .*"

You laugh. "Well, *you* are all those things. But, you know, it's just a high school show, right? It is what it is. I mean, Peter as Proctor? Come on."

I stop walking and your arm falls off my shoulder. We're outside the theater, standing on the wide steps leading to its entrance. You're a few steps below me. I stare at you and you look back, confused.

"What?" you say.

Just a high school show? I repeat. "That's kind of a dick thing to say."

Now you get it.

"Oh, hey, I didn't mean it like that. It's just, you know, not really my thing anymore."

"You've been in college for, like, two months, Gav. Suddenly theatre isn't your thing?"

You've pretty much given up acting to focus on the band, which is fine, but I didn't know that meant you didn't care about theatre at all. Or at least about *my* theatre stuff.

"I love you," you say with a sigh. "And I'm sorry. That came out all wrong. I'm really proud of you." You kneel down and clasp your hands together, extra dramatic. "Forgive me?"

My lip twitches. "Get up, you idiot."

"I'm taking that as a yes." You stand and adjust my cat ears. "How about we go somewhere, and you take everything off but these?"

"Alas, we have a cast party to get to." I smile. "But I'll give you a rain check."

We get into the car and you tap your key against the steering wheel. I can tell there's something you want to say and that it's maybe serious. My stomach turns. The past few times we've hung out we've been on the verge of a fight, but at the last minute one of us caves and it's okay. I wonder if that will happen tonight. If we can keep pretending nothing's changed.

"I don't want to go to the cast party," you say.

"Why?"

You sigh. "Because I'm in college, Grace. Because I don't want to go to some lame-ass party with a bunch of drama nerds who don't know *how* to party."

"You mean you don't like that it's not a kegger."

You never really drank much before college—just a beer or whatever at a party—but suddenly you're drunk-dialing me in the middle of the night or hungover on our dates. You grab a cigarette from a pack lying on top of the dashboard, another new habit of yours.

"What, you expect me to get excited about fucking pizza and Spin the Bottle? Or wait, a dance party where Peter grinds against you?"

"Seriously? You're bringing that up?" I shake my head. "Just drop me off, then, if we're all suddenly too lame for the great Gavin Davis to hang out with."

"What's that supposed to mean?"

I grind my teeth. "Nothing. Whatever. It's too late to get a ride from someone else. If you can take me, I'll go home with Nat and Lys."

You lower the cigarette. "Wait, you're seriously gonna go to this party when I haven't seen you in a week?"

"Gav, it's our *cast party*. Come on, you know how important this is. I've worked my ass off on this show and I want to celebrate. Remember how my mom made me miss the last one?" I roll down the window as your cigarette smoke wafts toward me. "And, seriously, put that shit out."

You growl something inaudible and throw the cigarette out the window, then peel out of the parking lot, going way too fast.

"Gavin!"

You don't say anything, just turn up the music and drive. We stay silent as you navigate out of downtown and head toward Peter's house, which is in the country, ten miles outside of town. I was so high on adrenaline during the show, watching the final performance, the culmination of all my hard work, but now I'm just tired.

I watch you out of the corner of my eye. The lights on the dashboard play across your face and your headlights cut through the night, which is darker now that we're in the country. I check my phone. I have two and a half hours before I have to be home.

"This is so stupid," I say. "What are we even fighting about?"

"I don't know," you say.

I unbuckle and lean across the console, my lips against your cheek, your ear, your neck. You smile and put a hand on my hair, your fingers running down the length of it.

You pull off to the side of the road near a stand of birch trees.

"What are you doing?" I say as you cut the engine.

You smile. "What are *you* doing?"

I lean toward you and kiss the tip of your nose.

"The party . . . ," I whisper.

You lift your chin so my lips land on yours.

"Screw the party," you say.

I let you kiss me some more and I'm tempted, I am, but I pull away.

"Gav. I'm the assistant director. I have to go to this party. I *want* to go."

I should have gone with Nat and Lys. I feel trapped in this car with you and for the first time since we've gotten together, I want to be somewhere you're not.

"Please just take me to the party," I say. "I'll get a ride home from Nat if you don't want to stay."

"I haven't seen you for a *week*."

"That's not fair—"

"You know what's not fair? What's not fair is that I have a girlfriend whose parents won't let me see her. It's not fair that she has a ridiculous curfew and that she doesn't come to any of the shows I play. It's not fair that I see the fucking baristas at Starbucks more than her."

"I can't control any of that," I snap. "And I've snuck out of the house for *three* shows since school started."

You turn your head away from me and stare out the window. I grab your hand and gently turn your face so you're looking at me.

"Hey. I want to be with you all the time. But I *have* to be at this party. Not going would be like a slap in the face to the whole cast and crew. You know that."

My phone buzzes, but before I can read the text from Lys, it's out of my hands and in your pocket.

"Please, can it just be us?" you say quietly.

"Gav, give me my phone."

"The party or me—which one is it?"

A plane flies overhead, its red taillights blinking. I watch it arc across the sky before I answer. I wish I were on it.

"Can't we do both?" I say, my voice small. "Compromise?"

You check your phone. "You have to be home in, like, two hours. If we go all the way out to Peter's, that's a half hour of driving. So what, you'll stay at the party for forty-five minutes, then save fifteen for me? That's all I get with my girlfriend this week?"

"But if you came with me, then we'd be together."

You explode. "I stayed in this shitty town for you and you won't even skip one party!" You hit your hand against the steering wheel. "What the fuck, Grace?"

"Wait. *What?*"

You get out and slam the door. I sit in the car by myself for a minute, fuming. I think about Nat and Lys and the rest of the cast and crew hanging out. I can't believe I'm stuck here on the side of the road, arguing with you, and I can't even text anyone about it because you still have my phone. I take a breath and slide out of the car, then walk around to where you're leaning against the driver's side.

"Gav. What do you mean you stayed here for me?"

You glance at me, then shake your head. "Nothing. Never mind."

"I never asked you to stay here. Why would you say—"

"I turned down LA schools so you and I could be together. Okay?"

I stare at you. "Are you being serious right now?"

You sigh. "I didn't want to tell you. Ever. I knew it would only make you feel bad. . . ."

"You didn't . . ." I swallow. "You didn't get into UCLA . . . right?"

Your dream school.

"Gavin. Right?"

You don't say anything.

I wait, staring at you, my breath suddenly coming out in labored clumps.

"I got in," you say quietly.

Something in me sinks, falls down the length of my spine like a stone.

"But we'd just gotten together," I say, almost to myself.

You shrug. "I'd already fallen in love with you by the time I got my acceptance letter. It wasn't even a question, not really. You're the most important thing. Always."

And I know this: if I get into NYU, I won't be strong enough to do what you did. I'll be on the first plane out. I think about the NYU application I've already started. The personal statement essay that I've written approximately five hundred times. Miss B's promise to write me a letter of recommendation.

"You gave up your dream school for me," I whisper, stunned. I had no idea how much you love me.

"I'd give up anything for you." You run the backs of your fingers across my cheek. "Anything."

My mind's reeling, like I'm on one of those merry-go-rounds in the park, going faster and faster and trying like hell not to fall off into the sand.

"I didn't ask you—didn't expect you—to do that."

"I know." You give me a half smile. "Guess I'm a romantic like that."

"But when I move to New York, what are you—"

You stand there, waiting. There's something I'm missing, something I . . . *Oh.* I lean against the car, the realization of what's happening right now washing over me, cold as the Pacific. It suddenly becomes harder to breathe. To think. To feel.

And then I feel everything all at once.

How can you ask this of me? Before you, this was the one thing getting me through. And you want to take it away. Nobody knows more than you how much I need to go to New York.

"Gavin . . ."

You are very still. Watching me. Waiting.

"I love you," I whisper. "I love you so much, but—"

"*But?* It's like that now?" you say. "I love you *but?* But what, Grace?"

I start crying. Big, messy tears and I don't even know what they mean. Grief. I feel something like grief. Because I know what you expect now. I can't go to New York, can I? Because if I do, then I don't love you as much as you love me. Then we're over.

After a minute you reach for me. "Hey. Baby, it's okay. The band's starting to get good gigs in LA," you say as you wrap your arms around me. "If you get into a school there, I'll transfer. I swear. We can get an apartment together. Can you imagine?"

I'm sobbing, my whole body shaking, and you just hold me, murmuring nonsense like I'm a spooked horse. I cling to you even though you've just stabbed me in the gut with a dirty knife, quick, out of nowhere. But then this still, small voice inside me starts to get louder.

Louder. It's shouting and I pull away from you, staggering back. Dust swirls in the headlights and clouds drift over the moon. Cars pass on the highway, oblivious to the drama on the side of the road. We could sell tickets.

I know I have to fight for this. It wouldn't be my life if I didn't have to go into battle for what I wanted. The universe doesn't hook me up. It doesn't give a damn about me. I'm lucky if it puts a sword in my hand before throwing me out into the shit.

"Gav." I swallow, take a breath. "This is my *dream*. Like my whole life, I've wanted to live in New York and do theatre. It's . . . it's who I am. You know that."

A lone car passes by us on the highway, its lights cutting through the darkness. I hear a snatch of music, loud rock with jagged edges.

"LA drama schools are just as good," you say. "Plus there's the whole film industry." You take my hands and intertwine your fingers with mine. "I already talked to the band. They're not willing to go to New York. LA's a better scene for us, it's cheaper, easier to get into the clubs . . . I tried. I swear I tried."

"When were you going to tell me any of this?"

"I thought . . . I didn't think you were still seriously planning on going to New York. I was waiting for you to change your mind. Or I thought, you know, maybe you wouldn't get in."

Was this a test? If it was, I failed it.

"You don't think I'd get in? What, like I'm not smart enough—"

You're not very deep.

"No! I just . . ." You sigh and pull off your fedora, run your fingers through your hair. "I mean, we've talked about living together."

We went to Ikea once, for fun. We picked out all the furniture for our imaginary apartment and your bought me the ugliest stuffed heart with arms coming out the sides of it and a big grin on its face. You named it Fernando and when you came over that one time when no one was home, we had to hide the thing under the bed because it was weird having sex in front of it.

"I thought the apartment and all that was for after college. I mean, of course we're going to live together someday."

"Someday," you say, your voice flat. "Five years from now? Really?"

"What if we did, like, a long-distance thing—"

You shake your head. "Those don't last. Everyone I know at school who had a boyfriend or girlfriend at the beginning of the semester has already broken up with them, and we've barely finished midterms. You know what they say happens over Thanksgiving break? The 'turkey drop'—when everyone in college dumps their boyfriend or girlfriend from home. We wouldn't even make it to Christmas."

"Yes we would. Those people aren't us," I say. "We're soul mates. Nothing's going to come between us."

This is my dream. My future. My life. How can I just give that up?

"We'll get there someday," you say. "I promise. New York's not going anywhere."

My head is pounding and I pull off the stupid cat ears. I can't believe I've been talking about the most important thing in my life looking like an ensemble member of *Cats*.

"We're probably fighting over nothing. I might not even get in—"

"Don't apply," you say. "Please."

I don't say anything.

"Four years is a *really* long time, Grace. You won't be at any of my shows. I won't get to know your friends. I wouldn't be able to come by and pick you up after rehearsal and go out for Denny's. You'd be going to bars and clubs and I wouldn't be there to dance with you, to buy you drinks and make sure you got home safely. Our lives would be totally separate. I mean, look how hard it is now, and we live five minutes from each other."

I honestly had never thought about it that way and I realize you're right. I don't want to spend the next four years on the other side of the country. I want to be with you. I see it play out: the time difference making it impossible to call each other, you getting upset because there are pictures of me on social media with guys you don't know. And then some cool, arty, hot girl who starts going to your shows finally gets your attention. You run into her at parties, maybe have a class together. Then one night, you drink a little too much and she's right there and her lips look so soft. . . .

You rest your forehead against mine. "Choose us. You won't regret it."

"For where thou art, there is the world itself . . . And where thou art not, desolation," I whisper.

The corner of your lip turns up. *"Romeo and Juliet?"*

"Henry IV." Ironic, isn't it, Gav, me quoting a star-crossed lover at the very moment we were doomed for good? I didn't realize it then, of course. I just knew the moment was important. A game changer.

I hold the image of me riding the subway and traipsing through the Village close, then let it go. It wouldn't matter if you weren't there to share it with me. I'd be miserable, and so would you.

"I need a minute," I say, and I walk over to a tree standing at the edge of the field you're parked beside.

You're supposed to sacrifice for the people you love. It's what my mom did when Beth and I were little, pre-Giant, working three jobs to keep food in our bellies. It's what Fantine did for Cosette in *Les Mis. I dreamed a dream in times gone by, when hope was high and life worth living.* I love you. And the fact of the matter is that you have to be with your band and your band doesn't want to come to New York. That's not your fault. It's not like you're asking me to move to Omaha. There's tons of theatre in LA and maybe I can try my hand at film. Get an internship or something. It doesn't have to be forever.

So why does it feel like I'm drowning?

189

"Okay," I say when I walk back to you. "No New York."

You kiss me, hard. "I love you so much."

Something in me is dimming, something that I already know I can't get back. But you're worth it. You are. I will tell myself this for several more months. And when I realize you aren't worth it, it'll be too late.

"I love you, too."

"Do you still want to go to the party?"

I shake my head. "No, you're right. There's not enough time."

"Are you sad?"

I nod. "Yeah. A little."

A lot.

My eyes fill and you wipe my tears away with the tips of your fingers. "We're gonna have the time of our lives in LA—promise."

You tell me a bedtime story about late-night taco runs and sunsets on the beach. An apartment with our clothes in the same closet. You say maybe we can get a dog. We'll wake up next to each other every morning and sometimes you'll even bring me breakfast in bed.

"It'll be perfect," you say.

"Perfect," I agree. Then I tell myself to believe it.

TWENTY-TWO

I'm having a dream—something involving an otter and my world history test on Monday—when I suddenly come awake. You're leaning over me, a smile on your face. The room is dark and at first I think you've snuck in somehow, but then I see that the bedroom door is open and the hallway light is on.

"What?" is all I can manage.

"Happy birthday," you say as you pull back the covers.

I sit up, rub my eyes. "What's going on?"

You point to the clock. "It's officially your birthday."

"It is?"

"Yep. You were born at exactly three-twenty a.m. on November fourteenth, eighteen years ago." You stand and grin. "How much time do you need to get ready?"

"For what?" I ask, immediately suspicious.

"We're going on an adventure. Top secret."

"My mom's okay with this?"

"I got parental clearance, don't worry."

You hold out your hands and help me up, then pull me against you for a second before letting go. I'm wide awake now, and smiling.

"What do I need to wear for this adventure?"

"Normal stuff. But bring a coat."

"You're being very mysterious."

You blow me a kiss as you back out of the room. "I'll wait for you in the dining room."

Things have been weird between us since the night of the cast party. I'm trying not to resent you for asking me to stay in California. It was my choice, you didn't force me, and yet it felt like I had no choice at all. But more than going to New York, I don't want to end up like my mom in failed and loveless relationships. I found you, the One, and I'd be stupid to let you go. But it's hard, giving New York up. I don't listen to *Rent* anymore—can't. I threw away all the pamphlets from NYU. I tell myself that you're worth it all.

When I'm finished getting ready, I grab my purse and coat. The door to my mom and The Giant's room is firmly shut, so I turn off the lights as I go back down the hall.

"How'd you get in?" I ask.

"Your mom left a key under the mat for me." You grab my hand. "Let's go."

There's coffee for me in the car, with lots of cream and sugar, just how I like it. We seem to be the only people in town awake this early—there isn't a single car on the road.

"It's kind of creepy this early in the morning," I say. "Like, apocalypse creepy."

You laugh. "Getting up this early is a sign of how much I love you, that's for sure."

I take a sip of my coffee. "So . . . where are we going?"

The only place open is Denny's, but that doesn't seem like something worth getting up at three in the morning for. Then we turn on a familiar street and you park in front of Nat's house.

"Okay, now I'm *really* curious," I say.

Nat and Lys come bounding out of the house.

"Happy birthday!" they say in unison as they get into the backseat. Nat holds up a pink pastry box. "I come bearing doughnuts."

"Okay, *what* is going on? I'm dying over here," I say, grinning.

You pull away from Nat's house and head toward the freeway.

"We're going north," you say.

"I need you to narrow it down a little bit more for me."

"Oh, let's play twenty questions," Nat says, clapping her hands. She hands me a tiara covered in pink rhinestones. "Also, you have to wear this, birthday girl."

I put it on, giggling. "Okay, question number one: is this place far away?"

Lys nods. "Yes and no."

"More than two hours?" I ask.

"Yes," you say.

"Is this place near the ocean?"

"Yes," Nat says.

I start smiling before I even ask my next question. "Does it have a really big bridge?"

"Yes," they all say.

"Oh my god, are we seriously going to San Francisco?"

"Hell yeah we are," you say.

"You guys!" I squeal. "Best birthday ever!"

"Well, you only become a legal adult once," Nat says.

"Your mom made me promise that you wouldn't get a tattoo," you say.

"For real?"

You laugh. "For real."

Lys hands me her phone. "Here. I made you a birthday playlist."

A playlist from Lys is a serious thing. She spends hours on them, finding the perfect mix of songs that she puts in a very specific order. Sometimes she goes for a theme, but it's always an eclectic mix. The last one she made had bluegrass, Rihanna, and the Beatles, with a little bit of Radiohead and Yo-Yo Ma thrown in for good measure.

I plug Lys's phone into your sound system. The first song that comes on is the Beatles "Birthday." I laugh as you sing along and dance in your seat. We break open the box of doughnuts, and I get first choice: chocolate with sprinkles, of course.

The three-hour drive goes by fast. There's no traffic this early and we're fueled by sugar and caffeine. The first thing we do when we get there is grab breakfast at an old-school diner in the Mission. Pancakes, hash browns, bacon, and more coffee. We're across the street from an entire building covered in street art—swirling flowers, a huge sun, ocean waves. These are my people.

"I cannot tell you how good it feels to be almost two hundred miles away from my family," I say as I take the last bite of my hash browns.

You wrap an arm around me and pull me closer. "Ditto."

"Think about it this way," Lys says. "This time next year, you might be in New York City, drama major extraordinaire."

I feel you stiffen beside me. I haven't told Nat and Lys yet. I know they'll be mad. They'll think I'm crazy. And maybe I am. But what's more important: a city or a person? The love of my life or the city that never sleeps? Mostly, I just don't want them to hate you. They didn't understand why I never made it to the cast party, why you'd even be cool with me skipping it.

Strike two, Nat said. You definitely lost their vote somewhere between the bowling alley and the cast party. But I think you bringing them to San Fran was a good call. I can see them softening.

"Speaking of drama," Lys says, looking at you. "Did you tell her yet?"

You shake your head, a small smile playing on your face.

"What? More secrets?" I say, bumping my shoulder against yours.

You reach into your jacket pocket and hand me four tickets—to see *Rent* today.

"Are you freaking *serious*? Oh my god!" I throw my arms around you and you laugh, hugging me back, tight. Then I hit you. "You jerk! You told me they'd sold out."

You laugh. "Well, I didn't want to ruin the surprise!"

"Aw, you guys are so cute," Nat says as Lys snaps a photo of us.

"I'm so posting this right now," Lys says. "Caption: Roosevelt High alumnus Gavin Davis wins Boyfriend of the Year award."

It is a perfect day. Before the show we go to Fisherman's Wharf and eat clam chowder in sourdough bread bowls. We take pictures with the Golden Gate Bridge in the background, hair whipping around our faces in the wind. We go to Chinatown and the Castro, where I buy a crazy pair of orange sunglasses.

"It's like gay Disneyland!" Lys says, grinning at all the paraphernalia: T-shirts with gay pride slogans, rainbow-colored everything. She buys a button that says *Born This Way* in rainbow letters.

Rent is amazing, of course. I don't let myself think about college, about the promise I made you.

"We'll get there someday," you murmur against my hair during intermission. "I promise."

I squeeze your hand and nod. "I know."

No day but today, they sing. I wonder if by not sending in that application I made the biggest mistake of my life. But then you lift my hand

and kiss my palm and I tell myself—again—that I made the right decision.

I did.

I CAN HEAR them shouting from the street.

First, The Giant's baritone, a threatening growl. Then my mom's voice, softer and uncertain.

You've just dropped me off and I'm tired and birthday happy, but as soon as I hear them I slow down and stop a few feet from the door, immediately tense.

"She already pays her cell phone bill, buys her own clothes," Mom's saying. "She's just a kid—"

"No, she's not. She's eighteen. I was helping my family when I was sixteen. You're spoiling her."

I stand there on the walkway, unable to move.

"She's in *high school*. I'm not going to make her pay rent, Roy, that's—"

"Who owns this house?" he shouts. "Whose name is on the deed?"

"Roy—"

"Who pays the mortgage every month?"

"Honey, please—"

"*Who, goddammit?*"

"You," she says, so quiet I can barely hear her.

"A hundred dollars a week," he says. "She needs to learn to be a responsible adult."

"I understand where you're coming from," she says, her voice quivering. I've never heard my mom go to bat for me like this. "But why don't we have her put that money aside for college? She's going to need so many things—"

"This conversation's over."

"But—"

"Get the fuck out of my face, Jean. I've had a long day."

There's the sound of a cupboard slamming and ice falling into a glass. I lean against the garage door and close my eyes. Why can't I have one day, just one *day* without The Giant stomping all over my life?

I force myself up the walkway. There's a cold wind and it blows through the big tree in our front yard, the bare branches shaking like angry fists. I pull open the door and walk inside. The Giant is sitting on the couch now, watching golf. Mom is in the kitchen, doing dishes. She turns around when I come in.

"How was it?" she asks. The smile on her face doesn't reach her eyes.

"Great. It was really fun. Thanks for letting me go."

"There's a little something for you on your bed," she says. "It's not much, but . . ."

"Thanks."

I'm a little dazed, numb. Does The Giant really expect me to start paying rent? Once the next show starts, I'll be working less than usual. I won't even *make* four hundred dollars a month.

I head into my room, suddenly exhausted. I wish it were this morning again, with you waking me up so we could go have an adventure.

My birthday present from my mom is in a bag with flowers on it. It's the one we reuse time and again. I can't remember who got it first— I think Gram put Mom's birthday gift in it a few years ago. Inside is a dark green sweater, almost the exact color of my eyes, soft, with wooden buttons. It's funny—I always feel like my mom doesn't get me, but every present from her is perfect. It strikes me that my mom might know me better than I realize. I try it on. It's cozy, with the sleeves going a little past my wrists. I set the sweater aside, then get ready for bed. My mom pokes her head in as I'm turning down the covers.

"Does it fit?" she asks, glancing at where the sweater lies over my desk chair.

I nod. "It's really pretty. Thank you."

She looks like she wants to say something else, but then just shakes her head.

"I'm so glad you had a good birthday. I'm sorry we couldn't do more for it."

The Giant had nixed our ideas for a party, reminding us that he wasn't made of money and that it didn't grow on trees.

"Mom," I say, just as she's about to shut the door. Her eyes slide to mine. "I heard you guys talking. About the money."

She sighs. "Shit. I didn't want to tell you on your birthday. I'm so sorry—there wasn't much I could do."

"I know. Thanks for sticking up for me."

After she closes the door, I collapse onto my bed and call you.

"Hey," you say, soft. "I thought you'd be asleep by now."

I tell you what The Giant said and you are livid.

"What the fuck is wrong with him?" you growl.

"I don't know," I say.

We talk for a few minutes, but I'm falling asleep, so I tell you I'll call back in the morning. What feels like minutes later, my phone starts vibrating. Two a.m. It's you.

"Open your window, baby."

"What?"

"I'm outside."

I sit up, disoriented. Sure enough, I see you peering through the window. I carefully slide it up and you crawl inside, then pull me into your arms. I melt into you.

"They'll kill me if they find you in here," I murmur.

"They've been asleep for hours," you say, just above a whisper. "It'll be fine."

I take your hand and pull you toward the bed and we get tangled up in each other for a good long while, skin against skin, our lips locked.

We have to be careful because my bed creaks. We touch and hold and kiss in silence, the only sounds a gasp, a sigh, a quiet groan. When I come, you press your palm against my lips because it feels so good and for a second I forget we're not alone in your house or your backseat and I can't help but cry out. You roll off of me and pull me against you. I breathe you in: Irish Spring soap and your boy smell. Your hair is a wild mess and it makes me immeasurably happy to run my hands through it.

"I'll always take care of you," you whisper. "Always."

When I wake up in the morning, you're gone. There's an envelope propped against my alarm clock. Inside are four hundred-dollar bills. And a note.

Rent for November. Fuck The Giant. I love you.

TWENTY-THREE

*T*his is how I love you best:

You're onstage, flinging your body around as your pick cuts across your strings. You and your electric guitar dance a wild, ecstatic round and then your mouth is against the mic and you're singing about us, about what it feels like to make love to me, and it's too dark for anyone to see me blush and I'm proud and embarrassed all at once.

> *Closer, closer I want inside*
> *You're the place where I can hide*
> *Steamy windows, my backseat*
> *You're all mine, my love so sweet*

This is one of Evergreen's most popular songs. It's got a sexy bass beat, drums that make hips shake, and you sing it like one long suppressed moan. Your guitar comes in every few seconds, like it just can't help itself. It reminds me of the way you'll suddenly lean over and kiss me full on the lips when I'm mid-sentence.

"God, he's so hot," a girl near me says to her friend.

I smile to myself. This is fun, getting to be the girlfriend in your world. I should have made a T-shirt: Gavin's Girl.

Kyle—the ride you arranged, breaking your own rule about me being alone with a member of the male species—looks over at the salivating girls near us and cracks up.

"Girl fight! Girl fight! Girl fight!" he chants.

I laugh. "Shut up."

"Better watch your man, Grace," he teases. "Those girls look like they came to play."

I listen to the songs, listen to how much you love me. When your eyes search for me in the crowd and you smile a secret smile just for me, all the crap my parents put us through is suddenly worth it.

"This next song," you say, "is for my beautiful girl, Grace. Can I get a *Fuck yeah* for my girlfriend?"

The entire room swoons and yells, *Fuck yeah!* I shake my head, laughing, almost crying because can you be any more wonderful? Your eyes never leave mine as you sing. It's like we're the only people in the room. In the *world*.

> *Your skin against mine*
> *Let go and let love*
> *Let go and let love*
> *Let me be your anthem, baby*
> *Let me be your song*

The crowd sings along, your fan base getting bigger every day. All of a sudden it becomes real, the fact that you might actually become a legit rock star. Girls will ask you to sign their boobs with a Sharpie. I push the thought away and sing along, too. Almost all the songs are about us, and I wonder if anyone outside the band realizes it. Kyle must. I can't tell what he thinks about them, though. What picture do your words paint? What he and Nat have is so tame compared to us. It's sweet, innocent. We're anything but.

You have a few more songs left in your set, some I've never heard. They're about being exhausted, sad beyond belief, horny. They're about confusion and love and the sense that something's not quite right. Ryan's bass feels like a heartbeat—frenetic, stressed. Dave's drums remind me of you hitting your hand against the steering wheel when you're angry, throwing shit around in your room when you're jealous. I start to come down off the high of your nicer songs but then you play the sweetest one of all, a lullaby you wrote for my toughest nights at home. When you finish, I blow you a kiss and you catch it with a smile, grabbing it out of the air and putting it in your pocket. It's something you've always done with me and the familiarity of it puts me at ease. We are still Us.

I check my phone—it's almost two. I'm praying my mom doesn't come into my room for some reason. Watch: with my luck, the house will catch on fire tonight. I can just picture the look on The Giant's face when he realizes the body sleeping under the covers of my bed is a series of perfectly shaped pillows.

You guys do a rendition of the Beatles' "Happiness Is a Warm Gun" as your last song and it's breathtaking and scary. You sing the words with such longing—I can almost see you willing the gun into your hands. I hate this song. It makes me think of you and that bathtub filled with your blood. The first time I used the guest bathroom in your house, I couldn't stop staring at the tub. I couldn't believe it wasn't stained. I couldn't reconcile what had happened in it with the fruity shampoos and bars of soap.

The last note of the song fades into the audience's loving roar and then you're done. Wild applause. Every girl in this room wants you.

I worry that I don't look cool enough, deserving enough. I've got bloodred lips. A short skirt. Heels. A tight T-shirt. It's all for you.

The club you're playing in is like a big black-box theater. There's a bar all along one side where I get a Coke with Kyle while we wait for you and the band to break down your stuff. There are posters on the wall—Pearl Jam, the Arctic Monkeys, Modest Mouse. Everyone here is older than me and I wonder if I stick out. This is your world, but it doesn't have a place for me. Not yet.

Arms around my waist, sweaty hair against my neck. You, you, you. I turn and wrap my arms around your neck and press myself against you.

"You were fucking brilliant," I say. Gush.

Right now, you are *the* Gavin Davis, the boy I loved from afar. Unattainable and yet here I am, with my tongue in your mouth. I'm never like this. You love it. Your arms tighten around my waist and I feel you go hard and I don't care that everyone's watching us.

I kinda want them to.

Kyle coughs. "Um. Guys. This is very romantic and all, but—"

"Jealous?" you say, only half kidding.

Normally this would bug me, but I like you territorial tonight. I like you sweaty and sneering at anyone who comes too close to me.

Kyle laughs, uncomfortable. "Uh . . . whatever, man."

You let go of me and wrap an arm around his neck.

"I love you, brother—I'm just giving you shit."

I watch as you accept hugs and congratulations and free drinks. The words to your songs thrum through me, some of them at odds with you being the life of the party:

Mud up to my neck, swimming in dirt, gotta get outta here

You cut me to pieces, you spin me around, you push me off a cliff and smile as I go down

Lay down, close my eyes, think of all the ways I can die.

How can the same guy who wrote these songs be the Gavin who's clearly having the time of his life? I can't keep up. But then there are your other songs, the ones that take my hands and spin me around until I'm delirious:

> *God, I want her so bad, she's mine, she's mine, all mine*

> *Kiss me again, tell me you love me, hold me close and don't let go*

> *She's perfect, gets better every day. Love her, don't care what they say.*

"We're going to Denny's," you say, grabbing my hand. You turn to Kyle. "You in?"

"No, man, I gotta bail. Good show," he says. He salutes me, then heads out to the parking lot.

"Gavin Fucking Davis," says a girl in a tiny black dress and knee-high boots. She wraps her arms around you, her fingers lingering as they slide around your waist. "You are *such* a rock star."

I like that you don't hug her back and as soon as she lets go, you reach for my hand.

"Thanks, Kim." You nod to me. "This is my girlfriend, Grace."

Her honey-brown eyes go to me and a slight frown turns down her lips.

"Hey," she says. "Gavin and I are in the same freshman comp class."

"Cool," I say, a clear dismissal. Then I turn to you and tug on your hand. "We have coffee and greasy food waiting for us."

"Right. See you later, Kim," you say, letting me pull you away.

We go to Denny's and you keep your arm around me the whole

time, making sure I don't feel left out with the band and their girlfriends. Then we go to your house, sneaking past your parents' room.

You open your old-school record player and put the Beatles on—*Abbey Road*. "Because" comes on and you take me in your arms and dance me around the room as you sing along.

"Love is all, love is you."

We collapse onto your bed and it is a perfect moment, just breath and lips and the feel of your body against mine.

For a little while, we are infinite.

TWENTY-FOUR

Halfway through my shift at the Honey Pot I'm dripping sweat. It's Black Friday and instead of decorating the tiny tree in my bedroom or eating Thanksgiving leftovers, I've been stuck here all day, fueling shoppers. As soon as there isn't a line, I'm whipping through the notecards I made for my AP World History test on Monday. We've moved on from the medieval plagues to the Renaissance. I love seeing the cause and effect, the way dots connect over long spans of time. *This* happened because of *that*. Like us. If you hadn't tried to kill yourself, we wouldn't be together right now. It's weird thinking you had to go through that pain for us to fall in love.

You saunter up during a lull in the evening, when people are hungry for dinner, standing outside Hot Dog On A Stick (winner of the worst uniforms ever).

"Hello, beautiful," you say.

I look up and grin, already scooping up oatmeal raisin cookies into a bag for you.

"What brings you here?" I ask, feigning surprise.

"Oh . . . you know. I was just in the area."

I raise my eyebrows. "What a coincidence."

"Indeed."

"Matt," I call into the back as I take off my apron covered in dough, "I'm going for my fifteen. Can you man the store?"

"Only if you bring me back a hot dog on a stick," he calls.

"She'll be too busy," you snap, and grab my hand, pulling me away from the shop.

"Gav, that was rude," I say.

"Do you know he checks out your ass when you take the cookies out of the oven?"

I smile and bust out some *Rent* in my not-so-great voice. *"They say that I have the best ass below Fourteenth Street, is it true?"*

"This isn't a joke, Grace. If I see it again, I'm gonna have to do something."

I almost laugh. *"Do something*? What is this, *West Side Story*? Baby. I'm sure you're just imagining—"

"I'm not."

"Well, then take it as a compliment. I mean, you want a girlfriend with a nice ass, right?"

You don't say anything. You just frown and lead us toward some benches in the center of the mall near the huge Christmas display. I decide to drop it, which is what I decide most of the time now when you get overly jealous. I don't want to ruin the few minutes we have with petty fighting. There are only a few pockets of time we can carve out for each other during the week. Things with your band are ramping up and you're playing shows a few times a week now on top of your full class load and your job at Guitar Center. I have my insane workload from my classes and the Honey Pot, not to mention my chores and babysitting, and whatever else my mom and The Giant decide to throw my way.

"It feels so good out here," I say as I plop down. Working at the Honey Pot is like being in a furnace. The oven never stops running.

You nod, distracted. You fiddle with your car keys, won't look at me.

"What's up?" I quickly scan through the day—I can't think of anything I've done to piss you off. I try not to feel anxious, to acknowledge the cold knot in my stomach.

You readjust your fedora, then look down, clasping and unclasping your hands. Whenever you got all antsy like this, I know something's wrong. God, I get enough shit at home. Why can't things be simple with you? Nat and Kyle never fight. They just have fun and are cute and normal.

"Someone posted a picture of the scene you did with Kyle in class," you say. "I saw it this morning."

"Oh yeah? I think we did pretty good. I mean, you can't go wrong with *Barefoot in the Park*—"

You snort. "Do you think I'm an idiot?"

"Huh?"

I play dumb, but I know what you're talking about. My face warms and I turn my gaze from you to Santa and his elves. A little girl is sobbing on his lap and one of the elves is doing a silly dance to get the kid to smile. Why does no one care that she's miserable and wants to get off that creepy dude's lap?

"How was it? Was he good?"

"Gavin. No. Nothing's going on. We tried it with a stage kiss and everyone said it looked too fake. Even Nat, and she's his girlfriend."

You look up, your eyes pushing against mine. "Doing a kissing scene with one of my *best friends*—that's kind of slutty, don't you think?"

My eyes widen. "What?" I whisper.

"Slutty," you repeat. "Which makes you . . . a slut. Right? You have a boyfriend, in case you forgot."

Slut. The word jabs into me, hard and fast. I sit there for a minute, my eyes on the shiny Christmas ornaments that hang from the ceiling, the fake snow in the store windows. Slut. Bing Crosby's singing about a white Christmas and there's a sale at the Gap and I can't believe this just happened. I can't.

"How could you *say* that to me?" I whisper, my voice trembling.

You look away, the faintest bit of shame in your eyes.

"I'm sorry. I'm fucking tired and I saw Matt looking at you and . . . it's just too much, Grace. I'm losing it."

"I have to go," I say.

You nod, lips set in a thin line. "As usual."

I throw up my hands in frustration. "It's my job. I can't leave Matt stranded there."

You stand. "It's fine. I'm gonna hang out with the guys. Later."

I watch you walk away. You don't look back. Your hands hang at your sides and you drag yourself along, zombie-like. No rock-star swagger. What's happening to you? For days now you've had dark circles under your eyes. I'll wake up in the morning with texts from you that were sent at three, four, five in the morning. Telling me you're depressed, that you have to get out of town, that you hate all the fakes at your school. I want to believe you didn't mean what you said. But I think you did, Gav.

When I get back to work, Matt is leaning against the counter, drinking a glass of ice-cold milk. I don't even like milk, but the stuff we sell is downright delicious.

"Spill," he says, looking at my dejected face.

And I do. Even though he's my ex and it's maybe not appropriate, I pour out every worry, all my frustrations. I forgot how easy he is to talk to. I tell him things I can't even tell you or Natalie. But especially not you. Like how I think you might be having Peter spy on me at school.

"Your boyfriend's creepy," Matt says matter-of-factly.

"No he's not!"

209

Maybe I shouldn't have said anything.

"Do you know how long Gavin was watching you before he came up to say hi today?"

I don't think I want to know the answer to this. You've admitted that sometimes you "keep an eye out for me" when I go places with my friends, but you don't tell me you're there. Once, you slept outside my house in your car late at night, just to make sure I'd be okay. You didn't want to wake me up because I had a big test the next day, but you'd had this horrible dream about me dying in a fire and so you'd gotten into your car, just in case. We got doughnuts and coffee for breakfast before you dropped me off at school. I thought it was sweet, but when I told Nat and Lys, they just rolled their eyes and said *crazy* in several languages.

"Dude. He was there at least an hour," Matt says, "standing over by Carl's Junior."

I shiver. I don't want to believe him, but that sounds like you these days: you have a flair for the dramatic.

"What am I supposed to do?"

I look over my shoulder, just to make sure you haven't come back. If you ever heard this conversation . . .

"Break up with his ass."

"No. I love him."

You're the only person who loves me. If we broke up, who would be left? Things are hard with us right now, but my life would be ten times worse without you. Sometimes the only thing that gets me through what's happening at home is knowing I'll be going on a date with you later in the week or just knowing you're out there, missing me as much as I'm missing you. I may not matter much to my mom and The Giant, but I'm everything to you. And it's addictive, being someone's everything. Letting them be yours. You're the only drug I take.

Still, it *would* be nice not to have to walk on eggshells with you all the time—I have enough of that at home to deal with. I never know when I'm going to set you off. And that *slut* comment really hurt.

"Look," Matt says, "I know I'm your ex and all, so this might sound weird coming from me, but . . . him checking up on you like this, the way he won't let you hang out with other guys—that is some hard-core possessive shit right there."

I've told him about the time I got a ride to rehearsal from Andrew, one of the guys who'd been in *The Crucible*. You came to the house as a surprise, but we'd already left. You were so angry that you wouldn't speak to me for days. It wasn't until I climbed through your bedroom window with nothing on under my dress that you forgave me.

When I finish closing up with Matt, I go outside to wait by the front entrance of the mall for my mom. Only the minivan's not there; you are. You're leaning against a streetlight, looking miserable. When you see me, you straighten up and take a tentative step toward me.

"Hey. I asked your mom if I could pick you up. I felt bad about . . . about everything."

"I thought you were hanging out with the guys."

"Yeah, I was, but you were upset and I . . . I dunno, I guess I just didn't want to leave things like that." You move closer. "You're not a slut. And I can't believe I fucking said that. I will regret that until the day I die."

I bite my lip. "That was a really shitty thing to say to me."

"I know. I'm, like, the world's biggest asshole." You grab my hips and tug me closer to you. "Forgive me? Please?"

I can't look at you. I focus on the cars that are scattered around the parking lot, the red light at the corner. The streetlight beside us that's spilling a pool of fluorescent light onto the sidewalk. All I can think is, *I gave up New York for you.*

"I don't know, Gav."

How can you be the boyfriend who gave me four hundred dollars when The Giant demanded rent *and* be the boyfriend who calls me a slut?

"I will seriously do anything to make this right," you say.

"I mean, that's the kind of thing The Giant would say to my mom. It's super fucked-up."

"I know," you say, soft. "I can be crazy jealous. And I'm sorry. I'm just so scared I'm gonna lose you."

"Well, calling me a slut isn't a good way to keep me."

"I know." You hang your head. "This isn't an excuse, but lately I've been feeling so fucking low. You're, like, the only good thing in my life." You look up at me, eyes glistening. "I don't know what I'd do without you."

Break up with his ass, Matt said. I flirt with the idea, just for a second. You slide your hand to the back of my head, pulling me closer.

"Grace." You whisper my name like a prayer, a cure.

And though everything in me is telling me to walk away, I let you press your lips against mine. The parking lot is dark and you pull me into the backseat of your car.

Gentle kisses become more and, for the first time, I realize I'm not in the mood.

Your lips, your hands, your skin—I don't want any of it. Suddenly I feel claustrophobic, that word—*slut*—pushing up against me as your hand slides up my skirt and pulls at my underwear. Who is this girl, lying in the backseat of a car that smells like McDonald's and sweat? Who is this boy who smells like cigarettes and won't look her in the eye? This is my great epic romance? This is what I spent my whole life dreaming of?

I sit up, fast. "Gavin, I can't. I can't."

You stare at me, confused. "You can't what?"

I gesture helplessly at the backseat, at us. "This." The words burst out of me, words I didn't know were there until I said them. "I don't

212

know who I am anymore!" I literally wring my hands—people actually *do* that. Not just in movies.

This, I realize, is the problem. It's not your jealousy or our different worlds or my parents' rules—it's that I've become a dandelion. You blow on me and I scatter in a million directions.

"You're my girlfriend," you say, your voice sharp.

You're right. That's all I am anymore. I'm Gavin Davis's Girlfriend. All that seems to matter is keeping you happy. Seeing you. Finding a way to be together.

"I want to be more than that," I whisper.

You push off me and I scramble back and pull my knees up to my chest, leaning against the door. Your hat is on the floor, your hair curling around your ears, and even now I want to run my hands through it.

You zip up your pants, then open the door and slide out. You lean in to look at me.

"I'm taking you home."

"Fine."

"Fine." You slam the door.

And I feel—relief. I won't have your hands on my skin, pushing into those dark corners of myself I can't acknowledge in the daylight.

We're silent the whole way. Ten agonizing minutes.

You pull off on a side street, a block from my house. "We need to talk."

I've already opened my door, shivering as cold autumn wind flows past me. It smells like dirt and campfires.

"Gav, I'm tired. I just want to go home."

"Why do you have to be such a fucking bitch?" you say.

I get back in the car and slam the door. "Why do *you* have to be such a fucking asshole?"

"I'm just watching out for you. Grace, you have no idea what guys think about. What fucking Kyle thinks about. He's trying to take you away from me—"

"He's my best friend's boyfriend! And he's one of *my* best friends. There is *nothing going on.*"

You shake your head. "Baby, you trust people way too much. You don't know how guys *think*—"

"Why can't you just trust me?" I growl.

"It's not *you* I don't trust, it's *them.*"

"This is bullshit," I say.

I move to get out of the car but you grab me then and pull me against you, rough. I push you away, my palms against your chest, but your grip tightens, bruising.

"Gavin, *stop*—"

You kiss me so hard our teeth hit and you force my mouth open and then I taste you, cinnamon and cigarettes. I keep trying to push you away, but you hold me tighter and somehow I'm kissing you back, my palms against your cheeks. You sigh, your grip loosening. *I love you, I love you*, you say when we come up for air, and I don't know whose tears are on your face, mine or yours, because we both start sobbing and I climb on top of you because I need to be close, I need to remember what we have, and this—you inside me, a part of me—is the only thing that makes sense.

What happens is not tender. It's punishing and fast and it feels so good. You burn through me, a fire scorching everything in its path. When it's over we're both slick with sweat and I'm sore and bruised.

"So *that's* what make-up sex is like," you murmur against my neck. "Maybe we should fight more often."

I lean my forehead against yours. "I hate fighting."

"I know. Me too." You sigh. "This whole college–high school thing is harder than I thought it would be. It kills me, not being at school with you. I feel like I'm not a part of your life and it drives me nuts."

"You are the *biggest*, most important thing in my life," I say.

"Promise?"

I nod. "Promise."

You run your hands through my hair, twisting the locks around your fingers. "I'm sorry. About everything."

"I know." I slide off you and back into the passenger seat, searching for my underwear. "I have to get home. My mom's going to be pissed I'm so late." I grab my bag, then open the door.

"Grace?"

"Yeah?"

"Nobody in the world loves you as much as I do. You know that, right?"

I nod, kiss you once more, then get out of the car. I don't know what just happened. I'm shaking and I'm scared and confused. I do know that I used to feel safe with you—and I don't anymore.

TWENTY-FIVE

*E*very year, Nat, Lys, and I have a Christmas sleepover at Nat's house where we exchange gifts, watch *Love, Actually*, and eat Christmas candy. This year, we're buying one another books, even though Lys doesn't read unless it's for class (we put it to a vote and majority ruled). Nat and I have extra fun shopping for her.

We get her a torrid romance novel (*The Flame and the Flower*—classic historical romance) and a picture book (*I Want My Hat Back* because she's morbid and when she read the book to Sam, the ending made her laugh so hard she cried).

Lys gets me the *Kama Sutra*.

"Weirdo," I say, laughing as I swat at her with the book.

Nat gets me a fancy edition of *Leaves of Grass* because she knows how much I love Walt Whitman.

She gets an annotated *Anne of Green Gables* from me and *Fifty Shades of Grey* from Lys. Nat, of course, is scandalized.

"Did you buy our books at an actual bookstore? Like, you had to hand them to someone?" I ask.

Lys grins. "Oh, yeah."

Soon, she's twisting her body into all kinds of weird shapes as I read the directions out loud from the *Kama Sutra* like it's a naughty game of *Twister*.

"Ohhh," I say, "this one's called The Lotus Blossom. *Sit backward on top of your partner and wrap your legs around his waist—*"

Nat plugs her ears and starts singing "You're a Grand Old Flag." By this point I'm rolling on the floor, tears streaming down my face as Lys turns into a contortionist. She cries out as she topples over and she laughs so hard her face turns bright red. Lys has the best laugh— it's like a baby's belly laugh. It comes from somewhere deep inside her, an endless well.

We eat pizza and drink way too much Pepsi. We paint our nails bright red and dig into the dozen cookies I snuck out of the Honey Pot and I seriously almost pee my pants when Lys pretends to give a candy cane a blowjob.

It gets late, that hour when it's time for confessions. I take a breath and tell them what you called me—*bitch, slut*—I tell them how you were watching me while I was at work.

"What. The. Fuck." Lys stares at me. It's weird seeing someone with so much rage on their face wearing flannel pajamas with rainbows all over them.

"He actually *said* those things?" Nat asks.

I nod. "He didn't mean it, but—"

"That is *so* not an excuse," Lys says. "I could seriously chop off his dick right now."

"Um. Don't?" I say.

Nat leans forward. "This is serious, Grace. That was exactly how my dad used to be with my mom before she left him. And after the name-calling came the hitting."

"Gavin would *never* hit me!"

I tell myself the bruises on my arms from that night in your car were an accident—you didn't mean to hold me as hard as you did. You just didn't want me to go.

"Yeah, my mom used to say that, too."

"And don't think we've forgotten how insane he was at the bowling alley," Lys adds.

"Or how you ditched the cast party to hang out with him," Nat says.

"Okay, that's old news now. I told you, he knows he screwed up," I say. "He wouldn't be like that if Summer hadn't been so—"

Nat raises a hand. "Hold up. It doesn't matter what went down between him and Summer. Even if she did screw around on him, that doesn't mean he gets to treat you as though you're her."

"There is, like, *no* excuse for saying that shit to you," Lys says.

I know they're right. I think I told them because a part of me knew all this, but needed to hear it.

"I don't know what to do," I say.

"Do what Matt said you should—break up with his ass," Lys says.

I shake my head. "He doesn't mean to be like this." They just look at me. "I love him. Like, so, so much."

You beautiful, sexy, talented, stupidly crazy boy. My enigmatic, fucked-up rock god. I can't give you up. I won't.

"Grace. He called you a *slut*," Nat says. "I get that you love him. I do. He's an amazing person. But his jealousy, the watching you—it's scary."

"Creepy," Lys adds.

"Besides," Nat says, "not to be harsh, but you guys are probably gonna break up once you move to New York. Long-distance relationships don't last, everyone knows that. I mean, do you guys have a plan?"

I can't look her in the eye, so I study my nails, rubbing my thumb over each finger.

"Yeah, we do," I say, soft.

"And . . . ," Nat says.

I finally meet her eyes. "I'm staying in California."

She stares at me. "Please tell me you're joking."

"I didn't apply to NYU. Just schools around LA."

Lys looks at me like I've just spoken in Russian. "But . . . New York is . . . what?"

I shrug. "I can wait a few more years. I'll get there eventually. And there are some really good theatre schools in LA. USC, UCLA, Fullerton . . ."

The doorbell rings. It's a little after eleven.

"Who the heck is that?" Nat growls.

"Maybe it's Kyle," I say, relieved there's a distraction.

"He knows better than to interrupt girl time," she says.

I really wish you hadn't called me a slut. I can't imagine Kyle ever doing that to Nat. Or Nat putting up with it if he did.

Lys and I follow Nat to the door. Her mom is already in bed and her brothers and sister are hanging out in the den. She stands on her tiptoes and looks out the peephole.

"Oh, brother," she says.

I'm pretty sure Nat is the only teenager in the world who uses expressions like that.

She turns to me. "It's your boyfriend."

I catch the note of reproach in her voice and I shake my head, voice lowered. I promised them I wouldn't see or call you.

"I swear to God I turned off my phone."

The bell rings again.

Nat glances at me and I make a split-second decision. I grab Lys's hand, pulling her into the hallway beside the door.

"Good girl," Nat whispers.

The door opens and I watch you and Nat in the mirror on the opposite wall. You're wearing a black leather jacket and your fedora, pulled low. I move away before you catch me looking.

"Hey. I need to talk to Grace," you say.

"Um. We're kinda busy right now," Nat says. She keeps the door half shut, one hand on the knob. Like she might slam it in your face any second. I know she wants to.

"I need to talk to Grace," you repeat, speaking slowly, as though Nat's native tongue isn't English.

"Look, I'm sure whatever it is can wait, like, twelve more hours—"

You sigh. "Natalie. I've had a really long day, so can we stop playing games? I want to see my fucking girlfriend. Please."

I have to make sure you're okay. You sound exhausted. Something must have happened. I walk down the hallway and come to the door.

"Hey," I say.

You scowl at Nat before turning to me. "Can we talk for a minute? Out here?"

I look back at Nat, as if I need permission.

She purses her lips. "You've got ten minutes. Then we get her back."

You don't answer her. You just turn and start walking across her front lawn to where your Mustang is parked out front.

Nat turns to me. "Don't think what he's doing here is romantic— it's possessive and controlling and *rude*."

Lys nods. "Word."

I sigh and slip on my Doc Martens. "I'll be back in ten. Promise."

I walk across the grass and immediately realize I should have put a sweatshirt on. It's freezing out here. I can see my breath in the air.

You're leaning against the hood of your car, arms crossed. A street-light streams down on you like we're onstage. The houses all around us have Christmas lights and blow-up Santas. It'd be kinda romantic if you didn't look so pissed off.

"What's wrong?" I say. "What happened?"

It's been weird since that night in the mall parking lot. We're not fighting, but things are tense between us.

"Nothing. I needed to see you. What was that shit with Natalie?"

"I promised her it would be just us girls tonight. Remember?"

"She didn't have to be such a bitch."

"She's not a bitch," I say, my voice hard. "She's my best friend."

"Look, I tried calling you, like, ten times, but it went straight to voice mail. There was no other way to get in touch with you."

"Girl's Night is sacred," I say. "And you didn't have to be such a dick to her."

"She wasn't going to let me see you!"

I stand there and just look at you until you roll your eyes and say, "Fine. I'm sorry."

You notice me shivering and you shrug off your jacket and put it over my shoulders. It's warm and smells like you.

You take my hands and pull me closer. "Don't be mad. I love you."

I keep hearing my best friends tell me to break up with you. The word *slut* plays through my mind, looping over and over. I take my hands out of yours.

"I told the girls what happened the other night—when I was at work." I bite my lip. "They're pretty pissed about it. That might have something to do with Natalie being less than welcoming."

You stare at me. "Why are you talking about that shit with them? That's private—it's only *our* business."

"Because it happened and even though we've made up or whatever, I'm still upset. You called me a *slut*, Gav. I can't just forget that."

"I didn't mean it," you say. "I told you that. I was angry." You reach out and draw me closer. "Come on, don't hold that against me forever."

My eyes meet yours. "If you ever talk to me like that again, I'm gone. Okay?"

You swallow. "Yeah."

You look so sad and repentant that I can't help but cup your face in my hands and press my lips to yours.

"Are we good now?" you say, your eyes pleading.

"Yeah, we're good." I tilt your fedora back so I can see your eyes better. "Why are you even here?"

"I know you're having a Girls Night and everything, but I was hoping I could steal you away—just for a couple hours. I'll bring you back, promise."

"Gav . . . I'm not gonna just leave them. We have very important girly things to do."

You give me your sexy half smile. "You sure? My parents aren't home, there's mistletoe in the house . . . I even wrote you a sexy Christmas song."

I lean forward and kiss your nose. "Don't tempt me, you evil man."

Your grip tightens and the little spark that was in your eyes disappears. "Grace, I've hardly seen you at all this week. It's just a few hours. You see them every day at school—I'm sure they'll understand."

"I'm sure they *won't*. I love you, but I have to go back in there, not least because it's cold as balls out here."

"Did you just say *cold as balls*?"

"I did."

You shake your head, laugh softly. "Such a dirty mouth."

Relief surges through me—that laugh means we're not getting into a fight.

My lips turn up. "I think you know *exactly* how dirty my mouth is."

There's a scraping noise behind me and I turn just as Nat whisper-yells down from her bedroom.

"Time's up!" she says.

You lift your finger and flip her off.

I hit your arm. "Gavin!"

And Natalie—good, pure, old-lady Natalie—she returns the gesture.

Then, as if to prove to her that you've won, you pull me against you, but instead of a crushing kiss, you softly kiss the corner of my mouth, the tip of my nose, my eyelids as they flutter shut. You whispersing bits of "All I Want for Christmas Is You." Then you take your jacket and let go of me and I stumble back, drunk on you once more. The streetlight rains gold dust on you and with your film noir hat and leather jacket you look like a boy up to something delicious, something no good.

"From now on your weekends are mine except for very special circumstances," you say. "And don't put your phone on silent."

"Don't boss me around, Gavin Andrew Davis."

Your lips turn up. "I love you, Grace Marie Carter." I turn around, but I've only taken one step when you grab my hand. "Call me before you go to sleep."

When I get back inside, Nat and Lys are sitting cross-legged like two Buddhas, waiting for me.

"What did he want?" Lys asks.

"For me to ditch you guys and come hang out with him for a few hours."

"And you said no," Nat says. "Right?"

"Of course I did. What kind of friend do you take me for?" I grab a tree-shaped Reese's Peanut Butter Cup from our pile of candy. "Were you guys talking behind my back while I was gone?"

"Hell yes, we were," Lys says.

"I can't *believe* you didn't apply to NYU," Nat says. She reaches for one of the stuffed bears on her bed and hugs it to her.

"I love him. We're practically engaged," I say. "I don't want to be on the other side of the country for four years."

"Are you forgetting the part where he called you a slut? Oh, yeah, and a bitch, too, if I remember correctly," Nat says, pursing her lips.

"He feels really bad. About everything. I promise."

"That's what you said last time," Lys says softly.

"I'm sorry to say, he's lost the best friends' stamp of approval," Nat says.

"Please don't hate my boyfriend. It would so suck if you guys didn't get along."

Lys throws an arm around my shoulder. "Then he better not give us another reason to."

TWENTY-SIX

I don't quite know how bad things are between my mom and The Giant until the beginning of February. Something fucked-up is going on, but I only get hints of it, like I'm watching their relationship between the slats in a wooden fence.

I rarely see them in the same room together and most nights he comes home late from work, snarling.

I swear to God, Jean, you nag me about fixing the van one more time . . .

Fine, leave me. Let's see how well you do in the real world.

Maybe it's time your fat ass got a job.

One night I throw my history book down in disgust and march out to the living room.

"Don't talk to her like that," I say, my voice trembling.

I can't watch him whittle down my mom so that she's nothing but Silent and Subservient Wife.

The Giant turns around, the drink in his hand sloshing over the side. The lamp by the couch throws his shadow on the wall by the fireplace. He looms over us. *Fee fi fo fum.*

"Shut the fuck up, Grace."

I glance at my mom, but she just stands there, her eyes shifting to a picture on the mantel, ignoring me. In it, Beth, Mom, and I are jumping on a trampoline, our mouths wide open with laughter. A pre-Giant day.

"Mom . . . ," I say. She looks at me and just shakes her head.

Sam starts crying and I pick him up, holding him to me. I take him back to my room, away from the arguing.

It seems like every night there are raised voices behind shut doors, the sound of breaking glass. Twice now I've caught my mom organizing the kitchen cupboards in the middle of the night. Last week it was the garage—a complete makeover that she began on a Wednesday at midnight when she was trying to find her sewing kit. She doesn't get up early in the morning anymore—sometimes she's still in bed when I get home from school. One minute she'll be smiling, the corners of her mouth pulled tightly across her face (*Roy bought me flowers—isn't that sweet?*). But the next, there are shadows under her eyes and she moves around the house like an old woman (*I'm just tired, that's all*).

It's a Saturday afternoon and I have to go to work, but I can't leave my brother alone. My mom has been in the bathroom for over an hour.

"Mom?"

I knock softly on the bathroom door. Nothing.

I knock again, louder this time. "Mom? I have to get going."

I press my ear against the door. The shower is still running.

I open the door a crack. "Mom?"

I can see her blurred outline in the frosted glass door of the shower.

"*Mom.*" Now I'm annoyed. "I have to get to work. I already fed Sam lunch and—"

Then I hear it above the water—sobbing. I don't think. I yank open the shower door, panicked, thinking of you and razors and blood. My mom's sitting on the tiled floor, huddled in a corner, her knees drawn up against her chest, her long hair plastered to her head. She looks up, her face distorted, eyes red.

"What happened?" I ask. "Are you okay?"

She just shakes her head, lowering her forehead to her knees. Her sobs push her shoulder blades together, as though she's trying to fly without wings.

I'm already dressed for work, but I don't care. I step into the shower and crouch in front of her. I'm soaked through in seconds. The hot water must have run out forever ago. The sharp stream rushing out of the showerhead is freezing and I reach up to turn it off. In the sudden silence her breathing is ragged. She's shivering uncontrollably—even her teeth are chattering. They sound like pearls being rubbed together.

"Hey," I say, gentle. I forget all the times she's called my own sobs overdramatic. I forget that I've been punished for my tears. "It's okay. Whatever it is, it's okay."

I reach out and place my hands on her elbows. Her skin is cold, refrigerated.

I've only seen her like this once before. When I was ten, there was this brief period when my mom and dad were maybe going to get back together. He was sleeping over every night and taking us out to dinner. Then one day he was gone. So was the can of money my mom had been putting cash into for months. We were trying to save up to go to Sea World.

She's mumbling something over and over.

"What?" I say, leaning in.

"I give up," she says softly.

The words fall out of her mouth, heavy and dead. Tears spring to my eyes.

"No you don't," I murmur. "You never give up."

I think about Mom before The Giant, before he smashed our world to smithereens. The way she'd throw overdue bills in the trash and take us to McDonald's, or how she cheerfully marched my sister and me a mile after our car ran out of gas. We sang Christmas carols even though it was April.

My hand reaches toward her without my permission and I run my fingers through the strands of her hair, dark brown like mine. I don't let myself think about how just a few days ago she pulled my hair, hard. *I'm tired of your attitude, Grace Marie.* I don't even remember what she was so mad about. I forgot to take out the trash, something like that.

"Mom." I shake her a little and she lifts her head.

"He's angry no matter what I do," she says, not to me but to herself. *Fee, fi, fo, fum.*

Her face crumples and she starts crying again. I wish Beth were here. She'd know what to do. I look at her, helpless.

"What did he do?"

She shakes her head. I reach over and grab a towel off the rack.

"Let's get you dried off."

Her mascara and eyeliner have bled over her skin so that it looks like she has two black eyes. She struggles to stand, as though her legs are too weak to hold her up. I put my arm across her shoulders while she wraps the towel around her body. She can't seem to stop shivering.

Once she's out of the shower she looks at me.

"Don't you have work?"

I nod, then look down at my soaked uniform. I'm going to be late. I feel like I need to stay with my mom, but I can't call in, since I'm the closer.

"I'm gonna change," I say. "I'll be right back."

She nods and I go to my room and peel off my wet clothes, then grab yesterday's work clothes out of the laundry basket. Sam is still taking his nap and The Giant is golfing, so the house is silent. When I'm done changing, I head back to her bathroom.

Mom's wearing a robe now, her hair twisted up in a towel. I remember Beth and me pooling our money together to buy her the thick terry-cloth robe for Mother's Day a few years ago.

"Sorry about that," she says, gesturing vaguely toward the shower. She's looking in the mirror, taking off her eye makeup.

It's been a long time since my mom and I talked openly about anything, but I decide to press my luck.

"Mom, why don't you just leave him? He's, like, the *worst*. You deserve better. We both do."

She doesn't look at me. Her eyes are glued to the mirror.

"It's not as easy as all that," she says.

"But—"

"Can I borrow twenty bucks?" she asks. Her eyes find mine in the glass. "I won't be getting any more money from Roy until the end of the week."

The Giant gives her an allowance. Like she's a kid. He controls everything.

"Yeah," I say. "Sure."

She will never pay it back. In fact, she will pretend this conversation— and the shower before it—never happened. It wouldn't be the first time.

"I love him," she says. "When you're older, you'll understand."

How could I possibly understand? What kind of person would put up with this shit?

"If he hits you, I swear to God, I'm calling the police, Mom."

I haven't seen him do it, but I wouldn't be surprised if he did.

She smiles, sad. "Roy doesn't hit. He doesn't need to."

And I remember something he said a few nights ago: *Go, then. But there's no way in hell you'll get custody.* She will never leave him—not until Sam's out of school, anyway.

I think about you—about the way you hold me like I'm something precious and rare, the little gifts you're always sneaking me, the way you sing me to sleep over the phone at night. And I suddenly feel desperately sad for my mother. Maybe she's never had what we have. Maybe she never will.

I swallow the lump in my throat. "I'll go get the money."

I give her two twenties, then walk to work, the cold February wind slicing through my layers, numbing me. I don't think about how I'm just barely going to make rent this month.

When I get to work, Matt throws me a concerned glance as he puts fresh cookies onto the trays.

"What's wrong, *chica*?"

I make it to the back of the store before I burst into tears. He rushes toward me, ignoring the customers that have just walked up. Without a word, he pulls me into a tight hug. I hold on to him, grateful. He smells like sugar and the musky cologne he always wears.

"You want me to stay here and close?" he asks. "Go home if you need to."

"That's the last place I want to be," I mumble into his shoulder.

"You want to talk about it?"

I shake my head. He holds me tighter for a second, then lets go. A soft smile plays on his face.

"You're even pretty when you cry, you know that?"

A smile sneaks onto my face. "Shut up."

"Grace?"

I look up and there you are, standing in the doorframe between the kitchen and the shop. Your arms are crossed and you do not look happy.

I turn to Matt. "Can you give us a minute?"

230

He nods. "Sure. Come out whenever you're ready."

You walk in and brush past Matt without a glance while the door swings shut behind you.

"He was all over you" is the first thing you say to me after Matt's back out front. "What the hell?"

"I was upset," I say. I'm pissed that you don't seem to care. I thought it was only The Giant who ignored my tears. "He was just being nice."

"That didn't look like *nice*," you say. Your eyes are a storm-tossed sea, your lips just a slash in your skin.

I think of my naked mother, the way her face crumpled like tissue paper, and I lose my temper.

"You know what? I don't care what it looked like. If you haven't noticed, *I'm crying*. I'm having a fucking terrible day and you're being a jealous idiot."

We stare at each other for a moment and then you cross the kitchen in seconds and wrap your arms around me.

"You're right," you say. "I'm sorry."

I sigh and breathe you in. I haven't seen you in days and the smell of you is like coming home, in a good way.

"What happened?" you murmur against my hair.

I shake my head. "I don't want to talk about it."

"Something at home?"

"Yeah."

Your fingers run down my spine, like you're playing guitar, easing the tension out of me.

"On a scale of one to ten," you say, "how much do you like this job?"

"I guess six. Sometimes seven or eight. Why?"

"I was thinking maybe you could come work at Guitar Center with me."

I smile, looking up at you. "I don't know anything about guitars."

"I'll teach you."

"I'd distract you. We'd both be fired." I pull out of your arms and grab my apron. "Besides, I have seniority here. They work with my schedule when I have shows. I like everyone—"

"I don't want you working here anymore," you say softly. "Okay?"

You shove your hands deep in your pockets. Bite your lip. Your eyes are trained on me, waiting.

"Why? Because of Matt?"

You nod. "How would you feel if I worked with Summer?"

"I mean, I wouldn't like it, but—"

"Grace. You would freak out if she looked at me the way Matt looks at you."

"Matt doesn't *look* at me any way."

"He does. I told you, he stares at your ass when you lean down to take cookies out of the oven. He touches you all the time."

"What?"

"Please." You step forward. "Even if you don't want to work at Guitar Center, just . . . work somewhere else. I'd do it for you."

"But I just got a raise. I get good shifts—"

"Don't worry about the money," you say. "I can make up the difference."

"Gav, I can't let you do that."

"You tell me you love me more than anything, but then you won't leave this shitty job. What am I supposed to think, Grace?"

"Hey." I move closer, wrap my arms around your waist. "I *do* love you more than anything."

"Yeah. Whatever."

You pull away from me and head to the door.

"Gavin! Come on."

But you keep walking.

Later, when I'm in bed, I stare at the slats that hold the bunk bed above me. There are still a few stray glow-in-the-dark stars stuck to the wood. I remember putting them up there when we first moved here. They don't glow anymore. Now they're just cheap plastic.

There's a tap at my window. I pull back the covers, slow. I don't really know if I want to talk to you right now.

I open the window and you look up at me, penitent. I step back and you hoist yourself over the short ledge and slip into the room.

"I shouldn't have walked away from you," you whisper. "I'm sorry." We sit on the bed and you take my hands.

"Have you . . . thought more about it?" you ask.

I nod. "Yeah."

"And . . ."

"Gav, I'm not quitting my job. It sucks that you don't trust me—"

"How am I supposed to trust you when you break the rules we agreed on? We said we wouldn't touch a member of the opposite sex and then you go off and kiss Kyle—"

"For a scene in class!"

I can't believe you're bringing that up again.

"And let Matt fucking *hold* you—"

I press my hand over your mouth. "Gavin, my parents!"

You close your eyes and I let my hand drop.

"I don't want to fight," I whisper.

You glare at me. "Then stop working there."

I keep my eyes on yours. "No."

It feels so good to say that word to you. You look like you're going to say something else, then just shake your head.

"All right, Carter. You win."

I lean forward and kiss you, magnanimous in my victory. "Besides, what would you have done without all the free cookies?"

"That's a good point," you say grudgingly. You kick off your shoes and crawl into bed with me. "Tell me why you were crying."

And just like that, we're not fighting and back in love. You hold me tight against you as I tell you about my mom. I wonder if she's curled up against The Giant or if she's all alone on her side of the bed, her eyes wide open.

"I feel so bad for her," I whisper.

She doesn't have someone who will make the clouds go away and the sun come out. She doesn't have you. I hold you tighter, kiss you all over your face.

"What was that for?" I can hear the smile in your voice.

"Just because," I say.

You press your lips against my forehead and soon your breathing is soft and even.

I lie awake for a long time, listening to the beat of your heart.

TWENTY-SEVEN

Ever since I refused to quit my job, you and I fight every single time we talk—being with you is like walking a tightrope all day, every day. I'm always tensed for the fall. If I don't respond to a call or text from you right away, you freak out. I changed the passcode on my phone because I was afraid you'd see Nat's and Lys's emails. They're engaged in a full-on campaign to get me to break up with you. It was also kind of a test, to see if you're actually as unreasonably jealous as they say you are. One night when we're out at a restaurant, I go to the bathroom and purposely leave my phone on the table. When I get back you're seething. *What are you trying to hide from me?* you say. *It was a test*, I answer. *You failed.* I refuse to give you the passcode and we end our date early and don't talk for three days.

End this shit, Nat and Lys say.

I can't. I just . . . can't. People who make each other this unhappy should break up. Duh. But right when I think I'm going to do it, something good will happen. Something that reminds me why you're my soul mate, like convincing the person who runs the mall's audio to let you sing a song for me, live, during one of my shifts at the Honey Pot.

"Attention, everyone in the mall. This song is dedicated to my favorite cookie baker."

Matt and I look at each other. He mouths, "What the fuck?"

"I think . . ." The first chords of "Anthem" play and I know for sure it's you. "That's Gavin."

"Let me be your anthem, baby, let me be your song," you sing.

A customer in line gestures to the speakers above us. "You know that guy?"

I blush crimson and nod. "That's my boyfriend."

"He has a beautiful voice," she says.

I smile, proud. "He does."

IT'S THE MIDDLE of February—only four months until graduation—and now that rehearsals for the spring play are in full swing, we don't have as much time together. I find myself feeling relieved that I don't get to see you and I know that's a bad sign. But I still can't give you up. I made the biggest sacrifice of my life for you when I didn't turn in that NYU application. That can't be for nothing.

At school we're doing Shakespeare's *Twelfth Night*—one of my favorites. Miss B's mother is sick and she's asking me to fill in for her a lot, since I'm the assistant director. I love every second of it: casting, running rehearsals, working individually with the actors, meeting with the crew and designers. And I realize something important about myself that I didn't know before, or at least maybe it wasn't true before: part of why I love directing is that it's just mine. And I like having something that has nothing to do with you. It makes me feel like . . . like *me* again.

A few weeks into rehearsals, I'm on my way to Ashland, Oregon, a special trip for drama kids that only happens once every four years.

Since all my paychecks go toward paying rent, I've had to borrow the money for the trip from my gram. *I don't want you to pay me back*, she said. *It'll be our little secret.* Just one more reason why Gram is my favorite relative. For a whole weekend we'll be immersing ourselves in Shakespeare, seeing several shows, taking workshops, and—best of all—being in a town expressly designed for theater (*ahem*, I mean *theatre*) nerds.

You are furious that I'm going on the trip. It starts the day after Valentine's Day, which, instead of being a mushy love day, has turned into the year anniversary of when you tried to kill yourself. You took me out to dinner, but you were distracted and not entirely sober. I (stupidly) made the comment that my trip was perfect timing because it would be good for us to have a little space. Now you're convinced I'm going to break up with you when I get back. You begged me not to go, said you'd take me after graduation. *We're more important than this trip*, you said. *I have to play a show. I need you there.* But I'm sticking to my guns.

The next morning I grab my little suitcase and rush to the school parking lot, late because of being up half the night worrying about us. Since I'm one of the last people to arrive, I end up sitting with Gideon Paulson on the bus ride there instead of in the back with Nat and Lys. He's a junior, a guy I hadn't really talked to much before we started *Twelfth Night*, but he's Count Orsino, one of the leads, so we've gotten to know each other a lot better this semester. We've actually become pretty good friends, not that I would ever tell *you* that. Gideon has my back and helps wrangle people when Miss B's not around and he runs lines with the actors who are struggling. He was formerly more of a choir geek but transferred into our advanced drama class in January and now he's part of our little group. It's crazy how doing a show with someone can make you so close so fast.

Gideon is my kind of people. We pretty much like all the same things except he's obsessed with manga and kung-fu movies, neither of which interests me. But that's okay because he loves Radiohead, reads even more than I do, and wants to travel the world someday. As our bus passes through California's drought-ridden Central Valley and into the lush green of Northern California, we sit slouched low in our seat, heads bent close together as we create an imaginary itinerary for a round-the-world trip.

"Okay," he says, pushing his glasses up as they slide down his nose. "We have a big decision to make here. Switzerland or Prague?"

"Prague is non-negotiable," I say.

"Oh, really? And why, pray tell, is that?"

"I'm part Czech. There's, like, a statue of one of my ancestors in a small town near there."

Gideon nods, all business, as he adds Prague to the itinerary.

"Fair enough," he says. "I won't stand in the way of rediscovering one's roots. But since you got that choice, I get first choice in Asia."

"By all means," I say.

He does research on his phone for hostels and we discover that in Asia, it'd actually be cheaper to share a room at a guesthouse, since they don't really have hostels there.

"Are you a bed hog?" I ask.

He grins. "Oh yeah. You better bring a sleeping bag."

And that's when I realize—we're flirting with each other. I have that light-headed, butterfly feeling I used to get with you and I'm suddenly very aware of how my knee is touching Gideon's and the way his hair curls just over his ears. He's wearing a shirt covered in Chinese characters and he's written FUCK WAR on the toes of his high-top All-Stars, an outfit so totally him—nerdy iconoclast. I like the fact that he carries a messenger bag instead of a backpack. It adds to the whole hipster/scholar vibe he's got going on. I'm a sucker for guys with style—you're evidence of that.

Gideon's hand brushes mine as he sketches in Mount Fuji on the map we've been making. I go still, every part of me aware of the warmth his touch leaves behind.

I want him to touch me again.

Fuck.

We spend the next four hours carefully detailing our itinerary, squabbling over cities and travel routes, laughing at our growling bellies. We should be stopping for lunch soon, but I don't want to stop because I'm having so much fun flirting with Gideon. Shitshitshit. I've always been like this: a fast faller. The first time I saw you I turned into one of those cartoon characters with popping heart eyes. I went from not knowing you existed to thinking about you every second of every day for *three years.*

"I'm telling you, we *have* to go on the Trans-Siberian," he's saying.

"But that won't leave us very much time to go to Moscow and St. Petersburg," I argue.

He frowns. "Riding across Siberia in a train would make me an official badass."

"I think swimming in the Great Barrier Reef will take care of that."

"Oh, so you're totally cool with *great white sharks* but we can't go to the Sahara because of scorpions?" he says, genuinely incredulous.

I laugh and Peter peeks over the seat in front of us. I hadn't noticed he and Kyle were sitting there. I guess I was . . . distracted.

"You know Gavin will never let you go on a round-the-world trip with another dude, right?" Peter says because he's a nosy bitch.

Gideon snorts. "*Let?* That's a bit 1840, don't you think?" He turns to me. "He's joking, right?"

I ignore Gideon and scoot closer to the window as I glare at Peter. I hope he didn't notice how close we'd been sitting.

"This is a purely hypothetical enterprise," I say.

But I break out in a cold sweat. Will Peter or Kyle tell you I sat with a boy on the bus? Does this count as being "alone" with another guy?

Peter just lifts his eyebrows. "If you say so . . ."

He turns around and sits back down. Gideon looks at me, his head cocked to the side. He turns to a fresh piece of notebook paper and scrawls across it in his scratchy handwriting.

You okay?

Yeah.

How did Gideon know that my good mood had suddenly disappeared? It was almost as if he knew it had happened before I did.

Was he kidding—about your boyfriend being mad?

When Gideon puts it in black and white like that I'm reminded of how absurd your rule is. There's nothing wrong with hanging out with someone. Or hugging them. I haven't hugged another boy in almost a year, except for when Matt gave me a hug that day I was crying at work.

No. Gavin is . . .

I bite my lip, look up at Gideon. Which is a huge mistake because if you look past his glasses he has the biggest, brownest, kindest eyes I've ever seen and I kind of fall right into them. I feel warm, like I do after I've had a nice big cup of hot cocoa. With marshmallows.

I like the planes of his face, the mixture of long Roman lines and soft cheeks, rounded, like they still have a little bit of baby fat left in them. I like his straight white teeth, tidy where the rest of him is gangly and adorably awkward.

Gideon takes the pen out of my hand.

Possessive?

There it is in black and white.

Yeah. Kinda.

The bus lurches to a stop and I rip off the piece of notebook paper he's written on and ball it up.

Gideon raises his eyebrows. "Destroying the evidence?"

"Very astute, Dr. Watson."

Nat grabs my hand as we all head out of the bus and surge toward the travel center with five different fast-food joints. Gideon goes on up ahead with Peter and Kyle.

"Dude. You and Gideon?" she says. Her smile is disgustingly huge.

"Oh my god, stop it," I say. "He's such a dork."

I feel terrible saying that about him because that's not even what I think. But I'm starting to realize that we all wear strange armor to get through the day. Mine is denial. Denial that I'm feeling something for Gideon. Denial that you and I need to break up, like, yesterday.

"No," Lys says, putting on her heart-shaped sunglasses. "You two are adorkable—there's a difference."

"Guys. I have a boyfriend. I know he's not your favorite person in the world right now, but I love him, okay?"

I tell myself I'm not going to flirt with Gideon anymore. It's wrong, I know that.

I'm just finishing lunch when I realize my phone has been on silent this whole time. There are six missed calls from you. And one text:

Who's Gideon?

Fucking Peter. I knew you were having him spy on me, but now I have proof.

When I get back on the bus, Gideon slides in next to me. I throw my phone into my bag and keep it on silent. For once, I'm going to ignore you. I don't realize this at the time, but I'm taking my first step toward leaving you. Baby steps.

"So where were we?" I say, holding up his notebook.

"We're in Tokyo and I was selling you on the merits of South Africa," Gideon says.

"I'll give you South Africa if you give me Morocco."

He holds out his hand. "Deal."

I take it, press my palm against his.

We hold on longer than we need to.

TWENTY-EIGHT

*L*ys has fallen in love with a girl from Birch Grove High. Her name is Jessie and she has curly brown hair and the kind of laugh that lasts so long it gets everyone around her laughing, too.

"I just can't believe this is finally happening to me," Lys says, awed. She's been walking around in a daze for half the day.

We're in our hotel room, just a short walk from the Oregon Shakespeare Festival. A pile of candy we'd gotten at the grocery store is sitting in the middle of one of the beds. My stomach already hurts, but I keep eating Red Vines.

"How glad are you the Birch Grove drama students tagged along on our trip?" I say. Initially, Lys had been a hater about it, since Birch Grove is the rich kids' school. (Even though she's rich, she says she's one of the *people*. Whatever.)

"I know, right?" Lys says. She falls on her back and practically swoons.

The next day we meet up with everyone at a local diner, squishing into five booths. Gideon is in the booth next to mine and he calls, "Canada! We totally forgot about Canada!"

I laugh when Jessie looks at him like he's crazy.

"We're planning a round-the-world trip," I explain.

"Oh, he's your boyfriend, right?" she asks.

I choke on my too-sweet coffee and Natalie grins.

Because your timing is impeccable, my phone rings and I hold it up so Jessie can see the picture I snapped of you playing guitar.

"*That's* my boyfriend," I say.

"He's pretty hot," she says. Then she winks at Lys. "Not my type, of course."

"That's just the packaging," Nat mutters.

We only have two days in Oregon and things are planned out to the hour. After the diner it's time for an improv class with some of the actors at the festival. They put us into two groups and we play what they call the "Yes/No" game. Two people are chosen and they stand in the middle of a circle. It happens to be me and Nat. I'm only allowed to say the word *yes* and she's only allowed to say the word *no*. That's it. We're supposed to respond to each other's cues to make it seem like a real scene.

"No," she says matter-of-factly.

"Yes," I say, firm.

"*No,*" she says.

"Yes?"

"NO."

It's at about this point that I realize this is the conversation she and I have been having about you for the past few months. Nat, cheating, glances in Gideon's direction. She smiles at me.

"No?"

I am going to kill her. Because there's only one word I'm allowed to say:

"Yes," I growl.

I grab her after, on our way to a clowning workshop.

"Dude, not cool," I say.

"What?" She is the picture of innocence.

"Look, I know you don't want me to be with Gavin—"

She stops me in the middle of the sidewalk and puts her hands on my shoulders.

"I love you. Let's not talk about this. Let's have the time of our lives."

I glare at her for a moment, a hand on my hip. I'd been so angry, but why? Because my best friend is watching out for me? Because she's teasing me about a cute boy?

Finally, I nod. "Okay. Challenge accepted."

For the first time in my life I feel totally free. My parents are hundreds of miles away (in a whole other *state*!) and it's just me and my friends having, as Nat said, the time of our lives.

We drink way too much coffee, filling our cups with loads of sugar and cream. We pop in and out of cute stores that sell all the theatre stuff you could ever want. We talk about method acting and read each other our favorite Shakespeare quotes from books in the bookstores. Our time is our own for the most part and we spend it helping Lys and Jessie fall in love and eating good food and laughing a lot.

You call me more than usual and I let myself ignore the calls, even though I know you'll be pissed. It feels good to just do what I want.

"This is what college is going to feel like," Jessie says, her hand in Lys's. "I mean, think about it: no parents, studying theatre, hanging out with new people."

We talk about where we've all applied—acceptance and rejection letters will be coming in next month.

"So how do you go to school for directing? Is it the same as acting?" Jessie asks me.

I nod. "I'll be in acting classes and stuff, but I'll take whatever directing classes there are, too. I'm gonna try to get some assistant-directing gigs and then—fingers crossed—I'll study in France. There's this school in Paris named after its founder, Jacques Lecoq—"

Lys bursts out laughing. "Le COCK? Shut the fuck up—that is *not* his name."

"I swear to God!"

Jessie and Lys collapse into a pile of giggles.

"Ladies, compose yourselves," Gideon says as he walks up to us.

We're all sitting outside one of the town's many theaters, waiting to go inside. He looks really good with an anime T-shirt under a long-sleeved button-down.

Nat shakes her head. She's trying not to smile at the word *cock* and I love her for it.

"Fools," she mutters.

Gideon glances at me. "Do I even want to know what's so funny?"

"LE COCK!" Lys screeches in overly accented French.

I roll my eyes. "Ignore them."

My phone rings—you. I'd let the last two of your calls go to voice-mail, so I really need to take it.

"Be right back," I say, hurrying over to a bench a few feet away.

"Hey, baby," I say, answering.

"Hey." Your voice is gruff, but I can tell you're trying to hold your annoyance in. "Having fun?"

"Yes! There's so much to do here. We took this improv class and—"

"I miss you so much," you whisper.

"I miss you, too." But I realize I'm lying. I don't miss you at all.

"Why aren't you answering your phone?"

"It's just really busy here and—"

"Grace!" Natalie calls, waving her hands back and forth.

"Hey, I gotta go," I say. "The house is open and everyone's going inside."

246

"Fine."

"Baby, don't be like that," I say. "Please. I'm having such a good time—"

"All right, enjoy the show." And you hang up.

I shove my phone into my pocket and take a deep breath. Paris, Lecoq—it's a pipe dream. You freak out with me a few *hours* from you—there's no way you'd let me go abroad. *Let.* As if I need your permission. But I do, Gav, don't I?

Someone coughs quietly behind me. I look up and Gideon's standing there, the setting sun outlining him in gold.

"I've been sent by Nat and Lys to escort you into the theater," he says, holding out an arm.

I grin as I take it. "Why, thank you."

"The boyfriend?" he says, nodding toward the phone.

"Yeah. He kinda hung up on me."

"Whoa."

"Not his finest hour."

Gideon reaches into his messenger bag and produces a pack of Red Vines. "Word on the street is that you love these things."

"I do!"

He hands them over and I happily start munching. If this were a play I was directing, I'd have the two actors walk upstage as the lights dim. Just before they enter the theater they stop and gaze into each other's eyes as a spotlight slowly warms over them.

Then: blackout.

TWELFTH NIGHT BEGINS with a shipwreck.

Viola finds herself washed ashore on an unknown land with nothing but the tattered clothes on her back. Behind her: a vast ocean. Beyond that, the life she left behind. She thinks everyone else on the ship must have perished because she's alone on this deserted beach. The land, she will soon discover, is called Ilyria.

I want to go there. I want to be like Viola—weather the storm, then start over, using nothing but my wits and charm to see me through to my happy ending.

Destiny is hard at work in Ilyria. Cosmic love and mistaken identity and strange serendipities. In Ilyria, nothing is what it seems, yet despite this confusion, it is a land of wonders. This production has turned Shakespeare's island into a lush Turkish outpost, with jewel-toned pillows piled on the floors, low tables, hookah pipes, and stained-glass lamps that cast ruby-colored shadows over the stage. The actors all wear flowing costumes—harem pants and elaborately embroidered corsets. My mind is spinning with ideas for our own production and part of me can't wait to get home and get back to work.

As I sit watching the Oregon Shakespeare Company perform, my mind wanders not to you but to Gideon, who's sitting next to me. Whose knee is slightly touching my own after he shifts in his seat. I feel a little like Viola does at the beginning of the play—storm-tossed and wary, trying to find her footing in a complicated world. And, also like Viola, I can feel something hopeless and fragile and terrifying bloom in my chest—a feeling I'm not supposed to have because I'm not allowed to have it, not while I'm with you.

"If it be so, as 'tis," Viola says, *"Poor lady, she were better love a dream."*

Viola is in love with Count Orsino, but she can't tell him because she's posing as a boy. She's essentially his manservant and Count Orsino is decidedly straight, which means her chances of him falling in love with her are slim to none. Viola can't come out and tell Orsino who she really is because being a woman alone in a world where that's not the norm could be potentially dangerous. Scene after scene I watch as Viola struggles in vain to hide her feelings, forced to help the count woo Olivia, a woman he thinks he loves but who has actually fallen in love with Viola (Olivia thinks Viola is a dude named Cesario—it's like this whole complicated thing: mistaken identity, star-crossed love, the whole shebang).

Gideon leans over to me, his lips close to my ear, his hot breath trailing down my neck.

"Even though we know the ending, I'm like, Oh my god, if they don't get together . . . This is killing me," he says.

Me too, I think. But I know he's only talking about the play. I turn my head slightly and our lips are so close—

"Me too."

Our eyes lock and the soft darkness makes me bold. I don't look away. I should, this is wrong, but in his eyes I see a spark, an intensity that wasn't there before I boarded the bus to Oregon and sat next to him, planning a trip around the world.

"Oh time," Viola is saying onstage, *"thou must untangle this, not I. It is too hard a knot for me to untie."*

TWENTY-NINE

Gideon is teaching me about God.

And Björk.

For the past few weeks, he's been getting me into the crazy music and poetry he digs, bringing me books and giving me playlists every few days. I write him long letters and he writes me back. Turns out, we both like to keep it old-school with pens and paper instead of impersonal emails. I love touching the lined notebook paper and knowing he's touched it, too. I like tracing the grooves he runs into the paper with his pen.

I'd forgotten how much fun it is to have a guy friend. I like seeing the world through his eyes: to Gideon, the universe is a messy delight. He's interested in deep stuff: the Big Questions, like why are we here and what are we supposed to do with our lives? I realize I suddenly want to know the answers to those things—or at least be asking the questions. I like what Gideon shakes up in me. In his universe, there is no judgment, no rules that take you away from yourself. He's fucking Yoda, is who he is. He's making me hungry for my future, for all the things I've dreamed of.

Gideon and I are just friends. I swear.

Except.

In those few minutes before I drift off to sleep, I don't think about you—I think about him.

This is a problem.

"You're sort of my guru now," I say, handing him back the collection of Rumi poetry he lent me.

Gideon laughs as he puts the battered book into his messenger bag—I wonder how many times he's read it. "Man, I'm gonna have to get some guru clothes, then."

"Nah," I say, pulling a little at his shirt because it's an excuse to touch him, "this is perfect."

His eyes fall to mine and we do that thing we've started to do—look, look, look until I break away, flustered and scared and so alive I can barely stand it.

Today he's wearing a shirt that looks like an old GameBoy screen—Tetris, the one where you have to get all the bricks to match up as they come down the screen, faster and faster. My friendship with Gideon feels like that game: like those bricks in Tetris, we're trying to fit together as quickly as possible. Quick, before you find out about us and then Game Over.

You're joy, Rumi says about God. *We're all the different kinds of laughing.*

You'll be given love, Björk sings out, sweetly innocent: *you just have to trust it.*

I don't know what you'd call the thing Gideon gives me every day, but it makes me happy.

Until I think about you and then I feel sick to my stomach because I am the worst girlfriend ever. It's taken me weeks to admit this to myself, but I'm emotionally cheating on you.

"So you liked them?" he asks. "The poems?"

"I *loved* them," I say. Gush. And here I go again. I forget all about you. "Rumi is so . . . *happy*."

"Right?"

Gideon and his parents are what you'd call *spiritual* but not religious. I haven't been to his house, but I can imagine incense burning next to a statue of Buddha, which sits against a wall with a cross on it. There's probably a yoga mat on the floor and, I don't know, Indian Hindu songs playing in the background.

"I love how he doesn't discriminate," I say. "Like, you get the impression that, for him, God doesn't have all these rules and boundaries and stuff. You can be a Muslim like him or a Christian like Nat or nothing specific like you and me . . . whatever. It's all good."

We drift over to a corner of the drama room, as is our habit these days. A little away from everyone else, but in public.

"Yeah, like, come one, come all," he says as he sits down and rummages through his brown paper lunch bag. "I'm really into this idea of universal salvation. I mean, he doesn't use those words, but you get the impression that everyone's going to heaven."

"Right. Like, why would God make all these people and then send most of them to hell?" I say. I remember once I saw a street-corner preacher describing the horrors of hell and it's stuck with me ever since— wailing and gnashing of teeth. Scary stuff.

"Dude, you guys are so freaking weird," Lys says as she plops down onto the carpet beside us.

"Says the girl wearing a neon-green dress with kittens on it," I say.

Lys laughs. "All right, touché."

I want to be alone with Gideon, but I'm glad she's here: I need a chaperone or else Peter will tell you I'm eating lunch alone with Gideon.

Gideon pops a chip into his mouth, then hands me the bag. "Have you ever thought, dear Alyssa, that *we're* the normal ones?"

She looks from him to me. "No," she says, deadpan. "I have never thought that."

We talk about our production of *Twelfth Night*, which opens next week.

"So what do you say, Ms. Director?" Gideon asks. "Are we in good shape for opening night?"

"You guys are in awesome shape," I say. I mean it. Everything is coming together at the last minute, which always happens in the theatre. It's like clockwork. How? I don't know. It's like Geoffrey Rush's character says in *Shakespeare in Love*: *It's a mystery!*

I love directing. I love watching actors do their thing, then trying to figure out how they can do it better. The best part is when I'm right or when we come to a whole new idea together. We brainstorm magic.

"It must be nice," Lys says, "not having to memorize lines and shit."

"Dude, it's the *best*," I say. "I used to get so nervous onstage. Just doing scenes in class freaks me out."

Lys and Gideon start talking about a scene they're in and I get distracted, playing my silly game with the apple in my hand. I hold on to the stem and turn it around and around, counting off the letters. A, B, C, D, E, F, G. *G* again. When I was a kid, we'd say this is the person you're going to end up with. I look over at Gideon. Maybe *he* was the G way back when I played this game before you and I got together. What if I've gotten it all wrong, Gavin? What if we aren't meant to be?

G, G, G.

The drama room door opens and Nat strides in, looking frazzled. Her normally perfectly smooth hair is in a messy bun and there are wrinkles in her dress (she usually irons her dresses every morning before school—she says it gives her a sense of control in a world full of chaos).

Between midterms and rehearsals, none of us have slept more than four hours a night. I like this energy—it zips through me, kinetic, frenetic, and I latch on and let it take me for a ride. It helps me forget to dread the hours I've promised to you this afternoon.

"Hey, when do you guys find out about your colleges?" Gideon asks.

"Next month," Nat says. "Except Grace didn't apply to the one school she really wants to go to."

I shoot her a glare. "It's too expensive."

"That's a bunch of malarkey," Nat says.

Gideon laughs. "Oh man, I need to add that one to my vocab. Takin' it way back."

She sticks her tongue out at him.

"What she means," Lys says, giving me the stink eye, "is that's total and complete bullshit." She turns to Gideon. "Did you know Grace's number one school was NYU but she didn't apply because her psycho boyfriend told her she couldn't?"

My face warms as Gideon looks at me. "It's more complicated than that," I mumble. "And I object to the word *psycho*."

The bell rings before anyone can give me more shit for not applying to NYU. Gideon and I walk together, since our sixth-period classes are across the hall from each other. He's uncharacteristically quiet. I know he's working through something—he's got that little furrow between his brows. It's not hard to guess what he's thinking about. Goddamn Natalie and Alyssa.

We get to our classes and I start to move toward mine.

"Okay. Um. See you later," I say.

But Gideon's not having that. He reaches out and pulls me into a hug. I go stiff, as if you could see us from wherever you are. What if Peter sees and, like, sends you video of it? I'll be in so much trouble. I try to pull away, but Gideon holds on a little tighter.

"You might think you have to follow your boyfriend's rules," he says, his lips against my hair, "but I don't have to."

I've told him all about you—not *everything*—not about backseats and how you know just where to touch me to make me gasp—but Gideon knows about your rules. He knows because I've had to explain why I can't study at his house, or why I dodge his hugs or can't talk to him on the phone. I think he's told me to break up with you approximately five thousand times.

"You're gonna get me in trouble," I mumble against his shirt. But I melt against him.

We fit perfectly together.

He's so tall and skinny. Smells so different from you—instead of the rock-god scent of cigarettes and rare showers, he smells like soap and incense. Clean, full of possibility.

He tightens his hold on me for a second before letting go.

"You know what I'm gonna say right now, don't you?" he asks, pushing up his tortoiseshell glasses as he walks backward toward his class. Somehow he doesn't knock into anyone—it must be all the meditation he does. He's a total Zen master.

"Don't say it." But I'm smiling a little because I sort of like to hear it.

He mouths the words *Break up with him*, then looks at me for a couple of heartbeats before he turns and heads into his class.

For the next two periods I don't think about NYU. I've made my peace with that.

I think about God. About how he/she might be so much bigger than I imagined. How maybe if I thought about God differently, I could think about you differently, too. I could go back to being the real Grace. Before you, I craved city lights and airplanes that went to exotic places. Before you, a reel played through my head constantly, a movie of me doing epic things: studying in NYC, traveling to Africa to help orphans, walking down red carpets, marrying a hot French guy and moving to Paris. But after you, my world has been whittled down to your hands, your lips, the sound of your voice singing songs you've written for me.

And this scares me, what I've become by being with you: my *no*s turned to *yes*es, my *never*s to *maybe*s. In the almost year we've been officially together, I've somehow morphed into my mother. I walk on eggshells, glass, coals—all to keep you happy.

Gideon asks me: *What are you so afraid of?*

He asks: *What would happen if . . . ?*

He says: *You deserve better.*

Do I? I don't even know anymore.

THIRTY

I know something's wrong as soon as you pick me up. Just a sixth-sense thing. But when I jump into the car and press my lips against yours, you kiss me back. You ask me how my day is. You almost trick me, but I can tell something's off.

"You okay?" I ask as you pull away from school and head to the park. Even though it's only the middle of March, it's already getting warm, so we've decided to have a picnic before I have tech rehearsal at six.

"Yeah, fine," you say.

But your hands tighten on the steering wheel, your knuckles white. I don't want to fight today. We haven't seen much of each other since I got back from Oregon. Your band is playing lots of shows and I hardly have any free time, now that rehearsals are taking over my life. There's distance between us, a widening crack, and I don't know what to do. You've started partying—a lot. You want me to be a rocker's girlfriend who smokes out with the band and gets drunk and gives you blowjobs in the dirty bathroom of whatever club you're playing at. Having a girl-friend with a curfew is a buzzkill, I get that. But whether you realize it or not, you blame me for being in high school, as if I have any choice in the matter. I can't be in your world right now, no matter how hard I try.

You park and we grab the blanket and food you brought, then head over to a secluded patch of grass under an oak tree. We kick off our shoes and I go through the grocery bag as I sit down.

"Nice job," I say, holding up a pack of Oreos.

You nod, picking at the grass. I set the cookies down.

"Gav. What's going on? There's obviously something wrong."

You sit there for a minute, quiet, and I think you're not going to get into it when you suddenly explode.

"I saw you. Yesterday. You were talking to some guy and he put his fucking arm around you."

Gideon's been slowly breaking down the wall I've built between me and every guy I know. I remember that half hug because I was sad when it was over.

"What do you mean you saw me yesterday? Were you on campus?"

A knot of worry grows in my stomach. I still haven't forgotten that day you secretly watched me at the mall. It's made me paranoid at work, especially when Matt and I have the same shift. But how are you watching me at school? It was during *lunch*.

"I just wanted to see how you were with other people when you're not with me," you say.

"You were *spying* on me?"

"No. I mean, I was gonna take you out later, but after I saw that guy all over you I was like, fuck it. Who is he?"

"Just Gideon—he's in the show." I sigh. "Honestly? I think it's a stupid rule. I have friends that are guys. You have friends that are girls. I don't see what the big deal is."

"The big deal is that I don't want other guys trying to get down my girlfriend's pants." You grab my hand. "You're mine. I don't want to share you."

I pull my hand away. "Gav, it's just not realistic."

You raise your voice and a couple of moms over by the playground look over at us. "I put up with so much shit and you can't even do this one thing for me? You have no idea what this does to me. No idea. I can't sleep at night, okay? All I can think about is you, surrounded by all these guys at lunch, at rehearsal, at the mall."

I decide right then: I'm breaking up with you. I am so fucking over this bullshit. I want to be with Gideon. I have to stop lying to myself, to you. I don't care how much we've been through, what we've given up to be together. Nat and Lys are right—you are controlling. And it's only going to get worse. I will not turn into my mom. I will *not*.

I brush invisible crumbs off my skirt. I need to channel Lady Macbeth. *Screw your courage to the sticking-place.*

"Gavin . . ." I swallow. "Gavin, I think . . . I think we should—"

But you don't let me finish because you know what I'm trying to do, don't you?

"If you break up with me, I swear to God I'll kill myself."

My mind just . . . freezes.

Kill.

Myself.

How could I have once thought trying to kill yourself was beautifully tragic? I saw you as the spurned lover, the ultimate romantic. God, what was I thinking?

The freeze breaks and suddenly I'm angry. Fuck you for telling me this, for putting a gun to your head and telling me it's my finger on the trigger.

"No you won't. You won't kill yourself." I whisper these words, as if saying them more quietly will calm the sharp-beaked thing inside you.

"Yes. I will." You say this slowly, as if you're talking to a child, as if me still being in high school and you being in college automatically makes you the mature one. This is your Calm Boyfriend voice. I hate it.

"I've thought about it," you say. "I have a plan." You look at me. "You know I'll go through with it."

"Jesus fuck, Gavin."

"Do you want to know how I'd do it?"

"*No.*" Then I lose it, anger trumping fear. I'm shouting and the sound of my voice punches the air and I don't care that we're in a park and that people are staring at me. "What the hell is wrong with you?"

"Do you think I like being like this?"

You turn away, but not before I see tears sliding down your cheeks. I want the anger to stay, but it's going . . . going . . .

I can't stand seeing you in pain. You cry messy tears and you're breaking right in front of me and I did this, *I did this*. I reach up and put my arms around you and you wrap yours around me and this is how it's supposed to be, this is where I belong, in the circle of your arms.

"I love you, I love you," I whisper.

How many times have you been my protector? How many times have you talked me off the ledge? I can't abandon you now.

You press your lips against mine and they're salty with tears and I breathe you in and the smell of you whisks me away from that lonely shore and back to you.

"I love you more than anything," you say.

I think about you in that bathtub. The razor, the blood . . .

I pull away. "Gav, you need help," I say. "Let's talk to someone. Miss B or your mom or—"

"I don't need *help*. I need *you*."

"If you won't talk to someone, I will," I say.

"What, you'll tell your school counselor your boyfriend is crazy—"

"I don't think you're crazy," I say. "I think you're depressed and—"

"Because of *you*, because you let these guys all over you—"

I stand up then. Fuck it. *Fuck*. *It*. "You know what, Gavin? I am so fucking tired of this stupid jealousy. I haven't cheated on you, but if you can't stop treating me like I have a fucking scarlet letter on my chest, then that's a pretty good sign that we shouldn't be together." The words fall out of my mouth. I want to vomit them all over you. "And telling me that I'm basically responsible for whether you live or die is fucked-up and I don't deserve that shit."

You stand up, just inches away from me. "I wasn't lying, Grace. That's how much you mean to me. You're not just some girl I fuck once a week, you're my *life*."

I turn away as frustrated tears pool in my eyes. Why can't you trust me? Why can't we be happy? Why can't I stop thinking of Gideon?

"This stuff," I say, my voice soft, "is pushing me away from you, Gav. I need space. I need to breathe."

"What does that mean?"

I look at you. It's hard being angry at the most beautiful boy I've ever seen. But not impossible.

"It means I don't want you spying on me or freaking out if I hug one of my guy friends. And . . . you need to get help. Like, real help. Meds. Something."

"I don't need fucking meds."

"Yes. You do. Last year you were in the hospital. And now you're threatening to do it again?" I step forward, lean my forehead against yours. "Please, baby. I'll go with you if you want."

We stay like that, holding each other, your breath against my neck, your heart beating against my chest. The thought of you not being alive hurts, makes it hard to breathe. You're the only person in the world who would rather be dead than not be with me. Nobody loves me like that. If I were in a burning car that was about to blow up, you're the only one who'd try to save me, the only person who would risk their life to save mine. I have absolutely no doubt that my parents wouldn't go near the car—they'd come up with excuses and tell themselves they couldn't have saved me anyway. And my friends, Beth—they'd want to save me but would be too afraid of dying in the process. But you. You wouldn't think twice, would you?

"I'm sorry," I whisper.

"I'm sorry, too."

I kiss your chin, your neck, your earlobe. Breathe you in.

"Did you really mean it?" I ask softly.

"Yeah, I think I did."

You're a maze, all high hedges and endless loops. I can't find a way out, can't see where I've been. It's all running, lost in the dark of you. Trapped. Everywhere I turn is a dead end. I keep winding up back where I've started.

I GO TO rehearsal after we leave the park. For the first time since working on a show, I have no desire to be there. I just want to curl up and make all this confusion go away. I want to not fall for Gideon. I want to not be thinking of breaking up with the guy I've considered my soul mate for the past year.

I push open the door to the theater's lobby. Cast members are milling around, running lines, practicing sword fights. I wave back at the calls of *hello* and go into the theater itself. Miss B is standing on the stage, shading her eyes.

"Grace, is that you?"

"Yep," I call.

"Can you go in the greenroom and get everyone who's in there onstage?"

I throw my stuff down on a chair and head backstage. Lys, Nat, and Gideon look up from something they're watching on a phone as I poke my head in. I can't look any of them in the eye. Especially Gideon. If I do, I'll start crying, I know it.

"Hey, guys. Miss B wants you onstage."

I leave before they can grab me.

"Grace!" Nat's in the doorway, looking at me, frowning in concern. "You okay?"

"Yep. Totally."

"Liar," she calls.

I give her a backward wave and head to the front row so I can get my clipboard and notepad. I jump onstage and Miss B starts listing things she needs done. I jot everything down as she walks around the stage, inspecting the set.

"We have to call the designer. This door won't shut properly," she says.

I see Gideon out of the corner of my eye. He's talking to Kyle, his eyes flicking toward me every now and then. Lys pulls me aside before the run-through starts.

"Dude, what's up?" she asks.

"Nothing."

"Bitch, please." She crosses her arms. "I know you."

I sigh. "I'll tell you tonight. We still on for a sleepover at your place?"

"Of course."

I'm packing up my stuff after rehearsal when Gideon drops down onto the chair next to mine.

"Want to talk about it?" he asks, psychic as usual. He's scarily good at reading my moods.

"Nope."

He studies me for a minute. "Fair enough. You coming tonight?"

Gideon's parents are out of town and he's having the cast and crew over. I've been debating all week about whether or not to go.

"I'm staying at Lys's, so it's her call."

We go, of course we do. On the way to his house I tell Nat and Lys everything.

"What the motherfucking fuck?" Lys says from the backseat.

"Not how I would put it," Nat says, "but I agree with the sentiment."

"You have to break up with him," Lys says. "I bet this is the shit he pulled with Summer."

"Yeah," I say, "and he *almost died*."

The car goes quiet.

"He can't put this on you," Nat says. "It's not fair."

"In my professional opinion," Lys says, "I say he's codependent with narcissistic tendencies and major depression. I'm pretty sure that's a fair diagnosis. This has nothing to do with you. He's gotta work through this shit on his own."

"Do you want to break up with him?" Nat asks.

I throw up my hands. "I don't know. I mean, I really *really* don't know. I love him, but . . ."

"But . . . ," Lys says.

"Gideon," Nat finishes quietly.

I hesitate, then nod. "Yeah. Gideon."

Nat pulls up to Gideon's house and shuts off the car.

"I think that was smart—about telling him to gets meds and stuff," Lys says.

"I mean, maybe that's all it is," I say. "A . . . what do you call it?"

"Chemical imbalance," Lys says.

"Yeah, that. Maybe he'll get meds and be the Gavin we all know and love."

"Maybe we never really knew him," Nat says. "Maybe *this* is the real Gavin."

Someone knocks on the window and we jump. Peter and Kyle are waving us inside.

"Hey," I say, putting my hand on Nat's arm. "Don't tell Kyle about this, okay?"

"I would never," she says. "He's my boyfriend but you guys always come first."

When she jumps out of the car, he picks her up and spins in a circle. She throws back her head and laughs, carefree and happy. I swallow the sudden lump in my throat.

Gideon's house is just like I imagined it would be. There's a Buddha statue in one corner and the whole place smells like incense. There's a small room off to the side of the entryway with meditation cushions and a yoga mat. Masks from all over the world hang on the walls along with pictures of him and his parents from their travels. There they are in front of the Taj Mahal, the Great Wall of China.

"You made it!" Gideon says. He has a bottle of vodka in one hand and a bottle of gin in the other, but he wraps his arms around me anyway. I don't push him away.

When he lets go, I turn to Lys. "I think this is the night."

"The . . . *Oh*." Her eyes go to the bottles in Gideon's hands. "*The* night."

I'd promised Lys that I would have my first drink with her. I want to have fun. I want to forget you. I want to do something that's just for me.

Nat shakes her head. "I don't know, Grace. Maybe you should wait until you're not, you know . . ."

"I'm fine," I say. "I want to. I'm eighteen, we're graduating soon. I need to be, I don't know, inducted or something."

"You're all speaking Girl," Gideon says. "I have absolutely no idea what you're talking about."

"You'll see," Lys says, grabbing my hand. "Direct us to where adult beverages can be found."

"Come, fair ladies." Gideon leads us through the living room, which opens up onto the kitchen.

As soon as we walk farther inside, we're greeted by cast members, all in various stages of tipsy. The main room is airy and bright, with a large Persian rug in the center and tapestries from India on the walls. Comfy couches in earth tones make an L shape, and a stack of art and travel books are in the center of the large coffee table. Two cats lie curled up beneath it, eyeing the room with suspicion.

When we get to the counter where all the drinks are, Lys scans the bottles, then grabs orange juice and the vodka in Gideon's hand.

"I'm making you a screwdriver," she says.

Nat looks at the vodka and wrinkles her nose. "That sounds dangerous."

"It's just vodka and orange juice," Gideon says. He glances at me. "You've never had one before?"

"She's never had *anything* before." Nat grabs a Sprite. "I'll stick to this."

Gideon leans against the counter, his arms crossed. "Is this really your first drink?"

I nod. "The very first."

"Okay, wait," he says to Lys. "We can't let her drink that shit."

He opens the fridge and pulls out a tiny bottle of champagne, then gets a champagne flute from the cupboard.

"Won't your parents realize that's missing?" I ask.

He waves his hand, then opens the bottle. "There are, like, ten in there."

Gideon pours champagne into the glass, then hands it to me. His fingers brush mine and his touch is electric.

I'll kill myself if you break up with me.

I take a sip. It's delicious and cold and wonderfully bubbly. Liquid gold. I feel warm inside almost immediately. I take another, bigger sip.

"Well?" Nat says.

"A perfect first drink," I say.

Gideon grins. "Success!" Someone calls him over and he hands me the bottle. "Be right back."

"Oh my god," Nat says as soon as he's out of earshot. "How freaking cute is he?"

Pretty cute, I have to admit.

"Consider yourself off matchmaking duty for the night," I say to her. "Seriously. I just want to hang with my girls and get tipsy. No more boy talk. Please."

They hug me so that I'm sandwiched between them and I am so in love with my best friends. Maybe I was wrong. Maybe they'd try to rescue me from a burning car, too.

And then I realize: *you're* the burning car.

I finish my glass of champagne, then grab both of their hands and pull them into the backyard. It's quiet here—everyone is inside doing dance party karaoke stuff, which is good because I might just fall apart and I don't want an audience for that. Gideon doesn't have a pool—he has a Zen rock garden, a swirl of white and gray stones, and I'm momentarily distracted by the moonlight bouncing off the rocks.

"Wow," I say.

"Now I get why he's so . . . Gideon," Lys says. "I'd be a fucking Zen master, too, if I had this shit in my backyard."

Nat doesn't care about the rock garden. She's the only one out of the three of us who realizes I'm shaking.

"Grace." She holds on to my hand, tight.

I lose it then. Messy tears and sobbing and I don't want to be with you anymore, Gavin, I don't I'm sorry and I love you but I can't do this anymore I can't can't I hate my life and I want everything to just stop, why won't it just stop?

"That motherfucking *bastard*," Lys says. "Look what he's *done* to her."

I can't stop crying and I cling to Nat while Lys paces back and forth.

"You can't stay with him," Lys says.

"You know he'll do it," I say. "He's not fucking around."

"Then let him," she snaps.

"*Lys,*" Nat growls. "Not. Helpful."

"I still love him," I say as my sobs die down.

"But you don't want to be with him anymore, sweetie," Nat says. "That's okay. People grow apart. It just happens, you know? Wanting to break up with him doesn't make you a bad person."

I shrug. "I don't know. If he wasn't so . . . And Gideon . . . I don't fucking know."

The sliding door opens and Nat turns, still holding on to me.

"Hey, Gideon," she says. "Sorry. Girl emergency."

"Is she okay?"

"No," Lys says flatly.

I turn to him, wiping my eyes. "Sorry. I'm fine. I mean, I'll be fine."

"Anything I can do?" he asks, handing me another glass of champagne. "Other than keep the bubbly flowing, of course."

I take the glass, grateful. "This is perfect."

He smiles. "Okay. I'm going back inside. But if you need an assassin or code breaker or Jedi Knight, you know where to find me."

I laugh. "Okay."

He goes and when he's gone, Lys glances at me. "Girl. You can bag you a Jedi *Knight*. This is a no-brainer."

I down the glass of champagne in one go and set it down.

"Whoa now," Nat says.

"What are you gonna do?" Lys asks.

I feel calmer now and I decide I like champagne.

"Make sure he gets on meds," I say. "And I'll see if that changes anything."

"And if it doesn't?" Nat asks.

I swallow. "Then . . . I'll break up with him."

I will, Gavin. Get your shit together because I swear to fucking God I will end us.

THIRTY-ONE

I'm on my hands and knees, cleaning the baseboards in the dining room. It's five-fifteen and you're going to be here at five-thirty.

It's a few days after the party at Gideon's, your birthday. Since it's a Tuesday, we don't have a show tonight, so I'm taking you out to the new Italian restaurant by your school. I tell myself that if you don't have meds by the end of the week, I'm breaking up with you. But I'm already thinking about extending the deadline. It's not right to kick someone when they're down. And it feels impossible when it's someone you love.

I try not to get my dress dirty as I spray all-purpose cleaner on the boards and then run a cloth over them. No dirt comes up on the cloth because *there is no fucking dirt there.*

Mom's new thing is that the whole house needs to be cleaned from top to bottom every day. Mopping and vacuuming and dusting and toilet cleaning and all that. Yesterday, there was some dried pasta sauce on the counter and she started screaming about the house being a pigsty. Between work and school and rehearsal and now this cleaning crusade, I am totally beat. When I saw you on Sunday after our matinee, I fell asleep halfway through the movie we were watching at your house. You covered me with a blanket and just held me for the longest time.

I really don't know how'd I'd get through all of this without you whisking me away or sneaking into my room at night, visiting me when I'm at work. When I call, you pick up on the first ring. You're the first person I go to when things get ridiculous and hard at home. You have been my lifeline and now it's time I'm yours. I've promised myself that I'm going to stop falling out of love with you. I'm going to fall back *in* love with you because if I don't you will kill yourself. I know you will. I don't want to be selfish. Or rash. I want to do right by us. You deserve that—we both do.

I won't let my mind wander to Gideon. Every time it does I feel guilty. I love you and we have been through so much together. You've had a lot of shit to put up with—my family, my schedule, me still being in high school. How could I let you go, after everything you've done for me? How can I break up with you right when you need me the most? So I force Gideon to the back of my mind. Again and again.

When I'm done I straighten up.

"Mom?" I call. "They're clean."

I hear her come down the hallway, Sam not far behind. She has dark circles under her eyes and her hair dye is fading. I can see strands of gray in her ponytail. It's weird seeing my mom looking anything less than perfect. She's practically religious about her hair and nails. She leans down and inspects the baseboards.

"You missed a spot," she says, pointing to a little smudge on the wall above the baseboard.

I lean down and rub the rag over it, two seconds away from losing it. I think of you and our date and how much I need to get out of here.

But then she stands and shakes her head. "You should probably go over them one more time," she says.

I can't help it. My eyes fill with tears.

"Mom, *please*. Gavin is gonna be here any minute; we have a date—"

"The sooner you get to working, the sooner you'll be finished."

"But we have reservations—"

"WHAT DID I SAY?"

Her whole face is suddenly contorted with rage and I can't help it, I give in and say everything I've been wanting to for the past few months.

"This entire house is clean, Mom, *perfectly clean*. And I am tired, *exhausted*, and I can't do this anymore. I can't. There's something *wrong* with you—"

She raises her hand and slaps me, hard. I stumble into the entryway, staring at her in shock, my hand against my burning cheek. She grabs my shoulders, shaking me so hard I bite my tongue.

"Why is it always a fight with you?" she screams.

I see movement in the corner of my eye and you're there, standing in front of the screen. My mom opened the door earlier today because the weather was so good. I look back at her, panicked. Mortified.

"Mom. *Mom*. Gavin's—"

"You bitch," she screams at me. She raises her hand and I hear the screen door open.

"Hey!" you say, but you can't stop the slap, this one so intense my head knocks against the wall behind me.

"What the fuck?" You're shouting now. I've never seen you so angry.

You grab me and pull me behind you. I'm sobbing and I can't stop and my head is pounding and my cheek hurts and I love you so much, Gavin, I love you so much for wanting to save me.

"What the *fuck*?" you yell again.

I can feel you shaking, pure fury rolling off you, and I'm so grateful to you, to finally have someone stick up for me.

My mom looks at you and there are no words.

"If you ever, *ever* do that again, I am calling the fucking police," you say. "I should call them right now."

Mom blinks, as if she's coming out of a trance. "Gavin, you need to leave," she says.

"Gladly." You grab my hand and push the screen door open. I'm crying so hard I can barely breathe as sob after sob comes out of me.

"Where do you think you're going, Grace?"

I turn around and look at her and I can't believe that after this I have to stay home.

"She's coming with me," you say.

I look at you, shaking my head. I don't even want to know how much trouble I'll be in if I leave.

"Grace Marie Carter, you get your butt back in—"

You ignore Mom and take my face in your hands and you are quiet and gentle.

"Baby, you're coming with me. I'm not leaving you here when she's like this."

"But if I go, I'll be in so much—"

"We'll deal with that later. Come on. I'm gonna take you to my place."

I cry even harder. "The restaurant . . ."

"It's okay. We'll go some other time."

My mom slams the door shut and you lead me to your car. I stumble, my eyes blurry, and realize I'm not wearing shoes. You get me into the car and then we're gone, heading toward your house.

"I'm sorry," I sob. "I'm so sorry—"

You pull over to the side of the road and unbuckle your seat belt.

"Come here," you say.

I fall into your arms, soaking your shirt in seconds. You wore a tie and that makes me cry even harder. You rub my back and it's only when I start calming down that I hear you softly singing my favorite song, "California Dreamin'."

I pull away and try to rub the tears off my face.

"I must look horrible," I say.

I hiccup then and you reach over and smooth my hair.

"You're perfect." You put your seat belt back on and soon we're pulling up to your house. Both of your parents' cars are here.

"Gav, I don't want them to see—"

You firmly grip my hand. "They can help," you say.

I follow you into the house and your parents turn away from the TV when the door opens.

"Did you forget something, hon?" your mom asks.

You shake your head and pull me closer. Just seeing the shock on your mom's face sends me back into tears. You explain what happened while your mom pulls me into a hug.

"Oh, honey," she says. "It's okay. It's gonna be okay."

She leads me to the kitchen and grabs a bag of peas out of the freezer.

"Put this on that bump on your head and I'll go get you some Advil."

You sit down next to me and when I raise the peas to the place where my head smacked against the wall you take the bag from me.

"I've got it," you say.

Your dad is pacing the living room. He stops and turns to me. "I think we should talk to your parents," he says. "Let them know that they'll be held accountable for their actions."

I shake my head. "Thank you so much, Mark. Really. But I think that will just make everything worse."

"She can't do something like that and get away with it," you say.

I rest a hand on your knee. "It's okay."

You reposition the peas and wrap one arm around my waist, pulling me to you so that I'm sitting on your lap.

Your mom comes in with the Advil and gets me a glass of water.

"I don't understand," your mom says. "What was it that set her off?"

I tell them about the cleaning and your mom frowns.

"Your mother should go see someone. Is she on medication?"

I shake my head. "No. She doesn't have health insurance. I mean, we don't, like, talk about this. It just . . . is what it is."

A buzzer goes off. "That's the laundry," she says. "I'll be right back."

"I don't want you to go back there," you murmur. "You're eighteen—you don't have to stay."

I lean my forehead against yours. "And where would I go?"

"Here." Your mouth turns up. "I'm sure I could squeeze you into my bed."

Your dad hits the back of your head with a newspaper and you smile.

"I need to go splash my face with some water," I say, slipping off your lap. "I'll be right back."

When I get to the bathroom and see my face in the mirror, I'm surprised you didn't fall out of love with me. My nose is bright red, cheeks splotchy and still stinging from those slaps. Red-rimmed eyes with mascara running down both my cheeks. Hair a frizzy mess. I grab some soap and scrub my face, then put my hair into a ponytail. When I go back out, it's just you waiting for me in the kitchen.

"Come on." You take my hand and lead me to your bedroom.

We lie down, two spoons curved against each other, and you hold me while I try to make sense of everything.

"Has stuff like this happened before?"

I sigh. "Not like this. I've been slapped before, but not that hard. But the way she was shaking me . . ."

I grip your hands, happy to have this Gavin tonight. You're protective and sweet and I love you for everything you said and did. Why can't you be this Gavin all the time? I feel horrible for crushing on Gideon. I don't deserve you. Maybe I never did.

I turn around so that I can look into your eyes.

"I ruined your birthday," I say, my voice cracking.

"No you didn't. Baby, come here." You wrap your arms around me. "This has been the best year of my life, being with you. All this shit with your parents will be over once you graduate."

I think about how many times you've been there for me when I'm dealing with stuff at home. All the late-night phone calls and songs and little presents. You, climbing through my window, taking me on adventures. I don't know how I would have survived my mom and The Giant this year without you.

"Hey, I have something that might make you happy." You open the drawer in your bedside table and take out a bottle of pills. You shake it in front of me. "Meds. For depression. You were right."

I lean forward and kiss you. This, this right here is why I can't give up on us. Gideon is probably just a silly little crush. How could I possibly kill what we have for something that probably wouldn't last anyway?

"I'll never let anyone hurt you again," you murmur against my lips.

Safe. For the first time in a long time I feel safe with you.

"I'm sorry," I say, my eyes welling up.

"For what?"

"I don't know. Everything."

Gideon. My parents. Not having faith in you.

You press your lips against my forehead.

"It's all right now," you say. "Everything's gonna be all right."

I wish I could believe you.

I GET HOME before my curfew. I left my phone at home so I have no idea if my mom's been trying to call me. I don't even have my keys. I try the front door—locked.

Fuck.

I ring the doorbell, hoping it doesn't wake Sam up. About a minute later, my mom opens the door. Her hair is wet and she's in her bathrobe. I feel nervous and defiant and tired. So tired. But I've mentally prepared myself for this fight. If she wants to have it, I'll go out swinging.

"Sit down," she says, pointing to the dining room table.

I'm scared. I try to remind myself that I'm eighteen, that they can't control me like they used to. I could walk out right now and there's not a thing they could do about it. *Courage, dear heart.*

The Giant's already there, a vodka tonic in hand. I pull out a chair and fall into it and I'm literally shaking because there's something very final about the way he's looking at me and my mom won't meet my eyes.

"I want you out of here," The Giant says.

"I don't under—"

"The last day you live under my roof is graduation. Then you're gone."

I stare at him. "But . . . where will I go? I don't start school until *August*. I don't even know where I'm going to school."

"Not my problem," he says.

I look at Mom. "Is this for real?"

She just looks at me.

"I didn't do anything *wrong*," I yell.

"Keep your voice down," she growls. "If you wake up your brother, you're the one who has to be up with him all night. I just got him down."

"This is insane," I say. "*You're* insane. The baseboards were clean, I had a date—"

"She told you to come back," The Giant says.

"You weren't even here," I say. "You don't know what happened."

"Did your mother tell you to come back inside?"

"Yes, but she was slapping me, and Gavin—"

"Did you go back inside?"

"No," I say, soft.

"Then this is on you," The Giant says.

I stand up, fast, and all the anger that's been in me ever since we moved here comes pouring out, shaping itself into words.

"I DIDN'T DO ANYTHING WRONG."

The Giant raises his hand. It's inches from my face, ready to slap me. Mom lets out an inarticulate cry, but for once I'm not scared. This time, I *want* him to hit me. I want to call this giant's bluff.

"Go ahead," I say, gripping the edge of the table. I smile, tilt my chin so my cheek is in prime slapping position. "Hit me. I'd love it if you did."

Because then I could call the police. I could tell the school. *He'd* be the one in trouble for a change.

We stare at each other. His eyes are a watery brown—diarrhea, dirt. His lip curls into a sneer, more comic villain than true terror.

"You're grounded," he says.

I throw back my head and laugh and laugh.

All this time I never realized: he isn't a giant at all. *Roy* is just a man with one trick up his sleeve.

And it's played out.

THIRTY-TWO

For the first time in days I feel happy. Natalie told me this morning that she talked to her mom and I get to come live with her this summer. Nat's mom didn't blink an eye when she asked if I could stay. *Of course*, she said, as if it hadn't even been necessary to ask. There is no yelling in Nat's house, no demands, no strings. Just a lot of love and good food and laughter. I can't wait.

"I love how The Giant's plan totally backfired," Lys says. She does a fake karate kick and slices her arm in the air. "Take that, bitch."

Nat grins. "Score one for Grace."

I'm almost glad things went down like they did. I feel like I have this enormous weight off my shoulders. All day I go through my classes in a daze. The countdown begins. Two and a half months until graduation.

It's the end of the school day and I'm loading up on books from my locker when a paper triangle falls to the ground—thick and folded with care. A letter from Gideon. The paper burns my fingers and all I want to do is read it, but I can't keep you waiting. I tuck it into my jacket pocket, then think better of that—what if it falls out? What if you find it? I should throw it away, not read it because he's not my boy-friend, but I bury the letter in the middle of my French book, then shove that into my backpack.

Not that I have anything to hide.

Gideon and I are just friends. We *are*. I love you and I have to keep telling myself that we're gonna be okay. You have meds now; I'm grad-uating soon. The rest of our lives is about to start. It's starting already. You saved me from my mom. I was in a burning car and you jumped in and pulled me out. Not Gideon—*you*.

I head out to the front, where you're waiting, and that letter seems to send out shock waves from inside my backpack. I hurry, and a part of me knows it's not because I'm anxious to see you—it's because I don't want to see the look on Gideon's face when you kiss me hello. I get into the car, quick. Slam the door shut. I hate my fickle fucking heart.

"Let's get out of here," I say.

You lean in.

I lean in.

You taste like cigarettes and I pull away.

"What?" you say, narrowing your eyes.

Can you see it? See my desperation to go, go, go?

"Gavin—you taste like a freaking ashtray."

"I never heard you complain about it before," you say.

"Well, now you have." My voice is testy.

"What's with the bitchiness?" you say.

I shrug. "Bad day. Sorry."

You pull out of the parking lot and turn away from your house, toward the university. There's a coffeehouse near there that you take me to sometimes. It makes me feel grown up, ordering a latte and hang-ing around the college kids. This will be me in just a few months.

After about fifteen minutes of driving, you pull into an apartment complex near your school. My heart sinks. The last thing I want to do is hang out with your friends. I always feel like a kid around them, like me being in high school is so lame.

"Gav, I thought we were hanging out. Just us two."

You grin. "We are."

You park, then jump out of the car and run around to the other side to help me out, ever the gallant gentleman.

"This," you say, taking in the apartment building with a sweep of your hand, "is our new home."

"YOU GOT AN apartment?" I say.

You're so happy right now. You're practically bouncing.

"I'm just subletting from a friend of mine from school. He's studying abroad and the guy who was supposed to be living here fell through. I'll have it until the end of the summer. Come on."

You reach for my hand and I follow you up to the second floor. It's a new complex, with peach stucco walls and balconies where people stash their grills or small patio furniture. Someone's blasting pop radio and somewhere a kid is throwing a tantrum, but otherwise it's quiet. I don't see anyone else.

"There's a pool, too," you say. "I thought we could have people over when it starts getting hot."

I smile and nod and why do you keep saying *we*? You open the door and step aside.

"Welcome home."

It's a small one-bedroom with bare walls, the living room littered with guitars and take-out containers and half-unpacked suitcases.

"Yeah, the guy who lives here never got around to decorating," you say, watching me as I check the place out. "And I promise I'll try not to leave my shit everywhere."

You take my hand and lead me farther into the apartment, stopping at a closed door at the end of the hall.

"And this," you say, gently pushing it open, "is our bedroom."

Our.

The only thing in the room other than piles of clothes on the floor is a double bed with a striped comforter.

"I've never seen you make a bed before" is all I can say.

You laugh, soft, and wrap your arms around my waist, rest your chin on my shoulder.

"I wanted it to be nice for you."

Sex.

It's the last thing I want, but how could I possibly say that to my boyfriend who I've been with for almost a year?

You lead me to the bed and gently lay me down. I'm trembling, as if we've never done this before and it feels like that, like that sharp pain is going to radiate through me all over again.

You're gentle today, excruciatingly slow. I kiss you harder, try to hurry things up, but you just laugh softly against my lips and murmur, "Patience, Grasshopper."

You tug at my jeans and slide them down my thighs, my knees. Next is my shirt, the one Gideon said made me look like a naughty librarian.

Gideon.

I close my eyes and try to forget him, but closing them just makes him more real and suddenly I know how I can get through this.

Your tongue slips into my mouth, but it's not yours anymore, it's Gideon's, and I pretend I don't taste cigarettes and coffee. It gets easier as your mouth moves down my neck, as your hands slide all over me, expert in my anatomy.

I bite my lip as you press against me and I want you—not you, Gideon—I want the you that is Gideon and this is wrong, I know it is, but I can't do this any other way.

You reach across me and grab a condom and you take my hand to help you slide it on and I watch as you close your eyes and lean back your head and I forget about Gideon. Screw you for being beautiful.

I keep my eyes open now and pull you closer and we are a storm that tears through the room and I hold on to you because otherwise I'll fly apart and your hands and your lips and don't stop, don't stop.

You collapse on top of me, our sweat mixing.

My stomach hurts all over again and I slip out from under you. You pull me close, my bare back against your bare chest and we lie there, huddled against each other. I'm so mixed up. First I'm imagining you're Gideon, which is wrong and pervy, and then I'm wanting you, and now I just feel sick.

You'll get me in trouble, I say to Gideon.

You'll be given love, Björk sings, *you just have to trust it.*

I slip away from you, mumbling about taking a shower. You watch me walk away, grinning.

"You sure are pretty," you say in a Southern drawl.

I stand in the shower, hot water stinging my skin. I try to wash you off as best I can. But soap doesn't work for everything. I don't know how to explain to you—even to myself—why being here feels so wrong. It's almost like stranger danger or something.

I'm not supposed to be here. Not now. Not yet.

I am filled with a fierce longing for Natalie and Alyssa and Gideon. I want to be at rehearsal and talking about how dumb it is that we still have to take the Presidential Fitness Test, running a mile because the government says we have to. I want to be laughing about the ridiculous dress code, how Alyssa got sent home because her tank top straps were one and a half inches wide instead of the required two or more inches.

Why can't I just be honest with you? Why can't I just let you go, stop all this misery? If I feel this bad, we have to be over.

But I can't do it. I grab the skin on the inside of my arm and pinch it, hard.

You stupid fucking idiot girl. I hate you. You're just staying with him because you're a coward, a whore who's too scared to be alone. Fuck you, Grace. Fuck. You.

282

I wish I could explain to myself why I'm such a pushover, why I'm so goddamn weak and spineless. You're on meds. Maybe you'd be okay if we broke up. It's a simple exercise: *Let's break up. I'm breaking up with you. We are not together anymore. I love someone else.*

But my mouth goes dry; my heart stops. I don't know if my body is telling me not to do it or if I'm just too much of a coward to say what needs to be said. The sad thing is, it's just easier to stay together. To not shake things up. To not shatter your heart.

I don't want to be a murderer. I don't want to be the girl who pushed you back into that bathtub. I am so messed up right now, it's not even funny. I can almost understand why Dad escapes with his drugs and those bottles of scotch. I want to be numb now, too.

I dry off and get dressed and you're waiting for me in the living room and you're holding a jewelry box with a ribbon wrapped around it.

"What's this?" I say.

You press it into my hand. "Why don't you find out?"

Inside is a brand-new shiny key.

You shove your hands into your pockets, your telltale nervous gesture. "I was hoping . . . Grace, I want you to move in. We could box up your stuff this weekend—"

"This *weekend*?"

You run your hands down my arms. "Baby, we have to get you out of that house. They already kicked you out for the summer. Are you seriously going to stay there until *June*? Your mom *beat* you—"

"She didn't *beat* me and also, Gav, I'm in *high school*."

"You're eighteen. Listen, I can drive you to school and pick you up. I'm sure Nat can give you rides to rehearsal and stuff. I can get more shifts at Guitar Center and instead of paying rent to The Giant, you can chip in here if you want. I've got it all figured out." You rest your lips against my forehead. "Move in with me."

I imagine waking up to you every morning. Cooking eggs for you in my pajamas. Making love without worrying about getting caught. Playing house. All it does is make me dizzy, like I'm on that horrible carnival ride that spins like a top and I need to get off, I need to get off *right now*.

I slide out of your arms. "I can't, Gav."

You stare at me, confused. "Yes, you can. Don't you see? You don't need permission from anyone. You won't get grounded or in trouble or any of it *ever again*. I made it so you're free. I told you I'd never let anyone hurt you and I meant it."

"I know," I say gently. "And I love you so much for protecting me. I do. But, Gav, I need to be a high schooler right now. I don't want to be the girl who ran away from home and lives with her boyfriend."

"Why not?"

I wrap my arms around myself, suddenly cold. "It would feel so . . . I don't know. I'd feel weird."

"Weird," you say, your voice flat. "I just got an apartment for us and made love to you in our bed and you feel *weird*."

"It's not *our*—"

"Yes it is!" you explode. "Everything I do is for you, don't you get that?"

See, that's the thing. You say these perfect lines—and you really mean them. It's not bullshit.

"I do get it," I say, quiet.

I am so bad at loving you.

"So you'd rather live with those fuckers and be their slave than be here, with me?"

You're angry. Furious.

"No, it's not like that," I say.

A year ago I thought I wanted a Serious Relationship. But I don't think I do anymore. I want sleepovers with my friends and drinking Gideon's champagne and random dance parties where I can get down with whoever I want.

But: *If you break up with me, I swear to God I'll kill myself.*

I rest my hand against your chest. I can feel every bit of your anger, your frustration.

"It's just really intense," I say softly.

You relax a little.

"Explain," you say, your voice surprisingly gentle.

"I just . . . Everything's happening so fast. I thought I'd never get to senior year and suddenly it's, like, *boom, real life*. You know?"

"Look, Grace, if you want to wait until you graduate, we can wait." You sigh. "It's been a year. I can wait a few more months."

"Actually . . . I'm moving in with Nat for the summer."

"What the *fuck*, Grace?"

"I'm sorry," I say. "I didn't know you got an apartment. Her mom said it was cool and—"

"So tell them you changed your mind."

Late nights with Nat and Lys watching movies, gorging on sugar, laughing so hard we can barely breathe.

"I need to think about it," I say.

You yank the key out of my hand and shove it into your pocket. "Fine."

"Gavin. Come *on*."

"You're going to be late," you say and you're walking out the door and I follow you down the stairs. Of course this is the one day I need to be at the theater by four.

We don't talk the whole way to the theater and when you screech to a stop in front of it, you barely look at me as I say good-bye.

I'm not worried. You'll text me, penitent. Maybe sneak into my bedroom after my mom and Roy are asleep. Or you'll be waiting outside tomorrow morning with doughnuts and coffee and kisses that make promises. I know you, Gavin. I know you think it's enough.

But it's not. Not anymore.

THIRTY-THREE

y mom and I are at Lucky Dragon Chinese, just the two of us. I can't remember the last time we did something like this. Ever since Roy decided to kick me out she's been acting weird. As in, she's being nice. And not yelling half as much. And giving me permission to go out and do stuff. It makes me sad. Why couldn't it have always been like this?

It's a Wednesday night, nothing special, but she had a friend watch Sam and left Roy a plate of leftovers. We're having dinner before I have to be at the theater.

Come on, she said, standing in the doorway of my bedroom. *We're having a girls' night.*

"I can't believe you're almost a high school graduate," she says as she bites into a spring roll. "A little over two months away."

Are we really going to just sit here and pretend that the slap night and me getting kicked out didn't happen?

"I know. It's kinda crazy."

I've been waiting so long for graduation that I'm kind of reeling, being so close to it. I wish we had the kind of relationship where I could talk to her about that, where she'd tell me about her anxiety when she was graduating from high school.

"When will you find out what schools you got into?" she asks.

"Any day now—they said by early April."

I've been obsessively checking my email, but so far I haven't heard a thing. You've already filled out the paperwork for UCLA, so we're waiting to hear back from them, too. It feels weird, continuing to go through with our LA plans when I don't even know if we'll make it through the summer.

I watch my mom out of the corner of my eye when she's not looking and I see—really see—what these years with Roy have cost her. Gray hairs, wrinkles, a permanent downturn of the mouth. I see some of myself in that weariness and it scares me. I think about how Roy doesn't discriminate between treating me like shit and treating her like shit. He's very even Steven about that. I imagine what it'd be like to be married to someone like him, to live my life flinching every time that person came near. I wonder if that would make me mean sometimes, if I'd be obsessed with invisible dust and forget what it was like to be young.

When I was little, Mom used to turn on the Supremes and sing along as she cleaned and she'd bake cookies in the middle of the night, just because. We'd eat them for breakfast. One time, when I was in sixth grade, she called me out of school to go ice-skating. She once spent an entire month sewing the perfect Snow White Halloween costume for me.

Somehow, in the past five years, that mom disappeared. Little by little, she floated away, a leaf on the breeze.

Now, the air between us is heavy: it's been too long since we've laughed together, talked. How do you relearn love?

"Thanks for this," I say, pointing to my dinner.

It's very rare to get a treat like this from my mom. Roy controls her money, so she never has the cash for extras like dinner out with her daughter. She nods, spearing a piece of tofu with one chopstick. She pops it into her mouth, swallows.

I laugh a little and she looks up. "What?" she says with a small half smile. "It's easier to use them this way."

I hold up my chopsticks. "Don't you remember *Karate Kid*?"

It was my go-to movie when I was little. I must have watched it at least three hundred times, no joke.

"That scene where he has to catch a fly with the chopsticks?"

I nod. "Yeah. You just need practice." I hold up my hands like Mr. Miyagi, the karate instructor. "Wax on," I say, making a circular motion with my right hand. "Wax off," I say, making the same motion with my left hand.

She laughs. "God, I used to have to put that movie on for you *every day*."

"I know." I pause. "We should watch it sometime. Together."

She smiles. "That'd be nice."

Neither of us says what we're thinking, but I bet it's the same thing: we will never get a chance to do that, will we? I can't imagine having a movie night with my mom under Roy's roof. But it's a nice thought, sitting beside her with a bowl of kettle corn between us.

"I'm sorry about the other day," she says, with difficulty. "Things . . . got out of hand. And I don't want you to move out. But . . . I don't have a lot of control," she says, "over . . . the situation. With your stepfather."

"It's okay. I'll have fun at Nat's."

Her mom's going to be away at a summer camp she works at until the end of August, so it'll be just me, Nat, and Lys. Funny how things work out. I get kicked to the curb and it results in what is probably going to be the best summer of my life.

"Plus," I add, because I can't resist a little dig, "she doesn't want me to pay rent. So I'll be able to buy some of the stuff I need for school."

"Oh." Mom nods, takes a sip of her iced tea. She looks unbearably sad. "That's . . . that's very nice of Linda."

We eat in silence for a bit. An old eighties power ballad comes on—the Police's "Every Breath You Take." For the first time, I actually hear the words.

"This song isn't romantic at all," I say. I've heard it a million times but I'm only just now getting it. "He's a total creepy stalker."

Every breath you take, every move you make . . . I'll be watching you.

Sound familiar, Gav?

I snort. "Gavin could have written this crap."

Mom raises her eyebrows. "I thought things were maybe not going well. . . ."

Then TALK to me about it! I want to scream. If there wasn't this wall between my mom and me, would you and I still be together? If I wasn't so desperate to escape my house, would I have let myself go on dates where I knew you'd probably treat me like shit, but that were still better than a night in with the stepfather from hell? Because sometimes—a lot of the time—you've been the lesser of two evils. That's not true love. Not even close to it.

I want the real deal.

"Yeah, not so much," I say. "He's—we're just growing apart, I think. He's not very nice."

"Honey . . ." Mom bites her lip, looks away. "Trust me, you don't want to be with someone who doesn't treat you well."

I nod. "I mean, honestly, I don't know that we'll stay together."

This semblance of closeness gives me such a warm, unexpectedly cozy feeling. I grab onto that. I want to make it last. So the floodgates open and all this stuff I haven't told her bursts out. I tell her as much as I can about you and me without admitting to sex and sneaking out and other rule breakage. I tell her you're suffocating me.

She takes a sip of her tea, then bursts into tears.

"Mom!" I reach over, put a hand on her arm.

"I'm sorry," she wails as she tries to hold in the sobs.

"Here," I say, handing her the little pack of tissues in my purse.

"Thanks, honey."

She wipes her eyes, blows her nose. For a minute, she looks like this little girl I saw in the mall last week who was lost. Lip trembling, eyes full of panic, she walked in a daze, trying not to cry. Then she sat down right where she was and sobbed. It was the saddest thing I'd seen in my life.

"Are you okay?" I ask.

She takes in a shuddering breath. "I'm just so sorry things have worked out this way." A wistful expression crosses her face. "Do you remember the purple house?"

Now I'm having trouble keeping the tears in. I nod and at the same time, almost as if by silent agreement:

"*Ewww*, the purple house!"

The words are magic and they work through me, burning away all the pent-up bitterness I've had toward her. I'm still angry, still hurt, but the words remind me of the bond we have. Even a giant can't break it.

"I'm sorry, too," I say. It's forgiveness, as much as I can give at this point. I take her hand and squeeze it.

She doesn't let go.

THIRTY-FOUR

Natalie loops her arm through mine and rests her head on my shoulder. "I love this time of year," she says.

Spring. It's all about new beginnings, but I feel like autumn inside. Tomorrow is our closing night, and it's bringing me down. When I have a show to work on, I spend less time at home. Now it's back to long afternoons filled with chores and yelling. It's also April, which means we'll be finding out what colleges we got into any day now. How could I have not applied to NYU?

"So, what's happening with Sadie's?" she asks.

The Sadie Hawkins dance is next week. The girls ask the guys and all the couples wear matching clothes.

I shake my head. "It's a no-go for me. Gav has a show that night."

Natalie stops, dropping my arm. "Dude. Senior year. You promised."

I did. Nat, Lys, and I said we would do every senior activity together and now I'm breaking that promise.

"My boyfriend can't come," I say. "What am I supposed to do?"

"Um. How about *go*?" She gets a sneaky look in her eye. "Gideon doesn't have a date yet. I have a feeling he wouldn't mind going with you at all."

I bump my hip against hers. "Stop it, you."

"Okay, but seriously," she says. "Fly solo. I'll ditch Kyle and dance with you all night, I promise."

"I'm sorry," I say. "I can't go. And it totally sucks because I really want to."

I love school dances. I love getting dressed up with my friends and dancing the night away.

"Then freaking *go*," she says, pulling open the door to the theater. "Seriously, Grace. It's like you have no control over your life anymore. Are you really gonna let your psycho boyfriend take this away from you?"

Her voice is raised as we enter the lobby and I wince. Gideon catches my eye and I fall into the dark wood of them, forget that your best friends and my best friends are watching as we stare at each other, as Gideon leaves the people he was talking to mid-sentence. As I float away from Nat. We break out into simultaneous smiles, giddy and reckless.

I can't breathe. It's like an entire battalion of soft winged things have settled all over my skin. Like I said, when I fall, I fall hard.

"Hey, you," he says when he reaches me.

I force myself not to touch him. Not to throw my arms around him and press my lips against his, and what am I thinking, I'm a terrible person, I'm leading him on and hurting you and—

"Hey yourself."

He reaches into his pocket and hands me papers folded into a small rectangle. Another one of his epic, wonderful, smart, talented, perfect letters. It's his turn to give me one—I wonder what he'll say about my ode to Radiohead, what he'll think about all my confusion regarding . . .

everything. Home and school. You. I wonder if he's read between the lines, how much I like him, but how I can't say that because it'd be wrong. We can't be together.

When I reach out to take the note, he holds on to it a second longer, waiting for my fingers to settle against his. It's unspoken, these secret ways of touching each other. No one will see. We can pretend that *we* don't even see. I look up and he's watching me blush, a question in his eyes.

But I can't answer it, I can't.

"Did you write me a book?" I tease.

"Working on it." He grins and I slip his letter into my pocket.

Kyle and Peter come up, eyes like X-rays, and without intending to, Gideon and I step away from each other. I feel frazzled, certain they can see everything I'm starting to feel for Gideon right there on my face.

"Hey . . . guys," Peter says, looking from me to Gideon. I sort of hate Peter now.

"Hey." My tone is deliberately casual. "Only two more shows. Can you believe it?"

Kyle shakes his head. "It's so freaking crazy that this is it—the last one."

"There's still the dance concert," Gideon says.

Peter shakes his head. "Doesn't count. Not like this."

Huge things are happening in the world—terrorism, refugees, disease—and yet here I am, obsessing over my small, stupid problems. Seriously, my boy troubles are nothing. But they feel like freaking everything.

Soon Miss B is corralling everyone onto the stage. I lead the actors in their warm-ups, doing tongue twisters like "You know New York, unique New York, you know you need unique New York." My favorite one is from *Hamlet*: "Speak the speech I pray you, as I pronounced it to you, trippingly on the tongue." I leave the actors to their stretching and running of lines and I lose myself in checklists and lighting cues and yelling at the crew, and for the first time in days I feel like myself.

But then the show is over and my mom is late and I have too much time to think about you. What are we doing, Gav? Why can't we let each other go?

"Where's your ride?" Gideon asks, coming to stand beside me.

I'm in front of the theater, leaning against one of the Greek-style pillars. I should have taken Nat up on her offer to drop me off at home, but I assumed my mom was already on her way.

I breathe out a frustrated sigh. "Who knows?"

"I just so happen to own a vehicle that could transport you to any location you so desire," he says. "I even put it through the car wash yesterday, so you'd be in for a treat. I only clean Fran on the night of the full moon."

"I'm not sure which is weirder—the fact that you named your car Fran or that you base your car washes on the lunar cycle."

"What can I say? I'm a man of mystery." He nods toward his beat-up VW Golf. "Come on. Your carriage awaits."

Like you wouldn't totally freak out about me getting a ride home from Gideon.

"My mom's on her way, but thanks anyway." I smile. "I'll have to meet Fran some other time."

Gideon sets down his bag and stretches his arms over his head. "Well, all good things are worth the wait."

I don't think he's talking about his car. He moves closer and I shiver a little when his arm brushes mine. *Stupid girl, stop it.*

"You don't have to wait with me," I say.

Don't go.

"I'm not waiting with you. I'm ... taking a break. Before I go home. I might meditate here after you leave."

I raise an eyebrow. "That is such bullshit."

He laughs, soft. "Yeah."

We stand there for a little, quiet.

"Grace—"

"Don't," I whisper. I know what he's going to say. It's time and it can't be because I don't want to break any hearts.

"We have a situation," he says quietly. "You know that."

I cross my arms, hugging myself. "I love him."

I don't look at Gideon as I say this. I don't want to see the look on his face.

"I know that. But you're not *in* love with him—and that's where I come in."

I turn to him, staring. He just said it all out loud, just like that.

And the world didn't fall apart.

"I can't break up with him," I say.

"Why?"

"I don't know."

Kill. Myself.

"Try," Gideon says, gentle. "Try to explain it to me."

"It's been so hard," I whisper. "And we both keep saying that once I graduate, it'll be okay. I mean, you know my parents, how strict they are."

"Yeah."

"And, like, if all those rules weren't in place, maybe everything would be fine."

"Okay . . . but there's still the question of—"

He points to himself.

"I know." I stare up at the stars, wishing I had courage. Wishing I could take his hand.

My mom pulls up then and I give her a quick wave.

I grab my backpack, relieved and disappointed at the same time.

But Gideon, I'm learning, doesn't give up so easily. He hands me a note written on the back of the rehearsal schedule.

"Sweet dreams, Grace," he says.

He's walking away before I can say anything else.

> *Grace—*
>
> *Did you know there's a place in Zagreb, Croatia, called the Museum of Broken Relationships? I read about it in <u>National Geographic</u>. People from all over the world send in objects and tell the story of their breakups. Isn't that sort of sad and weird and beautiful?*
>
> *G.*

I FIND MYSELF wondering what I'd send in after you and I break up. That's the scary thing—not *if* we break up, *after* we break up. Gideon knows me better than I realized.

The star necklace, I decide.

> *G—*
>
> *It is sad and weird and beautiful. I can't help but think this is a hint of some kind.*
>
> *—Grace*

> *Grace—*
>
> *Hint? Who, me?*
>
> *G.*

I WALK INTO the drama room on the afternoon of closing night and the whole cast is here because we're all a little sad that it's almost over and we want to be together as much as possible before the show spell is broken. Gideon is at the piano, playing a velvety jazz tune I don't recognize. He's intent on a handwritten sheet of music in front of him, oblivious to the whole world, squinting a little—he must have forgotten his glasses at home again. His long, thin fingers fly over the keys, and every now and then he stops and makes a note on the music sheet, then starts back up again. I lean against the piano and he looks up at me and smiles, like he's now utterly content, and without missing a beat he scoots over on the bench and I sit next to him. You know I'm a sucker for musicians. The music flows into me and it's like skipping down a sunny city street, but I catch the melancholy flowing under the bright notes, an enigmatic underneath. *Oh*, I think, *I have to write that in a letter to him.* He'd love that phrase—we trade words like kisses: *enigmatic underneath.*

He finishes with a flourish and glances at me. "What do you think?"

"I love it. You know I love it. I charge you with fishing for compliments."

He laughs, and am I imagining it or is he scooting a little closer to me? His arm rests against mine.

"What's it called?" I ask.

Gideon plays the refrain: I hear raindrops and the sound of clinking glasses. Laughter and sighs.

"Still thinking of a title," he says.

"Wait, you *wrote* that?"

I just assumed he'd copied it from somewhere onto a sheet of music paper. I often see Gideon noodling around on the piano and he's good—really good—but I had no idea he could do something like this.

He shrugs. "Not that hard—notes on a page, you know."

"No, I definitely do *not* know. Gideon—that's . . . I mean, that's amazing you can do that."

He looks down at the keys, runs his fingers through a scale.

"Give me your hand," he says softly.

I place mine in his, and there's a jolt, soft and sudden, and we both look up, right into each other's eyes. I hear warning bells in the back of my head, but they're muffled by the blood rushing through me, the beating of my heart.

He clears his throat, his lips turning up a little. "Here," he says, placing my fingers on the keys. He shows me a few notes and I try to mimic him.

"I sound like a stampede of elephants," I say.

"Um . . ." He laughs and I bump my shoulder against his.

"You weren't supposed to agree with me! That is so not, I don't know, *chivalrous*."

He covers my hand with his own and presses my fingers down slowly. It's better together.

I slip my hand out from under his, confused and guilty.

"I'm ruining your song," I say.

"Well, technically you're ruining *your* song."

"What—" Oh. *Oh*.

"Gideon!"

We turn around, both jumping a little. Peter and Kyle are staring at us. Oh god. Your best friends just saw . . . whatever this was.

"We gotta run through the sword fight," Kyle says. He won't look me in the eye.

Before I can say anything, Gideon scoots off the bench and grabs the sheet music. "It's not ready yet."

His rests his hand on my shoulder for just a minute before he goes to join the others. I stay on the piano bench, staring at the keys. Black and white. No gray.

Natalie sits on the bench almost as soon as Gideon gets up, straddling it.

"Yes," she says.

"What?"

She nods to where Gideon is. "Yes to him. *Si, oui, ja*, darling."

I shake my head, face burning. "Stop it," I growl. "I love Gavin." She gives me the stink eye. "I *do*."

"No, you're brainwashed by him."

"Dude—"

"Everyone can see it—you and Gideon. You don't just like each other. This is something . . . big. He gets you, Grace," she says. "You're not fooling any of us."

My heart snags on her words. "Please tell me that's not true."

Because if that's the case, it's only a matter of time before you find out. *Oh god*. What have I done?

"It's true," Natalie says, soft. "And it's *okay*. You're only eighteen; you can't stay with Gavin the rest of your life just because he says he'll kill—"

I shake my head. "I have to go."

"Grace—"

I give her a backward wave. "See you tonight!"

I don't look back to say good-bye to Gideon because I don't trust myself around him anymore.

I rush to the library and it's only there that I see the tiny square of paper tucked into the pocket of my jacket.

THIRTY-FIVE

Grace—

Okay, it's like this: the universe is huge, right? And we're just the tiniest speck on a tiny planet and we'll live for not even a second of a star's life. And yet. We're stardust. I read it in a science magazine, I'm not being poetic here: you, me—we're the stuff of stars. So keep that in mind when shit's getting you down.

Meet me by the gym after school, okay? Promise? Double pinkie swear?

G.

The bell rings and I find myself rushing to the gym, books clasped in my arms, stomach hurting in a good way because I'm going to see Gideon and then everything will be all right. But that's wrong, wrong, I should go home. Wait by the phone for you to call. You're coming to the show tonight and I'm here doing—what, exactly? It's not technically wrong to talk to my friend, it's not. Your rule is unrealistic and childish. It's a rule that's meant to be broken.

Gideon's already there, leaning against the gate that surrounds the pool across from the gym. He's reading one of his thousand manga books, engrossed. Nerdy and cute, and I love how he purses his lips when he's concentrating. Gideon drops into other worlds the way other people walk into rooms.

"Hey," I half whisper.

He looks up and smiles. "Hey, you." He throws the book onto his backpack, which is leaning against the gate. "Tell me your day."

It's this phrase he only uses with me. We tell each other our days like it's a story, embellishing, as though we were sitting around a campfire.

"Well, a gentleman wrote me a song," I begin. God, here I am flirting with him. *Again.*

He raises his eyebrows. "Do tell."

And off we go. We laugh, sometimes so hard my stomach hurts. We speak in whispers about things that are easier to say backstage, where the darkness surrounds us like a cloak. In these moments, our heads are close together, conspiratorial.

"I have a proposition for you," Gideon says.

"Okay . . ."

"Thespians are usually hungry before an evening performance— this is common knowledge, you understand."

I fight back a smile. "Of course. Everyone knows thespians get hungry from time to time."

"So, I'm just curious—taking a survey, actually: do you like food? A yes or no answer will suffice."

"You take beating around the bush to a whole new level."

"Dinner," he says, stepping closer. One hand is on the gate, gently clutching the metal. "With me. Tonight." He checks his watch. "Actually, in two hours, because we have to get to the theater early."

I shake my head. I should go. Gavin. My boyfriend. I should go.

"It's just dinner, Grace," he says gently. "I mean, let's be honest—it's the ninety-nine-cent menu at Taco Bell. Pretty innocent, all things considered."

"I don't even know what we're doing here," I say.

"We're doing this," he says. Then he wraps his arms around me.

"I hate you," I mumble, my forehead leaning against his shoulder.

"Liar," he says, soft. He presses me closer and we both sigh at the same time. I'm glad he can't see the smile on my face.

He's wearing a soft old T-shirt with a picture of Albert Einstein on the front and he's warm and something is swirling between us, in us, I don't know what it is but I don't want to let go. But I have to. This is wrong, this is almost cheating. If you saw—

I try to pull away but not really and he holds me tighter, runs his fingers through my hair.

"Choose me," he says.

I look up, startled. Our lips are inches apart. If he kisses me, I don't know what I'll do. My eyes fill with tears and I don't know what to say. I don't fucking know.

He tucks a strand of hair behind my ear. "I adore the hell out of you," he says. "You've become my closest friend in a matter of weeks. You're the first thing I think about when I wake up. Choose me. You won't regret it. I promise on Radiohead and Shakespeare. And even on Pepsi Freezes, if that will sweeten the deal. Pun intended."

My forehead falls to his chest. *Yes, yes*, I think. But also, *no*. I can't. Even if you weren't threatening to hurt yourself if I leave, would Gideon really want to be with me if he knew what my parents were like? Would he still feel this way if he knew how shitty I am at loving people, how selfish I am? I feel used up, tainted, hollow. I gave you everything, Gavin. I don't think there's anything left for me to give Gideon. He deserves better.

"Don't go back to him," Gideon says. "Even if we . . . even if you decide this isn't . . ." His hands slide down my arms and he interlaces his fingers with mine. "He hurts you. And it's killing me to see it."

I like holding his hand. I like that he wants to touch me as much as he can. I like the soft look he gets in his eyes whenever they settle on me. I'm cheating on you, aren't I? This must be cheating. I thought I was better than this.

I pull away. "Gavin and I have been together for almost a *year*. He's a part of me. Leaving him would be . . . I mean, you make it sound like I can just—" I make a sweeping motion with my hand. "It's not that easy."

Go away, I beg him. *I will ruin you. I'm broken.*

Gideon's fingers slip away from mine and he leans against the gate, arms crossed. "Why not?"

He doesn't say this with anger or frustration; his eyes don't narrow like yours do when you're pissed at me. It's like me staying with you is a math problem Gideon can't figure out. And he's really, really smart. I'm not the only one utterly, completely, totally baffled here.

"Because . . ." I frown and reach down and grab my books and my backpack. "Because I just can't, okay? I . . . I love him." I lift my chin and try to say the words with more conviction. "I love him."

Gideon shakes his head. "You say you love him like it's a question, not an answer."

He pushes off the gate and steps forward. I should move back but I don't. He grabs a piece of paper out of his pocket and slips it between the pages of my statistics textbook.

"You're worth the wait." He smiles, crooked. "See you tonight."

He starts to walk away and something in me crumbles, but then he turns back and closes the distance between us, resolute. Before I can move or protest or anything, he leans down and presses his lips against my forehead, his fingertips resting against my jaw.

I stare at him when he backs away.

"Speechless. Nice—just what I was going for." Gideon grins. "I've been wanting to do that for a while."

Then he walks away for real, hands in his pockets, messenger bag slung over his shoulder.

A part of me wants to run after him, turn him around, and give him the kiss I catch myself imagining whenever I'm bored in class.

Choose him.

Do it.

You stupid goddamn fucking girl, don't let him walk away.

I wait until Gideon has turned a corner, then make my way through campus. I only get halfway across the quad when I see the figure stalking toward me. That walk, so familiar. Long strides, hands swinging.

I stop. Stare.

"Where have you *been*?" you demand.

"Um . . ." Worst nightmare. WORST NIGHTMARE. "Just . . . getting my stuff together. You know. For tonight."

How could I have let Gideon *kiss* me? Forehead kisses count, of course they do.

"It's almost three-thirty," you say.

School lets out at two-forty. How was it possible that Gideon and I were together for almost an hour? It felt like minutes. Seconds.

"I—"

"Peter and Kyle said they saw you with some guy from your show. Gideon. Who the fuck is Gideon? Is he that guy from the bus ride to Oregon? The one who put his arm around you?"

Did I just cheat on my boyfriend? Am I a cheater?

"Yes, he's that guy. I mean, just . . . he's in the show and—"

"Look at you," you say. "You're lying to me. I know you. What are you hiding?"

You grab my shoulders like you want to shake the happy right out

304

of me. I think of how my mom did that, the rage in her eyes. Would you hurt me, Gavin?

"Nothing," I say. "I swear, nothing."

My eye catches on the note Gideon tucked into my book. Diversion. I need a diversion. I don't know what that letter says, but whatever it is, you will demand to read it and then you'll know, you'll know . . . Gideon says stuff like *I love your mind. You're the only person who gets my weird.*

You drop your hands. "I got here to take you out for fucking ice cream." I flush, guilty. "To celebrate your closing night."

"Gavin. We were talking about the show and about this album we both like and I lost track of time, that's all!"

"What album?" Because it's you, because it's music, the way this afternoon goes actually hinges on my answer.

"Radiohead. *Kid A.*"

You snort. "Of course. That mopey shit."

I wonder if Radiohead is a deal breaker for me. I don't get how you can't love them.

You fix me with a look so cold it turns my stomach. "Are you cheating on me?"

"Gavin." I reach a hand toward you, but you slap it out of the way. My skin stings.

"Are. You. Cheating. On me?"

I shake my head. "I love you. I would never cheat on you. I can't believe you would say that."

Deflecting. That's what cheaters do.

You bite your lip, eyes filling. How could I do this to you?

"Hey . . ." I pull you against me. It's not like with Gideon, who held *me*. I have to hold *you*. Have to hold you together so you don't break.

Kill. Myself.

"I can't lose you," you whisper. "I can't."

After who knows how long, you pull away and reach your hands out for my books.

"I've got it—" I start to say, but you take them out of my vise-like grip.

"What's this?" you ask, pulling out Gideon's note.

I pluck it out of your hand, smiling.

"Excuse me," I say. Tease, flirt, divert. "That is super-secret girl stuff from Natalie."

You narrow your eyes. "Right."

I'm not a gambling kind of gal, but I have no choice. I hold it out to you.

"Read it if you want. It's all about cramps and boy drama and—"

You look at it for a long moment and I think you know, but maybe you don't want to. You wave the note away.

"I'm good, thanks."

I tuck Gideon's note into my pocket, hands trembling. You're so smart, Gavin. If you hadn't threatened to hurt yourself, I would have chosen Gideon the moment he said *Choose me*. Or better, I would have chosen *myself*.

You put your arm around my shoulders. "I'm sorry," you say quietly. "It's just when Peter and Kyle—"

"I get it," I say. "I'd freak, too."

Your hand slips into my back jean pocket, rests there.

"Gavin," I say, dancing out of your arms. "Someone will see. . . ."

"So?"

My stomach hurts.

You're worth the wait.

"I have to get home," I lie.

You're wearing the shirt that says ROCKSTAR across it that I bought you right after we got together. You love it. Sometimes you ask

306

me to sleep in it so it'll smell like me. It's faded now and has a hole near the shoulder and isn't that us, I want to say, *Isn't that us?*

You sigh. "Let me drive you, at least."

I get into the car, but instead of driving me home, you drive to your apartment and park in the lot.

"Seriously," I start, but you stop me with a kiss and unzip my jeans.

"Here?" you whisper against my lips. "Or inside?"

We haven't been inside since my first time over. But I owe you. The guilt swims inside me, threatens to take me over.

I shift away from you. "Inside," I whisper. I am powerless. And maybe I want to be. "I really don't have much time."

Your lips snake up. "We don't need much time."

When we get inside I surrender to your touch, to sweat and spit and sloppy kisses. Because you deserve this. Because it's the least I can do. I think of Gideon's letter in the pocket of my jeans and I hope it doesn't fall out. You push me onto my knees. Slide off your underwear. Your eyes beg. Demand.

You're right. We don't need much time.

THIRTY-SIX

I'm standing backstage waiting to call the last cues. Kyle's onstage doing the clown's final speech. I'm in a dark puddle of blue light and Gideon comes up and hugs me from behind, his arms crossed over my chest, his chin resting on the top of my head. He's so tall.

"Gideon . . . ," I whisper. Anyone could see. But I don't push him away. This is the last night of the show. No more hiding together in the dark.

We stand like that for a few minutes, me sinking into him. He whispers funny stuff in my ear, tries to get me to laugh. His lips brush my hair as I call for a blackout. This is all highly unprofessional and I love every guilt-ridden second of it.

"And . . . lights up," I say into my headset.

The stage is blindingly bright and Gideon runs out, along with the rest of the cast, to center stage. They lift up their arms and bow. They motion for me to come on, and Miss B, too. Tears spring to my eyes and it suddenly hits me that this is my last show. The next one I do will be in college.

Backstage again, everyone's floating. It was a good final show and the house was packed. The guys head to their dressing room and I follow the girls into theirs to help out with costume stuff. It's small and it smells like perfume and makeup.

"I can't believe this was our last show," Lys says. "We're graduating in *ten weeks*."

Unreal.

Natalie glances at me as she reapplies her lipstick.

"So . . . ," she says.

"So . . . ," I say back.

She rolls her eyes. *"I adore you?"*

I've told them everything that happened this afternoon, except that very last part with you. I hate myself when we mess around now. It's like I lose another piece of me each time. Soon, there won't be anything left. *You stupid, stupid girl. You deserve what you get.*

"I don't deserve him," I say. "He's . . . I have so much baggage."

"You have daddy issues," Lys says.

"Like I said: baggage."

Nat's eyes flash. "Just . . . stop. Stop being dumb. You're going to hurt Gideon. You already are."

"I know," I whisper. I've been trying to ignore the longing in Gideon's eyes, the hurt when I try to stay away from him.

"I'm siding with Nat on this," Lys says, adjusting her pink babydoll dress, then sliding on a pair of knee-high socks with bows on them.

"I love you," Nat says. "And I get that this whole Gavin thing is effed up. But you can't have it both ways. It's not fair to put Gideon in the middle."

She's right. It's not fair. I'm stringing him along. He's not going to wait forever. And I'm not going to break up with you anytime soon. I have to believe that these feelings for Gideon will pass. They will. It's just a crush and I've taken everything too far—

There's a shout outside and we rush to the stage door that leads to the private outdoor courtyard for the cast and crew. You're there, gripping a baseball bat. Peter and Kyle are holding you back.

"Are you fucking my girlfriend?" you scream at Gideon. "I will kill you. *I will kill you*, you little fuck."

"What is this?" Gideon says, gesturing to the bat. "You think you're gonna challenge me to a duel or something? This is bullshit."

He glances at me and it's a punch to my gut. I realize that he's not just talking to Gavin—Gideon's talking to me, too.

He hurts you. It kills me to see it.

"Gavin!" I yell, running toward you. "Stop! What are you *doing*?"

"Shut up, whore," you say to me, your voice dangerous. I stop. The word echoes and I hear Nat and Lys gasp.

"Enough," Gideon says, his voice low. He takes my hand and gently pulls me away from you. I let him. Electricity surges through us, between us.

"You don't talk to her like that," Gideon says.

You stare at my hand in Gideon's. I let go, palm slapping against my thigh. My skin tingles. I can't breathe.

"She's *my* fucking girlfriend. I'll talk to her however I want." Your words are tough but your face—the look in your eyes. You want to kill *me*, not Gideon.

"Asshole," Nat mutters beside me. Then louder, "Get him out of here or I'll bring Miss B." She holds up her cell. "Or, better yet, I'm calling the cops."

"Come on, man," Peter says to you.

You look at Gideon for a long moment.

"Is this what you want?" you say, nodding toward Gideon. "This skinny fucker who can't even grow a beard?"

Gideon's seventeen, a year younger than me, two years younger than you. Here, now, you seem even older, with the cigarettes in one pocket and the keys to your own apartment in the other.

I know I'm supposed to say something—tell you to fuck off and run into Gideon's arms, or tell you *No, I love you, stop it*. Or, better yet, go off by myself. But I don't say anything.

Because I don't know what to say.

"That's it." Nat holds up her phone. "I'm calling."

"Jesus Christ," you mutter. "I'm going, Natalie. Stop." You take one last look at Gideon. "Stay away from her."

Gideon's lip turns up. "I think it'd be better for all concerned if *you* stayed away from her."

Peter and Kyle drag you away, but not before you fix me with the angriest, most vile glare, the bat still clutched in your hand.

Gideon barely waits for you to leave before he pulls me against him. Everyone's watching but I don't care and he doesn't, either.

"He's psychotic," Gideon says. "I mean, clinically. End it. You deserve better."

Maybe better, but not Gideon. He's good—kind, pure. I don't think he's ever had a girlfriend. Me? I can't even count how many blowjobs I've given the guy who just threatened to bash Gideon's head in with a baseball bat.

I feel so used up and empty, and this well of sadness that's opening up in me is getting deeper every second.

"Grace," Gideon says in that soft, kind way of his, "you have no idea how great you are. Just trust me, okay? You've got to break up with him."

I finally nod because I want to trust him. So much. "Okay."

The words fall out of my mouth and they taste like something spicy, waking me up.

He pulls away enough to look at me. "Really?"

"Yes. I'll do it. Tomorrow."

Gideon wipes the tears from my eyes and he can't hide the smile on his face. It's the kind of thing that you could see from miles away.

"Does that mean I get to kiss you for real?" he says. I laugh-sob and he puts a comforting hand on my shoulder. "You've got this."

Something in me releases. I can do this. I sigh and lean against Gideon. We stay like that until it's time to go.

~

Grace—

I'm not mad. I promise. I knew you breaking up with him was a long shot. Although I have taken to reciting the Duke's opening lines from Twelfth Night. *Do you remember us in Oregon, sitting next to each other during the show? You smelled like grapefruit and I was sorely tempted to lick your cheek, just to see if you tasted like you smelled.*

If music be the food of love, play on;
Give me excess of it, that, surfeiting,
The appetite may sicken, and so die.
That strain again! It had a dying fall:
O, it come o'er my ear like the sweet sound,
That breathes upon a bank of violets,
Stealing and giving odor!
Enough; no more:
'Tis not so sweet now as it was before.

I miss you, Grace. I don't want to lose your friendship. Stop avoiding me, eh? I promise I won't quote any more Shakespeare. It's just two a.m. and I can't sleep and I . . . I don't want to make all this harder on you than it already is. Anyway. Friends?

G.

hey baby—

I recorded this song for you. it's going on the LP! have a listen. it's all acoustic, just like you always want. can't wait to see you at the show tonight. i love you more than life.

<u>Grace</u>
I know I'm not perfect
But I'll sure as hell try
Just give me one more chance
To prove that I'm your guy
You're my saving Grace
You're my saving Grace
This love doesn't grow on trees
But I'll get down on bended knee
To prove my love to you
To prove I want you—only you
You're my saving Grace
You're my saving Grace
Baby, come closer now
Don't give up on me
We're so close to everything we want
We're so close to everything we need
You're my saving Grace
You're my saving Grace
I need you
I want you
I love you
You're my saving Grace
You're my saving . . .
Grace

Dear Ms. Carter:

On behalf of the University of Southern California, I'm delighted to invite you to join us next Fall to continue your academic career. Out of hundreds of applicants, you were one of the few students that have been chosen for our prestigious School of Dramatic Arts. You will soon receive a packet in the mail with more information. Congratulations and welcome to the Trojan Family!

Fight on,

Eleanor Hopkins
Dean
USC School of Dramatic Arts

Racy Gracie!

Your BFF Nat here. Look, I know things are crazy right now with boys. You know which one I'm rooting for. But—and I know this is going to sound insane—they're just BOYS. You're not going to marry either one of them, I PROMISE. I know this for a fact because I heard a rumor that a certain Calvin Klein underwear model is MADLY in love with you and wants you to have his babies. Shhh, don't tell.

I miss you, my dear friend. It's been weeks since we've hung out just the three of us (and, coincidentally, three weeks since The Bat Incident). We're supposed to be having senior year fun times, remember? It's almost MAY! Don't push everyone that loves you away, okay?

Because you can try, but we're not going ANYWHERE. (I mean that totally literally because this town freaking sucks, so, like, where could we even go—the water tower?).

I Lovvvvvvvvvvvvveeeeeeeeee Youuuuuuuuuu—

Nat

grace |grās|
noun

1. *simple elegance or refinement of movement:* she moved
   across the stage with effortless grace.
   - *courteous goodwill:* at least she has the grace to
     agree Radiohead is the best band ever.
   - *(graces) an attractively polite manner of
     behaving:* she exhibits all the social graces
     when directing a play (except when Peter
     doesn't learn his lines).
2. *(in Christian belief) the free and unmerited favor of
   God, as manifested in the salvation of sinners and the
   bestowal of blessings.* You deserve all the grace in the
   world.
   - *a divinely given talent or blessing:* she has the
     graces of Dionysus, god of theatre.
   - *the condition or fact of being favored by
     someone:* you can never fall from grace with
     me—no matter how hard you try.
3. *(also grace period) a period officially allowed for
   payment of a sum due or for compliance with a law or
   condition, esp. an extended period granted as a special
   favor:* my feelings are getting stronger for you
   during this grace period.

*You're one of my most profound friends and a wonderful
person with a beautiful soul. Whatever happens, don't
forget that.*

                                                    G.

grace—

my therapist told me it'd be a good idea to write you a letter, to tell you everything I'm feeling. at first, I was, like, fuck that, but then I started thinking about everything and realized, yeah, I have to get some stuff off my chest. I mean, I'm seeing this therapist and taking fucking meds for you. do you even appreciate that? pretty shitty that you basically coerced me into going, saying it was the only reason you'd stay with me, which, by the way, was a lot to ask of me after what you did.

HIM. you know who I'm talking about.

I thought I was okay, you know, after we made up and you promised me nothing happened and I realized I needed some help because I seriously would have bashed his fucking face in if it weren't for Kyle and Peter, but I can't get him holding your hand out of my head. and how you let him. I talked with my mom about it and we both agree that that's not "nothing," as you say. I am in literal fucking agony over this, grace. like, I can't sleep at night. my doctor had to up my meds because they just stopped fucking working. I can't write any songs except total emo shit.

you are ruining my life.

and I'm letting you. you're like a goddamn drug that I can't get enough of. do you have any idea how addictive you are? I should turn you into pills, sell you on the street.

I don't know what to do. I love you so much. like, I would die for you. I really think I would. but you're driving me crazy. I would never do this to you. how would you feel if you found out I was with some girl all the time? holding

her hand? that bad feeling you just had reading that—it's
what I feel all the time.

    and don't read this and say we should break up. you're
not the only one in this relationship. so here's the deal:

    stop being a tease. stop stringing me along. no more
contact with him. no fucking letters or after-school talks or
sitting together at lunch or phone calls or whatever the hell
is going on over there behind my back. yeah, peter told me
everything so don't even try lying. and stop listening to your
bitch friends who hate me and want you to be with HIM.
why are you turning your back on me and not them?

    grace, I love you. can't you see that? what more do I
have to do to show you that we're meant to be together? soul
mates. you're the one. please don't fuck around on me.

Gav

Grace—

Are you even reading these? Sometimes I think the letters I write you are diary entries that wind up in the trash. Did he find one? Is that why you won't write me back?

Listen, I know this whole situation is screwed up. And I know you say we can't be friends. But that's CRAZY. You're one of my best friends. The only person who I can talk to about all the stuff going on in my head—God, Radiohead, the world—all the shit that matters. Can't we keep that, at least? I promise I won't talk about "the situation" or try to kiss your forehead or even say stuff like "I really, really want to kiss your forehead." I swear on all the gods.

You're not okay. I can see it. And what's with spending lunch in the library? It's <u>your senior year</u>. Nat and Lys are super worried about you—Miss B, too. Are you not doing the spring dance concert because I got cast? I'll totally quit if you need me to. I know he doesn't want us around each other and even though you know how I feel about him and all of that, I don't want you to lose your last chance to do a Roosevelt show.

There's this expression the teachers in my mom's yoga class use: Namaste. It means "The light in me recognizes the light in you." Namaste, Grace.

Come back to us.

Come back to me.

G.

Gav—

It's our year anniversary and I woke up this morning and wished I were dead. For a second there, I really wanted to be. I wanted to wake up in the clouds or into oblivion or whatever happens when we die. That scared the shit out of me. There isn't any good way to say what I'm about to say. So I'm just going to say it: I'm breaking up with you. As of this moment, we are no longer together. I still love you, but I'm not in love with you. Or maybe I am, I don't know. That confusion is reason enough to break up, don't you think? What I do know is that we fight all the time. I know you're angry at me—hopelessly, endlessly angry at me. I know that no matter what I do, it's never good enough for you. I know I hurt you so bad about the whole Gideon thing. And I can tell you now that even though nothing happened, I like him. A lot. I'm so sorry.

I'm not getting with Gideon after writing this. I'm not getting with anyone. I need time to be by myself, to figure out who I am and what I'm going to do with the rest of my life. We've been together so long—I have no idea what's me and what's you. We've both sacrificed huge parts of ourselves—me with NYU, you with UCLA—and it's time to stop doing that. We are <u>so young</u>. Gav, I'm desperately unhappy. I practically start crying the moment I wake up and I cry myself to sleep most nights. Nothing brings me happiness. I'm a zombie, just walking around school in this depressed haze. I can't keep on like this. It's my senior year and I've worked so hard to get where I'm at.

I'm sorry I'm doing this in a letter, and on our anniversary, which is the shittiest timing and seems purposeful, but isn't. It's just I know I won't be able to *break up with you when you're standing right in front of me being sweet and hot and mine. I don't know if there's a future for us. Maybe in a few years we'll figure it out. Maybe we won't. Please just give me space and I'll give you space, too.*

I love you, Gav. I love you so much. But I can't do this anymore. Please don't hurt yourself. Please.

Grace

THIRTY-SEVEN

I clutch the letter I wrote you in my hands and stare out the window as Nat speeds to your place.

"I am so effing proud of you, Grace," she's saying. "I know how hard this is, but seriously, don't you feel better already?"

I nod, but I'm not so sure.

"You're positive this isn't the equivalent of breaking up with someone over text?" I ask, holding up the letter. It just says *Gavin* on the front.

"Dude," Lys says from the backseat, "the only reason you have to do it this way is because we now know he threatens to bash people's heads in when he's pissed."

This is true.

"But it's our year anniversary. Maybe I should wait a day? It's so harsh."

"Okay, imagine this," Lys says. "You don't give him the letter. He's going to pick you up tonight and take you out. You're going to pretend that it's all good the whole time, but he's not stupid, so he'll ask what's wrong, and you'll get in a huge fight. And you'll try to break up and then he'll cry and ask for one more chance. . . . Am I on track?"

I nod, miserable.

Nat glances in the rearview mirror. "I think it's time for the breakup playlist," she says.

"Hells yeah." Lys takes her phone out of her backpack and hooks it up to the car stereo.

"You guys made me a breakup playlist?" I ask.

"Oh, did we ever," Lys says as Lily Allen's "Fuck You" comes on.

The three of us have a dance party and by the time we reach your apartment, I have the courage to get out of the car. Your Mustang isn't in the parking lot, so you're going to get this when you get home from rehearsal with the band. You guys are playing a show later tonight, a few hours after our planned date, so I know you won't be able to get too depressed. In some ways, the letter is coming at a perfect time because you can get your sadness and anger out in the best, most healthy way: through your music. I don't know if you would try to kill yourself again, like you did with Summer. You're older now, and on meds and in therapy. And it's not like this is coming out of nowhere. I can't remember the last time we saw each other and didn't fight.

> *"You go to school with him every day," you said, just a few days ago. "How do I know that you're not making out in between classes, screwing in his car during lunch?"*
>
> *This language, it doesn't rile me up anymore like it used to. I've become quite accustomed to you flinging this shit my way. Gideon's letters burn inside me:* Namaste. Come back to me. *I haven't talked to him for the entire month of April. I miss him. I miss the me I am with him.*
>
> *"I don't understand why you're staying with me if that's*

the kind of person you think I am," I say. "Break up with me if you can't trust me."

Now I feel like I don't have the right to be the one doing the breaking. I'm the one who emotionally cheated on you. I don't get to hurt you like that, then dump you. I deserve to be dumped. I'm waiting to be dumped. (Please dump me.)

"Break up with you," you snort. "That's what you want, isn't it?"

"I love you," I whisper. Then a tiny bit of courage rears up in me. "But I'm fucking tired of fighting with you every day—"

"I hate you." You say this quietly and when you look over at me, the malice in your face sends a chill down my spine. "I hate you almost as much as I love you."

I stare at you. There are no words, just this fear spreading through me. You're so much bigger than me and you have those strong guitar-playing hands. My fingers move to my neck, clutch at my collarbone. I think about the foresight it took to find a baseball bat and bring it to the theater. If no one had stopped you, would you have used it on Gideon? Me?

I don't know who you are anymore.

Panic blooms in my chest and I think about how I forgot my cell phone at home and how we're in the middle of an abandoned housing development after dark, since some of the guys from the band are crashing at your apartment. No one would hear me scream.

I inch toward you because that is the only thing that ever calms you—my touch. I reach out and place my palm against your cheek. Bring my lips close to yours. Your eyes are two narrow slits and I don't know what that means, only that I have to tame you somehow.

"We're soul mates," I whisper. "Soul mates don't hate each other."

I take your hand and pull you toward the back of the car. I open the door and lie down, pulling you on top of me. This always works—your skin against mine, your breath in my mouth.

"I want you," I whisper. "Only you. Always."

After, you drive me home, silent, and when you drop me off, I close the passenger door softly behind me, as though you're The Giant now and I'm afraid to wake you.

I go into my room, grab a sheet of paper, and start writing:

Gavin—

I STAND IN front of the door to your apartment and it hurts to remember the happy look on your face when you brought me here for the first time. Just past this door is the future you've been trying to build for us. I'm about to knock it all down. My phone buzzes in my pocket and I feel sick because I know it's you. I pull it out and look at the text—a picture of you holding up a tiny gift bag from the jewelry store in the mall. I am such an asshole.

Nat honks and when I look back, she and Lys pose with Lady Gaga claw hands and huge, you-can-do-it grins. I give them a thumbs-up. I *can* do this. I *will* do this. I tuck my phone back into my pocket and rest my palm against the door for a minute, a year of memories running through me: you serenading me in the hallway at school as you ask me to prom, you kissing me under stars, drenched in moonlight. Birthdays and holidays and shit times and beautiful times. Your songs and your smiles and the way your hands touch me like I'm a priceless treasure. But then I think about you saying *I hate you* and a year of tears and yelling and punishing kisses and sex for the purpose of forgetting.

A year of a hopelessness that's rooted itself deep inside me. Five hundred twenty-five thousand six hundred minutes of riding a roller coaster that refuses to stop.

My eyes well up as I tuck the letter under the corner of the welcome mat your mom bought you. Then I run back to the car and Nat turns the stereo up full blast: Taylor Swift's "We Are Never Ever Getting Back Together."

"I say this calls for some Pepsi Freezes," Lys says.

For the rest of the day I feel light as air. *I'm single*, I keep thinking to myself, over and over. *I'm free.*

I meant it in my letter when I said I wouldn't get with Gideon, but a part of me wants to run into his arms and stay there for a good long while. It might be too much to hope that he'll forgive me for shredding his heart and then ignoring him for the past month just to protect my own. I'm so used to having that now—a boy to hide me from my problems. Except . . . the boys *are* the problems.

"Don't let me get with Gideon," I tell the girls. "I know I need to be on my own."

Lys nods. "Chicks before dicks."

I laugh. "Yeah, I kinda like the sound of that."

Nat turns up the radio as Beyoncé's "Sorry" comes on.

Middle fingers up, put them hands high, wave it in his face, tell 'em boy bye . . .

I don't hear from you. I thought I would—endless texts or calls I'd have to ignore. But there's nothing. I feel disappointed. Not that I wanted you to fight to get back together, but I thought our year together warranted some kind of response.

When I get home, I turn off all the lights in my room and light a few candles. The *Rent* soundtrack is on and I'm putting everything related to us in a box. Letters, gifts (the star necklace, the infinity bracelet). I take pictures of us off my phone. Take them out of frames.

Then I lie on my back and close my eyes, dreaming myself to Paris. To Jacques or Raoul, to baguettes and café au lait and picnics along the Seine. I go to Notre Dame and the Louvre and the top of the Eiffel Tower. Then I'm in New York, in a boat in Central Park, at a late-night diner with friends. In a sound booth, calling a show on Broadway.

And only once I'm looking out over all of New York at the top of the Empire State Building, just a speck among the thousands of twinkling lights, do I fall asleep.

MY MOM PULLS up in front of the hospital and I'm out of the car before she's even stopped. I sprint to the information desk. Words tumble out of my mouth—I don't even know what I'm saying.

"I need—my boyfriend—he's been in an accident—"

The receptionist nods, calm.

"What's his name, sweetheart?"

"Gavin. Gavin Davis."

She does something to the computer while I stand there, breathless and terrified.

"Fourth floor—room 407. Visiting hours are almost over—"

"Thank you," I say as I run to the bank of elevators on the other side of the lobby.

The other people in the elevator give me a wide berth. It's one of the few days that it's rained in our region and I'm soaked, my ratty old pajama bottoms and tank sticking to me. I forgot to put on a bra and it's freezing in here, why are hospitals so cold? I don't know how you are. I only know what your mom's text said when I woke up this morning: you were in an accident last night, you were in the hospital, come immediately.

Right now there is no anger. That will come later. All I know is that I love you and you're maybe very badly hurt. I will do anything to make sure you're okay. I never should have written that letter.

The elevator doors slide open and I rush through. The nurse at the main desk hands me a visitor's badge and points down the hallway. I'm running, my wet flip-flops smacking against the linoleum, but when I get to your room I stop, scared. Your mother must hate me for that letter, for ending us on paper. You deserved a conversation at least, but I'm a spineless coward.

Please be okay.

I just need to know you're okay.

I stop in front of the closed door, hesitating. Who am I kidding? If I go in there, we'll get back together. That letter, all the courage it took to write it, will mean nothing. And we'll both be right back where we started. I listen hard, but I don't hear anything. I know your mom is probably in there with you. Your dad, too. I know I should go in right now because you need me and you're hurt, but I don't.

I turn around and hurry back to the elevator and when that doesn't come right away, I bolt down the stairs, as if you could somehow chase after me. I'm halfway across the lobby when my mom walks in.

"What happened?" she asks. "They won't let you see him?"

How can I explain? She knows about the letter and already told me that had been a terrible way to break up with you, that it was wrong of me. *I'm so disappointed in you*, she said. *That poor boy.* And then the accident happened and it felt like it was my fault, like my hands had been on the wheel, my foot on the accelerator.

"I can't go in there, Mom," I say. "If I do . . ." I break down, crying. "We'll get back together and—"

"Grace Marie Carter. I raised you better than this. Now you get your butt into that elevator and go see if Gavin is okay."

"But—"

"*Now.*"

She's right. I'm a horrible person. Selfish beyond belief. I can't imagine a scenario in which you wouldn't come to make sure I was okay. Just because we're broken up doesn't mean I don't care if you live or die.

A few minutes later, I'm knocking softly on the door.

"Come in"—your mother's voice.

I push open the door and the first thing I see is you in a hospital bed with bruises and scratches all over your beautiful face and I lose it.

Your mom stands between me and the bed, your dad slumped in an armchair in the corner, and all I want to do is throw my arms around you and make it all go away, the accident and the pain you're in and that letter. Because I did this. It's my fault. How could I have been so stupid?

"Maybe now isn't the best time—" your mom starts, but you reach out a hand for me with the arm that doesn't have an IV hooked up to it.

"It's okay," you say quietly. To her, to me. Your eyes never leave my face.

She looks from me to you, frowning, uncertain.

"Mom, it's okay," you say. "I want her here."

Your dad stands up, but he doesn't say anything to me. They walk out of the room together, but not before your mom throws me an accusatory you-almost-killed-my-son glare. I deserve that, but it hurts. They've both been so good to me, so good. And I realize, too late, that I haven't just hurt you: I've hurt your whole family. They'll never forgive me, and I don't blame them.

When she shuts the door behind her I run to you. The right side of your face is one big bruise and when you try to sit up more, you wince.

"Gav—Gav—"

"Shhhh," you say, wrapping your bandaged arms around me.

"I'm sorry, baby," I sob, "I'm so sorry."

I had underestimated just how freaked the hell out I'd feel seeing you like this.

"Are you completely broken?" I ask.

You shake your head. "Just banged up. No internal bleeding or anything. They said I can probably leave tomorrow. The car's totaled, but whatever. Guess I have a guardian angel or something." You pause and your voice goes soft. "I should be dead."

I press my lips to your neck and breathe you in. You smell like hospital and it's wrong, so wrong. You tell me what happened: you read my letter and then got wasted. Around one in the morning you stumbled into your car.

"I was out of my mind," you say. "I just . . . saw the streetlight and decided, *Fuck it.* I don't remember what happened after that."

The doctor says you're the luckiest kid in town. That hitting a streetlight at ninety miles an hour should have killed you. A miracle.

"That's what I wanted it to do," you say, soft.

My heart stops. I go cold all over. I think of the look on Summer's face when she came into the drama room last year and told us what you'd done.

"Let's make a deal," you say. "We stay together until the end of the summer. If you still want to break up when you start school, okay. But give me the summer—without your parents and rules—to prove that we're right for each other."

"Gav, you said you *hated* me."

You shake your head. "I didn't mean it. Come on, you know I didn't mean it. I was angry—"

"You're angry all the time," I say gently. I reach out and brush your hair out of your face. You catch my hand in yours.

"I love you, Grace. I love you with all my heart." Your eyes plead with me, eyes I've gotten lost in so many times. Glaciers and Popsicles and the sea, a blue so particular to you that I haven't seen the color anywhere else.

"Okay," I say. "Until the end of the summer."

You draw me down onto the bed beside you and in minutes you're asleep, exhausted. I stay there until the nurse tells me I have to go. I slip out of your arms, brush my lips against your forehead, then quietly shut the door behind me. Your mom is sitting by herself in the empty waiting room. When she sees me, she stands.

"I read the letter," she said. "It was . . . in his pocket. They gave me his clothes after . . . There was so much blood."

Tears slide down her face and I wrap my arms around her like she's done so many times for me. Losing you would mean losing your parents, too. I hadn't thought about that. I wait for her to push me away, but she doesn't.

"I'm so sorry," I say. "I didn't know what to do."

She pulls away. "Grace, why didn't you tell me what was going on? You know how fragile he is. I could have kept an eye on him."

I hang my head, ashamed. I'd been so caught up in myself that it had never occurred to me to talk to your parents. Or maybe I was just afraid to.

"I'm sorry," I say again. "It's just been so hard and . . ." I start crying and she takes my hands in hers and squeezes them.

"Honey, we love you both so much. And Gavin loves you more than anything in the world."

"I know. I love you guys, too."

"How . . . how did you leave things?" she asks quietly.

"We're staying together. We're going to work it out."

Middle fingers up, put them hands high, wave it in his face, tell 'em boy bye . . .

I was so close.

She frowns. "I can't say that makes me feel better. You really hurt him. That Gideon boy . . ."

"I didn't cheat on him," I say. "I would never."

She sighs. "I won't get in the middle of it. But . . . you're part of this family now, Grace. You're like a daughter to us. When you do stuff like this, it's not just Gavin you're affecting."

I nod, chastened. "I understand."

"We're going to take him back to Birch Grove for a week or so. I want him to come home after that, but he said he wants to stay in that apartment. I need your help keeping an eye on him, make sure he's taking his meds. And I need you to *tell me* if anything is the matter. You can talk to me, about anything. Okay?"

I nod. "Okay."

"I'm going downstairs to find Mark and get some coffee. Do you want any?"

I shake my head. "I have to go, actually. My mom's waiting for me."

"Okay. You'll come by later, after school?"

I nod. She gives me another hug and is gone. I open the door to your room and watch you for a minute. You could have *died*, Gav. I would have had to stand by your grave and know it was because of me, that there would be no more songs because of *me*. But you didn't. We have another chance. Your chest is moving and your eyes slide beneath your eyelids and I wonder what you're dreaming about. The heart monitor beats steadily. Medicine drips into your veins and you are alive.

I quietly close the door and head toward the elevators.

THIRTY-EIGHT

I am sitting on the floor of my kitchen holding a knife.

You don't know this. You're practicing being a rock star while your girlfriend crouches against the dishwasher wondering if she has the guts to do herself in.

I can barely breathe, sobs crashing through my throat, an avalanche of tears. I will bury myself alive. I will cut my skin to shreds. I swear I will, I will. And I'll burn this fucking house down if it means I can cut you loose, be free, be without Gavin Davis. It's been a week since your accident and already I'm falling into this dark pit and I can't crawl out of it and pretend to be okay anymore, I can't. Why do you have to make this so hard for me? Why does your life have to be in my hands? They're not big enough to hold you.

My phone is pressed hard against my ear as I wait for my best friend to pick up. Nat answers: bright, cheerful.

"Hello, dahling!"

"I can't do it anymore," I say. My breath hitches and another sob breaks free.

They say that slitting your wrists is the best way to go. They say it doesn't hurt too bad. It's like falling asleep, only messier. But you know all about that already.

Nat immediately changes her tone. "Grace? What's wrong?" She's mama bear angry. "What did he do?"

So many things. What *didn't* you do—today, every day?

I ignore her question. "I'm so tired. I can't. I can't."

"Grace. Break up with him. This has to stop."

My entire body shudders, this darkness inside pulling me down in the muck. "It's not that simple."

"It is. And if he fucking dies, who the fuck cares."

"Holy shit, Nat."

"I'm sorry," she growls.

You play on a constant track in my head, the volume too high. *Bitch. Whore. Slut. I love you, don't you understand? One more chance, just one more chance. I hate you.*

I can't stay with you until the end of the summer like we agreed, I know that. But you'll say *I want forever with you, we'll be better this time, you promised you'd give us a fair chance* and I will chicken out because I can't see you in a hospital bed again.

"Should I come over?" she says. "I can come over."

This house is a prison, a suburban Alcatraz. Nat would make it better. She'd make the bars disappear. But my mother would never allow it. Not on a school night.

"Grace?"

I look at the knife. Sharp blade, dark black handle. It scares me. It's real. It can do some damage if it wants to.

"I'm holding a knife," I whisper. I say it again so I can hear the words, take the next step. "I'm holding a knife."

Someday I will remember this. This cry for help. Even now some part of me knows I just want to feel the heft of that knife in my hand, to know there *is* a way out, if I need it. To know I can control this one thing. *This is* my *life*, I want to growl. To you, my psychotic boyfriend, to my family that only speaks in yells and punishments. *I can end it if I want.* It feels like the only decision that's all mine and no one else's.

It feels like power.

Nat and I talk for an hour. She guides me off the ledge with her soft voice, her warmth, her assurance that it won't always be this way. *We* will *get the heck out of here*, she says. And I believe her, at least a little. Because, Jesus Christ, what if we don't?

When the sun finally slips below the horizon, I realize I have to stop crying, have to pick myself up. Mom and Roy will be home soon. I'm supposed to make dinner. To make sure every little thing is perfect: spines of books lined up just so, every blade of grass in the yard watered, the edge of place mats flush with the edge of the table. All of this so when my mom and Roy wheel through the door, they might not lay into me right away. I need to be Perfect Daughter. Perfect Stepdaughter. Or else.

"Are you sure you're okay?" Nat asks, unconvinced.

"Yeah. I'm fine. Really. Promise. I'm sorry I'm being a drama queen."

"Break up with him."

A whisper: "I can't."

I have a million reasons why. I have none. It doesn't matter. This feeling of *can't* is stronger than anything else, like you're some dark lord who's put a spell over me. (Are you? Because that would explain so much. Tell me you're magic, Gavin. I'll believe you.)

I hang up. I stand and put the knife back where it belongs. The blade winks at me as it slides into the block. I wish I could stab it into your heart, put us both out of our misery. Instead, I dry my eyes and set the table for dinner.

I ROLL THE window down all the way, then stick my head out the car and yell into the wind because I am two hundred miles from you and it feels So. Fucking. Good.

"Yesssssssssssssssssssss!!!!!!!"

I slip back in and Natalie grins. "*Hell* yes."

I never thought my mom would let me take a road trip to LA with my friends but when my sister said she'd put us up for the weekend and introduce us to the college life, my mom said, and I quote, *You're eighteen now. The choice is up to you.*

An alien attack would have surprised me less.

This is all Nat's doing. After I called her holding that knife, she insisted we get out of town immediately. Then she called Beth for reinforcements. And Lys, obviously. Three days later: here I am, speeding away from everything that keeps me up at night.

You, of course, are pissed that I'm going. You don't like the idea of Nat and Lys spending so much time alone with me. You're scared they'll come between us. News flash, Gavin: they already have. It doesn't help that you've been a broken record about them. You want me to stop hanging out with them. You don't trust them and you shouldn't. They are not Team Gavin. Not by a long shot.

I can't get your newest song out of my head. You played it for me the day after you got out of Birch Grove, where your parents made you go for therapy after you were discharged from the hospital. Our date ended in a screaming match because you found out I'd been to a party that Gideon was also at. Doesn't matter that he and I barely exchanged three words and that he has a girlfriend now. It was still *Fucking whore, I hate you.* You're so smart, Gav. You knew that if you survived that accident, there's no way I could ever leave you again. Not unless I want your blood on my hands. You're lucky your gamble paid off. Now you can do or say whatever you want, can't you? You've got me right where you've always wanted me.

You win.

This was your song:

I watch you sleep at night
Wonder what you dream
Put my hand against the glass
Want you here with me
There's a window between us
Thick glass all the time
Can't seem to remember
The days when you were mine

"Okay, so I need specifics," Nat says as we sit down at a roadside taco stand. "Exactly how many times has he watched you sleep?"

"A lot, it sounds like," I say. "I think he's trying to be romantic, but . . ."

"Nu-uh," Lys says. She grabs a chip and scoops up some salsa. "That is so creeptastic. Like, *beyond* creeptastic."

I don't admit this, but I agree. The thought of you standing outside my window at night didn't fill me with butterflies and rainbows, as I think you assumed it would. I mean, you weren't trying to hide that you were doing it—you played the song for me, proud of the guitar solo halfway through.

"Let's talk about something else," I say.

"No, dude, I think we should role-play this," Lys says.

"Let's not and say we did," I grumble. Lys and her psychoanalysis.

"Hey, in a few years, you're gonna have to pay me, like, a hundred and fifty bucks an hour to untangle your shit. Get my expertise free while you can," she says.

I imagine her sitting behind a desk, wearing the same outfit she has on now: a tank top that says I Slay, dangly pineapple earrings, and neon pink jeans with white stars printed on them.

"I really don't—"

But Nat cuts me off. "I actually think Lys is right—this could really help."

I roll my eyes. "Fine."

Lys grins. "Okay, I'll be Gavin, obviously." She lowers her voice and slouches—it's a pretty good impression. "Hey, baby."

Natalie snorts.

"Hey . . . Gavin."

"So . . ." She motions for me to start talking.

"I, uh, really love your song, but . . . maybe you shouldn't watch me sleep. I mean, my parents will be pissed if they find you—"

"NOPE," Lys says. "Tell him how *you* feel."

"I don't want to do this," I say. I shove a chip into my mouth, then another.

Lys gives an overdramatic sigh. "You're hopeless."

"I'm gonna put up curtains."

Nat reaches across the table and grips my hand. "We love you. Why are you so crazy?"

"I don't know," I whisper.

But I do. All of this—the fighting, the tears, breaking Gideon's heart—will have been for nothing if we don't at least try to see what life would be like when I graduate. How many times have I pictured myself being able to go to all your shows, to the after-parties, without having to worry about parents or curfews? How many times have you fantasized about waking up next to me, meeting me for lunch between classes? You have an illness and you're trying to get better. Maybe if we found the right meds, the right therapist . . .

Breaking up with you is too hard right now. Going away with my friends, doing senior year activities—even planning on flying solo for prom since you have a show that night—all that stuff I *can* do.

UCLA has a huge, sprawling campus in Westwood, a trendy part of LA. We find parking on a palm-lined street, then make our way to

Beth's Spanish-style apartment, which is located five minutes from campus.

Music blares out of an apartment on the ground floor and a guy in nothing but board shorts saunters out and lights up a joint, right there in front of us.

"Ladies," he says, tipping an imaginary cap.

Nat stares in shock while Lys giggles uncontrollably as she heads for the stairs.

"I can't take them anywhere," I say to the guy with a small smile.

He grins as he holds the joint out to me. "You want?"

I shake my head, quick. It's the first time I've ever been offered a smoke. I only know the smell because of the few parties I've gone to with you.

"She's in *high school*," Natalie says with her customary disapproving tone. She looks like a camp counselor in her khaki shorts and polo shirt.

I kick her shin.

The guy nods, unfazed. "Sucks."

"You got that right," I say.

Nat pulls me up the stairs after Lys. "Oh my gosh, that druggie was totally *flirting* with you," she says.

"Right?" I grin and shake my hips. "Off the market, but I still got it."

"Oh, brother."

Sprouting wings begins with a tingle that spreads across your chest, then your whole body, all the way around to your back. It doesn't hurt at all.

Beth opens the door on the first knock. She and I scream simultaneously and jump around.

"Your hair is blue!" I screech.

"I know!" she yells back.

My sister's place is my dream apartment. White Christmas lights line the inside windows and the furniture is all really modern stuff from Ikea that screams *We are young and broke, but cool.* She and her roommates have draped the walls with colorful sarongs and hung Chinese lanterns throughout.

What follows is pretty much the best weekend of my life. There's an impromptu bonfire on the beach, a doughnut run at two a.m., mornings spent drinking coffee, and thrift-store shopping. We check out nearby USC and I can't stop talking about the great French program there with a study-abroad option and how their drama school is one of the best in the country. I buy a sweatshirt and pose for a picture in front of Tommy Trojan, the USC mascot, and try not to think about how I'm going to manage to pay my tuition.

"Okay, little sis, I gotta ask," Beth begins. We're sitting on a blanket on the beach, watching Nat and Lys splash around in the frigid Pacific. "Why are you still with Gavin? I know I tell you to break up with him all the time, but seriously: *break up with him.* You're obviously *miserable.* You've, like, lost weight and have crack-whore eyes."

"Thanks for the confidence booster," I say.

"Anytime."

I lean my head on Beth's shoulder and she wraps an arm around me.

"I'm trying to break up with him," I say. "I promise. I really am."

Beth shifts and brings her hands to my shoulders so that we're face-to-face.

"The only reason you should stay with someone is because you make each other happy. Any other reason is bullshit."

I shake my head. "You don't get it, Beth—he almost *died.* The doctor said it was pure luck he made it. If we break up, who knows what he'll do? I couldn't live with myself if he—"

She throws up her hands. "Your job is not to keep Gavin Davis alive. That's *his* job."

I don't say anything. There's nothing to say.

"Like I told you before: you're turning into Mom," she says. "Can't you see that? Gavin is your Giant. Your man is abusive and dangerous and one hundred percent insane. And you just take it."

Tears fill my eyes. "This is some seriously tough love you're dishing out."

She shrugs. "I love you. And this shit has got to stop."

I don't call you to check in. I don't even think about you, other than that talk with Beth. I imagine what my life in LA would be like, talking to cute, shirtless boys who live downstairs, meeting up with friends on the quad between classes. I picture getting on a plane bound for Paris, taking classes at La Sorbonne.

We're standing in line for cookies at Diddy Riese, this famous place near UCLA, and Nat hooks her arm with mine.

"I haven't seen you this happy in a year," she says.

"I know," I admit.

Other than with Gideon, I can't remember the last time I laughed so hard my stomach hurt. I can't remember not freaking out that you'd see me having a conversation with another guy. I haven't looked over my shoulder once, worrying that you're around to catch me doing something that will piss you off.

This trip does something to me. It gives me a peek into the future. This is what life could be like without you.

It's not as bad as I thought it would be. In fact, it's not bad at all.

THIRTY-NINE

You are so mad that I decided to go to prom without you. You refused to go because you're twenty and *I'm not going to a fucking high school dance* and I refused to not go.

"Fine," you say. "Go find that little fucker in his tux—"

"Gavin, like I've told you a million times, if I wanted to cheat on you, I could have. So what does it matter if I go to prom and he's there?"

"You'll dance with him, for one."

"No, I won't, because he has his own date. Her name is Susan and—"

"So the only reason you wouldn't dance with him is because he has a date."

"That's not what I meant," I say. "You're putting words in my mouth."

"Look, I don't want to argue anymore. I'm just saying, shit happens on prom night and that's why I want to keep you close, okay?" You look down at me, slightly paternal.

"I'm sorry if I'm not comfortable with the possibility of my girlfriend screwing some guy because she had too much to drink and he looked good in his tux."

"I only drank that one time!" I yell.

"At HIS house," you say. "Don't think I've forgotten that. Your first time should have been with me."

"I'm well aware of the fact that I have a boyfriend and that means something to me, like not screwing other guys on prom night. Jesus, Gavin!"

"Are you really gonna do this?" you say, quiet.

"It's my senior prom. You're welcome to come. If not, I'm going without you."

You stare at me, dumbfounded, then jump into your car, a new Dodge Challenger that your parents surprised you with when you got out of Birch Grove. You're lucky they didn't suspend your license after the DUI you received when you woke up in the hospital.

"Find your own way home," you say before peeling off.

I wait until you're out of sight and then I jump up, a fist in the air. I did it. I fucking DID IT!

I walk the two miles home from the Pot, grinning the whole time.

NOW I'M POSING with my best friends and Lys's girlfriend, Jessie, grinning for the photographer. We're standing in a little chorus line, holding one another's waists. He takes the picture when we're all mid-laugh.

"I love that the photographer thinks you guys are lesbians, too," Lys says when we're done. "Best group photo ever."

I give Nat a big smacking kiss on the cheek. She's the best prom date a girl could ask for. I was planning on flying solo, but Kyle got the stomach flu at the last minute, so Nat and I decided to be each other's dates.

The four of us move away from the prom backdrop. The theme is *Arabian Nights*, so it looks like we're on the set of *Aladdin*. Star-shaped lanterns hang over the dance floor and there are pretty cutouts of elegant windows surrounding the room. The hotel ballroom is packed.

A slow song comes on and we all go onto the dance floor. Nat and I do a tango while Jessie and Lys get all cute and cuddly.

"I love that they met on our Oregon trip," says Nat, with a nod to our friends.

"Yeah," I say, soft. Thinking about that trip always hurts a little.

Perfect timing: I catch sight of Gideon near the refreshments table and my heart lurches. As if he can sense me, he turns his head and his eyes find mine.

"Who are you—" Nat says, turning around. "Oh."

I give a little wave, then look away. I don't know if he waves back.

"You should talk to him," Nat says. "Clear the air, you know?"

I shake my head. "I treated him like such shit."

"So go over there and say you're sorry."

"Empire State of Mind" comes on, and just hearing the lyrics makes my eyes fill with tears: *In New York, these streets will make you feel brand-new, these lights will inspire you.* Nat wraps her arms around me.

"I'm sorry about NYU," she says.

"Me too."

I should never have let you push me into not applying.

"It's my own damn fault," I mutter.

"Yeah. But it still sucks," she says. Nat pulls away. "Bright side: we'll be in the same state!"

I nod. "It'll be great—we can pretend to hate each other during football games."

Apparently, USC and Cal have it in for each other.

The night passes in a blur of laughter and dancing and feet hurting. By the end I'm barefoot and sweaty and happy. You've called me seven times and I've only answered twice.

"Is he there?" is the first thing you say to me when I pick up.

"Yes. Literally across the room, as far away from me as possible. Happy?"

I hang up on you and don't respond to the text you send me a few minutes later.

I'm sorry. I love you.

A slow song comes on and I'm about to sit down when someone grabs my hand. I turn around. My heart stops.

Gideon.

"May I dance with your date?" he asks Natalie, who's sitting with her feet propped up on another chair, drinking punch.

She grins. "By all means."

He looks at me, his eyes asking permission, and I nod. It feels so good to have my hand in his again.

The song is Adele's "Someone Like You" because the universe likes messing with me like that.

Never mind I'll find someone like you, I wish nothing but the best for you too . . .

Gideon leads me to the center of the floor, then takes my arms and drapes them around his neck. His hands slide around my waist. His cheek rests against mine.

"I've been working up the courage to do this all night, you know," he says softly.

I smile. "You have?"

"Uh-huh. Mostly, I was worried about getting jumped with a baseball bat afterward. But then I decided it'd be worth it."

345

I lean back a little so I can look at him. "I'm so sorry. For everything."

"I know." He pushes up his glasses and then his grip around my waist tightens. "Let me guess: he didn't want to come to a high school dance."

"Bingo." I laugh, and its bitterness surprises even me.

"You know what I'm gonna say, right?"

I smile, remembering our little ritual before sixth period.

I nod. "Yeah."

He mouths the words: *break up with him.*

"I will. I feel like . . . really close to doing it."

Gideon gives me a pitying look. "That's great."

I hate that he doesn't believe me. I want him to know I'm going to do it for real this time. *I* want to know that I'm going to do it for real this time.

"Wanna make a bet?" I ask.

"Okay. What's the bet?"

"If I break up with him by graduation . . . you have to write me an email every week this summer."

"And if you don't break up with him?"

"Um . . . what do you want?"

"You still have to be friends with me," he says.

"Deal." I glance over to where his date is chatting with a group of girls. "Susan okay with you not dancing with her?" I ask. He seems happy, which is good. What he deserves.

"She's not like Gavin," Gideon says. "She trusts me."

I nod. "That's good."

"It is."

We don't talk much after that. It feels like everything we can say has been said. When the song ends, Gideon keeps his arms around me and gives me one of his wonderful bear hugs.

"Good luck, friend," he says.

"Thanks."

Nat, Lys, Jessie, and I stay until the very end, dancing as a group to Katy Perry's "Part of Me."

"It's your song, bitch!" Lys yells over the music.

I double cross my fingers and hold them up as we shout the lyrics: *This is the part of me that you're never gonna ever take away from me, no!*

At the end, we all fall into one another for a group hug. We have sweet perfumed sweat and smeared makeup and dresses that are too long, but we don't care because this is our night and, for once, I didn't let you ruin it.

"Proud of you," Nat whispers in my ear as we make our way to the car.

I sling an arm around her shoulder. "By graduation," I say.

"I've got your back."

I smile. "I know. You've had it the whole time."

"Damn straight," she says.

"You cursed!"

Her eyes twinkle. "Fuck him."

Lys turns around and grins. "Fuck yeah fuck him!"

We laugh and laugh and laugh.

And they're right: Fuck you, Gavin.

EVERY YEAR THE senior classes of schools all over California get to go to Disneyland after hours. For this one night, the park is all ours. Nat, Lys, Peter, Kyle, and I go on every ride at least once, take pictures with characters wearing graduation robes, and eat way too much over-priced food. We don't leave until the sky lightens and by the time we get back to Birch Grove, I'm exhausted—that overcaffeinated kind where you're so tired you can't sleep.

I'm so surprised when you show up at school to give me a ride home that I don't protest. But instead of taking me home, we go to your apartment, even though I say I don't want to. You're pushing and I'm too tired, so as soon as we get there I immediately collapse on the bed and fall asleep. As soon as I wake up, I'm going to break up with you.

Sometime later, I jerk awake. You're spooning me, one hand inside my underwear. Your finger moves inside me. Up, down, up, down. I can feel your erection through my thin T-shirt, your quick breaths against my ear.

"What the fuck?" I say, pushing you off me.

Your eyes narrow. "You liked it."

"I was *sleeping*."

That half smile of yours flits across your face. "Trust me, I can tell you liked it."

I feel . . . violated.

> *I watch you sleep at night*
> *Wonder what you dream*

"Gavin, that's . . . I mean . . ."

There are no words. Disneyland suddenly seems like it happened years ago. Now this is what I'll remember: not the fun I had with my friends, but the after—you, touching me without permission. Getting off on getting away with it.

"You're my girlfriend," you say. "Since when do you not want me touching you? You're acting like I'm some kind of . . . kind of *creep* or something. Jesus Christ."

"Well, maybe you are! I mean—"

I stop as something shifts in your expression. I can't quite put my finger on it, except . . . *malice*. That's what I see. Just like that night you first told me you hated me. And I am suddenly hyperaware of the fact that I'm alone in an apartment with a boy much stronger than me. A boy who looks like he wants to hurt me.

Calm him down, a panicked voice inside me says.

I'm suddenly terrified as you crawl closer to me, push me against the pillows.

"Tell me you love me," you whisper, your eyes turning to slate. You straddle me and pull off your shirt, then lean down, your lips barely brushing mine. "Grace. Tell me. Or I swear to fucking God I will go hang myself in that bathroom."

I start to shake. Your eyes burn into mine as your hands curl around my wrists and pin me to the bed.

"I . . . I love you."

You pull at my pants. Slip them down. This isn't happening. It's not. It's not.

"Gavin, no, please . . ."

"Tell me you want me," you growl. I flinch. *"Grace."*

"I wa-want you."

You take my hand and put it on your belt. I close my eyes and pretend you're Gideon. I pretend I'm somewhere else, far away from this apartment and you and your heart beating against my skin.

Let me go, I want to scream. *Please let me go.*

You are not gentle.

After, I take a shower, holding my fist to my mouth so the sobs won't echo off the tiles. I'm so fucking scared. I pray you won't have another go at me. If you do, I'll shatter.

You pull open the glass shower door and step inside, smiling as you dunk your head under the stream of water. You're acting like everything is fine, like what happened in your bed was us making love. I become Contrite and Subservient Female. You ask me to wash your back. I do. Then you turn around and watch as I wash you off me. The soap travels from my breasts to my hips, my thighs, my feet. Finally, it goes down the drain. I stay in the shower long after you get out. I wait until the water runs cold. Until all of you is gone.

FORTY

I am breaking up with you today.

I am breaking up with you even if you start to cry and your electric-blue eyes turn extra bright, your eyelashes heavy with tears. I am breaking up with you even though I will never again see you onstage, your lips kissing the mic, and think, *That's my boyfriend.*

Pull out every trick you have, every sweet word, every wounded glance. Throw me your best excuse, your wildest promise—throw it hard so I can knock it out of the park. Give me everything you've got. It won't be enough to keep me by your side.

"Five words, sweetie. Just five words. You can do it," Nat whispers. *I'm. Breaking. Up. With. You.*

She grabs me in a fierce hug, then goes to hide with Lys behind a nearby SUV in the Roosevelt parking lot. She's promised to break up with you for me if I don't do it. I gave her permission to drag me away from you, if need be. She would do it, too.

I've asked you to meet me in the high school parking lot because it's a public place. Because I don't trust you anymore. I'm scared to be alone with you.

I'm breaking up with you right before graduation. Because I won't let you ruin this day. I won't let you take one more thing away from me.

I'm going to spend the whole summer with the friends I've neglected for the past year. And then I'm going to go to a college far away. And I'm going to find someone I don't want to break up with.

As soon as we're over, I'm going to call your mom. If you try to hurt yourself, that's on you. I can't carry you anymore. I won't.

You're walking toward me now, fedora pulled low over your eyes. You smile when you see me and dance a little jig because this is the day we've been waiting for. But I'm going to make it the worst day of your life. I'm sick with nerves. For once, there isn't a part of me that still loves you, that still lifts a little when you walk toward me with that slacker shuffle. I want nothing to do with you ever again.

"How's my girl?" you say when you reach me.

I feel the cracks spreading through my heart as it starts to break. You're wearing the tie I bought you for Christmas—the one with the skull and crossbones. I know you love it. I know you're wearing it for me. And it's so weird, the you that I used to love superimposed over the guy who pushed me down on that bed and shoved himself into me while I tried not to cry. I'm so sad for us. For what we were. For what we maybe could have been.

"Grace?"

It's too late for Gideon, but it's not too late for me. *For me.* It feels good to be selfish, but it's hard.

I open my mouth, but the words won't come. Despite everything, I don't want to break your heart. I wish I wanted to. It would be so much easier to cut you down with a smile on my face. But I'm not an ass-kicking ninja warrior queen.

Yet.

"What happened?" you ask. You are Concerned Boyfriend.

Tears are filling my eyes and I shake my head, as if the words could just fall out so I won't have to say them. Nat will have to put more bobby pins in my hair—I can feel my mortarboard slipping off.

You reach for me, your hands gripping my arms, your skin warm on mine. "Baby, what's wrong?"

Oh god, you think it's not you, that there was some kind of graduation drama. Your voice is so sweet, the question so innocent. You want to protect me and it's too much. The end of high school, the end of us. The beginning of everything else. *I don't know if I can do this.* After what you did to me the other day, this should be the easiest thing in the world. Why isn't it? What's wrong with me? I turn my head and see Nat and Lys. It makes me feel strong, knowing they have my back.

"I'm breaking up with you. Right now. Please don't say anything."

The words come out in a rush and sweat's dripping off me and *Please, god, please let me really do it this time.* All those times I'd tried to do this and, in the end, it's such a simple thing: five little words. *I'm breaking up with you.*

You have no idea how hard it is to love you.
Bitch.
Whore.
Slut.
Stop being such a child.
You're lucky I love you so much.
I hate you.
I'll kill myself if you break up with me.

You stare at me. No threats. No tears. For once, you don't say a word. Because you know I mean it this time.

And then I walk away from you.

I don't look back.

EPILOGUE

*I*t is Christmas in August.

Natalie and I trim a fake tree. Alyssa puts on her favorite Christmas music. The house smells like sugar cookies and the stockings are hung by the chimney with care.

We're having a party tonight. Lys is inviting Jessie and Nat is inviting her childhood friends who went to a different high school, and Kyle, who now knows the whole story of you and me. He's been hanging out with us a lot, our go-to guy when things go bump in the night.

The three of us—Nat, Lys, and I—have been living alone in Nat's house since graduation. Her siblings are at camp, along with her mom, who's the summer camp nurse. We are given free rein, we are trusted, we are worthy of that trust.

Our days bleed into one another, one long strand of perfect moments: lip-synching to the *Rent* soundtrack, waking up to full glasses of Pepsi, overcooking and undercooking everything. We live in a cocoon of awesome, protected from you and Roy and anything else that dares to rain on our parade. We are young and free and we will never die.

My best friends stitch me back together one hug, one laugh, one dance-off at a time. The past year melts away under their care. There are days when I wake up sad and angry at all the time lost, at the wasted months of loving a ticking time bomb. They take me to get a Pepsi Freeze. They prescribe twenty minutes of jumping on the trampoline or force me into Nat's car late at night so we can drive by your apartment and flip it off. Sometimes I cry, wondering how it was possible that I could have been so goddamn weak, so fucking spineless. Without you around, I can finally see all the ways you'd kept my heart shackled to yours. The manipulation, the verbal and physical abuse, the mind games. And yet I still miss you. Isn't that fucked up? But I do. I miss being loved, even if that love was sick, terminally ill.

These girls, this summer—it's the best kind of medicine. They show me how I can be enough, how I don't need you to be me. They show me how to fill days with good memories, catching and trapping them like lightning bugs in a jar. They glow and glow and glow.

I help Nat put the star on the tree—the final touch—then she drives me over to the Honey Pot. She picks me up at the end of my shift—a double. I'm working as much as I can to save up for the things I'll need for school: computer, dorm decor, and anything else a proper college girl needs.

"Ugh, I smell like the Pot," I say as I walk into the house.

The living room explodes with laughter.

"I told you she always says that!" Lys says to the room.

I love this: being known, laughing, not worrying if I'll do something that will make you threaten me, hurt me, slice me wide open with your words. I don't have to look over my shoulder anymore.

It has been seven weeks since I broke up with you. I called your mom right away so that she'd keep an eye on you. If you tried to hurt yourself, I never heard about it, but she's texted me a few times, telling me how much she and your dad miss me. I wonder if you put her up to it. You scared us for a while there, pounding on the door in the middle of the night, coming to visit me at work. One night we came home late from the movies and we're certain you broke in—I could smell my perfume in the air, as though it had just been sprayed, and my favorite shirt was missing, the one you helped me pick out at the vintage store downtown. Once or twice we made Kyle sleep over so that we didn't have to sleep with butcher knives under our pillows. I'll never forget what happened the morning after Disneyland—the look on your face as you held my wrists. It keeps me up nights.

We pass out presents wrapped in Christmas paper we've foraged from Nat's garage. Silly Dollar Store stuff: Play-Doh, a shower cap with rubber duckies on it, six GI Joe figurines. Kyle crosses to the piano and runs his fingers along the keys. I think of Gideon and my heart hurts.

I'm sandwiched between Nat and Lys and I slip my arm around each of their waists as we sing carol after carol—rowdy, raucous versions of the old standards and the best cover of "All I Want for Christmas Is You" that I've ever heard. I don't let it bother me that you sang that song to me last Christmas because it's not yours and you can't have it. I direct the words to Natalie and Lys, the real loves of my life, who stood by me during my darkest moments. These girls are my lights at the end of the tunnel, guiding me back to myself every time I get lost stumbling around in the darkness.

In a few weeks, I'll be moving to Los Angeles. I've already purchased my leopard-print bedspread and red pillows with delicate gold embroidery: Chinese dragons, for good luck. I have my *Rent* poster carefully rolled up. My Paris-themed calendar. My French dictionary. All of it is neatly stacked in a corner of the living room, waiting. Waiting for me to start the rest of my life. I know you'll be there, playing shows with Evergreen, being a rock god. Your mom texted me that you were moving there in September but that you're not going to school. I'm worried you'll come to USC looking for me. Yesterday Lys handed me a bottle of pepper spray on a key chain and it goes everywhere with me now so I hope, for your sake, that you leave me alone. I wish I could warn every girl you're going to meet, tell them that your hotness and sexy songs and enigmatic smile aren't worth the cost of the ride. I wish I could put a warning label on you. I wonder if you'll always haunt me like this, a ghost with a baseball bat and a bad-boy car.

Natalie and Lys start rocking out to "Rudolph the Red-Nosed Reindeer" and a sob tears up my throat, my eyes instantly damp. I rush into the kitchen and splash my face at the sink, sick with the thought of leaving them behind. I wish I could pack them in a suitcase and set them up in my dorm room at USC. I wish I could have all the hours you stole from me back so I could spend every minute with them.

I need an excuse for being in the kitchen and so I grab an apple and begin idly twisting its stem, playing the little game with fate that I have since I was a kid. Once again, the stem breaks off at G.

And I suddenly get it.

G is for *Grace*. Not you. Not Gideon. *I* am the person I'm supposed to be with right now. I lift the apple to my mouth and take a big, noisy bite.

It's just as sweet as I thought it would be.

AUTHOR'S NOTE

When I was sixteen I fell in love. Hard. For the next two and a half years I would stay in my bad romance, desperate to get out of it. It wasn't until I'd graduated high school that I got the guts to break up with my Gavin. It can seem pretty crazy that anyone would stay in such an abusive relationship so long, but when you're in it, breaking up seems impossible.

The essence of this book is true even though much of what you've read is made up, wildly altered, or reimagined. As Stephen King says, "Fiction is a lie, and good fiction is the truth inside the lie."

I wrote this book because, as the incomparable Lady Gaga puts it: *I'm a free bitch, baby.* If you're stuck in your own bad romance, I want you to be free, too. I also wanted to raise awareness: dating abuse now affects one in three young adults. Young women ages 16 to 24 experience the highest rates of rape and sexual assault. That's messed-up and it needs to stop.

On the next page are some places where you can get help. I've also created a website for all of us to share our experiences and to get encouragement and inspiration. Blogs, art, music, and lots of love: badromancebook.tumblr.com. Our hashtag is #chooseyou.

Whoever you are, know that it does get better. You just have to take the leap. You've got this.

RESOURCES

Love Is Respect (loveisrespect.org): This site is amazing. It has quizzes you can take to see if you're in a healthy or unhealthy relationship, tons of resources on what you can do to get help, and how to stay safe. If you are in an abusive relationship, this should be your first stop for online help. Peer advocates are available 24/7 to talk. Text "love is" to 22522 or call 1-866-331-9474.

Break The Cycle (breakthecycle.org): This site has tons of info about dating violence. You can find out what the signs are and what you can do about it.

No More (nomore.org): This organization is great and also has information if you are the friend or family member of someone who is being abused. They need you more than ever. For some tips on how to help them, check out nomore.org/how-to-help/what-to-say/.

Girls Health (girlshealth.gov): This site has all the phone numbers you need, a great Q and A section, quizzes, stats, and more.

Day One (dayoneny.org): If you are—or think you might be—in an abusive relationship and live in NYC, go here to find out more. You can also call their confidential hotline at (800) 214-4150 or text (646) 535-DAY1 (3291).

These hotlines are free, private, and open 24 hours a day:

National Sexual Assault Hotline: 1-800-656-HOPE (4673)

National Domestic Violence Hotline: 1-800-799-SAFE (7233)

National Child Abuse Hotline: 1-800-4-A-CHILD (422-4453)

#CHOOSEYOU

badromancebook.tumblr.com

ACKNOWLEDGMENTS

Sarah Torna Roberts and Melissa Wilmarth: thank you for being my Nat and Lys. Thank you for saying BREAK UP WITH HIM a million times and for the best summer of my life and for holding me together and patching me up. I love you girls so, so much. Brandon Roberts, thank you for coming over that night when we were pretty sure the house had been broken into and for making me laugh and being the big brother I never had. Diane Torna, your generosity that summer knows no bounds.

To the teachers, counselors, pastors, and other adults who graced my life in high school—especially Susan Kehler (only the best drama teacher ever), Tricia Boganwright, Julie Morgenstern, Sonny Martini, and my Fire By Night family: thank you for your support and love during the very worst years of my life. (And for saying BREAK UP WITH HIM, even though I didn't listen for a long time.) And a huge hug to all the friends and mentors I had who were there through it all in one way or another: there were so many of you, so forgive me for not listing names—I hope you know who you are.

Love to my family, especially Meghan Demetrios, sister extraordinaire: thank you for foot wars, sticking up for me, and always being on my side. Zach Fehst: I am one lucky girl to have married you and become a part of your awesome family (hey, Fehsts!). I'm so glad you asked for my number after acting class freshman year at USC.

Stephanie Uzureau-Anderson, Jessica Welman, and Allison Campbell: oh, ladies, where do I start? I'm so grateful the USC dorm gods put us together. Who knew "tragic teen" would be the subject of a book one day? (Of course, I shall never forget that he was the subject of an excellent musical first.) You got me through my first year without HIM.

Last, but not least, thanks to Elena McVicar for beta reading; my VCFA Allies in Wonderland; my rockin' agent, Brenda Bowen; and, of course, my editor, Kate Farrell, who made this book so much better and was such a cheerleader on this rough journey. Also, love to everyone at Holt and a shout-out to all the amazing artists who are on my Bad Romance playlist (especially you, Gaga): you made reliving this mess a whole lot easier and are waaaaaaay cheaper than therapy.

GOFISH

HEATHER DEMETRIOS

What did you want to be when you grew up?
Growing up, I wanted to be anywhere but home. I'm a total romantic, so I longed for epic adventures and travels around the world. I made my peace with reality by telling stories. I've always wanted to be a writer of some kind, but there was a long period where I did a lot of theater, so then I wanted to be an actress, then a director. When I went back to writing, I realized that everything I did was about creating other worlds and escaping into them. I don't know of anything better than writing if you want to build castles in the sky.

What's your favorite childhood memory?
I was a figure skater for several years, and my grandfather would get up at four a.m. to get me to practice by five. In the afternoons, he'd watch me skate and then take me to Starbucks. It meant so much to me, how supportive he was of me and my skating. I didn't have a dad around, but he more than made up for that.

As a young person, who did you look up to most?
I looked up to my great-grandmother, who passed away just a few years ago. She traveled all of her life, and even

when she was very old she was taking classes in gourmet cooking and Spanish. She was always pushing boundaries, way ahead of her time. She showed me that your life is something that is supposed to be embraced to the fullest, something to revel in.

What was your first job, and what was your worst job?

My first job was working at this amazing cookie shop in Central California called Hungry Bear. Oh my god, those cookies were *divine*. My worst job was working as a telemarketer. Talk about soul-sucking. My happiest moment was when I quit my day job and started writing full time. I'd spent my life dreaming of doing what I love for a living, and when it happened, it felt like the entire universe was smiling down on me. Being able to do that is my greatest accomplishment.

How did you celebrate publishing your first book?

To celebrate *Something Real,* I got a tattoo that says YAWP. It's an important word in the book and pretty much my favorite word. It comes from Walt Whitman: *I sound my barbaric yawp over the roofs of the world.* It's all about being unapologetic about who you are and embracing your wildest side and sharing that self with the whole wide world. I do that through my writing. I love Whitman. He's the man.

If you could live in any fictional world, what would it be?

The world of the Harry Potter books, hands down. I also write fantasy, and it's my most fervent longing to be magical. When I read Harry Potter, I fall so deeply into that world that I really feel like I'm there, right alongside all those extraordinary characters. Reading Harry Potter got me back in touch with what I love most about reading: being so totally absorbed in the story that it feels like I'm living it myself. I was in college at the time and reading lots of heavy, boring stuff. My roommate convinced me to read the first Harry Potter book and it changed my life. I mean that literally. That's why I write YA, because I had fallen in love with the genre.

What was your favorite book when you were a kid? Do you have a favorite book now?
My favorite book was *Little Women.* I grew up in a broken home, and things weren't always easy for me. I think I gravitated toward that story because here was this wonderful, whole family that loved each other and enjoyed one another. And, of course, I loved Jo! My favorite book now is the whole Harry Potter series. They're my desert island books for sure. If I had to choose, it'd be the third book—I just love Sirius Black. *Prisoner of Azkaban* is also my favorite Harry Potter movie.

If you could travel in time, where would you go and what would you do?
I would travel to the 1920s and hang out in Paris, be a real bohemian artist. I would rock being a flapper so hard. When can we go?

What advice do you wish someone had given you when you were younger?
I wish someone had told me to just be myself, but—more importantly—that being myself was enough. When you're a teen, it's so hard. You're dying to be accepted, to fit in. It's really hard not to hide your weird. I wish I could go hang

out with teen Heather and let her know that she's cool as is and that she's going to do some pretty awesome stuff with her life. I wonder if she'd believe me.

What would you do if you ever stopped writing?
Is this a trick question? I could never stop writing! I literally feel unwell when I'm not writing. It's how I express myself best and how I make sense of the world. I think no matter what happens in my life, writing will always remain central. I love to travel, so that's something I would do if I were, say, taking a break from working on a book. And I've always wanted to open a coffeehouse. But you can write while doing those things!

Theater plays such an important role in *Bad Romance*—it's Grace's passion, and the narration is interspersed with musical references and stage directions. Can you tell us a little about your inspiration and the significance to the story?
I've been a theater nerd my whole life, and it was a HUGE part of my high school world (I also went on to get a BA in theater). Some of my very best memories are from either performing in or doing crew for shows during that time. When I was in my own bad romance in high school, theater saved me. It was my safe space, total magic. I wanted Grace to have that, too, and I wanted to show how one of the best ways to get through—and out of—a bad romance is to have a passion. To have something that is yours and gives you a life and an identity outside your relationship. It's also her ticket out of her crappy home life and away from her boyfriend. I think if Grace didn't have that, or such great friends, she might have been stuck with Gavin for a long, long time.

Natalie and Alyssa are so lovable—they're true friends through thick and thin. How did they develop as characters?

Well, I totally cheated because they're my real-life best friends who got me through my bad romance in high school—different, of course, because they became their own people as I wrote the book, but completely based on Sarah and Missy. For the record, Sarah would like everyone to know that she had better fashion sense than Natalie. ☺ I cannot say this enough, though: They saved my life. Truly, if I didn't have them, I honestly don't know where I'd be right now. Having friends to lean on during the horrors of an abusive relationship is priceless. I really wanted to show how imperative it is to keep your friends close when you're going through something like this. Sometimes when you're in an abusive relationship, you feel pressured by your partner to cut your friends loose. Or you turn your back on them because you can't handle their truth-telling. I wanted Grace to have the support I had, and I'm hoping readers will see that the real love of your life is your friends.

Although the book deals with dark subject matter, it also has genuine humor and ultimately remains hopeful. How did you strike that balance?

You know, despite it being a pretty awful time in my life, I had a lot of fun in high school. I think being in the drama crew was the biggest part of that. We laughed so much. And it was so cool to be doing what I loved and sharing that with my friends. So while Grace is having a tough time, she's still pursuing her dreams and having a blast doing it. The thing is, very rarely in life is everything terrible. It might feel that way, but there's always a silver lining. And hope. You can't let go of that. What gets Grace through—and what got me through—is knowing that there is more out there in the world than her small town and her bad relationship. She has goals and dreams. Part of why Grace loves the musical *Rent* so much is that it's all about living the life of an artist in NYC with a family you cobble together on your own. And I know she's going to have that someday, because *I* have that.

What scene from *Bad Romance* was most challenging to write?
Honestly, all the cute moments between Gavin and Grace were the very hardest for me to write. Because the book is inspired by my own bad romance, it was just impossible to create chemistry and sweetness and desire between the two of them because all I could think of was the bad stuff, of where this was all going. And I wanted to protect Grace from that! I had to create Gavin out of my own secret high school dream boy, the one who strutted down the halls and made me swoon every. Single. Time. (There was this musician we called "The Beautiful One"—and yes, he is *still* beautiful today. I based Gavin on him—I mean, the sexy parts of Gavin.) Eventually Grace and Gavin stopped being me and my ex, and I was able to let things play out.

You made a point to highlight how difficult Grace's life at home was. What part do you think that played in her relationship with Gavin?
You could have the most amazing family and still be in a bad romance, BUT I think that you are especially susceptible to abuse when home isn't a safe space for you. It certainly wasn't for me growing up, and I think that's part of why I was in my bad romance in the first place. One of the reasons Grace gets so attached to Gavin is that he's kind of

the shelter in the storm. When things are bad at home, she feels like she's got this knight in shining armor who has her back. And, despite him being a crap boyfriend, he *does* help her through some of the really awful things she deals with, whether it's being hit by her mom or verbally abused by her stepdad. Also, her mom and The Giant are in a bad romance, too, so Grace never gets the opportunity to see what a healthy relationship looks like. This is why her friends are so important, as well as her drama teacher: They're her real family, the support system she lacks at home. No one at home can see how much Grace is suffering because they're so caught up in the family hurt. I think if Grace had a healthy home environment, she might have felt safe to seek advice from her parents and get some of the help she needed— and they would have seen the toll the relationship was taking on Grace without her having to say a word. There's so much heartbreak all around, and what Grace deals with at home makes her especially brave and kickass for getting out of her bad romance.

What kind of response have you been getting from people who have read *Bad Romance*?
I *knew* this book would hit home with readers because whenever I talked about it as I was writing it, people would say *Me too, I had a boyfriend like that,* or *My friend/sister/ daughter is in a bad romance.* It's been so heartbreaking to see just how many readers are hurting or still in the process of healing. I've heard from so many readers who've been through a relationship like Grace's. I've heard from parents who are concerned about their daughters and want to know how best to support them. Some readers have a tough time because it brings up trauma for them but are ultimately glad they've read it, because they're survivors and it reminds them

of the fight they've won. More than anything, readers say, *I wish I'd read this when I was younger.* And that's why I wrote the book: Because *I* wished I'd read it, too. I was so alone. I didn't know anyone who was going through what I was experiencing. I was so ashamed and scared and confused. It makes me sad to see how many people have experienced what Grace and I have experienced, but I feel encouraged by all the women who are beginning to speak out about this kind of pain. The more we talk about this stuff, the more we protect ourselves from the Gavins of the world. We're so much stronger than the world wants us to believe we are: We can be our own knights in shining armor.

A TRAILER PARK GIRL WITH BIG DREAMS. THE COMBAT VETERAN
SHE NEVER EXPECTED TO FALL FOR. AND THEIR STRUGGLE
TO ESCAPE A LIFE THAT SEEMS PRE-DESTINED.

KEEP READING FOR AN EXCERPT.

chapter one

The Mitchells' backyard was packed, full of recent and not-so-recent grads in various stages of party decay. The girls leaned against one another, wilted flowers that looked on while the guys got louder, sweatier.

I craned my neck and scanned the crowd for Chris, but my wingman had disappeared.

"Shit," I muttered.

Like I needed any more confirmation of my loner status. I moved purposefully through the crowd, on a mission. The last thing I wanted was to have some drunk dude notice I was alone and try to hit on me.

A girl to my right stumbled, spilling her beer on my All Stars. I had to reach out an arm to steady her before she stabbed me in the toe with her stilettos. I sighed and shook my foot.

"Thanks!" she said, more to the air than me, as she turned back to the knot of girls beside her.

"Skylar!"

I turned around—Chris was over by the keg. When I raised

my arms like, *WTF*, he turned over his empty cup, then made a sad face and pointed to the line of red-faced guys in front of him. Obviously he hadn't taken me very seriously when I'd said, *Let's get out of here as quickly as possible.*

I pulled out my phone and started texting Dylan while I made my way to Chris. Knowing her, she was probably in the back seat of her boyfriend's beat-up Chevy Malibu, but I wanted Brownie points for coming out at all. Really, I was only here to see Josh Mitchell, this Marine I used to work with who had just come home from Afghanistan. I could have waited to see him some other time, but it seemed like a dick move; someone comes back from fighting a war, you go to their homecoming party.

U still here? Looking for Josh.

No answer.

People stumbled through the Mitchells' back door, probably looking for the bathroom or somewhere to hook up. Every now and then, someone would wander out grinning stupidly from Reggie Vasquez's hastily rolled joints. Linkin Park blared inside the house, and I wondered what the night would feel like if someone switched the soundtrack from angry kick-the-shit-out-of-stuff to Ben Harper or the Chili Peppers.

I stopped by the doorway when I saw a flash of long blond hair, but it wasn't Dylan so I backed away, ignoring the *what's she doing here* looks people were shooting at me. They weren't mean-girl looks—I just didn't belong. Didn't want to.

Drunken laughter erupted from groups of partiers at regular intervals, but not because anything was funny. It was like laughter was just something you were supposed to *do*. I scanned the faces around me: the usual crew of locals from my high school. There were also a lot of slightly older faces—Josh Mitchell's friends, partying with the teenagers, doing the same thing they had done every Saturday night since they were in junior high: Drink. Smoke. Screw. Repeat.

Chris walked toward me, sipping on his frothy beer as he picked his way across the lawn. He was wearing the shirt I'd given him for graduation, the words *mathematician* and *ninja* under the heading CAREER GOALS. He held out a can of Coke like a peace offering.

"Dude, *you never, never leave your wingman*," I said. "Didn't you learn anything from *Top Gun*?"

I had this thing about *Top Gun*—it was my dad's favorite movie, and I'd been obsessed with it since I was six.

"I told you I was getting a beer! I thought you were behind me when I made the turnoff at the kitchen." He gave me the puppy-dog eyes that always got me laughing, and I grabbed the Coke, trying to keep my lips from turning up.

"Well, thanks for this." I hit the can against his plastic cup. "To graduating," I said.

"Hell, yeah, to graduating!"

It had only been three hours since the ceremony ended, but it looked like any normal Creek View night. I shouldn't have expected it to feel different. I knocked the Coke back like it was eighty proof, keeping my eyes peeled for Josh Mitchell.

It'd been no surprise when Josh joined the Marines two years ago. Like most of the guys in Creek View, his choices had been limited: the military, truck driving, or crappy part-time jobs along the highway. We lived in a blink town—blink and you'll miss it—off California's Highway 99. It was just a trailer park, a few run-down houses, a couple of businesses that barely made enough to keep their doors open, and the Paradise Motel (aka my part-time job).

Though we'd worked together at the Paradise and I'd grown up around him, I'd been weirdly shy when Josh came up to me in his uniform, his head all shaved, calling me ma'am. I'd asked if he was scared, and he said no, that this was as good as it would get for him. He couldn't wait. For a minute we'd just looked at each other and then I kissed his cheek—which surprised both of us—and told him good luck. Then he was gone.